*New York Times* **Bestselling author Ace Atkins** has been nominated for every major award in crime fiction, including the Edgar three times, twice for novels about former U.S. Army Ranger Quinn Colson. He has written nine books in the Colson series and continued Robert B. Parker's iconic Spenser character after Parker's death in 2010, adding best-selling novels in that series. A former newspaper reporter and SEC football player, Ace also writes essays and investigative pieces for several national magazines including *Time*, *Outside* and *Garden & Gun*.

He lives in Oxford, Mississippi with his family, where he's friend to many dogs and several bartenders.

## BY ACE ATKINS

### QUINN COLSON NOVELS

*The Ranger*
*The Lost Ones*
*The Broken Places*
*The Forsaken*
*The Redeemers*
*The Innocents*
*The Fallen*
*The Sinners*
*The Shameless*

### ROBERT B. PARKER'S SPENSER NOVELS

*Robert B. Parker's Lullaby*
*Robert B. Parker's Wonderland*
*Robert B. Parker's Cheap Shot*
*Robert B. Parker's Kickback*
*Robert B. Parker's Slow Burn*
*Robert B. Parker's Little White Lies*
*Robert B. Parker's Old Black Magic*

### NICK TRAVERS NOVELS

*Crossroad Blues*
*Leavin' Trunk Blues*
*Dark End of the Street*
*Dirty South*

### TRUE CRIME NOVELS

*White Shadow*
*Wicked City*
*Devil's Garden*
*Infamous*

# THE SHAMELESS

ACE ATKINS

CORSAIR

First published in the United States of America in 2019 by G. P. Putnam's Sons

First published in Great Britain in 2019 by Corsair
This edition published in 2020

1 3 5 7 9 10 8 6 4 2



*All characters and events in this publication, other than those clearly in the public domain, are fictitious and any resemblance to real persons, living or dead, is purely coincidental.*



A CIP catalogue record for this book
is available from the British Library.

ISBN: 978-1-4721-5500-9

Printed and bound in Great Britain by Clays Ltd, Elcograf S.p.A.

Papers used by Corsair are from well-managed forests
and other responsible sources.

Corsair
An imprint of
Little, Brown Book Group
Carmelite House
50 Victoria Embankment
London EC4Y 0DZ

An Hachette UK Company
www.hachette.co.uk

www.littlebrown.co.uk

*For Patsy Brumfield*
*The News Queen of Mississippi*

"There ain't any explanations. Not of anything. All you can do is point at the nature of things. If you are smart enough to see 'em."

—Robert Penn Warren, *All the King's Men*

Don't stand up when the enemy's coming against you. Kneel down, lie down, hide behind a tree.

—Rogers' Rangers Standing Order No. 18

# THE SHAMELESS

**Tashi Coleman**
***Thin Air* podcast**
**Episode 1: BRANDON**

NARRATOR: Last year, Brandon Taylor's sister contacted me through social media with a simple but urgent question: WILL YOU PLEASE COME TO MISSISSIPPI TO FIND OUT WHAT HAPPENED TO MY BROTHER?

It was written in all caps, with little information about who she was or who her brother had been. She said she'd heard our earlier podcasts about missing people, murders, and botched police investigations. Over the course of the next several months, Shaina Taylor messaged me with countless newspaper articles, family photos, and details of candlelight vigils and walkathons to find out who killed Brandon.

On the last day his family saw him, Brandon said he planned to go deer hunting after school, a regular pastime in north Mississippi. He came home, grabbed a cold ham biscuit and a Mountain Dew and his Remington rifle. He parked his Chevy Apache pickup off a county road and walked into a large parcel of land adjoining a national forest. He never walked out.

For days, rescue crews searched the woods, crossing over the same thick forest time and again. More than a week later, Brandon's body was found, ravaged by animals, time, and weather. The local sheriff ruled his death a suicide after a brief investigation. His rifle was located nearby, fired once. A bullet in his skull.

His family and friends never believed it. His sister said every step of the police and forensic work had been a mess. A proper autopsy was never performed and possible suspects never questioned. Not to mention, she said, no one in their county ever wanted the case solved. The truth would only embarrass some important people and call into question the motive of the county sheriff, a good and decent old man named Hamp Beckett. Over a series of dozens of heartbreaking messages, Shaina Taylor turned to us and said we were her last hope.

We receive countless requests like Shaina's every day from all over the country. Thousands of people disappear or die without solid answers for their families. Shaina said her brother lived an idyllic life in a small Southern town. She called him a normal fifteen-year-old boy, with loads of friends, a classic old truck, and a girlfriend he'd met over the summer. She said he was a great photographer with a keen eye, a talented guitar player who idolized Garth Brooks, and a blossoming journalist.

The last part is what got me. Brandon Taylor had been a student journalist and a valuable member of the yearbook staff. He could've been anyone on our team of reporters, had he grown up. His family deserved answers.

So last summer, I packed up the few belongings I have and met up with my producer, Jessica Torres, to drive from New York City down to Tibbehah County, Mississippi. It's a rural place known for sweet potatoes and some recent sensational stories about drug dealers, bank robbers, and a young crusading sheriff—coincidentally or not, the nephew of the old sheriff. Some real *Walking Tall* meets Faulkner kind of stories. As always, we tried to make ourselves invisible as we worked, talking to Brandon's family members, friends, and local law enforcement, both retired and present. What resulted wasn't quite the story we hoped to find.

Instead, we uncovered something darker and more sinister, a true meditation on today's society. What do we value? Lies or facts.

Posturing or morality. But to explain all that now would be taking you way too far down the country roads of Mississippi.

First, I must tell you about this boy, Brandon Taylor, and his 1955 Chevy Apache truck. It was a cold, rainy day in November 1997, and there was a rumor about the largest buck in the county wandering somewhere near County Road 334 . . .

# ONE

Lillie Virgil had been bird-dogging Wes Taggart's sorry ass for most of the summer, from Panama City to New Orleans and now back to Biloxi. The top-shelf turd had left a trail of filthy motel rooms, unpaid restaurant tabs, and jilted strippers. The last one being his undoing, a cute little piece of tail named Twilight who he'd brought with him from Tibbehah County on his run from the law. He was wanted on charges of drug trafficking, racketeering, and the attempted murder of a close friend of Lillie's, a one-armed trucker named Boom Kimbrough.

"This is it?" Lillie said, pointing to the old neon sign reading STAR INN. It was early morning, not long past dawn, the two having made the drive all the way from Memphis through the night to the Gulf Coast. With the windows open, you could smell the salt air on the hot wind.

"Yep," Twilight said, playing with the ends of her bleached blonde hair, the tips tinged with a purplish hue. "We spent a week here last month. Eating shrimp po' boys and drinkin' Jim Beam. Now, do I get my money or what?"

"Depends on if he's here," Lillie said. "And sweetie? Would you mind not putting your feet on my fucking dash?"

The girl took down her bare feet, with those stubby purple-painted toes, as Lillie parked the gray Dodge Charger across the road, right outside the Sharkheads T-shirt shop, the entrance a wide gaping mouth with sharp teeth. Across the road, the Star Inn advertised LOW RATES. JACUZZI ROOMS. CABLE TV & SWIMMING POOL. Real class with a capital *K*.

"Did Wes at least spring for the Jacuzzi?" Lillie asked.

"No, ma'am," Twilight said. "That should've told me something. We got a cheap-ass room overlooking the fucking parking lot. I laid out on the beach every day while he laid in bed watching goddamn cartoons and smoking American Spirit Lights. I'd get in as the sun was going down, thinking we were going for a steak dinner, and he'd just be lying there drunk as hell and wanting me to suck his peter."

"That's some real romance right there, kid," Lillie said. "Bogart and Bacall shit. Now would you reach in the backseat for my binoculars? I think I spotted Romeo up there on the second floor scratching his nuts."

Five days ago, Twilight, whose real name was Tiffany Dement but went by Twilight to avoid professional confusion, checked in with her momma back in El Dorado, Arkansas. Lillie, a U.S. Federal Marshal, had visited Mrs. Dement in June and made sure the woman kept her on speed dial if she heard a word from her daughter, a former straight-A student and churchgoer. Momma was worried sick, as her baby had left town six months before high school graduation, sometimes sending home money but more often just postcards from Audubon Zoo in New Orleans, Panama City Beach, or Graceland.

The last one really impressed the woman as it contained a recipe for Elvis's favorite meat loaf.

"Looks like your boyfriend cut his hair."

"He ain't my boyfriend."

"If you suck a man's peter while he's watching SpongeBob playing his fucking nose flute, then y'all got some kind of personal deal."

"Damn, you're a hard woman, Miss Virgil."

"Just honest," Lillie said, turning and reaching down in the console between them for a pack of Bubblicious. She'd been chewing the hell out of it after she quit smoking. Damn, it hadn't been easy.

"Is that him?" Twilight asked. "Is that Wes with his shirt off? Can I see?"

Lillie handed her the binoculars and reached for her cell phone, calling in the Biloxi police before making the arrest. She could easily handle it herself but would rather not have to deal with some local fuckwads complicating things. Twilight lifted the binoculars up to the railing, where it looked like Wes Taggart was licking the frosting off a donut. He used to have a shaggy seventies-style look, an uglier version of Scott Glenn in *Urban Cowboy*, but now he was jailbird bald. Almost like he was resigned to his fate.

"I don't know what I saw in that man," Twilight said, shaking her head. The early-morning light catching the glint from the ruby stud in her pug nose as she shook her head.

"Probably reminded you of your worthless daddy."

"How'd you know my daddy was worthless?" Twilight said, still twisting at the ends of her purplish hair, her face a wide question mark.

Lillie leaned into the wheel of the Charger, eyes hidden behind a pair of Ray-Bans with big silver lenses, and just said, "Lucky guess."

"He didn't touch me or nothin', if that's what you're saying."

"Your daddy or Wes Taggart?"

"Daddy, of course," she said. "Wes Taggart humped me like a mangy damn dog first night we met. Took me back to the VIP room at Vienna's Place in Jericho and got five damn lap dances in a row. Had the DJ play nothin' but some old band called Def Leppard. You know, 'Pour Some Sugar on Me,' 'Pyromania,' all that shit? And then didn't pay me a dime. Said what was between me and him was personal. Wish I'd known what the arrangement was before I started shifting his gears."

"Next time get paid up front," Lillie said. "Don't be anyone's punch."

"Why are you so damn hard, Miss Virgil?" she said.

"You know what?" Lillie said. "I never gave it a second thought."

"You drive like damn Dale Junior and keep a loaded Winchester twelve-gauge in your trunk," she said. "I seen it when you loaded up our bags up in Memphis. You're taller than my daddy and most boys I know, got an ass like an NFL linebacker, don't talk much except for when you're cussin' or telling folks what to do. You don't back up for no man, do you?"

"That's enough, Sister Twilight," Lillie said. "My big ass is full of smoke. And I think I can take it from here."

"Money?"

"In the dash," she said.

Twilight looked kind of sheepish about it until Lillie nodded to the glovebox and she opened it to find a fat envelope inside stuffed with cash. "Can I at least stick around and see how it goes down?"

"Only if you shut your damn mouth," Lillie said. "And promise to stay the hell out of the way."

Senator Jimmy Vardaman arrived at the Neshoba County Fair that morning triumphant as hell after beating the establishment favorite two-to-one in the primary runoff in June. His long silver hair was slicked tight to his skull, and he'd dressed for success in khakis and a blue-and-white gingham shirt rolled to the elbows. A real man of the people, with a big toothy grin and a bright gold watch. It was a warm and muggy morning, Vardaman up on the dais as his supporters sat in church pews laid out underneath the Founders Square tin-roofed pavilion. He announced he sure was ready to dig deep into the muck in Jackson and serve the working folk of Mississippi. *Yes, sir. Yes, sir.*

Just the mention of the working man sent a sea of red bandannas swirling in the crowd, his symbol, worn around the necks of his supporters. Sweat spread under his arms and across his chest as he spoke like an old-time preacher. His face was flushed with sun and heat as if he worked outdoors, not hanging out at the Country Club of Jackson.

"We're all just foot soldiers in a long history of American exceptionalism," Vardaman said. "This past year I've been called a radical and a racist. But let me tell you something, friends, don't you listen to what the fake news tells you. We're on a rendezvous with destiny this fall. Those people want to tear down our flags. Our statues. But that dog don't hunt here in Neshoba. We know honor. We know truth."

Sheriff Quinn Colson turned to his wife, Maggie, her jaw muscles clenched so tight they looked like walnuts. Her pale green eyes scanning over the crowd, in disbelief and anger at what she was seeing and hearing, spinning her wedding ring around her finger. "Jesus God."

"Don't give him any ideas," Quinn said.

"I think I may puke."

Much of the crowd was on its feet, in the shade of the pavilion's wide metal roof, waving the red bandannas and yelling, most of them incomprehensibly, as Vardaman spread his hands wide, palms outstretched, and soaked in the praise. An elderly woman in a wheelchair, oxygen tubes going up her nose, held a WOMEN FOR VARDAMAN sign decorated with the stars and bars of the Confederate flag. Sweat trickled from Quinn's brow and he removed his Tibbehah County sheriff's ball cap to dry his face.

He'd been sheriff now for nearly a decade and he still wasn't sure the state was getting any better. It was the entire reason he'd retired early as a U.S. Army Ranger, believing he could make a difference, fighting corruption, drug running, and violence in his own backyard.

"If that man is elected governor, he'll set Mississippi back fifty years," Maggie said.

"Considering where we are now," Quinn said, "that'd put us somewhere during Reconstruction."

The scene around Founders Square on the Neshoba Fairgrounds looked as if it might've come from a Norman Rockwell painting. Shoeless kids ran wild with packs of dogs behind them, oblivious to the speeches going on under the big pavilion. Every summer, families gathered for two weeks of horse races, livestock shows, carnival rides, and deep-fried food, culminating in the most important stump speeches in the state. Maggie's family had been coming for decades.

Quinn was born and raised in Mississippi, but this was his first time at the fair, coming at Maggie's urging to meet his new extended family after their wedding in June. He was a tallish, muscular man with a chiseled face of sharp planes and edges, dark green eyes with a hard glint in them. He had on blue jeans and a starched sheriff's office shirt, despite it being nearly a hundred degrees. Compared to Camp Anaconda in Afghanistan, Mississippi in August felt like a cool spring day.

He shifted in his seat in the long wooden pew, feeling the Beretta digging into his hip.

"You think he'll start singing some hymns?" Maggie said. The old woman beside her shushed her and held her sign even higher in her frail arms.

"Maybe 'What a Friend We Have in Jesus.'"

"Jesus would think he's an asshole," Maggie said. "Nobody cares about what he's done or that he doesn't even have a real agenda. This is the most broke-ass state in the Union. How about you fix our damn roads before trying to sell me your Southern history bullshit."

"Don't blame me," Quinn said. "The Colson family joined up with the Union in Corinth. They didn't give a damn about supporting plantation owners. We were too damn broke."

"Rendezvous with destiny?" Maggie said, arching an eyebrow.

"This is a race about conviction and moral fiber . . ." Vardaman said, continuing, shaking his fist as he spoke, talking down from the lectern on the hundreds who'd gathered to hear him speak.

Quinn looked up and locked eyes with Vardaman, the man seeming to lose his place for a beat. He glanced over to a group of men hanging outside the shade of the pavilion, several of them dressed in military-style clothes, guns on their hips. Quinn had heard of them. Folks called them the Watchmen Society.

"Moral fiber," Quinn said. "Interesting choice of words."

"I don't think I can take much more," Maggie said, tugging at his arm. Her wrist was wrapped in thin leather bracelets and chains, nails cut short and painted black. Under her right arm was tattooed the words BE HERE NOW. Back in Tibbehah she'd been a bit of an anomaly, the kind of woman old folks might call a hippie. But Maggie was Maggie and Quinn loved her for it.

"Don't you want to hear the big finish?" Quinn said. "I think he might just be warming up."

"Not unless his head spontaneously combusts," she said, sliding her hand down on his knee. "Now, that's something I'd like to see."

Vardaman had kept a big hunt lodge in Tibbehah County for decades, the source of wild rumors and sustained fact, a place where he'd worked out deals with some of the most corrupt sorry-ass people in north Mississippi. Several times Vardaman had been on the fringe of people Quinn had either sent to jail or shot. But Vardaman always slipped clear of it, like a man who stepped in cow shit and came out smelling like Chanel No. 5.

"If we don't see this through," Vardaman said, "you will be forced to bury our rich history and tradition in the red clay of Neshoba. I think our moral fiber is too tough for that."

"How about me and you take a walk, Mags?"

"They sell daiquiris and margaritas by the Tilt-A-Whirl," Maggie said.

"Can't have an elected official drinking during daylight," Quinn said. "We'll have to be like regular folks and sip whiskey when the sun goes down."

"How about I buy you a sausage biscuit at the Piggly Wiggly?"

"Now you're talking," Quinn said. "And a tall coffee, too. I'd rather spend our time watching the livestock show."

"There'd be less bullshit."

Quinn pulled a Liga Privada cigar from his shirt pocket as he caught Maggie's eye and nodded, both standing and making their way out of the pew and past the Vardaman supporters, who were again on their feet, waving their red bandannas. Damn proud rednecks but with few who looked like they actually did manual labor. The Watchmen folded their arms over their chests and stared from behind their dark sunglasses as they left the pavilion. Walking away, Quinn heard something about the Southerners being pushed out of their home by immigrants and gangbangers.

Vardaman said he wanted his people to stand their ground and turn back the clock to a more glorious time.

"Turn back the clock?" Maggie said. "Christ Almighty. Is he really going to win?"

"Hate to tell you," Quinn said. "But he already has."

* * *

"You're going to kill him," Twilight said. "Aren't you?"

"No," Lillie said, watching the shadowed figure disappear from the railing and head back into his room at the Star Inn. "That's not my intention."

"But you want to?"

Lillie didn't answer. She'd wait until the locals got there, close off any exits, and then knock nice and polite on his door. How it all went down would be up to Wes Taggart's sorry ass.

"I'm sorry about your friend."

Lillie nodded and, damn, if she didn't feel herself tearing up behind her sunglasses, just thinking about the condition they left Boom in. Taggart and his late pal, J. B. Hood, had taken to Boom with a couple of Louisville Sluggers, the cowardly way of knocking a man who was six foot six and two-sixty to his knees. Nobody was sure he would make it, as he slid in and out of a coma, coming to and not being able to see or hear right for a while, having to go through therapy just to walk straight. Yeah, Twilight was probably right. She really wouldn't get too emotional if a shitbird like Wes Taggart happened to make the wrong play.

"I'm not what you think," Twilight said, removing the cash from the envelope and counting it out quick with a licked thumb. She tucked the wad into a pink lacy bra.

"Just what do I think?"

"I'm not damaged or trash," she said. "I know what I want. God gave me this body to flaunt. And I'd rather eat filet mignon than a meatball special at Subway."

"Preach, Sister," Lillie said, watching two patrol cars show up in her rearview right by the shark's mouth. She reached for her door handle and looked right at Twilight. "See you around."

"Promise you won't kill him," Twilight said. "He's a real asshole, but I kinda like him. He could be gentle. Said he loved me when he was real drunk on the Turkey."

"How far can you get on that money?" Lillie said.

"Why?"

"After the show's over, it's time for you to start travelin'."

"I can get drunk on less than twenty dollars."

"Damn," Lillie said, getting out and walking to the back of the Charger to retrieve her favorite shotgun and some extra shells. "A true talent. Good luck with that."

# TWO

Does Senator Vardaman ever come here for breakfast?" Tashi Coleman asked, not two days after arriving in Tibbehah County, Mississippi, from Brooklyn. She'd tried to keep a low profile since coming to town, renting a room at the Traveler's Rest Motel, dressing down in jeans and a threadbare black J.Crew tee she'd borrowed from her ex-boyfriend, a disgraced writer who famously sold a false memoir to HarperCollins. Steel-toe work boots purchased at a vintage shop, black hair in a bun, no makeup, and clunky glasses to make her seem more anonymous.

"Sure," said the waitress at a place called the Fillin' Station diner, an old joint actually housed in an old gas station. A true and authentic greasy spoon with busted linoleum floors and a single window air conditioner. "Likes grits and eggs, sausage on the side. Decent fella. Not a bad tipper. Why you asking?"

"Just curious," Tashi said. "His name's been in the paper a lot lately."

"Why wouldn't it be?" Mary asked, her hair the color of copper wire and permed tight like Tashi's mom from pics of her in the eighties. She wore a pale blue apron over street clothes—acid-washed jeans and a plaid top, plain white tennis shoes. "He's going to be our next governor. The man believes in setting us back on the right course, back to the way things used to be when I was a girl."

"And how was that?"

"Simpler times," Mary said, her wrinkled face softening. "Much simpler times. You could sleep sound at night without locking your doors. Neighbors spoke to each other. Families damn well went to church."

"And what's different now?" Tashi asked, glancing around the nearly empty diner. Just an old, black farmer-looking dude by the front door smoking a very long cigarette. He seemed to be contemplating time and mortality or perhaps the incoming rain. She hoped it rained, it would make for some nice audio for the podcast. "You mind sitting down with me? I'd like to ask you a few questions."

"Me?" Mary asked. "What do I know about any of this mess?"

"I don't think there's anyone better to help me figure out this town."

"First time in Mississippi?"

"First time down South."

"Signs and wonders," Mary said. "I knew you wasn't from here the minute you walked in the door."

Tashi felt her face color as she set her iPhone on record and set it across from Mary right by the salt and pepper shakers and Louisiana hot sauce bottle. She self-consciously touched the edges of her thick black glasses. "How?"

"What's your name?"

"Tashi," she said.

"What kind of name is that?"

"Indian."

"Like Pocahontas?"

"My mother was a yogi," Tashi said. "She told me it means 'good fortune.' You know, 'auspicious.' She said she always believed great things would happen to me. I guess she's all but given up on it now."

"Oh, yeah?" Mary tilted her head and studied her face. "Just where are you from, young lady?"

"New York," Tashi said. "Brooklyn, actually. But I plan to be here for a long time. I really want to settle into Jericho."

"Why on earth would you want to do that?"

"You don't like it here?" Tashi asked.

"'Course I like it," Mary said, closing one eye with suspicion. "Just love it. Can't you see it all over this old woman's face?"

"I want people around here to know me," she said. "I want everyone to know I'm not just some reporter passing through. I know some people down here don't like strangers asking questions."

"You've been watching too many damn movies," Mary said, wiping her hands on her apron and taking a seat. "This ain't no *Mississippi Burning*. Let me tell you, folks around here have nothing but time to talk and talk. Just don't talk to someone about something you don't want known. You say one thing on the Square and two hours later it's out all over Tibbehah."

"This is a rough place," she said. "I've read a lot about it. Prostitution. Drug dealers. Wild West shoot-outs."

"You mean those old Pritchard boys?" she said. "Unfortunate. Nicest damn boys you ever met in your life. They just got a little above their raising, trying to expand their farming on up to Memphis. Should've just stuck to what they knowed best."

"And what was that?"

"Dirt track racin'," Mary said. "Lord, Cody Pritchard could fly. Like a damn scalded cat."

"You know some more people around here who wouldn't mind being interviewed?"

"What kind of people?"

"People who've lived here their whole life," Tashi said. "I'd like to know how this town used to run back in the nineties."

"Way back then." Mary tapped at her waitress pad with her pen. She closed up one eye thinking about it and just shook her head. "Lots of folks. But Mr. Stagg and some of the supervisors are all in jail. Mr. Stagg's been gone for almost three years."

"And who is Mr. Stagg?"

"Christ Almighty," Mary said, setting down her pad and sliding into the booth across from her. She pulled a pack of Kools from her apron and set fire to the end of a cigarette with a bright pink Bic. "You want to know how things used to run around here and don't know Johnny T. Stagg? How much time you got, girlie?"

"Long as you'll give me," she said. "I want to know everything."

"Everything?"

Tashi nodded. "The present, the past, all of it."

Mary exhaled a long plume of smoke, resting her arm on the back of the booth. "Tomorrow morning there's a meeting with the supervisors about building the big cross."

"The what?"

"Some fella from Arkansas just came to town and said Jesus Himself told him to build a sixty-foot cross in Tibbehah County. He's already got the support of Old Man Skinner and other local wheeler-dealer types. Would it interest you?"

"You bet."

"It's what you'd call some real local color."

"What do you think about it?"

"Building a big cross?" Mary said. "Oh, I don't know. I think it's just Skinner trying to cover up the sign to the titty bar out on the highway. I think it might just class this town up a little. Let people see what we really stand for."

* * *

Wes Taggart wouldn't open the goddamn door, and after finding it dead-bolted, the locals were more than happy to kick it in. Lillie was inside the little motel room first, moving fast and hard, as she'd learned from Quinn Colson, checking corners, watching for that son of a bitch to come out of the shitter. But instead she saw Bugs Bunny on the television, rumpled sheets under the flowered bedspread, and heard singing coming from the shower. The dumb son of a bitch hadn't heard a thing, hitting the refrain of Waylon's "Drinkin' and Dreamin'."

She elbowed through the door and slid open the shower curtain just as he got to the part about never seeing Texas, L.A., or ol' Mexico.

"Nope," Lillie said. "You sure as hell won't. Either clean that little pecker or put it away, because I have warrants for your arrest, Wes Taggart."

Bald-headed and corded with muscle, a damn atlas of shitbirdism inked across his arms and chest, Taggart grinned and placed his right hand over his nuts. He held up the flat of his left. "And who the hell is Wes Taggart?"

"The fella who wouldn't come clean and got his nuts shot from here to Pass Christian."

"Are you willing to bet on it?" he asked. "You can get sued busting in here like this."

Lillie pointed the end of her shotgun at his privates. Taggart dropped both hands to cover his rather disappointing package and gave a big shit-eating grin. "You know me now?"

"If you ain't the famous Lillie Virgil. Calamity Fucking Jane of the Marshals."

"Damn straight, fucknuts." Lillie reached for the rack and tossed him a towel. "Don't worry about covering up that Vienna sausage of yours, just show me your hands and come with me."

"Christ Almighty," he said. "What kind of woman talks like that? Where we going?"

"Someone wants to talk to you back in Tibbehah County."

"The fucking Ranger?"

"You aren't as dumb as you look, Wes."

"You getting all this?" Mary asked. She lit her third cigarette in less than twenty minutes, sucking in the smoke with hollow cheeks and burning through nearly half of the fresh one.

Tashi didn't answer, only shrugged. She just kept on listening to the woman talk about the *Who's Who* of Tibbehah County, starting off with a man named Johnny Stagg—great name, by the way—who used to run the board of supervisors until some dumb-ass crooks broke into an associate's house and robbed his safe full of cash and important papers. Those papers ended up landing Stagg in federal prison on corruption charges.

"Sheriff Colson sure hated that man."

"You mean the sheriff who killed himself?"

"You don't know much, do you?" Mary said. "Quinn Colson is the sheriff right now. At this very moment. His uncle was the man who killed himself. His name was Hamp Beckett. He was a fine man, a loving man, and lots of folks aren't so sure he did himself in. I sure didn't see it coming."

"Were y'all close?"

"As close as can be," she said. "He was what you young folks call a significant other."

"Lots of secrets down here," Tashi said. "Aren't there? I heard a novelist once say Southerners don't like to talk about unpleasant subjects. Is that true?"

"You want some more coffee?"

Tashi shook her head, not wanting the woman to quit talking. She was onto something, getting right to the heart of what she wanted Mary to say without being prodded.

"Y'all mind me asking why y'all are here," Mary said, wiping a speck of tobacco from her lip.

Tashi swallowed and nodded. "Do you remember Brandon Taylor?"

"It'll be twenty-one years to the day in November," Mary said, spewing out smoke from the corner of her mouth. "The family has suffered every day since they found that boy."

"What do you think, Miss Mary?" Tashi Coleman asked.

"I don't know," she said. "I didn't know Brandon. I can't understand why any of God's creatures would take their own life. Young boy, his whole life spread out before him."

"Some people don't believe it happened that way," Tashi said. "Some folks believe he was killed."

"I've heard the same kind of talk," Mary said. "Oh, Lord. Twenty years. It was a long time ago. So much has changed. Sometimes I don't even recognize this little ole town on the Square."

Quinn and Maggie headed back to their cabin, passing by the Spinner and the Tilt-A-Whirl, the daiquiri and margarita stands. They stopped briefly at a shooting game and Quinn quickly won a giant stuffed dog for Maggie. He started to go for a second prize, but the old Mexican man who worked the game, looking lonely and sad with his ancient chihuahua, finally held up his hand to Quinn and said, *"No más."*

It wasn't noon yet but damn-near one hundred. Quinn had promised to stop by a few cabins and shake a few hands. Not his favorite part of the job, but a necessary part of being sheriff.

"What are you gonna name him?" Quinn said, nodding to the big dog as they walked back toward her family cabin.

"Cujo," Maggie said.

"That movie always scared the hell out of me," Quinn said. "I never looked at a Saint Bernard the same way again."

"My mother didn't like me watching scary movies," Maggie said. "Especially anything with the supernatural. I wasn't even allowed to watch *Gremlins* until I was fifteen. I was told those little bastards were satanic."

"Only when they got wet."

"My daddy didn't care so much," Maggie said. "Especially when he was home from the road. We'd watch all kinds of movies late at night. He loved *Smokey and the Bandit. Convoy. White Line Fever.* Did I tell you he named his truck The Blue Mule? Just like in the movie."

"Many times," Quinn said.

"Well, if we stay married, we're bound to hear the same stories," Maggie said. "I've heard all about your dad and his time out in Los Angeles. About how he jumped those Pintos back before you were born and how he worked as a double for both Burt Reynolds and Lee Majors."

"Did a lot of work on *The Fall Guy*," Quinn said. "He used to always tell me and Caddy the show was based on his life."

"Was it?"

"Hell no," Quinn said. "If you're ever unlucky enough to meet him, you'll understand why."

"I'm just proud we got through our wedding without any family drama," Maggie said. "I won't ever forget Lillie Virgil stepping up like she did, standing in for Boom as your best man. It was a hell of a thing."

"Best woman," Quinn said, walking with her side by side down a dusty path, back toward the cabins. The food trucks already starting to grill sausage and peppers, chicken on a stick, and barbecue, the air thick with grease. "She still thinks she can find the son of a bitch who did that to Boom."

"Hope she does."

"Me, too," Quinn said. "I have a few questions for him."

"I bet."

"More than just what he did to Boom," Quinn said. "These people from the Coast have been wiping their feet in Tibbehah County for years. They've been running drugs, guns, and women through here for too damn long."

"You said it was worse under Johnny Stagg."

"Not much difference," Quinn said. "Stagg was just better at keeping it secret. Tibbehah County has been wild and wide open since the white man swindled it from the Choctaw. Same shit, different crooks. If I can talk to Wes Taggart, I might get what I need to stop some of this."

"But can Lillie find him?"

"Lillie Virgil can find anyone."

Quinn and Maggie found their way back to the Sunset Strip, a long, narrow shot of two-story cabins perched alongside a hill. All the little coves and streets had names like that. *Happy Hollow. Groovy Gardens. Beverly Hills.* At night, Christmas lights shone down on the dirt paths, families sitting on their mini porches with their feet on the railings, listening to music and drinking.

Tonight was their last night. Maggie's mother and sister and her sister's kids had gone home. There was an Uncle Paul, who didn't do much but sit on the porch and drink beer and wander down to the track when the horses ran, but he was gone, too. Now it was just Quinn and Maggie. Quinn's soon-to-be-adopted son, Brandon, was back home with Jean, Quinn's mom. He was looking forward to finally being alone with his new wife.

"Oh, crap," Maggie said.

Quinn had seen the men before she had, not slowing a single stride as they walked up onto the Sunset Strip. Five men wearing Watchmen militia gear—black pants, black T-shirts with the rebel flag, and sunglasses—gathered at the mouth of the narrow street, blocking their way, waiting for Quinn. They had short hair and unshaven faces, two of them smoking cigarettes. Their dress and their attitudes tried to imply they were former military. But Quinn knew the difference.

Quinn either had to stop walking or move right through them. If Maggie hadn't been with him, he'd have head-butted the biggest guy and taken the next one out with a sharp elbow. Quinn had met a hundred guys like this, wannabe Special Forces operators who took online courses and drooled over gun magazines. Quinn appreciated a good gun, but it wasn't any more than a tool for him.

He reached down for Maggie's hand and squeezed it. She breathed a little harder and her freckled face shone with sweat. Quinn pulled the Liga Privada from his lips and blew smoke in all their faces.

The men stared at him. A short man, muscled and low to the ground, coughed and swallowed. "You know who we are?" he asked.

Quinn didn't answer. He just placed the cigar to his lips and drew in some more smoke.

"You ain't got no right coming to Founders Square," he said. "You ain't got no right trying to make Senator Vardaman uncomfortable."

"Uncomfortable?" Quinn said, trying not to smile. "Now, that just breaks my heart."

Another man stepped up by the sawed-off little fellow. He was a little taller, with wraparound sunglasses and a GLOCK hat. All the men wore guns on their hips and all of them probably carried permits. If they made any more trouble, he'd make sure to run all their records.

"Vardaman told you up in Tibbehah," the man said. "You can't stop what's happenin'. You thought you were real clever shutting down his talk. Permits, you said. That was just a damn lie."

Every man wore a red bandanna around his neck. Most of them tattooed, kind of shorthand these days to show folks you're tough. The tattoos were of shamrocks and Gaelic symbols. The Punisher logo from comic books.

"Come on, Quinn."

"Nice place you got, ma'am," the short man said. "A real pretty shade of blue."

Quinn slowly dropped his right hand to the butt of his Beretta 1911, slow and easy, nonthreatening. "If you speak," Quinn said, "speak to me. And if you want to threaten a law enforcement officer, you're gonna have to do a much better job."

"You don't feel threatened?"

"By you?" Quinn said. "Not at all. Only thing you boys threaten is my sense of smell."

"It's coming," another man said, piping up like he'd just thought of what to say. "Ain't nobody gonna stop it. Especially you. You ain't got the right to wear that flag on your sleeve."

Something broke in Quinn with them talking about his service. Pushing by Maggie, he walked up on the man, who was red-faced with spittle on his lip, and reached out and grabbed the loudmouth by his nose, twisting and pulling until the little fella dropped to his knees. The men yelling and threatening but not doing a damn thing.

"You boys can spend the rest of the fair in jail," Quinn said, twisting the man's nose more for good measure. "Or you can walk away. It can be all corn dogs and cotton candy. Doesn't matter a damn to me."

There'd been a time when Quinn would've taken them all on. He'd been in bar fights, hand to hand in combat, and even left in a pit to battle it out with other Rangers. But law enforcement wasn't like being a Ranger. Assholes weren't real threats.

Quinn let go of the man's nose and stepped back. He hadn't let go of the cigar in his right hand. He put it back in his mouth and took a draw. The men turned and dispersed, the short man looking hard at Quinn and spitting in the dirt. They walked toward Founders Square and the pavilion, where you could still hear the stump speeches from the PA system.

"Didn't even drop your cigar."

"Hope that didn't scare you," Quinn said.

"Would you think less of me if I said I liked it?"

Quinn drew on the cigar and squinted one eye in the harsh morning light. "Not a damn bit, Maggie Colson."

# THREE

"Don't kid yourself, Ray, this place is fucking dying," Buster White said, adding emphasis with the bloody steak on the end of his fork. "Enjoy it while you're here. The last days of Rome. Everything is burning. Goddamn Nemo fiddling."

"You mean Nero," Ray said, his petit filet in front of him untouched, a cigarette smoldering in a coffee saucer.

"Then who the fuck is Nemo?" Buster White said, chewing, reaching for a big glass of cab, wine and blood dripping down his fat chin.

"A fish," Ray said, picking up the cigarette. "From a kids' movie. My grandkids love all that crap. I've seen it a million times. Fish gets lost, gets caught, and then jumps into the toilet to save his life."

They sat in the back room of the Old Chicago Steakhouse in the far corner of Buster White's casino in Tunica. Officially under the ownership of Dixie Amusements, a corporation with offices in Biloxi,

New Orleans, and Memphis, a front for a Syndicate of good ole boy thieves who'd been running shell games in the Deep South since the mid-1950s. Buster was getting old. Ray could see it in his dark-rimmed eyes, bad, blotchy skin, fattened jowls, and continuous indigestion. He couldn't get through three sentences before belching.

"Are you closing us down?"

"Maybe," White said, sawing back into the T-bone and filling his mouth, not breaking stride in the conversation. "But that's not why I wanted to see you. Whether this place goes tits up or not isn't up to me. We've tried to move our casinos off the river and inland. But the religious nutsos think by taking gambling off the water, it'll just spread all the fucking and dancing. So we got what? The Coast. And the fucking Indians. But something else gave me a goddamn heart attack this morning."

Ray nodded, brushing some ash off his seersucker suit, legs crossed, cordovan loafers buffed to a high shine for a meeting with the boss. "Wes Taggart."

"You're damn fucking right," Buster said, belching into his fist and then running his tongue over his back teeth for some loose meat. "The dumb shit hillbilly went and got himself caught, not two miles from my fucking castle. He'd reached out to me, trying to make some kind of amends for fucking me right in the ass. Claimed stealing the tractor trailer wasn't his idea, he'd been set up. When he got busted, he had a cute little piece of tail with him from up in Jericho. What's her name, Amber? Cherry?"

"Twilight."

"Oh, Christ. Are you fucking kidding me? He should've known the puss would be his undoing. What do I always say, don't shit where you eat and don't fucking let the puss go to your brain. It makes you goddamn soft and fucking stupid. Hey? Aren't you gonna eat? Don't you like your steak? I hired this guy right from Pascal Manale's, doubled his salary after he cooked for me and the missus one night. Sharp black guy. Talks just like a white man."

"Wes Taggart won't talk."

"Glad you got the faith, Ray," White said. "But these younger guys ain't from the same mold as you and me. We were all raised different, from a different time, a different era. We knew all this shit would go around and come back around. You get caught, you shut your mouth, you do your time, and when you're out you get your reward. But Taggart and that shit-for-brains J. B. Hood . . . Christ Almighty, why did we ever send those guys up to north Mississippi? All they did was rob me fucking blind."

Ray had to be careful of what he said. He never liked or trusted those guys or ever thought in a damn million years they could do a better job than Fannie Hathcock. But goddamn Buster was sure of it at the time, although he wouldn't say shit now even if his mouth was crammed full of it. So Ray did what Ray had always done ever since he and Buster had been boosting cars from the airmen on the Coast and running shithole clip joints on Beach Boulevard. Back then they were full of piss and vinegar and wore crew cuts and worked out with weights and ate nothing but steak and pussy. But, goddamn, times had changed. Buster belched again and pointed to Ray again with the end of an empty fork.

"I couldn't have Fannie try and work with the Chief again," Buster said. "That man would've scalped the red hair right off her head if we hadn't made the damn peace after what she did. Christ. I'm going to send her back to work out the details of running our shit on the Rez now that Tunica is dying this slow and painful death. Did you see the outlet mall out there? I only saw two cars in the big parking lot. Two cars. Bally's is gone. Harrah's is gone. We need those red-skinned Choctaw bastards."

"Hood and Taggart couldn't do it."

"Those boys would've fucked up their own funerals."

"Fannie's doing a damn fine job," Ray said. "We did good putting her in charge."

"What goddamn choice did I have?" Buster White said. "Those boys shit the bed. And Fannie had to clean it up. It's fine. It's fine. At least for now."

Ray lifted the cigarette to his lips and squinted in the smoke. It had to be damn-near sixty degrees in the back room of the Old Chicago Steakhouse, but Buster was sweating like a hog. Sure, Taggart was a liability. But how much damage could he really do unless he knew some real cruel and current shit about Buster and those Cartel folks in Houston? Something was making his old buddy shit his drawers. Something dirty and nasty.

"Not much we can do now," Ray said, blowing the smoke from the side of his mouth.

"Would you fucking eat?" Buster said. "That's a hell of a piece of meat. A nice char, good and bloody on the inside. Better than barely legal puss."

Ray shook his head. As he'd gotten older and grayer, he had less tolerance for Buster's crude talk. He hadn't changed a bit since they were teenagers in the way he thought of money and women. The more, the better—in everything. Food, booze, pills. And Ray seriously doubted he'd ever see the businesses in Tunica close up. All of it would far outlast him. Buster sat there, a gelatinous hump, wheezing, the meat along the edge of the T-bone sliced away.

"How's the cooze?"

"Come again?"

"Fannie," Buster White said, giving a half laugh, a half burp. "Who the fuck've we been talking about?"

"Good."

"She still mad at me?"

"Fannie doesn't get mad," Ray said. "Fannie's all business."

"Just like you taught her," Buster said, grinning, putting down his knife and fork. "I'll never forget when you brought that little piece of country trash into my bar in New Orleans. Real *Coal Miner's Daughter* shit. I thought you'd lost your damn mind. She was nineteen? Eighteen?"

"Twenty-three."

"Twenty-three, with legs going on forever and long red hair. And those tits. Christ Almighty. The best tits I've ever seen. My mouth's watering just thinking about them. I knew she was trouble then. And, goddamn, I know she's trouble now."

"She cleaned up one hell of a mess," Ray said. "Wes Taggart and J. B. Hood could've gotten us all sent to prison. North Mississippi was her reward. We're not going back on that. Are we?"

"I haven't decided," Buster said, picking up the T-bone with his hands and chewing off those last bits of gristle. "You're pussy-blind, Ray. You've never seen what kind of creature you're dealing with. I'd watch my back, if I were you. That woman will be the death of us both."

Damn, the kid was good. Caddy Colson knew all parents thought their kids had special talents, but she'd never seen an eleven-year-old throw and catch the football like her son Jason. He was nearly a head taller than most of the kids and could zip it downfield flat-footed without much effort. He was fast, too. During the start of summer drills that night, she watched Jason lead the pack, tossing a football back and forth to his new cousin, Brandon, making sure the younger boy was feeling comfortable at practice. This was only his second year playing

Little League ball, but Caddy Colson truly believed, the Good Lord willing, the boy was going to get a college scholarship. Ole Miss. Or if he got really good, Auburn.

"Did you hear from your brother?" her mother, Jean Colson, asked. Both of them sitting high in the stands at Tibbehah High stadium. "He said they were coming back from the fair early."

"He called."

"Did he say what it was about?"

"No, ma'am," Caddy said, trying to watch practice. The fifty or so boys were lined up, in mismatched shorts and T-shirts, bear-crawling for ten yards. Jason again leading the pack, most of the boys a good five yards behind him.

"I hope he and Maggie didn't get in a fight."

"Why would you think that?" Caddy said, baseball cap down in her eyes, dressed for the hot practice in a white tank top and khaki shorts with pink flip-flops. She held her keys in her hands and they would rattle on her knee every time she got excited watching her son run.

"Brandon's daddy's been making trouble," her momma said. "He's working with some lawyer in the Delta to make sure he can appear in court. I can't imagine that sitting well with Quinn. A filthy, no-good killer and bank robber."

"Quinn knew what he was getting into when he married Maggie," Caddy said. The boys ran backward in the ninety-five-degree heat, the sky turning a soft pink and blue over the metal visitors' stands across the field. "That's why I'm glad I never had to mess with an ex-husband or some dumb ass who wants to get to know his son years later. No, ma'am. Jason is all mine."

Caddy knew her mother wouldn't follow up. As much as she adored her grandson, she'd only asked once who his father might be.

The hard truth of it was even Caddy didn't know, the boy born in a wild, spun-out fucking kaleidoscope time in Memphis filled with Jack Daniel's, little white pills, and boys. House parties and lap dances and waking up in places she never knew she'd visited. There had been a garage rock drummer, a boxer, two pro wrestlers, but all those she'd ruled out on account of Jason being half black. Caddy Colson returned home damn-near ten years ago to Tibbehah County toting a black baby and everyone wanting to know her business. But she'd gotten clean and straight after a couple of tries and God could've never blessed her with a better son than Jason.

"How'd you enjoy the fair?"

"It was hot," Caddy said. "Boys didn't want to leave. They spent all day running around without shoes in all the dust, chasing Hondo and living off hot dogs and funnel fries."

"You think Jason is fast on account of him being part black?"

"Momma, that's so wrong."

"Well, tell me you weren't thinking the same thing," her momma said. "I mean, he didn't get that speed from our side of the family. It's why Quinn ended up in the recruiting office instead of signing with Ole Miss."

"Quinn ended up in the recruiting office because he couldn't stay out of trouble," Caddy said. "Uncle Hamp gave him two options, jail or the Army. Do you really think he had a choice?"

"Look at those little boys run," Jean said. "My two grandboys. I couldn't be any prouder."

The kids all followed a long, straight route across the goal line, waiting for the coach's whistle, and then followed down the sidelines, up ten yards and across the field, up another ten yards and across the field again, snaking their way back and forth to the other goalpost. Caddy was glad she wasn't down there in the heat. There was barely any shade up in the stands, her mother bringing them seat cushions and travel mugs filled with iced tea. Although if she really wanted to make an issue, she was pretty sure her momma had filled her own mug with ice, margarita mix, and a double dose of tequila. The woman never missed happy hour. Jean's eyes shone a bit in the fading sunlight, pointing down toward little towheaded Brandon, three years younger than Jason, trying to keep up with the big boys. He reminded Caddy of herself, trying to keep up with Quinn and Boom Kimbrough when they were kids, never facing a trail or a treehouse that didn't need conquering.

"How about Hondo?" her momma asked. "Did he bring that dog to the Neshoba County Fair?"

"Hondo won't leave Quinn," Caddy said. "You know that."

An old brown GMC truck rambled down to the edge of the field and parked crooked by the goalpost. The front door opened and an old black man got out and walked around to the passenger side and held open the door. Boom Kimbrough, twice as big as his father, crawled out of the truck, his own, planting a big foot on the field and then a cane and hefting himself to his full height. He had on a ball cap, long khaki pants, and a plain white tee, loose on the right sleeve where he'd lost an arm in Iraq. He'd grown out his beard since he'd been beaten by those two thugs, walking slow and steady toward the team he used to coach.

"I can't believe it," Jean said, taking in a long breath of air and reaching for her special cup.

"Did you really think Coach Boom would miss the first day of full practice?"

Some of the boys broke from formation and ran toward him, the other coach on the sidelines blowing the whistle but soon stopping, seeing who'd arrived. The swarm of children enveloping the big black figure with the wide smile.

* * *

"Buster wants Wes Taggart gone."

"A little late for that," Fannie Hathcock said, on the fifth floor of the casino, looking through the windows at the flat roof over the conference center and out onto the Mississippi River, muddy and snaky all the way up to Memphis. "Don't you think?"

"He thinks you might can get to him."

"In federal custody?" Fannie said, resting on a little blue settee, a cigarillo lit in her long, manicured hand. "No thank you. Wes Taggart is Buster's goddamn dog. If it's Ole Yeller time, then he better be holding the fucking gun."

"You're right," Ray said, slipping out of his jacket and setting it across the king-sized bed. The soft gold light shone into the curtains and across the white carpet and dark furniture. He walked over to the bar and scooped out some ice into a glass and filled it full with Glenfiddich.

"When Wes was at your place did he talk much about us?" he asked. "Family business and all?"

"Not really," Fannie said, plucking the cigarillo back into her mouth and stretching out her long legs, studying the toenail job she'd gotten down at the spa, cotton still between her toes. "Man was too goddamn pussy-blind to talk about much else. He and his buddy Hood just wanted to let me know I was nothing but a yipping dog at the table. Did I tell you what they did to my office?"

"You did."

"A couple fucking animals," she said. "Food and cigarette butts everywhere. He screwed that girl Twilight so hard on my desk, they cracked the glass. Cost me nearly a thousand dollars to get it repaired."

"Send me the bill."

"I sent it to Buster."

"Tread easy, Fannie," Ray said, taking a seat across from her. "Buster White isn't in a joking mood. This casino is on its last legs and it looks like he's going to have to double down on our business at the Rez."

"Jesus Christ," she said. "Goddamn Sitting Bull and his tribe of thieves."

"Don't worry about all that," he said. "We made nice with the Chief."

"Only way to make nice with Chief Robbie is to ram a goddamn tomahawk up his ass," Fannie said, offering a sweet smile. "Would you be so good as to pour me some champagne, doll?"

Ray stood up, feeling a little light-headed and tired, holding on to the arm of the chair, before pushing on back to the bar. Fannie was on her feet, holding his arm and walking with him. "Are you all right?"

"Fine and dandy."

"Your face has gone a little gray."

"Two hours with Buster, him talking nonstop bullshit, and you'd go gray, too," he said. "Now, where'd I put my goddamn cigarettes?"

"That dumb son of a bitch," she said, letting go of his arm and making her way to the minibar, pulling out a bottle of Veuve Clicquot rosé. She twisted off the cork and poured a glass, making her way back to the little sitting area, pulling out the cotton between her toes, before taking a sip.

"Taggart has become a real problem," he said. "He knows stuff no one should hear about. He opens his mouth and he fucks us all."

Fannie snorted some rosé and shook her head. "No argument from me," she said, turning from the fluted glass. "I'd take out his ass pronto."

"No kidding," he said. "But here's the thing. I need ideas on how we get it done."

"From little ole me?" Fannie said, rolling the glass stem between her fingertips. "I'm just the hospitality queen. Or isn't that what that tub of whale shit Buster White called me?"

"You look good, Boom," Jean Colson said.

Boom took a seat up in the bleachers between Caddy and her mother, taking a damn long time to get off the field and make his way to where they sat. It was hard as hell watching him walk so slowly, but she knew he'd hate being helped. Boom told her he didn't want anyone's pity or anyone treating him like a goddamn invalid. He said he'd been hurt but it wouldn't slow him down a bit.

"Appreciate it, Miss Jean," Boom said. "But I feel better than I look. My therapist said it might take me six more months to get back to normal. Figure by Christmastime, I'll be ready to hit the road again. After all the news got out, I got plenty of offers to start driving again."

"Don't rush it," Jean said. "Don't you rush a thing. Heal up. Get yourself better."

"Jason's looking good out there, Caddy," Boom said, leaning his back into the bleacher behind him. "Boy sure is fast. Lots faster than your brother. Y'all know Quinn's slow as hell."

"I told you," Jean said.

"You see how fast he set up in the pocket?" Boom said. "Damn. If he can get a decent receiver, these boys going all the way to state."

Caddy looked over at Boom, the sun setting across his scarred face. The scars came from years before, back in Iraq, barely hidden under his patchy black beard. She wanted to reach out and touch his face, try to make him feel better, let him know there were better things than the meanness and violence that kept on stepping into his life. More than anything, she knew Boom just wanted to be left alone. Him and his truck and a long stretch of road in front of him.

"Wasn't too long ago when I was watching you and Quinn play,"

Jean said, leaning forward and setting her face on her hands, watching her grandsons split up into drills.

"Hate to say it, Miss Jean," Boom said. "But that was back in the Jurassic days. You wouldn't know from looking at this football field. Nothing looks like it's changed."

Jean Colson smiled, her hair getting longer and grayer over the summer. Her pale blue eyes crinkled at the edges as she smiled, putting a hand on Boom's leg. "Looks the same as when my ex jumped all those Pintos here back in '77. Lord, love is blind when you're wearing hot pants and suede boots up past your knees."

"Momma," Caddy said, the last thing she wanted was to hear stories about the wild old days of the seventies when her father split time between north Mississippi and Los Angeles, working as a stuntman. Or the time her mother visited an aging Elvis at Graceland, talking to him in the Jungle Room about the existence of God and man's place in the universe.

"You still seeing that nice girl from Memphis?" Jean said, having the sense to change the subject. "The one with the nice smile and all that wild hair?"

"Nat Wilkins?" Boom said, stroking his beard, the way he did when he got nervous. "She come down to visit from time to time. But she's a busy woman, a lawwoman like Lillie Virgil. Don't have much time for relationships. Especially with a busted-up dude like me."

"Hush your mouth," Jean said, taking a long pull from her tumbler. "You and Quinn have heads made out of steel."

"Shit," Boom said. "What you drinking there, Miss Jean?"

Boom looked to Caddy and Caddy grinned, having a little fun with her mother. At the far end of the football field, Jason dropped back for a pass but then just as fast ran it hard and quick up the middle for a touchdown.

Jean just shrugged and toasted them both with her cup. Boom looked over at Caddy and studied her face. "What?" Caddy asked.

"Saw you last night at the service," Boom said. "You and that Bentley fella seem real close."

"He's just helping me with some grants," she said, feeling her face flush, trying to keep her eyes on practice. She wouldn't turn to Boom because he'd known her his whole life and would see it all over her face. "His nonprofit in Jackson can be a godsend to communities like us. Helping get food and supplies where they're needed. We're getting hamburger meat. Cheese. Clothes for the schoolkids . . . Stop looking at me like that."

Boom laughed. It was good to hear him laugh, even if it was at her expense.

"Mmm-hmm," Boom said.

"What are y'all talking about?" Jean asked.

"Nothing," Caddy said. "Nothing at all. Besides, the boy is six years younger than me. He's just a damn kid."

Boom just grinned and the three of them sat back on the bleachers watching the Colson boys practice.

**Tashi Coleman**
***Thin Air*** **podcast**
**Episode 2: THE BIG WOODS**

NARRATOR: The first spot I wanted to visit in Tibbehah County was the old Hawkins place. This is where Sheriff Hamp Beckett found Brandon's '55 Chevy Apache the day after he disappeared, although Brandon's body wouldn't be found for nearly a week. The windows were open, seats covered in rainwater, according to an account in the Tupelo *Daily Journal*. His gun rack was empty, only his backpack and a few scattered CDs lay in the passenger seat. One of them was Garth Brooks, *Fresh Horses*. I'd thought about that album a lot when I first started looking into Brandon's death, the song "Beaches of Cheyenne" particularly staying on my mind. *They packed up all his buckles and shipped his saddle to his dad*, the song goes, about a rodeo rider who gets killed riding a bull. His girlfriend takes the news pretty rough.

The land is in the far northeast corner of Tibbehah County, a five-hundred-acre spread that had recently been divided up into four sections after Joe and Lorna Hawkins died in the late 1970s. Their kids moved to other states and rarely checked on the property. According to the same news story, one of the children had offered hunting rights to Tim Taylor and Taylor, in turn, let Brandon use it.

My producer Jessica and I decided to drive out to the land on our very first day in Mississippi. The cattle gate was still up, chained to a rotting post, and covered in thick kudzu. It's an eerie stretch of dirt road to the old house, much of it overgrown by weeds and partially blocked by downed trees. The house had fallen in on itself, windows boarded up with rotting plywood and the front steps broken and decayed. Brandon's mother told us about a deer stand sitting a quarter mile down a path from the old home.

> [BIRDS CHIRP. CICADAS TICK. REPORTERS' STEPS SHUFFLE ON PINE NEEDLES.]

We followed the same path, pushing through the vines, spiderwebs, and tree branches. It was August, almost oppressively hot, but there was a soft stillness as we walked on the rust-colored pine needles, following the trail Brandon Taylor had gone down many times. Even twenty years later, it doesn't seem like the kind of path you'd get easily lost on. We found the deer stand in about ten minutes and crawled up its old wooden ladder to see what was left. Inside, we discovered a stack of waterlogged *Penthouse* magazines, some empty tins of smokeless tobacco, several crushed soda cans, and two condoms.

> [SHUFFLING OF DEBRIS IN DEER STAND.]
> JESSICA: Brandon was here.
> TASHI: Looking out on this very same field. Maybe this was his Mountain Dew? Or can of Skoal. Did Brandon use that stuff?
> JESSICA: I'll ask Shaina.

NARRATOR: The view opened up into a slice of land that had at one time been clear, now filled with small trees and wild vines.

According to what the sheriff's office said at the time, Brandon, a kid who'd been hunting these same woods since he was eight, simply got turned around that night and stumbled into the Big Woods, a twenty-thousand-acre stretch of national forest populated by oak and loblolly pine, with creeks, a river, and thick undergrowth.

Brandon's body would be found nearly twelve miles away from

where he'd parked his truck in a completely different part of the county. Was he really lost? Did he purposefully wander into the Big Woods to kill himself?

The location of the body wasn't our only question. The idea Brandon somehow got turned around and wandered away on purpose could make sense. We do know he carried a Remington .308 on a shoulder sling, a high-powered deer rifle, the gun always cited as the weapon used in his suicide.

But what we'd later learn is the bullet found in Brandon's skull wasn't from a Remington .308 at all. A copy of Brandon's first autopsy released to us by his sister says the bullet that killed Brandon was a .38 caliber, bullets most commonly used in revolvers, sometimes in semiautomatic pistols. Officials would tell the Taylor family for years it was simply a typo. A zero missing in the report.

But with all other files lost, and no evidence related to the case in storage, we couldn't be so sure. That hot night in August, Jessica and I stayed up in the deer stand until it turned dark, listening to old Garth Brooks on our iPhones, drinking a few cheap beers, and thinking about how this fifteen-year-old boy ended up almost another county away. There was something mysterious and ominous about being so close to those Big Woods, which seem to spread out forever from the old Hawkins land.

> TASHI: It's getting so dark.
> JESSICA: No streetlamps or ambient light. I hope we can find our way back.
> TASHI: Brandon always had a flashlight. So do we.

NARRATOR: The only thing we could imagine driving us further into the unknown was if we'd been followed.

# FOUR

Cleotha handed Quinn a cup of coffee as he entered the sheriff's office, hot, black with one sugar, in his favorite mug. "Heard that new truck of yours from a mile away," she said, hands on her sizable hips. "Sounds like a damn monster growling. Shakes the whole damn building, Sheriff. You got to get those pipes fixed."

"Those pipes cost extra," he said. "Puts fear in the criminal element in this county."

"All it do is make a lot of racket, Sheriff," she said. "Why do boys like them big-ass trucks?"

"Makes us feel important," Quinn said.

He raised the mug toward her, heading on into his office right beside the entrance to the jail. The SO was pretty much split in half, with the office out front, inmates in the back. As of this morning, they had thirty-six. But he was expecting a thirty-seventh by noon if Lillie Virgil made her schedule checking Wes Taggart out of the

Harrison County lockup and heading north. She'd told Quinn she couldn't wait to make small talk with him on the way up, making a detour into Tibbehah County before getting processed onto his first appearance in federal court in Oxford. He and Quinn had a lot to discuss.

Quinn pulled out the unfinished Liga Privada from his shirt pocket and found a battered old Zippo in his Levi's. The Zippo had been given to him by his Ranger sergeant who'd gotten it from a Vietnam-era Ranger. He lit the cigar and placed his cowboy boots at the edge of the desk.

His office was as clean and orderly as always, with a polished wooden gun rack on the wall lined with shotguns and rifles. A few framed photographs of his family. His Uncle Hamp. Caddy, his momma. Even a publicity still of his daddy, Jason Colson, as sort of a Southern version of Evel Knievel, wearing a jumpsuit adorned with a rebel flag. He'd written to a young Quinn to *Stay in School and Mind Your Teachers* . . .

Reaching for a file on his desk, Quinn set about looking through the incident reports since he'd been away. He'd left his second-in-command, Reggie Caruthers, in charge, and Reggie had kept him up to date on the big criminal activity since he left town. Two pecker-heads had tried to kill each other outside the Walmart. The fight had started over a Ziploc baggie of assorted pills and a case of Busch Light. The argument got down to the split of the spoils and one of them decided to make his point with the sharp end of a Case pocketknife.

"Sheriff?" Cleotha asked.

Quinn looked up. As always, his door had been wide open.

"Woman here to see you," she said. "Said her name is Sashy Coles. Or something like that."

"Did she say what she wanted?"

"Said she come down from New York City to ask you some questions," Cleotha said. "Real serious-looking, with some big-ass Urkel glasses and carrying some kind of tape recorder. I don't know. Says she's some kind of reporter."

Quinn said to send her on in and kept on going through the narrative on the Walmart throwdown. Banks Ellard was apparently treated and released with fourteen stab wounds in his stomach. The man had been lucky the blade had been short and didn't hit any vital organs. Ellard was quoted in the report from Deputy Cullison as saying, "All I tried to do was chill the damn beer and the boy went off on me."

There was a knock on the door and Quinn looked up to see a young white woman, somewhere in her mid-twenties, with black hair up in a bun and heavy black-framed glasses on her delicate face. She was wearing a blue-and-white-striped T-shirt and wide-leg jeans hitting her high on the calves.

"I'm Tashi Coleman," she said, holding a small microphone, a recording device dangling from her shoulder on a strap.

Quinn stood and offered his hand. The office felt a little stuffy that morning, and Quinn walked over to raise the window. Outside, you could hear two of the inmates working on a new table for the break room, the saws making a high buzzing sound every few minutes. Some light hammering.

"I'm hoping you might help answer a few questions," Tashi said. She looked pleasant and eager.

"Just a few?"

Tashi smiled. "Maybe more than that."

"OK," Quinn said, nodding. "Take a seat, Miss Coleman."

"Wow," she said. "I figured I might have to call several times. Bug you until you'd agree to talk with me."

"Don't you know Tibbehah County is the hospitality capital of the South?" Quinn asked.

"I thought the motto was 'Native American name but All-American values'?" she asked.

"Maybe," Quinn said. "But I kind of like my slogan better."

The woman reached into her purse and pulled out a notebook and pen. She sat up straighter in the wooden chair and said, "I'm looking into an old case worked by your uncle. This was from more than twenty years ago. A boy named . . ."

"Brandon Taylor."

"How'd you know?"

"Miss Mary at the Fillin' Station," Quinn said. "Didn't she warn you news travels fast on the town square?"

Tashi smiled again. "Can you pull those files for me?"

"If I had them, I'd be glad to share them," Quinn said. "But it seems like those files were lost long before I took over here. I tried to pull them for a friend of Brandon Taylor's earlier this year."

"Was there a fire or something?" Tashi said. "I always hear about these famous fires that just happen to hit sensitive files."

"Ma'am, I've always found working with the press can be a two-way street," Quinn said. "Y'all sometimes find out things we'd like to know. And to be clear, I was only two years older than Brandon when he went missing."

"But your uncle was the sheriff."

"Right."

"And this is a small town," she said. "Surely you heard things. Did your uncle ever talk about the case?"

"I know my uncle found a rifle close by and his death was ruled a suicide," Quinn said. "And I also know Brandon's family has never believed it."

"Was the rifle sent off for testing?"

"I don't know," Quinn said.

"Was the body examined by the state?" she said. "Or just the local funeral home?"

"I don't know."

"Were there photos taken?" she said. "Evidence examined? Time lines established?"

Quinn held up his hands and shook his head. "I was pretty much just trying to get through my senior year and raising hell with my friends. I knew Brandon. But I didn't know him well enough to tell you what he was going through personally."

Tashi Coleman nodded, taking a long moment before saying, "So what you're saying is you don't know a whole hell of a lot, Sheriff."

"Yes, ma'am," Quinn said. "About all I can offer you right now is a hot cup of coffee."

"No thank you," she said, stuffing the notebook and pen back in the purse. "I'm fine."

"It's the only good coffee in town," he said, smiling. "Much better than the Fillin' Station. That stuff tastes like hot dishwater."

"You have to understand how frustrating this is," she said. "Files can't just disappear."

"I understand," Quinn said. "I'd be glad to ask around when I can. But I'm a little busy right now. We had a stabbing at the Walmart last night and I have a U.S. Marshal delivering a prisoner to me real soon. I've been wanting to talk to this man for a long while."

"I'll be in touch," Tashi said.

"You sure you don't want coffee? Get whole bean from a company in Oxford," Quinn said, smiling. "Dark roast they called Faulkner's Fury."

"OK," Tashi said, and her face softened a bit. "And maybe you can help me with a few general details?"

"You bet," Quinn said, reaching across the desk and offering his hand again. "You can call me Quinn. You might find my methods a bit different than some Mississippi sheriffs you've heard about. I like reporters. I keep an open jail log. Unless it's an active investigation, I'm happy to share with you what I know."

"Hard to believe."

"Did you think I'd wear mirrored sunglasses and chew Red Man?"

"To be honest," Tashi said, "I wasn't sure what I thought I'd find. I just spent the morning with the Tibbehah County supervisors. They talked about a dozen or so bridges being closed by the state for repairs. And plans to bring a sixty-foot cross to Highway 45."

"Just gets better and better, doesn't it?"

"You don't support building it?"

"Ma'am," Quinn said. "I support my country, my county, and my church. But I believe that money could be spent on more worthy projects for people in actual need. I also prefer to be a bit more quiet about my personal beliefs."

"They say it'll cut down on the glow from the neon of the strip club," Tashi said, looking behind Quinn at his pictures of his family and from his time with the 3rd Batt of the 75th Regiment. A framed American flag once flying over Camp Spann in Afghanistan hung on a far wall.

"Might have to make it a hundred feet, then," Quinn said. "That's a lot of neon."

"Don't be sore, Wes," Lillie Virgil said, driving with her right hand on the wheel of the Charger and cracking the window with her left. God, the son of a bitch smelled. "You gave it your best shot, shaving your head and all. Someone just needed to give you a road map to get off the Coast. Just think of me and Charlie here as giving you a nice nudge in the right direction."

Marshal Charlie Hodge sat in the passenger seat as Lillie drove, Wes Taggart in back shackled to a D-ring. He hadn't said two words since they got him rousted from the shower, out and dressed and processed through the local jail at dawn. She was supposed to take him on to Oxford, but due to some lost paperwork, he'd make his first appearance on the attempted murder of Boom back in Jericho.

"Air too cool for you?" Lillie asked.

Taggart said nothing.

"Charlie here has been a Marshal now for twenty-five years," Lillie said. "Ain't that right, Charlie?"

"Coming up on thirty," Charlie said, staring straight ahead. He was a skinny dude of medium height, and kept a thin little mustache and goatee. His hair was snow white.

"Don't you worry," Lillie said. "We plan on stopping off for lunch in Starkville. They feed you a good breakfast at the lockup?"

"Sausage biscuit and some piss-poor coffee," Taggart said, his eyes meeting Lillie's in the rearview.

"Ain't that a shame," Lillie said. "We can do better in Tibbehah County. Sheriff makes a mean cup of coffee."

Taggart's eyes shot back up to the mirror. "Tibbehah County," he said. "Shit. You're really fucking me, lady. I was told I'd make my first appearance in Oxford. I'm supposed to meet my fucking attorney. He's gotta drive all the way down from Memphis."

"I'm sure your lawyer won't mind the longer drive," Lillie said. "It's only an hour away. Hope your Syndicate folks set you up with someone good. Or did your buddies scatter like bottle flies on shit when you got on the phone?"

"I don't know what the hell you're talking about, woman," Taggart said, his pockmarked face working into a little snarl. "There's no more a Syndicate or Dixie Mafia than there is a fucking Santa Claus."

"And you didn't even know your name was Wes Taggart, either," Lillie said. "Can you believe that, Charlie? The man had amnesia when I found him at the Star Inn scrubbing his little ole peter."

Charlie chuckled. He was a good guy. He'd been Lillie's mentor since she came on with the Marshals last year, right out of Glencoe.

"I don't want to go to Tibbehah," Taggart said. "And y'all got no business to take me there. 'Cept the sheriff was friends with that big nigger y'all say I beat up. Which is a goddamn lie."

"You're a charmer, Wes," Lillie said. "Sheriff Colson's gonna love spending some time with you."

"My lawyer is a big damn deal," Taggart said, turning his head, watching the flat land along Highway 45 zip by, a sprawling cow pasture featuring a life-sized statue of Jesus with His arms wide. "A big damn deal. Y'all are wasting your time. This is all bullshit. I was on fucking vacation."

"You always bring thirty grand with you on vacation?" Lillie said. "And two handguns and a fake ID?"

"I'll be gone from that shithole town by morning."

"We'll see," Lillie said.

"If the damn sheriff lays a hand on a single hair on my head . . ."

"Don't worry, dipshit," Lillie said. "You shaved it all off."

"Your friends will say I'm too old," Caddy said. "I'm robbing the cradle."

"I'm twenty-nine damn years old," Bentley said. He was a handsome young dude, with straight white teeth and lots of thick brown hair swept back from his tanned face. "Where I'm from, that's not very young. Besides, how is it their business?"

"Momma likes you," Caddy said, tossing a big bag of cow manure from the back of her truck to Bentley's feet. "Momma can be hard on men I like."

"So you like me?" Bentley said, looking up at the tailgate of the old brown GMC Caddy drove. "You're going to go ahead and admit that right here and now? Because I'm getting tired of having to meet down in Jackson or in Memphis just to go to a movie and dinner."

"I'm not embarrassed of you," Caddy said, tossing another bag of cow shit toward Bentley, this time seeing the seam of the bag split open and spill on Bentley's nice shoes. He hadn't dressed for work, although over the last few weeks he'd been a big help at The River, sorting clothes, picking okra, and doing some basic repairs on the shacks. He was doing everything he could to show he wasn't just some spoiled little shit from Jackson who grew up in a house with a stable bigger than an airplane hangar.

"Then why won't you be seen with me?"

"I don't like folks knowing my business," Caddy said, wiping her brow with her forearm, her boots caked in mud, sweating in a tank top and cutoff jeans. "And we don't really have a lot of culinary options here besides Mexican, Chinese, catfish, and barbecue."

"What's wrong with barbecue?" Bentley tossed the hair out of his eyes, an Ole Miss frat boy move Caddy usually would've hated. The bag of cow shit he carried made it OK.

"Barbecue here is OK," Caddy said. "But it doesn't get much better than Memphis. How'd you like those Cornish hens we had last time?"

"At the Cozy Corner?" Bentley said. "It was pretty awesome. And the taco place over in Germantown. The one with that old guy who yelled at me for ordering cheese dip."

Caddy smiled, kicking the final bag off the tailgate and hopping down in the dirt of a barn that doubled as a church on Sundays. Everything at The River was about getting back to the basics of religion. No big-screen TVs. No light shows. No gossip or grandstanding. The church was founded by her love Jamey Dixon with the prime purpose of serving the Lord and the common man. It didn't matter if you were an immigrant who didn't speak English or a woman who'd made money selling her body. This place was about acceptance, love, and finding a purpose. The River had saved her life. And now it had expanded, with a big new building funded with money from Bentley's family foundation.

"There's this event in Jackson," Bentley said.

"Stop you right there, kid," Caddy said, walking up on Bentley, running a hand over her close-cropped towhead and smiling. "I don't do fund-raisers, mixers, glad-handing, or cocktail events."

"You should make this one," he said. "Don't you want to grow this place? These are the very people who contributed to the food pantry here."

"Do you remember when we first met?" Caddy said, placing the flat of her dirty hand on Bentley's white Polo shirt, smiling when she saw it left a mark. "And not when you claimed you saw me riding with my daddy. You didn't know Daddy until he'd left our family and I'd have had no more to do with him than the man in the moon."

"You're talking about on the Square."

"Yes."

"I walked up to you and told you you had a nice figure."

"And what did I say?"

"You told me to go to hell."

"After that."

"You said I had a nice figure, too," he said. "And a cute ass."

"You're lucky I didn't slap it when you walked away," she said.

"You handed me a bill for The River," he said. "Old-time gospel show. You were the most beautiful girl I'd ever seen."

Caddy nodded, slamming shut her tailgate. The inside of the old barn pleasant, cool and dark. The dirt floor worn as smooth and soft as talcum powder. The pews and folding chairs neatly stacked up by the pulpit, a simple handmade cross hanging from the rafters.

"Glad I showed up."

"I know who you are and what you do, Bentley Vandeven," Caddy said. "And I sincerely appreciate all the donations your foundation has given. We need every penny. But we stand on our two feet here at The River, and as long as you keep me and your high-dollar friends in Jackson separate, I think we'll continue to have a fine time."

Bentley had his hands on his hips, his face breaking a little as he looked down at the stack of fertilizer and manure she'd loaded up in the tractor to take down to the garden. He seemed to think on things for a moment before lifting his eyes and smiling. "You don't have to dress up," Bentley said. "You don't even have to be nice."

Caddy didn't answer.

"My mother is the one throwing the party," he said. "She wants to meet you. She thinks the world of your father. She said he's the best horseman she's ever seen in her life."

"My father is a charmer," Caddy said.

"Your father looked out for me when I needed him," Bentley said. "He taught me to ride, care for horses, and be a man. We used to watch those old movies he was in at his trailer in Pocahontas. If you stopped those VHS tapes at the right moment, you could see it was Jason Colson and not Burt Reynolds. He helped raise me."

"Funny how that works," Caddy said, the sunlight bright and glowing at the barn door. Everything else around them in darkness, smelling of hot old wood and leather tack. "I never really thought Jason Colson had it in him."

"Will you think about it?"

"Will you help me transport this cow shit?"

Bentley bent down and rolled up his khakis to his knees. "You got some work boots around here to fit me?"

"Can't have a man laboring in loafers," Caddy said. "Let me see what I can find."

"I brought you a little present," Lillie Virgil said. "An endangered shitbird from the Gulf Coast of Mississippi."

"What about your people in Oxford?" Quinn asked, picking up the cigar he'd neglected during Tashi Coleman's visit. He tipped the ash and relit the end. Lillie never really seemed to give a damn whether he smoked or not, understanding a little caffeine and nicotine was needed on the job.

"Fuck 'em," Lillie said. "His paperwork got lost. The original charges were filed in Tibbehah. And that's where he'll make his first appearance. They want this turd to answer to federal charges, you can FedEx his sorry ass up their way."

"As long as it doesn't get you in trouble."

"Shit," Lillie said. "After what he did to Boom? Just don't fuck him up too bad or I'll have to answer for it. But talk to him all you like. He softened up a little on the ride over, resigned to his fate."

"How'd it go with his girlfriend?"

"Little Miss Twilight?" Lillie said, sitting at the edge of his desk. Everything as smooth and easy as it had been when she'd been his second-in-command. Lillie looked tall and cool in a black linen shirt with her sleeves rolled up and dark jeans, Sig Sauer and Marshal's badge clipped to her Western belt. "Apparently, he wasn't much of a lay. I found her working at a shithole on Summer Avenue. Her mother told her I was coming. She didn't seem to have any issue with it. Sat outside the club as she smoked a joint and told me all about her time on the run with Kmart Butch Cassidy. He promised her champagne wishes and caviar dreams but only delivered Popeyes fried chicken and screw-top whiskey."

"What'd he say about Boom?"

"Denied it," she said. "Said it was all J. B. Hood."

"God rest his soul."

"Spoken like the man who shot him dead on Highway 45."

"Didn't have much of a choice."

"Guilt-ridden?"

"Terribly," Quinn said, blowing out a stream of smoke. "I wake up every morning crying to myself. You want some coffee before we do the meet and greet?"

"I sure missed your coffee, Quinn," Lillie said. "Marshals' office has one of those old Bunn coffeemakers, pumping out the same weak-ass shit since back in the day. I have to drive on down to South Main by the train station to get a decent cup."

Quinn started for the door, turning back around with his hand on the brass knob. "Before we do, I wanted to talk to you about something."

Lillie crossed her arms over her chest and nodded. "You still fixated on that fuckwad Vardaman?"

"Yep."

"I don't think Wes Taggart could find the state capitol with Siri jacked into his ass," she said. "He's a low-level turd. Nail his ass for what he did to Boom and flush the goddamn toilet."

"You know good and well his people are tied in with Vardaman."

"Of course they are," Lillie said. "They've been tied in with that asshole back when Stagg was running the show. I just think you're wasting your time with Wes Taggart. Only person around here who might connect the Syndicate with Jimmy Vardaman is Fannie Hathcock. And good luck with that."

"Won't hurt to ask."

"Ask nicely," Lillie said. "The whole ride up I wanted to crack that fucker's head like an egg. But I applied the utmost restraint."

"No kidding."

"Why the fuck are you surprised, Ranger?" Lillie said. "I'm the one who trained you to use compassion."

"Is that what you call it?"

# FIVE

"My family held out hope he'd gotten lost in those Big Woods," Shaina Taylor said, sitting in lawn chairs in front of her small white house. Her three-year-old daughter racing down a Slip 'N Slide and hooting with laughter. "But after the fifth, sixth, seventh search party didn't find nothing, they knew something bad had happened. Wasn't like Brandon was the kind of kid to hitch a ride out of town. And even though I was only nine, I know it wasn't the kind of house he wanted to escape. Daddy worked at the sawmill for Larry Cobb before he got into trouble with Mr. Stagg and them. Momma ran her daycare next to the Piggly Wiggly. Our sister Charlene was a senior at Tibbehah High. We weren't the kind of people who invited trouble into our lives. My folks worked hard, took us to church twice a week. Ain't nobody around here getting beaten or anything like that. Brandon wouldn't have just got up and left one day. He had a life here. Boy had lots of friends at school. Even had a girlfriend who used to spend her summers up here with her grandmother. Damn, he loved that girl. Traded letters every week."

"Maggie Powers."

"Yes, ma'am."

"You don't need to call me ma'am," Tashi said. "We're pretty much the same age."

"I didn't mean to imply you're older," Shaina said. "Just someone I respect."

"How so?" Tashi said, sitting side by side with the chubby little woman in the flowered dress, both of them wearing sunglasses and drinking bottles of Diet Coke.

"For one thing, you're the only person who's ever done one thing for Brandon."

"That can't be true."

"Of course it's true," Shaina said, standing up for a moment, telling her daughter to be careful about belly flopping on the hard ground. "I swear to you, that child don't have a lick of sense. She cut up her foot the other day at the swimming pool, refuses to wear them flip-flops I gave her."

Tashi looked down at her notebook, the microphone placed on a small wicker chair between them, catching the sound of the passing cars on the highway, the gurgle of the hose, and the laughter of the child. "How's Charlene doing with all this?"

"Charlene's never done well with any of it," Shaina said. "Momma and me ain't spoke to her in two years. Last time my sister came home, with her second husband, she was carrying on about some big job she was about to get down in Orlando. She swore to us she was about to be one of Cinderella's stepsisters in that Electric Light Parade they have. Charlene and me had been real big about Disney since they paid for all of us to come down after they found Brandon. There we were, three months after them finding his body and being treated like damn princesses. I was too young to know I couldn't have fun. Charlene and Momma crying the whole way through the fireworks. Me thinking maybe wishes do come true and Brandon'd be at home when we got back to Jericho. Silly stuff like that."

"Do you think your mother has changed her mind about talking to me?"

"Momma?" Shaina said, rolling her eyes. "Oh, hell no. She's still mad for me reaching out to y'all. I don't think she's scared or nothing. I just think she can't handle living all this again. 'Bout killed her. Definitely killed Daddy. Man was never the same after Brandon died. Got meaner than hell. Drank like a fish. Quit praying. Goin' to church. Believing in any damn thing."

"I'm sorry."

"Like I told y'all," Shaina said. "I'm not looking for a killer or any conspiracy theories. I just think Brandon deserves some answers. I can't find the state's autopsy. Only the one done here in town at Bundren's that I passed on to y'all. And I can't find no police report. I can't get a damn straight answer from the state people about Brandon's rifle. Did they test it? Did they give it back? Where'd it go? Why'd everything go and disappear? How could you possibly know Brandon walked into those woods to chase a big buck and then just decided to go and kill himself? Lost? That boy could never get lost. Not where he was headed, following the old crooked creek where him and Daddy used to go fishing."

"How'd your father die?"

"His heart stopped working," Shaina said. "Got all kind of medical reasons for Daddy. Doctor's reports, insurance denials for a preexisting condition, all that mess. But sometimes folks can just get so sad, they hole up in a place in their head and never want to get back out. Daddy blamed himself. Never got over it."

Her daughter was as slick as a sea lion, hair plastered back to her head, all elbows and knees, with a big, mischievous smile. The hose flooded through their yard and into a cleared lot next door with a single-wide trailer with a FOR RENT sign in the window. Shaina Taylor worked most days at the Dollar General, was off on Sundays.

"You said your parents blamed the sheriff?" Tashi said.

"Yes, ma'am," Shaina said, not being able to help it. "Daddy used to say Sheriff Beckett was big as an ox and dumb as a brick. Said the man never even questioned what happened to Brandon. As soon as they seen that rifle nearby, laying ten feet away, he decided on it."

"Hold on," Tashi said, holding her hand. She scribbled out some more notes and then checked the recording levels to make sure she was getting all this. "Who said 'ten feet away'?"

"The sheriff told Daddy that," she said. "Said some animals had moved his body some. But we don't know if anyone even checked to see if the bullet inside Brandon's head came from his hunting rifle. You know how it says on the autopsy that it was a .38, not a .308, and they tried to tell us it was a typo? Well, we don't have no bullet. No ballistics or whatever. And to this day, I don't even know how or why he'd even do such a thing. If that ain't Tibbehah County, I don't know what is. *Believe what you're told. Keep your mouth shut and don't ask no questions. And let the folks in power let you know what's best for your family.* I'm just glad Daddy lived long enough to see Sheriff Beckett be the one who really took his own life. After years of backstabbin', corruption, and dirty payoffs, the man just couldn't live with himself no more."

"Did he ever speak to you or your family again about Brandon?"

"Came by once after the fifth anniversary," Shaina said. "Tried to shake my daddy's hand and give my momma a hug. Daddy told him never to say Brandon's name again in his presence or he'd punch him right in the damn mouth."

* * *

Vardaman left Ray and Chief Robbie to talk while he got changed. He'd spent the morning in the woods with a CNN news crew, taking them on the deer runs and fire trails and talking about what Mississippi values meant to him. Ray walked over to the bar inside the hunt lodge and fixed himself a tall scotch. Chief Robbie wasn't one to drink. Ray heard he'd had some real trouble with the drugs and booze back in the day and now he was a workout freak. Tall and black-headed and built like a brick shithouse, he posted videos of himself online pulling weighted sleds and swimming in the Rez lake towing several canoes behind him. Chief Robbie was a real piece of work.

"I don't like to wait," Chief Robbie said. "I don't like to waste my time."

"Vardaman wanted to make sure we're comfortable with each other before we get down to the ass-kissing," Ray said, taking a sip. "That's what this shit's about. You know it. How you been, Big Chief?"

"All right," Chief Robbie said. "My youngest daughter is getting married next month."

"Congratulations," Ray said.

"Not for me," Chief Robbie said. He was dressed in denim on denim, a ceremonial beaded necklace around his throat and the open shirt showing a strong tanned chest. "This boy—a white man—is a loser. He owns a karaoke bar down in New Orleans. I had him checked out. He's a fraud. Cashing bad checks, selling drugs. I don't like it one bit."

"Then why don't you put your boot down?" Ray said.

Chief Robbie shrugged and crossed his right leg over his knee. He wore a pair of big, pointy alligator-skin boots. The legend was he'd wrestled the gator himself, only killing it when he'd flipped it on its back, field-stripping it right there, somewhere down in Louisiana.

"Mr. White sends his regards."

Chief Robbie nodded, looking at Ray with his serious black eyes, big silver watch studded with turquoise on his wrist. Ray had always thought of turquoise being more of a Southwest Indian thing than Choctaw, but didn't figure he'd ask about it. Chief Robbie had his own mysterious ways.

"Mr. White wants you to understand how important you are to all of us."

"I know that," Robbie said, flashing a big grin of perfect white teeth. "Tunica is about to fall into the Mississippi River. No one goes there besides the very poor and the very desperate. My place brings in families. Good people who want to have a good time. You should visit us sometime. We have a water park now."

"I heard."

"My grandchildren love it," he said. "We have a lazy river and everything. Sixteen slides across ten acres. It's all built within the historical context of the Choctaw lifestyle. Someday we'll have a theme park as big as Six Flags Over Georgia. I have the drawings. Things have really changed."

Ray took a swig, reaching into his coat pocket for his cigarettes. "Damn, Chief," he said. "That's impressive as hell. I'll have to stop by sometime."

"But I want you to know one thing," Chief Robbie said, leaning forward while Ray fanned out the match. "What you people pulled with the Hathcock woman still does not sit well with me. She was supposed to come up and run the skin for us. Nothing more. That woman is the devil, I tell you. She was a spy. A liar. She tried to turn my own people against me. Say things about me that were not true.

She stole. She ran drugs. She tried to get a young woman to infiltrate my bed, promising me things that come right out of the barnyard."

"Oh," Ray said. "Yeah. Well. Yes, she's been spoken to. It won't happen again, Chief. She's been demoted."

"Not how I hear it," Robbie said, pointing his index finger right at Ray. "She's running north Mississippi now. The drugs. The women. Working direct with Sledge in Memphis. And you handle these fucking power people."

The Chief pointed around the inside of the hunt lodge, with its tall wood-beam ceiling and mounted animal heads and fish. Expensive gleaming silver and polished walnut shotguns and rifles hung on the wall. The furniture was upholstered with thick leather and the tables and the bar had been handmade from old-growth oak and polished to a high shine.

"Business," Ray said. "It's all business. No different when you ran those swamp boat tours down in New Orleans. We all got to grease the wheel, don't we?"

Chief Robbie nodded with a serious face, craning his neck as Vardaman entered the room, shaved and clean and reeking of mint and intense cologne. The men stood and shook his hand as he joined them at the grouping of a table and chairs, finding a spot dead center in the middle of a big couch, his arms spread wide.

"We got a fine lunch planned for y'all," Vardaman said. "Elk steaks from Wyoming with field peas and fresh tomatoes from the garden. My cook, a tough old black woman, asked me what kind of animal did I kill this time? Some kind of tiger? And I had to pull up a picture of an elk on my phone. She about jumped out of her skin. Said it was the largest deer she'd ever seen in her life."

Ray nodded and grinned. Chief Robbie hadn't changed his position, still sitting there, leaning in to listen, alligator boot crossed over his knee, waiting for them to go on and get to the point of this luncheon. Vardaman's big toothy grin faded.

"I didn't want y'all to feel pressure to come," Vardaman said. His broad face ruddy, head too big for his body, like a bobblehead won at the state fair. "But I don't like to go through flunkies. And I know you don't. This is a crucial time for us at this election. If we want to protect and grow Mississippi, we all need to be on the same team. Not any different from when I played high school ball. How about you, Chief? I know you had to have played some football back in the day. Guy your size."

He shook his head. "Nope," he said. "Just stickball. And the wrestling."

"I heard that's where you got those boots," Vardaman said, his smile huge and welcoming. "Wrasslin' the big ole gator?"

"Maybe," Chief Robbie said. "We all pretend to be larger than life. Big-game hunter. Hero. Leader."

Vardaman's expression didn't fade this time, only grew a little larger as he laughed, settling farther back into the seat. The old black woman appeared from the door to the kitchen and he waved her away. "Just a minute, Lucille. Got a little business to discuss."

Chief Robbie's eyes were as flat as two-lane blacktop. Unmoving, a big piece of cut stone examining the smaller man.

"A man doesn't ever want to look back in a race," Vardaman said. "But you don't get too comfortable with the lead. Things can happen. I have enemies. Lots of enemies. Folks are still sore as hell over how my people took that primary election and left their guy with egg on his face. Couldn't have done it without y'all's help. The establishment never wanted a man like me. Someone who will challenge and uproot this whole broken system. They look at you people as outsiders. Enemies to a way of life that hadn't changed since the plantation days."

Robbie looked over to Ray. Ray nodded back.

"Enough bullshit," Chief Robbie said. "How much?"

"What's that?"

"We want to thrive," Chief Robbie said. "You want to win. We don't want a lottery. And we want to see more casinos inside the state and off the water. We must have your support and approval. And you need our money to beat the people in Jackson. Like I said, how much?"

"Chief," Vardaman said, nodding. "Chief. Come on, now. Let's just get to talking a little bit. This fella on the other side could upset the whole damn thing. He's an outsider. From goddamn California. And he wants to come down to Mississippi and tell us how Mississippians need to do business. I don't care for outsiders."

For the first time, Chief Robbie smiled. He nodded. "My people never did," he said. "Now we just want a seat at the table."

"You'll have one."

"And we want to grow," he said. "Beyond the Rez. Out of the goddamn Delta. Sorry, Ray."

Ray shrugged, showing no offense was taken. He set down his scotch and waited for Vardaman to put it all in perspective.

"My people have worked out an extended gift-giving plan that would last us into election day," Vardaman said. "I would be tickled to death if we might look over the details before our lunch."

"I'll give you a few days with Wes Taggart before his sorry ass is wanted up in Oxford for his first appearance there," Lillie Virgil said. "What he did to Boom was plain fucked up and we want him to answer for that more than anything. But Judge Biggers might have a different feeling about those racketeering and drug running charges at Sutpen's. That man sure can get crotchety about stuff like that."

Quinn nodded. Smoke twirled into the scattering blades of an overhead fan as he looked up at Lillie seated atop his desk. "Can I buy you dinner at the new Chinese place on the Square? Their General Tso's chicken isn't half bad."

"Appreciate it," Lillie said. "But I promised Rose I'd pick her up at school. She's stayed the last two nights with a friend. Hard to explain to a seven-year-old exactly what a U.S. Marshal does."

"Before you go—"

"No," Lillie said. "You may not splatter the walls with Wes Taggart."

"I can't find a file," Quinn said. "From back when my uncle was sheriff."

"What are you looking for?"

Quinn nodded. "Brandon Taylor."

"Christ Almighty," Lillie said. "How the hell did that come up? From Maggie?"

"Maggie had questions," Quinn said. "I looked around for the report and couldn't find a thing. And then today a woman from New York came to see me about looking into the case."

"I understand Maggie," Lillie said. "I know she and the Taylor boy were friendly. But why the hell does someone from New York give two shits about some old suicide?"

"You know the Taylor family."

"'Fraid I do."

"They can't let it go," Quinn said. "And I think Shaina Taylor reached out to these people to reopen the investigation as a podcast."

"They have anything?" Lillie said. "Other than a lot of questions from the Taylors?"

"This woman Tashi Coleman said the Taylor family has the original autopsy, the preliminary one done here," Quinn said. "She says the original report says Brandon Tayler had died from a .38 bullet."

"So?"

"Don't you remember?" Quinn asked. "He was supposed to have walked into those woods with his Remington .308. The family also says they found Brandon about ten feet from his rifle."

"Maybe the '.38' is a typo," Lillie said. "None of those Bundrens could spell worth a shit. That includes your little old honeybunny, Ophelia. She used to look over my shoulder in French class all the damn time and copy my answers."

"Before you left, I moved everything my uncle had squirreled away in the house and the barn out to a climate-controlled unit in town," he said. "There's the initial incident report, when Brandon's dad reported him missing, and two more follow-up reports after that. But most of what I know came from what I found online. Old newspaper stories."

"Did you happen to see the name Hubie Phillips?"

Quinn shook his head.

"But you know who he is?" she said.

"Sure," Quinn said. "He used to teach at Tibbehah High."

"You know what happened to him?"

"I heard folks ran him out of town."

"The whole damn county turned against him because they thought he'd been having an improper relationship with Brandon," she said. "He was a good English teacher, taught a lot of mouth-breathers around here that speaking properly wasn't a sin. You shoulda seen the man light up when someone used *ain't* or went for a double negative. My God, I loved that man."

"My uncle thought he had something to do with Brandon's death?"

"In one way or another," Lillie said. "He was a suspect before they found the body. People starting to whisper about how Brandon spent more time with him than he did his own family. And then there were the facts everyone else pretended weren't real."

"Like what?"

"Man in his forties, unmarried, who spent time up in Memphis taking on cultural pursuits."

"What's that mean?"

"It means I'm pretty sure Hubie Phillips was gay and that alone made him a suspect in whatever happened to Brandon Taylor. I mentioned it to Sheriff Beckett once and he got real angry with me. I think he felt bad about the association Phillips had with the case and the fact he'd been fired and had to leave Jericho in the middle of the night. Me and you were in school then. Don't you recall, Quinn?"

"I recall there was something about a teacher," Quinn said. "But I didn't remember who it was."

"What was going on while people searched wasn't exactly advertised," she said. "I didn't find out the whole story until I came on with the sheriff's department. But your uncle bowed to pressure from the local yokels and brought Phillips in for an interview. It was enough to send Brandon's daddy down to Tibbehah High with a loaded pistol and revenge on his mind. He dragged poor Mr. Phillips into a bathroom stall and stuck a .44 down his throat, asking him all kinds of vile questions."

"How do you know?" Quinn said. "This is a hell of a small town and I never heard that story."

"Fucking E. J. Royce."

"Shit."

"Yep," Lillie said, tilting her head to study Quinn. "Is that old turd dead yet?"

"Unfortunately, he's still with us."

"Try not to threaten Royce right off," Lillie said. "He can't help he was born a racist, misogynist peckerhead any more than a dog can't help licking its nuts."

"Will do." Quinn nodded and picked up his cigar. "You ready to talk to Wes Taggart?"

Lillie smiled. "Damn straight."

"You made your people sit out here in the heat, Chief?" Ray said. "You know they could've come inside, had a nice lunch made for them by Miss Lucille. Vardaman wouldn't have cared."

"I don't want my people to know my business," Chief Robbie said, standing in the shade of a huge twisted oak outside the hunt lodge perched on the hill. Ray had always heard how fancy it was, but, Christ Almighty, it looked like a glorified Cracker Barrel to him. It was true. Money can't buy good taste.

"You don't like this part," Ray said. "Do you?"

Chief didn't answer, his big hairless chest sweating as soon as they got outside. With the long hair and the bare skin, he reminded him of some kind of drugstore romance novel cover. Chief Robbie in *Savage Instincts*.

"Mr. White says we support this man," Chief Robbie said. "OK, then. That's part of our agreement. But his ideas, what he stands for, what he has said on his radio stations—"

"He does love to talk," Ray said, looking at the big Indian as he shielded his eyes from the sun. "And he may be the biggest goddamn crook this state has ever seen. But he's our crook. And after the election, we'll own his sorry ass."

The Chief nodded.

Ray stuck out his hand and the Chief studied it for a moment.

Ray knew he wasn't going to let go of the whole Fannie Hathcock debacle, knowing Ray and Fannie were intimate friends on occasion. The Chief once remarked to Ray that he could smell evil all over him.

Ray thought it was some kind of Indian trick, but then he realized he meant the Chanel No. 5. Not to mention, there was also the matter of a young kid named Mingo who had worked for both Chief Robbie and Fannie. When push came to shove, the kid went to Fannie. God forbid if the Chief ever knew how all that shit turned out.

The Chief nodded and accepted Ray's hand.

The big man's grip was like putting walnuts in a fucking vise. Ray could feel the old cartilage in his hands crack and pop. He squeezed back as hard as he could and gave the man a solid wink. They were pals now, friends again, the sun would shine down on Mississippi for their wonderful ole confederacy of crooks.

"Before you go," Ray said, smoothing down the edge of his silver mustache, "I have a favor to ask."

"For Vardaman?" he said. "Or for you?"

"For Mr. White."

The Chief folded his arms across his chest and listened as Ray told him about the unfortunate incident of Wes Taggart being arrested in the motel in Biloxi.

"Could he hurt us?" Chief Robbie asked.

Ray didn't say anything, just leveled a dead-eyed stare at the big Indian and nodded.

"I don't have to talk to none of y'all," Wes Taggart said. "My goddamn American rights have been shit upon ever since this dyke bitch busted into my motel room in Biloxi and aimed a pistol at my peter."

Lillie looked up at Quinn. "He's right," she said. "I didn't mirandize his pecker. But it was so damn small I couldn't see it."

"See what I'm talking about?" Taggart said. "You hear the kind of shit she's pulling on me? I'm a fucking white man in America and don't need to be treated like a crackhead."

Quinn stood over him in the interview room at the Tibbehah County Jail. The interview room wasn't much; an eight-by-eight cinder-block holding cell with walls painted a light green. Somewhere Quinn had heard the lighter color soothed the inmates, but his first suspect had taken off his pants and shit on the walls trying to spell out his name. They painted over it the same green as it had always been.

"You know me?" Quinn said. He left his gun on his desk and kept his clenched fists under his biceps.

"Naw," Taggart said. "Why would I?"

Quinn had thought about Wes Taggart every night since they'd found Boom beaten and bloodied and left for dead. He'd had unpleasant thoughts about what he'd do when finally faced with the man. Most of the time the damage would be done with his hands. Sometimes it was just a quick shot. But this is where Lillie had trained him. For all her big talk and jokes, Lillie had helped him make the transition from warrior to peacekeeper. And you didn't beat a suspect. You didn't torture them to get the truth. You just let the son of a bitch twist and turn with their lies and eventually hang themselves.

"You and J. B. Hood came into my county to teach Boom Kimbrough a lesson," Quinn said. "You damn near killed him."

"I don't know how many fucking times I have to say this, but I don't know any SOB named Boom," he said. "Why don't you go out and roust some other hardworking folks? Whatever shit you're trying to frame me with ain't gonna work. What do you got? You got a weapon? Some DNA? Some blood or shit? You see, I know my business. You can't let the word of a bleached blonde cooze make it so."

"Purple," Lillie said. "Your cooze has purple hair."

"I want to see my high-dollar lawyer and I want him now," he said. "I ain't saying no more to neither of you about something that happened to y'all's friend."

"What did you say?" Quinn said.

"Don't try to fuck me for your friend fucking up."

Quinn felt his jaw tighten and his eye twitch a little. He thought about reaching for Taggart and pulling his sorry ass to his feet, letting Lillie unlock his cuffs and let them just go at it inside the locked room until only Quinn was left standing. There would be blood and shit on all those pale green walls.

"We've got a Louisville Slugger with Boom's blood and your prints all over it," Quinn said. "J. B. Hood must've kept it as a trophy when he flipped his car."

"And you shot him," Taggart said. "You gonna shoot me, too? Call it an accident? Old-time frontier justice like when I used to watch *The Rifleman* with my daddy?"

"Would it make you shut up?" Lillie asked.

Quinn shook his head, let out a breath, tried to let his fists relax, untighten, let his hands drop to his sides and placed them on his hips. He looked at the muscly man with the craggy face, shaved head, and blue scrawl down his biceps and over his forearms. His eyes were a pale blue and his face had stubble about as long as the hair on his skeletal head.

"Are we done here?" Taggart said.

"Nope," Quinn said. "I'd like to talk to you a little about your relationship with J. K. Vardaman."

"You mean our next governor?" Taggart said, laughing. "How the hell would I know a fella like that?"

Lillie shook her head and walked out of the room. Quinn watched Taggart's face, the cocky laugh settling down into a shit-eating grin.

"You're facing attempted murder charges here in Tibbehah," Quinn said. "Not to mention what you and your late pal J. B. Hood did to Cody Pritchard. You're looking at murder for him, too. And that's long before you sit down with the Feds."

"Fuck me like a dang mangy dog."

"All I'm saying is if you know something about Vardaman working with your people on the Coast," Quinn said, "I'd be interested in hearing you out."

"Y'all are nuts."

"Loyalty," Quinn said. "Sure do admire that. Good luck to you, Wes."

Quinn walked from the interview room, waiting for the jail guard to buzz him back through the locked doors and into the lobby. Quinn headed outside to the flagpole in the parking lot and worked on taking in deep, even breaths and letting them go slowly. The air was hot and sticky and the sun reflected off the rows of vehicles out in the lot.

"You did good in there, Ranger," Lillie said. "I didn't know about the prints."

Quinn nodded. "Be great if it was true," he said. "Goddamn prints showed J. B. Hood's little monkey hands were all over that bat."

"And the other bat?"

Quinn shook his head. "We never found another."

Lillie smiled. "And what'd he say about Vardaman?"

"Claims he never met him."

"How did he look when he said it?" Lillie asked.

"Like a goddamn liar."

# SIX

Tashi picked up Jessica, her producer, researcher, and full-time partner in crime, at the Traveler's Rest Motel just outside Jericho. This would be the fifth time they'd worked together on an investigative story, starting off together at Columbia as grad students and then coming on as network interns at the same time. They'd both fetched coffee, done grunt work, and brainstormed ideas. *Thin Air* had actually been Jessica's baby, after watching one of those crazy *Dateline* shows about a missing woman in Iowa. Tashi remembered walking into her loft in Red Hook, Jessica already a little stoned, open boxes of Thai food all around her, and telling her to sit down and watch something.

When the segment was over, Jessica turned to Tashi and said, "Don't you think we could do better?"

And they did. Their investigation into that very same case led to the eventual arrest and prosecution of a deputy sheriff who'd been on the fringe of the case. He'd done his best to hide evidence, misdirect investigators, and cover up any trace of his relationship to the victim. Through Tashi and Jessica's work, the state police eventually learned of a shallow grave outside Iowa City where the lawman had buried her.

"How come everyone I meet knows I'm not from here?" Jessica said, Tashi driving them farther south into the county. Her GPS set to a place called The River.

"Maybe it's the blue hair," Tashi said, turning off of Highway 9 and onto Jericho Road. "And your big black Doc Martens. You definitely bring a certain vibe to the state of Mississippi."

"I'll have you know I've toned it down while you've been out doing your meet and greet," Jessica said. "I dressed down considerably for my little resupply trip to Walmart. Don't you see this T-shirt, 'Love it or Leave it'? But as I was in line at Walmart, waiting to check out, I got the same question, 'Where you from?' Like 'New York City' was tattooed on my forehead."

"Everybody seems to know everybody else down here," Tashi said, the road and terrain flattening out south of town, long stretches of cotton and soybeans all around them. The sun high and blazing hot. "Even with Brandon Taylor, look at all the connections. His former girlfriend is now married to the sheriff, who is the nephew of the old sheriff. And the sheriff's sister used to know Brandon. And Brandon's father worked at the sawmill owned by one of the town's biggest crooks. It's one degree of separation with everybody in town."

She slowed and put on her blinker as she spotted a hand-painted sign directing them to THE RIVER. ALL WELCOME.

"Are they going to try and convert us?" Jessica said. "Maybe you should let them know you're Jewish and I'm a lapsed Catholic. You know, straight off, so it's out there."

"This place is more of a community outreach than a church," Tashi said. "They have a decent online presence. It was started by a guy named Jamey Dixon. He had a pretty extensive history, spent some time at Parchman for manslaughter. He was convicted of killing his girlfriend in 2005. They found her on a back highway run over dozens of times. The body was so mutilated, there wasn't much of her left. Although he always claimed he was innocent."

"Maybe he was."

"Whatever happened, he started this church," she said. "It was supposed to be a throwback to old country religion. He had a bluegrass band every Sunday and apparently did a lot of good for this county. He'd become an ordained minister while in Parchman and spent the rest of his life on the outside handing out food, clothes, and money to the poor."

"And what happened to him?"

"All that money he gave away belonged to some other cellmates from an armored car job," Tashi said. "When they found out he'd double-crossed them, they broke out of prison and murdered him."

"Jesus," Jessica said. "Just where have you taken me this time?"

"His last girlfriend is the woman I wanted you to run a background on today," Tashi said, seeing the long wooden fence up ahead, a cattle gate wide open with a road curving into some small pine trees. "Caddy Colson."

"Who is the sheriff's sister."

"Correct."

"Not exactly an angel herself."

"What'd you find out?" Tashi said, seeing the wooden barn and a big skeletal metal frame of a building under construction, surrounded by several trailers and little shotgun shacks at the end of the road. She let down her window and she could hear the high whine of the cicadas and chirping of birds. Great Southern background sounds that would go well with trucks rounding the Square blaring country music.

"Drug arrests stretching out more than five years," Jessica said. "One arrest for solicitation."

"Oh, no," she said. "Really? Are you sure?"

"Absolutely," Jessica said. "But apparently she's clean and sober now. She's done some interviews over the last few years, talking about what she does here and how she has compassion for people of all walks of life. One guy interviewed, some local politician, joked she had a Mary Magdalene complex. You know who that is. Right?"

"Do you recall my last boyfriend?" she said. "Rob? And his super-Christian parents?"

"Oh, yeah," Jessica said, flipping through her notebook. "Super-Rob. What a dick. I thought they were Catholic?"

"They were."

"Big difference," Jessica said.

"What do you mean?"

"Give it a few days," Jessica said. "You'll see. When I was living in Georgia, I can't tell you how many people tried to save my soul. I kept telling them I was on their side. We just had a different interpretation of the same message."

"Didn't the blue hair scare them off?"

"Ha," Jessica said. "And for the record, back then it was pink. Only my tattoos were blue. Maybe I'll get one down here? There's a tattoo shop on the Square right by the Mexican restaurant. What do you think about Willie Nelson and a big fat joint?"

Tashi parked the rental and they both climbed out and looked around. At the mouth of the barn, they spotted a woman in her early thirties, blonde hair cut pixie short, dressed in blue jean cutoffs and a white tank top. She had on a pair of cheap sunglasses, which she pushed up on her head as she knelt down to talk to a little brown-skinned girl. The woman was lanky and sort of muscly, with a pointy nose, sunburned face, and freckled shoulders.

A battered blue pickup truck was parked nearby, where a short Latino man with a big black mustache and cowboy hat was piling boxes into its bed.

As she and Jessica walked up close, Tashi hit record just as the woman pushed up to her full height, removed her sunglasses, and smiled. "Hello," she said. "How can I help y'all?"

"I'm Tashi Coleman and this is my friend Jessica," she said. "We're from New York and have a few questions for you."

"New York?" Caddy said, looking the two of them over. "You won't believe this. But that's just what I was thinking."

"Pap's is the best catfish you'll ever eat," E. J. Royce said as Don the barber snipped black hairs from his ears. "I guaran-damn-tee you. I can't believe you ain't never been to Pap's, Don. I mean, where do you take your wife after church?"

"You know us," Don said, really having his work cut out for him. Royce had more hair in his ears than on top. He'd already worked the spacer all over the man's old shrunken head for the last five minutes. "We're pretty loyal to the El Dorado. I get the chimichanga most days. My wife likes the taco salad."

"I haven't eaten there since I seen a rat in the kitchen."

Quinn looked up from where he sat on a vinyl sofa under a television playing *Days of Our Lives*. He could tell the old man was lying, having some fun with Don, who was a good and honest man and often didn't see the dark side in people. And E. J. Royce, former deputy sheriff under his Uncle Hamp, had plenty of evil about him. The man exuded an odor not unlike sulfur.

"You didn't see no goddamn rat at the El Dorado," Luther Varner said, cross-legged and black-eyed. The wiry old Marine sat across the room, with a burning cigarette ash that looked to be about a foot long. "You're as full of shit as Christmas turkey, Royce."

Royce lifted his eyes from where he'd buried his chin in his caved-in chest. "You calling me a liar, Luther?" he said. "Goddamn thing popped out of the dang nacho chips and run under the buffet. Made me so sick I didn't eat for nearly a week."

"What color was it?" Luther asked.

"The nachos?" Royce asked, Don returning to work, lathering up the old man's neck and pulling out a straight razor. "Ain't but one dang color."

"No, the goddamn rat," Luther said.

"I don't know," Royce said. "Fucking rat-colored. I didn't take no Kodachrome."

Don stopped with the razor and pointed over to the plywood walls. Nestled among the deer heads and mounted bass was a small sign saying NO PROFANITY OR TRASHY TALK OF ANY KIND.

"Son of a bitch," Royce said. "Coming in here is worse than going to a Kool-Aid and cookie social. Then you and all these women you done hired to work at a man's barbershop sit around watching these harlots on TV with their damn titties pressed out, jumping from bed to bed. How's that any different?"

Luther Varner looked over at Quinn, ashing his cigarette in a Styrofoam cup, and shook his head.

"Would y'all please shut up," Don the barber said. "Today's the day we find out about Eric's baby. I do think Jennifer is the right woman for him. He should get up and marry her."

"Y'all have been neutered," Royce said, Don scraping across his thick red neck. "I knew it the minute Mr. Jim kicked the bucket and y'all started hiring hairdressers. What in the hell is the world coming to?"

Miss Gayle and Miss Tammy looked up from the spinning chairs where they sat without clients, watching the soap opera. They just leveled a hard look at the little man and then turned their attention back to the TV perched on top of the Coke machine. Before Don had even finished cleaning the shaving cream from his neck, Royce pulled off the barber's cape and stood up, reaching into his pocket and fishing out two five-dollar bills. No tip.

He handed it to Don and then walked toward the rack to retrieve his red MAGA ball cap. Quinn stood up.

"What the hell do you want?" Royce said. "You don't need no haircut. You always look like I did right out of boot camp."

"Came to talk to you, Royce," Quinn said. "Fellas at the VFW said I could find you here."

"Yeah, yeah," Royce said, screwing up his face like he might spit. "'Course they did. If you're coming to make some kind of trouble about them parking tickets, you can just stick it, Quinn. I worked my damn ass off in this county as a lawman before you ever popped out of your momma's coot."

Luther stood up quickly. Royce craned his head toward the big man with the silver crew cut, shrinking a bit. But he relaxed as Varner turned toward Don and ambled over to take a seat in the barber chair. The two hairdressers both exchanged looks with eyebrows raised. Luther was an old man, but nobody in Tibbehah County wanted to mess with him. Back in Vietnam, he'd been a top-tier sniper with more kills than he ever cared to remember.

Quinn walked into the hot parking lot with Royce toward the man's Chevy truck with mismatched wheels and tires, the gold paint rusted and dull. In the back of the truck, he had a Walker hound chained up to a cinder block.

"Little hot for the dog."

"You ain't one of them PETA folks, are you, Quinn?" he said. "I heard you done got married to some hippie woman."

Quinn widened his stance, turning down the radio on his hip, so they might talk a little in private. The old man's eyes were bloodshot and his breath smelled like a cheap-ass pocket whiskey.

"Came to ask you a few things about an old case."

"Should've known," he said. "That's the only time you come out and see me. Me and your uncle were thick as thieves."

"You may want to work on your choice of words."

"Shit," he said. "What is it you want? I done told you all I know about that nigger them bikers kilt."

"I don't like that word," Quinn said. "And you won't use it in my presence."

"Has the whole goddamn world gone crazy?" Royce said. "Everyone wants to be politically correct these days. Christ Almighty."

"I want to talk to you about Brandon Taylor," Quinn said. "The boy you and my uncle found dead up in the Big Woods."

"The damn kid who ate his gun?" Royce said. "Who the fuck wants to know about that?"

"Me," Quinn said.

"It was a hundred years back."

"Twenty."

Royce opened his mouth and then thought better of it, opening the door to his truck and leaning against it. He spit on the ground and lifted his tired old eyes to Quinn. "That was a hell of a goddamn thing," he said. "I walked them woods so long, I wore off the soles of my boots. Never thought we'd find that kid."

"I need to know who y'all were looking at," Quinn said.

"We weren't looking at nobody," Royce said. "Christ. If we was looking at someone, we woulda found out what the hell happened."

"You're a liar."

"Excuse me?"

"I said you're a liar, Royce," he said. "I need you to shake the cobwebs out of your busted old head, even if it means finishing that pint on your front seat. I need to know what you heard from Hubie Phillips. You and Uncle Hamp brought him in before y'all found the body."

"That old queer?" Royce said, cackling. "Just where'd you hear some bullshit like that?"

"Lillie Virgil."

"Oh."

"Now, you want to tell me what you know?"

Royce reached into the car and grabbed the small bottle of Fighting Cock. He took a long swallow and wiped off his white-whiskered chin with the back of his hand. "She ain't still around," he said. "Is she?"

"Is this about us feeding workers here?" Caddy said. "Did Old Man Skinner send you out to make trouble about taking money away from hardworking Americans?"

Tashi shook her head. Jessica said, "No way."

"Because folks around here have gotten scared to use vouchers," Caddy said. "Some fool has passed a regulation saying if you're a legal immigrant and you try and get government-assisted food, even for WIC, you might get in trouble with the Feds. Can you imagine? New mothers who can't feed their babies are afraid to go out and get the food they need. Do you have any idea what that does to early development? Sometimes I can't even keep track of the evil set loose in this world."

"We met with Skinner," Tashi said. "But only to hear about his plans to build the big cross on the highway."

Caddy Colson stood there, in cutoff jeans and a tank top, mud boots up to her knees, hands on her hips. "Did you women just drive out here to make me puke or do y'all have something to discuss?"

"We know who you are and what you do," Jessica said. "But this has nothing to do with The River or your charity work, Miss Colson. We just need a little bit of your time to talk about your uncle. Hamp Beckett."

"My uncle?" Caddy said, pushing her hands in her pockets and lifting up on the toes of her boots. "He's been dead for almost ten years now."

"We're working on a podcast about the disappearance of Brandon Taylor," Jessica said, smiling. "We're trying to learn anything we can about Brandon before he died. Your uncle didn't leave many files or notes behind."

"He never did," Caddy said. "Maybe y'all should talk to my brother. He's the sheriff. If he can help, he will."

"I have," Jessica said. "And he said he knew about as much as we did. He told us most of the files were lost."

"Well," Caddy said. "If y'all spoke to Quinn and he can't help you, I sure can't. I mean, I was just a kid when Brandon got lost. That was a lifetime ago. I was only fifteen."

"Did you know him?" Jessica said.

"Not very well."

"But you went to the same school?" Tashi asked. "In the same class."

Caddy looked at them both and nodded. It was kind of a solemn nod, Caddy with pursed lips like she was contemplating the whole thing. "Y'all want to get out of this heat?" she said. "My office has AC and we can get something to drink."

They followed her up the wooden steps of a nearby trailer, basic white and industrial-looking, and headed inside. There was a Latina moving some files from a table into some large boxes. Caddy whispered something to her and she disappeared out the front door. Caddy walked over to a mini fridge and pulled out three Cokes and set them by a half-dozen chairs set in a semicircle. Little pamphlets for AA waited on the seats.

"Yeah, I knew Brandon Taylor," she said. "But we weren't close friends or anything like that."

Tashi asked if she minded them continuing to record and Caddy shook her head, popping the top of her Coke and leaning toward the women with her elbows across her thighs. She was flushed with sun and sweaty. A simple silver cross on a thin chain dangled from Caddy's neck.

"What do you recall about him?" Jessica said. "We spent some time with his sister Shaina this morning. But she was very young when he disappeared. Most of her memories were just of him being the big brother. We want to know all about him from people who knew him best."

"Lot more folks knew him better than me," Caddy said. "He was kind of an odd kid. He kept to himself. About the only thing I recall is he drove this cool old truck. A black Chevy Apache . . . Did y'all really come all the way from New York to talk about Brandon?"

"We did," Tashi said. "The Taylor family has never been satisfied about what happened to him."

"And how long do y'all plan to stay?"

Tashi looked to Jessica and shrugged. "As long as it takes."

Jessica shrugged. "Pretty much."

"That's something," Caddy said. "I thought people had forgotten all about Brandon. It was a really big deal when it happened. We had news people here when he went missing, always hanging out at the high school or on the town square. But when they found him and learned he killed himself, they pretty much packed up and went home."

"I understand your brother got lost in those same woods," Tashi said. "A few years before Brandon."

Caddy looked up from where she'd been rolling the cold Coke can between her hands. "I thought y'all wanted to talk about Brandon and my uncle?"

Something in Caddy's face, a fierce look, made her know it was better to keep to Brandon. "Can you give us an overall impression of Brandon at the time?"

"I think he was fifteen, sixteen," Caddy said. "A little bit older than me. We were in a few of the same classes but never really hung out. I know he was close to a girl named Maggie Powers who visited during the summers. After he died, she didn't come back. Until a few years ago."

"And then married your brother?" Jessica said. "She's Maggie Colson now."

"Two days and y'all already know a lot."

Tashi smiled. "We do our best."

"As far as Brandon goes," Caddy said, "damn, I don't know. What was he like? What made him tick and all? I know he was really into music. He played country songs on his guitar. I remember one night on the Square. Y'all know it's where most of the kids meet up on the weekends? He played 'Friends in Low Places' and 'Shameless' exactly like the record. That and he was real into working for the school newspaper. He took yearbook pictures for Mr. Phillips. I think he was serious about photography. I was a cheerleader back then, if you can believe that. He was always on the sidelines at the JV games."

"What about his personality?" Jessica said. "How would you describe him?"

"Goofy," Caddy said. "He was funny, but really goofy, too. I mean when you'd see him in the halls, you just had to smile and laugh. He always had kind of a silly look on his face, kind of a smirk, like he knew all this was some kind of cosmic joke."

"What was the joke?" Tashi said.

"High school," Caddy said. "Life. Church and ballgame grind down in Tibbehah County. I think he was like most of us, couldn't wait to get the hell out of here."

"Did he ever seem depressed?" Jessica asked. "Like a kid who might wander off one day into the deep woods and kill himself?"

Caddy shook her head. "I knew him and didn't really know him," she said. "Jericho is a small town, but, believe it or not, we don't all know each other's business. We didn't run in the same crowds."

"Did your uncle ever mention his death?" Jessica asked. "Or about finding him in the woods?"

Tashi lifted her eyes to Jessica, who was watching the readers on the recorder, sliding the mic slightly to the left, closer to Caddy. Tashi took a deep breath and swallowed. The inside of the trailer smelled like an old classroom, all musty books and disinfectant. "I understand you were close to your Uncle Hamp."

"True."

"Would you call him a father figure?" Tashi asked.

Caddy shrugged and leaned back into the folding metal chair. "Sure," she said. "Quinn and I didn't have much of a father to speak of. At first, he was just gone. And then he came back for a while just to get divorced."

"And Uncle Hamp filled in?" Tashi asked.

"He did more than that," she said. "He and Aunt Halley pretty much helped my mother raise us. He took me and Quinn hunting and fishing. I worked in Aunt Halley's garden, worked with the cattle. I had the number two beef heifer in the state one year."

"I understand a lot of people in this county like him."

"I'm sorry," Caddy said. "I don't see what my uncle has to do with Brandon's suicide. If you're looking into something about the investigation, you need to keep talking to Quinn. I don't know a thing about it."

"We know about what happened to Sheriff Beckett," Jessica said, blurting it out a little too fast for Tashi. "Some have suggested he might have felt some guilt for what happened to Brandon."

"What?" Caddy said. "What in the hell are you talking about? Y'all get here for a couple days and listen to a bunch of gossip and innuendo and think you got this jerkwater town figured out. First off, I'll have you know my uncle didn't kill himself. Someone murdered him. I don't give a damn what anyone else has told you. Have y'all managed to look into the swamp of criminals who were here before my brother came back from the service? My uncle had gotten old and weak and someone took him out. They didn't want him making trouble."

"Could the same thing have happened to Brandon?" Jessica said. "Been involved with these same people?"

"My uncle was the county sheriff," Caddy said. "Brandon Taylor was just some punk kid. Nice kid. But still a country punk. Like us all. Who brought my uncle into this mess?"

Tashi pursed her lips and didn't say anything. Jessica combed her fingers through her blue hair, waiting for Caddy to continue, Tashi not sure either of them should comment on a source.

"I've told y'all all I know," Caddy said, standing up and walking over to the trailer door and holding it wide open. Hot air blew in from outside, scattering the little AA pamphlets across the room. "But rumor and lies aren't facts. You come back to me when y'all want to talk about something sensible. I don't have time for this. I have mouths to feed."

"How was your day?" Quinn asked.

"Interesting," Maggie said. "Had a woman come to the ER with a cell phone stuck in a very private place. The whole time the doctor was trying to get it out, it kept on buzzing. Her ringtone playing 'Turn Down for What.' I bet you don't know that song."

"Is it by Waylon or Willie?"

"Lil Jon."

"Then probably not," Quinn said.

"Probably sounded better when it's not coming out of the woman's privates," she said. "Not exactly a Bluetooth speaker."

Quinn held up his hand as Maggie stood in the doorway, dressed in light green hospital scrubs and clutching a bottle of wine from the new package store off the Square. She set the bottle down on the coffee table, where he and Brandon had been watching *Red River*. Quinn had felt part of his education was to make his new son fully versed in both classic movies and books. At night, he'd been reading him *White Fang* before Brandon went to sleep. The shelves in the study and Quinn and Maggie's bedroom sagged with paperbacks and old hardcovers: hunting and fishing books, classic novels, adventure and frontier stories, and thick books on Greek myths and plays. Quinn loved Homer about as much as he did Louis L'Amour.

"You want another beer?" Maggie said, nodding to the Coors can on the table.

Quinn shook his head, Brandon engrossed in the scene where Montgomery Clift helps out Joanne Dru while being attacked by Indians. "You're shooting too high, aim lower," Clift tells her from behind a wagon.

"Dinner's in the oven," Quinn said. "I picked up some fried chicken at Annie's. There's some greens and cornbread in the refrigerator I can heat up."

Maggie disappeared and Quinn followed her into the kitchen. He was still dressed in his uniform shirt, sleeves rolled up to the elbows, and crisp dark Levi's, but had left his boots on the front porch and locked away his sidearm. A can of Coors came flying from

Maggie and Quinn caught it in midair as she forked out some greens into a bowl.

"Sometimes I think we have a competition to see who's had a stranger day," Maggie said, setting the bowl in the microwave. "One day you have a crackhead dragging his butt down Highway 9 and other days I have a patient who's stuck a toilet plunger up his backside. Kind of makes me wonder who in the world are we trying to help."

"Protect and serve," Quinn said. "Hearts and minds."

"I still hear the Lil Jon song in my head," Maggie said, pulling her long reddish hair into a ponytail. "Good God. I can't get it out."

Quinn whistled the theme to *Red River*. "That woman had to be embarrassed as hell."

"If she was, she sure didn't show it," Maggie said. "Just kind of annoyed her boyfriend kept on calling her, knowing the damn thing was stuck."

"Make a plate and come sit down with us," Quinn said. "Brandon did his homework at my mother's and he's ready for bed. I think we can finish the movie. You'll like this one. I promise."

"Thank you, Quinn."

The microwave dinged and she grabbed the greens, the fried chicken and cornbread warming in the old gas oven.

"For what?" Quinn said, smiling. He moved in close and wrapped his arms around her waist, leaning down and kissing her on her freckled nose.

**Tashi Coleman**
***Thin Air* podcast**
**Episode 3: THE SEARCH PARTY**

NARRATOR: The days after Tim Taylor found the old Chevy truck on County Road 334, everyone was looking for Brandon. Family, friends, church groups, volunteer firefighters, Boy Scouts, police, and game wardens. Even a psychic from Tupelo. The psychic's name was Miss La Tonya, a palm reader and fortune-teller who claimed she spoke to Native American spirits who roamed the Big Woods. Those spirits, she said, had seen Brandon—alone, tired, hungry, and calling out for his family. WREG in Memphis covered the story from the start, Brandon's parents appearing haggard and worried on their front porch in the bright lights of the cameras.

> RHONDA TAYLOR [SCRATCHY TV AUDIO FROM 1997]: I just want my baby home. I know he followed that dang big buck way too far and got himself turned around.

NARRATOR: A week later, a National Guard unit was dispatched to Tibbehah County. Helicopters with spotlights flew overhead as searchers worked eighteen-hour days. Dog handlers were brought in, the baying of bloodhounds ricocheting off the distant hills. The sheriff at the time commented on a radio interview about the scene.

> SHERIFF HAMP BECKETT: This whole thing has been a nightmare for this family. I just pray to God we

> find the boy alive. If someone has heard something or seen something, please let us know. Right now, y'all just keep us in your thoughts and prayers. These workers haven't rested a wink since that boy went missing.

NARRATOR: For the searchers, everything meant something. A broken branch, a footprint that might've come from Brandon's shoe, a discarded wrapper from Brandon's favorite candy bar. Which, by the way, was a Nestlé Crunch. Or a windblown tarp spotted covering a fallen tree, a spot some thought might've been used as a shelter.

The searchers worked in the wind and the rain. The nights were cold and wet that November, many in the county recalling another boy like Brandon who'd been lost in the woods almost a decade before. This interview came again from WREG in Memphis in 1997.

> TEENAGE BOY: When I was lost, I just kept walking. I knew I'd cross a road or see someone. Everything was real dark.
>
> REPORTER: Weren't you scared?
>
> TEENAGE BOY: No, ma'am.
>
> REPORTER: And how old were you then?
>
> TEENAGE BOY: Ten.
>
> REPORTER: How did you eat? How did you live?
>
> TEENAGE BOY: I carried a .22 with me. There were plenty of squirrels and birds to eat. A rabbit, if you got lucky. I know Brandon will do the same.

NARRATOR: That was the voice of Quinn Colson as a seventeen-year-old high school senior, before he joined the Army. He would later come home to replace his uncle, Hamp Beckett, as sheriff of Tibbehah County. Colson liked to hunt even more than Brandon Taylor—that's something we'll revisit in future episodes. Despite what the sheriff told us, some said he might have been the very last person to see Brandon Taylor alive.

# SEVEN

Three days later, Quinn was behind his desk at the sheriff's office listening to Reggie Caruthers run down the overnight events: a bad wreck on County Road 229 with minor injuries, two domestic situations involving the same man and two different women, and an attempted robbery at the Dixie Gas out on Jericho Road. When Quinn had asked why the robber didn't get the money, Reggie explained the kid who walked into the store had been bluffing. He only had a pocketknife and a bad attitude and the clerk had chased him out of the store with her .357.

"And who was the clerk?" Quinn asked, drinking his third cup of coffee that morning. Still waking up, trying to get Reggie off shift and back home to rest.

"Miss Peaches."

"Peaches?" he asked. "When'd she quit Varner's Quick Mart?"

"Must've been three months back," Reggie said. "She and Mr. Varner got into it over her cut with the kitchen. You know how the woman can cook."

"Damn straight," Quinn said. "That's why I haven't seen her lately. I gained five pounds just by walking in the door and smelling what was for lunch."

"Varner is one tough old nut," Reggie said. "Miss Peaches left and took all her business on over to Dixie Gas. You know Varner is regretting it now. But you know how the old man can get."

"What's she have for lunch today?"

"Hamburger steak and butter beans," Reggie said, flipping through his notes on the attempted robbery. "Don't you want to know who did it?"

"Pookie Williams."

"Damn," Reggie said, closing his notebook. "Just how'd you know that, Sheriff?"

Reggie had left the 10th Mountain Division three years ago, already married with two kids at home and needing work. Since then, he'd turned out to be the best deputy Quinn had since Lillie left. Smaller than Quinn, muscular and tough, and good with the people out in the county. A black man born and raised on a farm, he could talk with rednecks up in Carthage or black folks down in the Ditch with equal ease. Everyone liked and respected Reggie Caruthers. He had a God-given cool, easygoing way about him.

"I heard Pookie's mom tossed him out," Quinn said. "He's been sleeping on his sister Latasha's sofa, smoking weed and playing video games. His momma called me and told me he'd be doing something stupid again soon and to please not shoot him."

"I went over to his sister's last night, but she said he was gone," Reggie said. "She kicked his ass out."

"Won't be hard to find," Quinn said. "Pookie doesn't have a car anymore. Ran the damn thing into a tree. Probably just hanging out at the Ditch. Maybe you could check up on it? Down at the gas station or at Club Disco?"

"Yes, sir," Reggie said, standing and stretching, tucking his notebook in the back pocket of his uniform. "Still trying to make some headway with Wes Taggart. Brought him a sack of burgers and fries from the Sonic last night, just like you said. He ate the burger, but wouldn't say two words to me. I tried just to shoot the breeze, talk about the weather and where he was staying down on the Coast. But he wouldn't even look at me while he ate. Looked like something rough was on his mind."

"Man's looking at a long stay at Parchman."

"I seen that look," Reggie said. "Wasn't it. This man looked scared as hell. Real nervous about me just standing close to his cell."

"Keep working on him," Quinn said, standing now, too, and reaching for his ball cap and what was left of his cigar. "I backed way the hell off the other day. If Lillie hadn't been there, I would've taken his head off."

"Probably what he's scared of."

"Maybe."

"Where you headed, Sheriff?"

"Something's come up," Quinn said. "Headed out to see Rhonda Taylor. I guess you know all about that story."

"Some," Reggie said. "I was just a kid when the boy went missing. You think there's anything at all to some kind of cover-up?"

"In Tibbehah County?" Quinn asked. "Hell, yes. But I got too much on my plate right now to reopen a twenty-year-old probable suicide. Wes Taggart knows the goddamn road map from those crooks on the Coast on up here to Vardaman. Maybe he'll break."

"You think?"

"I haven't met many crooks not willing to save their own ass," Quinn said. "He's all about money. Vardaman and his people are after something else."

"But they go hand in hand?"

"Long before you and I got home from the Sandbox."

"Miss Hathcock," Old Man Skinner said. "One of your waitresses—the surly woman named Christy—said you had some issue with me putting out a donation box for the Tibbehah Cross."

"Is that what you're calling it now?" Fannie said, taking a seat in a red vinyl booth across from him at the Rebel Truck Stop. "Has a real ring to it. Almost like y'all have a real purpose to this whole damn project."

"Sounds like you disapprove."

"Thought the supervisors might concentrate on fixing our shit roads and broke-down bridges before rolling out the welcome mat for His Second Coming."

"That's not what the cross is about," he said. "And as far as county projects, our work is limited to state and federal funding. For a poor county like Tibbehah, I think we're making a fine effort. We've poured more than a million dollars into improvement projects since I became head of the supervisors."

Fannie blew out some smoke and ashed the tip of her cigarillo in a tray. "I'll let my mechanic know," she said. "Last week I dropped my brand-new Lexus into a crater the size of the fucking Grand Canyon, busted an axle and about knocked my transmission loose."

"I'd prefer you not using profanity," Skinner said. "I'm not some of your employees next door. I don't mind working with a woman, but she needs to understand how to discuss matters in this town."

Two of her waitresses, Christy and Ruth Ann, stood by the cash register, trying to eavesdrop on her little meet with Skinner. They disliked the big, lumbering son of a bitch more than she did, with his reptilian eyes, bald head, and slow way of speaking. An affectation of Southern bullshit trying to dominate the conversation, to show he had an understanding of all things.

"I've complied with the law at Vienna's Place," she said. "And I've even made a donation or two to your reelection campaign. However, I draw the goddamn line at raising money for some Bible-thumping monstrosity that will block the view of one of the most famous signs in the Mid-South."

"What sign?"

"Vienna's Place," she said. "Or haven't you noticed the curvy mud flap girl done up in blue and red neon. I'll have you know the sign was featured on both the Travel Channel and *Playboy After Dark*. It's a damn Mississippi landmark."

"Of iniquity."

"Come again?"

"That means 'evil,'" Skinner said, reaching for his half-finished cup of coffee and slurping up what was left.

"I know what it means," she said. "But I really thought you were a realist. A businessman who wanted to put Tibbehah back on the map, like you said. The first thing you try to do is shut me down, cover up my only advertising, and now put out a tin cup in my business to fund the plan to make it happen. You must think I'm stupid as hell."

"No, ma'am," Skinner said. "I've never thought you stupid. But I'll offer you a fair warning. Times are changing around here, Miss *Hath-cock*. I figure you know that, but the only reason I was called back into public service was to help turn back the clock on the immorality and stain on this county. There's a hot wind of change blowing across Mississippi."

"I've seen the goddamn commercials," Hathcock said. "Your buddy Vardaman."

"A fine Christian man," Skinner said. *"He sees the sword coming against the land and sounds the trumpet to warn the people."*

"The Watchmen," Fannie said, leaning back into her chair. "I've heard that bullshit, too. A real interesting group of kooks, kind of like the Jaycees without the sense of humor. I get talk radio on my ride up to Memphis."

"Maybe you should just stick to that town," Skinner said. "Tibbehah won't be to your liking next year."

"We'll see."

"I'll leave a donation bucket at the front," Skinner said, not budging an inch from the best booth in the entire truck stop, a catbird seat's view of the diesel pumps and of Vienna's Place off to the side. "I'll get my folks to check on it next week."

"Can I get you anything else, Supervisor?"

"Not a thing, ma'am," he said, reaching in his pocket for a fifty-cent tip. "It's a fine and glorious morning. I do feel truly blessed. I'll be praying for you, Miss Fannie."

"You do that, Skinner," she said. "Just don't pray too damn hard and give yourself an aneurysm on the can."

"Mrs. Taylor?" Quinn asked.

Rhonda Taylor had her door cracked, seeming surprised to see Quinn, although he'd called ahead earlier in the morning. The chain was on the door and a small dog yipped from inside. Somewhere a television was playing the news out of Memphis. Two people shot at a tire dealership in south Memphis. Lots of rain in the future for the Mid-South. Details ahead.

"You mind if I come in?"

The woman didn't answer, but unchained the door, Quinn stepping onto thick white carpet and following her through a small living room and into a kitchen and family room area, an old-fashioned portable TV playing on a long counter. A little girl turned to him with a spoon in her hand filled with colorful cereal.

"That's Cassidy," she said. "Shaina's daughter. She's at work and I watch her all day. You want some coffee, Sheriff?"

"If it's no trouble." Quinn had removed his hat as any decent man would do inside a building and set it beside the little girl. She stared at him in a curious way, looking down at his polished cowboy boots, Beretta sidearm, and up to his face. She smiled when she got to the face, with its sharp planes and angles, and Quinn winked at her. A commercial played on the TV for a car dealer out of Tupelo featuring a blonde woman named DeLois Price and a Mexican man in a sombrero called Peso Little. The commercials had been on for decades and hadn't changed a bit. Even the same actors.

Mrs. Taylor poured him a cup of coffee and handed him the mug, advertising COBB LUMBER MILL, and he accepted the hot mug with both hands. She nodded her head toward the living room and a grouping of two blue chairs and a tweedy-looking sofa. Quinn had his notebook and pen out, making sure he nailed down all the specific dates and information for a new case file on Brandon's death. He wanted to limit the embarrassment to the sheriff's department as much as he could. That's all he needed, a couple women down from New York City wanting to think no one in the county knew how to type up a report.

"You want to talk about Brandon?" she asked. "Don't you."

"Yes, ma'am," Quinn said. "With it being twenty years now, some folks have renewed interest. You know I was only two years older than your son. And there isn't much left from back then at the sheriff's office."

Mrs. Taylor's eyes wandered away, nodding at nothing in particular.

"Not a lot of folks I'll discuss Brandon with," she said. "But I remember how you helped out in those early days. You worked with your uncle in the woods, walking those same trails from when you got lost as a boy. I believed Brandon would come out of those Big Woods same as you. You were the town hero after surviving all that time. Gave me some hope."

Quinn nodded, feeling his face flush.

"How's Maggie?" she asked.

"Just fine."

"I love that little girl," Rhonda said. "She never lost touch with me or Shaina. I don't think a month's gone by she hadn't called or sent me a letter. Birthdays, Christmas. So many of them. She never forgot our Brandon."

"Her son," Quinn said. "Our son is named for him."

"Oh, I know," she said. "I met him when he was just a baby. She brought him up here to see us with that man she'd married. I know I shouldn't say this, but I didn't care for that man at all. He had a wild look in his eye, always wanting Maggie to shut up and let him talk, walking around and looking at his watch, something on his mind."

"Say what you want," Quinn said. "The man was a liar and a thief. He was mean as hell to Maggie and Brandon and tried to kill me before blowing up my favorite truck."

"Sometimes the Lord works like that," Rhonda said. "Any man who'd blow up another man's truck oughta be in prison."

"Yes, ma'am." Quinn drank some coffee, the little room reminding him a lot of the house where he grew up, nearly the identical blueprint, probably built by the same people. Basic sixties ranch style, brick and wood, with a wide porch outside and a view of the forest. Brandon had had two sisters, Shaina and an older sister named Charlene. Charlene had been in Quinn's class, a heavyset girl who'd been manager of the town's Hollywood Video back when folks still rented movies. Last Quinn had heard, Charlene had moved to Orlando with her second husband, a used-car salesman named Tommy Reeves who played high school ball with Quinn.

"I'll tell you what Shaina told those women from New York City," Mrs. Taylor said. "I figure they've come to see you, too. I don't really know what to make of those folks. One of them has blue hair. Why do they care so much about what happened to our Brandon? Why would they come all the way down to Tibbehah County to start shining a flashlight in the dark, looking for an answer nobody seems to know? Just 'cause Shaina asked them? I don't believe for a hot second that's true. There aren't too many of us left, really. My Tim's dead, Charlene's gone to Orlando. About the only people still left are Shaina, Maggie, and me. Kind of a small club, ain't it?"

"Yes, ma'am," Quinn said. "I promised my wife and those women I'd do my best to find some answers."

Rhonda's face didn't change, her slightly opened mouth still, eyes looking right into Quinn. She looked as if he'd betrayed her in the same way, although he believed he was doing the right thing. What Maggie wanted him to do. What Shaina Taylor said she wanted.

"Why?" she said. "Just to get the blame off your uncle?"

Quinn shook his head. "Excuse me?"

"Hadn't you heard?" Mrs. Taylor said. "He let that awful old man go. Hubie Phillips had all the answers and he just let him go. Tail tucked between his bony legs and skittering on out of this county like some kind of perverted animal."

Quinn nodded as he wrote down some notes. "I heard he might be up in Memphis somewhere?"

"Why don't you ask those New York women?" she said. "Them Bobbsey Twins. Seems like those gals are two steps ahead of you, Sheriff."

* * *

Fannie took the call back at her office at Vienna's, which she had fumigated, painted, and filled with brand-new furniture after those shitbirds J. B. Hood and Wes Taggart vacated the premises. Ole J. B. Hood in a pine box somewhere in Alabama and Taggart now sitting in the county jail, probably with his teeth kicked in by the sheriff. As Ray came on the line, she stood from her glass-top desk and wandered out to the catwalk that looked over the show floor. It was a few hours from opening. Two new hires were vacuuming and scrubbing down the leather chairs of last night's party fun, men spilling drinks and exploding like champagne corks all over her rugs and finery. Damn, it was hell keeping a class place in north Mississippi.

"Sweet baby."

"Money is time, Ray," she said. "What you got for me?"

"Maybe I just wanted to thank you," Ray said. "Tell you how much fun I had at your last visit. Mimosas. Bloody Marys. Maybe take you for a big T-bone dinner at the Como Steakhouse and get you some New York cheesecake for dinner."

"I thought you liked cherry pie, Ray."

"Sometimes it's so damn hot, I just might burn my tongue."

"Shush your mouth," Fannie said, spotting a nasty new stain on the rug leading into the VIP room. She whistled for one of her workers, a Mexican man named Jorge, and pointed to the stain. "I just might blush."

"Since when?"

"Money," Fannie said. "Time."

"You're gonna have a couple guests check in at the Golden Cherry tonight," Ray said.

"OK?"

"They won't be in town long. But perhaps you can arrange for some company to help them while the time away."

"How important?"

"Why's that matter?"

"Depends on if you want the damn Junior Varsity or my starters, Ray," she said. "My talent doesn't come cheap. Longer I keep those girls off the floor, the less we all make."

"Whatever they want," Ray said. "Just make sure they're girls you can trust. They may have to account for some lost time in the next twenty-four hours. Good to know they were being serviced all throughout the day."

"Oh, shit," Fannie said. "What the fuck is going on now?"

"Don't you worry your pretty red head a bit," Ray said. "I can't tell you what's happening, but you'll sure like the outcome."

"Then why won't you tell me?"

"And spoil the surprise?" Ray said. "Not a chance, doll."

# EIGHT

It took Jessica less than two minutes to find Hubie Phillips on Facebook. The profile matched the age, education, and background for the source they hoped to find. Although some details were blocked, they saw his profession was retired educator and that he'd been in Memphis since 1998. Although there had been no mention of Jericho or Tibbehah County, they decided to take a flyer and Jessica sent out a friend request. Within fifteen minutes, they heard back, asking, *Do I know you?* Tashi and Jessica decided direct and honest was the best way to proceed and answered back they were journalists looking into the death of Brandon Taylor.

For two days they heard nothing, but on the third day Jessica received a message from a man named Arthur Kelm from a Gmail account who said he'd like to meet and find out if they had the best interests in mind for his friend Hubie. He wanted to meet in Memphis at a public spot and they chose the food court at an aging mall in east Memphis on Poplar Avenue. Tashi went alone with her recorder and a notebook and found a small table outside a Starbucks, on the first floor, right by the entrance to Macy's.

She drank a matcha green tea latte and checked her phone, waiting for thirty minutes and then an hour. She texted Jessica back at the Traveler's Rest Motel saying, *Looks like a no-show.* But Jessica remained firm, saying, *Kelm said he was running late. Stick tight. He'll show.*

Nearly an hour and a half from the agreed meeting time, a slight, older man with thinning gray hair, dressed in a short-sleeved plaid shirt and khakis, walked up to her table. He looked as bland and inoffensive as an insurance salesman. "Are you Jessica?"

"Tashi," she said, giving her best welcoming smile, pointing to an empty chair. "Jessica is my producer. She couldn't make it."

The older man looked worried, his sagging cheeks ashen, his eyes, a clear blue, darting around the mall, looking as if a SWAT team might swoop in at any moment, knocking over coffee cups, muffins, and Danishes. "I agreed to meet Jessica. I don't know you."

"You don't know Jessica, either," Tashi said, still smiling. "But we showed you who we are and what we're working on. Can I buy you some coffee or something to eat? There's a Chick-fil-A right around the corner. We could talk there."

The man didn't sit, just kept on looking around the mall. Foot Locker, U.S. Apparel, a GNC store offering BUY ONE, GET ONE 50 PERCENT OFF! LIT ON-THE-GO IN TANGY ORANGE. He was skinny and slump-shouldered. His tennis shoes were sensible white canvas with spotless laces.

"I promise, I don't bite."

The man shook his head and turned, walking fast back toward the center of the mall to the water fountains and glass elevator she'd passed on the way in. Tashi grabbed her purse and recorder and left her empty cup, following Arthur Kelm through the few people who still came to malls, walking and window-shopping for shit no one needs. Cart vendors tried to sell her bootleg fragrances, cheap sunglasses, and 3-D family portraits etched in glass. Kelm turned toward a staircase heading up to the parking lot and she pursued, the air smelling of the Auntie Anne's pretzels at the corner, free samples wafting right in front of her face.

"Mr. Kelm," she said, yelling up the steps. "I believe Hubie Phillips might know what really happened. I know he was Brandon's friend."

Kelm quit walking. He didn't turn, just stood there on the landing, holding the handrail, staring up at the daylight as he bowed his head. Tashi took the steps two by two and got within earshot. "Can you please just relay a message?" she said. "We only want to know about Sheriff Beckett. We need to know more about his investigation. Everything has been destroyed. We are starting from the very beginning. November 1997. Sir?"

The older man turned to her, out of breath, face drained of color. He looked down at a cell phone in his hand and then back at Tashi. "OK," he said. "Just don't lie to me. You lie to me once and I'm done."

"Mr. Phillips?" Tashi asked.

The old man nodded. "I sure loved that boy."

Work didn't stop in Tibbehah County, not for Wes Taggart or Brandon Taylor, and that afternoon Quinn had been tipped Pookie Williams was spotted up in Blackjack milling about the new Dollar General, shoving candy bars and beef jerky into his pant pockets. He radioed into dispatch he was headed into the store, but as soon as he was through the door, the clerk, a chubby, balding dude named Buddy Smallwood, leaned against the register and pointed to the far back corner. Smallwood had a toothpick hanging from the side of his mouth and somehow looked curious and bored at the same time.

The store seemed empty except for some loud music playing down the cereal aisle. A big Bluetooth boom box perched above a Lucky Charms display blasted a Kane Brown song Quinn had heard all summer. "Used to Love You Sober."

Quinn reached down for his mic and radioed in that Williams was inside the store.

Cleotha radioed back, asking if Tibbehah 1 needed backup.

"No, ma'am," Quinn said, turning down the radio and walking down the far wall filled with refrigerators and freezers.

"What's that shit you listening to?" Cleotha said, radioing back.

"Keep this channel clear, please."

The glass cases held about everything you needed to get by in the country: milk, sausage, ice cream, Popsicles, and big sacks of frozen biscuits. He looked up at the circular mirror in the corner and spotted a man, two aisles in, moving fast toward the front of the store. Quinn walked back the way he came to cut him off, past the bags of potato chips, cheese puffs, beef jerky, and mixed nuts.

Pookie had his head down, hands cradling his bulging sweatshirt like a pregnant woman as he walked. When Quinn called out his name, Pookie looked up, said, "Oh, shit," and dropped sacks and cans of food on the floor. He darted back the way he'd come and disappeared around the corner.

Quinn knew he wasn't armed, but letting Pookie Williams escape the sheriff in the Blackjack Dollar General might prove embarrassing as hell. He moved back toward the front of the store and nodded to Buddy. "Back door locked?"

"'Course it's locked," Buddy Smallwood said. "Dang. You think I like getting robbed just for the fun of it?"

"Exit door?" Quinn asked.

"Fire door?" Smallwood said. "Oh, well. Yeah, but it'll set off the alarm."

Quinn ran back toward the far corner of the store, toward the big paper towel display. Pookie had gone in the opposite direction, back where they sold kids' clothes, T-shirts, and underwear. The back displays offered Christmas and Halloween decorations year-round for fifty percent off.

"Pookie?" Quinn said.

He heard feet in the next aisle and turned to see Pookie running down the toy aisle, knocking down boxes of Barbies and action figures behind him as if it would block Quinn's path. He got nearly to the front of the store when Buddy Smallwood blocked Pookie's escape with a revolver in his hand. Quinn called out for Buddy to put it down but Buddy wouldn't listen, standing there in a Dirty Harry pose, legs wide and chomping on his toothpick. If Quinn didn't get him settled, they'd be picking up Pookie's brains on aisle 6.

"Pookie," Quinn said. "Son of a damn bitch."

Pookie ran so fast he got tangled up in a Mylar balloon display, tripping and falling but getting back to his feet, running like hell with several pink and green balloons wrapped around his legs. Quinn headed for the fire exit, knowing that it was the only way out, but Pookie was hopped up and ready, beating him there and busting through the door, the alarm going off in the store. Quinn finally caught him by the dumpsters and throwaway boxes outside, tackling him to the ground, balloons and all.

They fell in a heap, crushing boxes under them, as Quinn flipped Pookie onto his face and searched his pockets for the knife he knew he'd find. He pulled out a retractable blade inside a pair of brass knuckles etched with a profile of a dragon breathing fire. A nasty little setup anyone could buy at their local gas station for five bucks.

"Damn it, Pookie."

Pookie turned his head and spit. His lip was busted and his face scratched as he looked up at Quinn. "Damn," he said. "I sure am sorry, Sheriff."

"Buddy Smallwood almost shot you in the back."

"I didn't steal nothing," he said. "I dropped everything but these damn balloons all over my ass."

"You robbed Miss Peaches at the Dixie Gas station," he said. "You pulled this knife on that nice old woman."

"Did I?" Pookie said. His eyes were glazed, as Quinn helped him to his feet, and he looked authentically confused.

"You sure did."

"Shit, Sheriff," he said. "Last week's sure as hell been a blur. I can't really say what I done or not done."

"We got you on video."

"Oh."

"And your momma's worried sick about you," Quinn said, opening up the back door of his truck. Pookie's hands were cuffed behind him and Quinn had to help him up onto the rails. "I would've hated to tell her you got shot over some Slim Jims and Cheetos."

"I'll get straight," Pookie said. "I promise you, Sheriff. I'll get straight."

They walked toward Dillard's.

"I'm sorry," Hubie Phillips said. "That wasn't exactly a time in my life I want to remember. It was pure and absolute humiliation."

"How soon after Brandon's death did you leave Jericho?" Tashi asked, glad to have some of the mall sounds on the recording. A little side action always made things sound better. You could hear the fountain, the slight murmur of people talking and walking.

"I left around graduation in '98," he said. "I didn't want to go. I loved teaching. I'd been at Tibbehah High for more than twenty years, but no one made it comfortable. The principal, the school board—everyone was against me except for a handful of students. I was guilty in the eyes of everyone in town."

"Was it because you were gay?"

"Is it that obvious?" Phillips said, smiling for the first time. "Is it my sensible shoes?"

"I've talked to several people," Tashi said. "They say that's why you were the first suspect."

"That," Phillips said, "and also because Brandon and I were genuine friends. He could talk to me like he couldn't speak to his father. Have you met his dad, Tim?"

"He died a few years ago."

"That man was a piece of work," Phillips said, as they passed a Sunglass Hut and a Bath & Body Works, the smell of the cinnamon pretzels now replaced with Sweater Weather and Pumpkin Waffles candles. "A mean SOB. I'm sorry. I don't mean that. But he did try to kill me once. He stuck a gun not only into my mouth but down my throat. If it hadn't been for the school resource officer and the football coach, I think that man would've pulled the trigger."

"Did you file charges against him?"

"I wanted to," he said. "But the principal and the Taylors' pastor talked me out of it. Said Tim Taylor had been through enough already. Damn, Brandon hated that man."

"He and Brandon didn't get along?"

"Not at all," Phillips said. "Brandon tried to embrace all those things his dad loved. Tim Taylor was typical Tibbehah County. Liked to hunt and fish, drink beer, and watch football. He did some kind of manual labor at the Cobb family sawmill. Typical roughneck who couldn't understand his son had broader interests. You do know Brandon was an excellent photographer? That's probably what he was up to in the woods. The hunting story was probably Tim's own interpretation. Or maybe Brandon said it so they'd leave him alone."

"How did you get pulled into all this?" Tashi said. They sat down in a little grouping of leather massage chairs offering shiatsu for a buck. Neither one of them leaned back or relaxed.

"Sheriff Beckett," Phillips said. The skin on his face as pale and thin as parchment paper. "Tim told him Brandon and I had an unnatural relationship. He said Brandon and I spent more time together than the boy did with his own family. That was very true. But Brandon was curious, working in the darkroom as a member of the yearbook staff, talking about music and art. He loved playing the guitar. To a man like Tim that just meant you were a queer."

"Did Beckett seriously consider you?"

"He kept me at the sheriff's office for two days straight," he said. "I didn't have an attorney or ask for one. I answered all his questions. I took a lie detector test. I accounted for my whereabouts. I mean, I had nothing to hide. And I wanted to do my best to help find Brandon. I told Hamp Beckett if he wanted to look at someone who had the motive, it was Tim Taylor. Brandon used to come to school with bruises on his arms. He came one time with a black eye. That man was pure walking evil."

"What charges did he hold you on?"

Hubie Phillips shook his head. "I don't even know," he said. "After two days, the sheriff let me go. I thought that was the end of it. I took part in nearly every search party they put together. But I heard the rumors, saw the looks when I'd go out to eat. I hate to break it to you, but a confirmed old bachelor like me is something of an anomaly in Jericho. People called me witty and eccentric to my face and just a crazy old queer behind my back."

"And when they found Brandon?"

"It only got worse."

"That's why you left?"

Phillips started to cry and wiped his eyes with the back of his hand. He took a few moments to compose himself, let go of the shakiness in his voice. He cleared his voice a few times and nodded. "Not much else you can do when the sheriff drives you way out in the county to have a heart-to-heart and gives you twenty-four hours to get out of town."

"What did you do?"

"I drove straight up to Memphis and stayed with a friend," he said. "I sold my place in Jericho through a realtor and had my friends collect all my belongings. I left town with nothing but my car and the clothes on my back. Hamp Beckett wasn't any different from all that crew. Tim Taylor, Johnny Stagg . . . Do you know about Stagg?"

"Oh, yes," Tashi said. "His shadow looms large."

"That town," he said. "That whole county tries to act like it's all Mayberry. Main Street USA. But there is a streak of mean that's been there since the town was settled. Did you know they lynched a black man in 1977 and no one said a damn thing? It's not a civilized place. And I doubt anything has changed."

Tashi swallowed, feeling for the man, wondering what else he'd been up to. Wanting to know about his life now, where he worked, how he escaped the rumors. But there were more pressing questions and she always centered back to the focus. "Do you believe Brandon killed himself?"

"Not at all," he said. "At first, I believed it could've been his father who drove him away. Or even killed Brandon himself. But when Tim came for me that day with the gun, it changed my mind. The look in his eyes as he stuck the barrel down my throat, he wasn't play-acting. He believed I'd done it."

"Why do you think he believed that?"

"Besides me being gay?"

Tashi nodded.

"Nothing," he said. "They just needed someone to blame for that boy never coming back and I was one hell of a target."

Quinn had met Reggie at the sheriff's office, heading back toward the locked gate and through the gauntlet where the jailers worked, watching video feeds and running dispatch. Two more metal gates led into the cells themselves, Wes Taggart set off by himself next to Pookie Williams, who'd already made himself at home, watching television with two guys there on public drunk charges and unable to make bail. All of them entranced by *Family Feud*, Steve Harvey asking, *Name something that comes strapped to you.* The boys snickering at the question.

"Understand you wanted to see me?" Quinn said.

"Yes, sir," Taggart said, rising up off his bunk, looking at Quinn between the bars, rubbing the stubble on his head. "Sure do. How about you get me out of this shithole and let me sit down face-to-face like a white man."

Quinn shook his head, exchanging a glance with Reggie. "I understand that high-dollar lawyer from Memphis still hasn't come to see you," he said.

Taggart's cocky grin faded, nodding as he pondered the situation. "I could use something decent to eat," he said. "Shit on a shingle and an old cup of coffee ain't cutting it. You think you might wrangle up one of those Sonic burgers again?"

"Sure," Quinn said. "Reggie, radio up Kenny and tell him to stop by Sonic."

Reggie nodded and walked back toward the jailers and dispatch, leaving Quinn standing alone in front of Taggart, looking uglier than ever with his bald, skeletal head.

"Except for the part when you about ripped my head off, I'll be kind of sad to leave Tibbehah County," Taggart said, his teeth big slabs discolored by coffee and cigarettes. "I can't imagine the folks in Oxford being so downright hospitable."

"You got something to discuss, Wes?" Quinn said. "Or you just looking to bullshit for a free meal?"

"I don't know," Taggart said, kind of laughing to himself. "What you got on the menu, Sheriff? How about you spell it out for me."

"Your people left your ass hanging in the wind," Quinn said. "You're looking at attempted murder and murder charges here and then racketeering, drug running, and human trafficking up with the Feds. Altogether, I don't see you getting out for a good long while. You might just want to lose the attitude and look at your situation. You really that good of friends with Fannie Hathcock and her people down on the Coast?"

Taggart didn't say anything, just turned his head and spit on the floor. Reggie walked back up, nodding to Quinn, Quinn punching the key in the lock and opening up the cell. Taggart seemed surprised by it, taking a few steps back. His bed was unmade and his lunch sat picked apart and nasty by the seatless toilet. Someone had brought him some free religious comic books and they lay splayed open on his bunk. The tale of Bathsheba and King David. Taggart noticed Quinn staring and said, "Boy, that woman sure got David's pecker out of joint. Damn near destroyed his kingdom after seeing her nekkid. Men will do things like that. Toss away everything for a piece of tail."

"Are you saying you're like David?" Quinn said, grinning.

"Maybe," he said. "I had lots of things going for me. Nice strip club, truck stop, and a trucking company, before little Miss Twilight gave me a little private show. You know the dumbest damn part of it?"

"Not really," Quinn said.

"I thought that little girl loved me."

Quinn looked to Reggie and Reggie just shook his head, having little patience for Wes Taggart. Reggie wanted the man gone as quickly as they could arrange transport.

"Your people aren't going to help," Quinn said. "They didn't send a lawyer. They won't show you a bit of support. If you got something, now is the time to talk."

"Maybe I'd rather talk to the Feds than some two-bit Andy Griffith in some hick town," he said. "Just what in the fuck can you do for me?"

"Besides getting you a double cheeseburger with extra pickles?" Quinn said. "I might be able to talk to the prosecutors about the charges against you. I don't think you and Hood went after Boom on your own. I think your people down on the Coast cheered you on. How about we talk a little about them? And their relationship with Jimmy Vardaman. They've been a pain in my ass since I came home."

"People on the Coast?" Taggart said, sitting down on his bunk and tossing the biblical comic book to the floor, the pages fluttering like a wounded bird. "Shit. You really don't understand who they are and what they do. They'd just as soon kill you, Sheriff, as look at you. Why the fuck do you think they sent me and J.B. up to Shithole USA anyway? It sure as shit wasn't just to watch truckers titty-fuck some truck stop women. Oh, hell no. We got sent to take care of you, Sheriff."

"And whose idea was that?" Quinn asked.

"When's that burger getting here?"

"Soon."

"You get me tater tots and shake, too?"

Quinn looked at Reggie and Reggie nodded. "The works, Wes," Quinn said. "You know nothing's too good for an important guest like you. You're absolute shitbird royalty around here."

"How about you let me ask you a question, then," Taggart said. "How the hell did you piss off so many folks in Jackson? It ain't the goddamn honest crooks who are after your ass, it's the fucking Moral Majority. My friends are just hired hands for some fat cats in the capitol."

"Vardaman," Quinn said.

"Some old swinging dicks across this state sure would've liked to seen that fucker lose," Taggart said. "But he's got a lot of friends. They even have a name for themselves, the fucking Watchmen Society. Have you heard about those morons?"

"I just met a few down at the Neshoba County Fair."

"As long as business is booming, as long as we're able to run drugs and gash around the Mid-South, everything is copacetic, Sheriff. But you don't need to start pointing your fingers at some honest crooks. You know where we stand. It's the goddamn suit and tie crowd, thumping the Bible and looking to turn everything back into the plantation, who're going take your ass out one day."

"You got some names?" Quinn said.

"You already know some," Taggart said. "One big name with his eyes on the big prize. But hell, man. It sure is hard for me to talk on an empty stomach."

# NINE

Sam Frye and Toby hit the Tibbehah County line just as the rain and thunder started to roll across north Mississippi. They'd been listening to the news out of Tupelo on the ride, Toby being Toby and wanting to ignore the weather or the news, and instead planned to play a shuffle from his iPhone he'd made with his buddies on the Rez. His straight job was a party DJ and the boy had some kind of plan to be the first big Choctaw rapper out of the South, claiming he had more than five thousand followers on YouTube who'd listened to a song he'd made called "Tribal Woman."

"This shit is lit."

"But will it make you rich?"

"It'll get me laid," Toby said. "A damn Indian who can rap. Think about it, old man."

"Why'd you quit at the water park?"

"Too damn hot," Toby said. "Cleaning out filters, checking pH levels, being told not to stare at the white girls in their bikinis. I mean, shit. What's the damn point? This thing I'm about to play for you, this music I made over the last few weeks, it's gonna put me and the whole damn tribe back on the map. We'll be able to sell out shows all over the Mid-South."

Sam Frye didn't believe half the shit the kid had told him. But Toby, born Tobias Williams sixteen years earlier, was the son of Sam's best and oldest friend, and when the boy's father had been eaten up with cancer, Sam promised he'd look out for Toby. "Show him the old ways," Big Monte had said. The old man meaning take the boy out to the burial mounds, introduce him to the elders who still spoke the language, and maybe teach him some dirty stickball tricks.

But Sam Frye had never been much of a stickball player. And most of the elders he knew had passed on, besides some of the women who sold baskets at the big Choctaw Carnival every year and talked about the days when the Choctaw Nation covered half of the state. The white men arriving with treaties and a little money, forcing most of the tribe west to Oklahoma. A few of the tribe hiding in the woods, staying away from the white man, while their people were forced onto the Trail of Tears, and waiting more than a hundred years before they could claim their land again, put up casinos and water slides and dance for the entertainment of tourists. Frye figured he would do what Big Monte really wanted and teach the boy an honest trade.

"OK, Sam," Toby said. "Who's the guy they want dead?"

"Didn't ask," Sam Frye said, hitting the windshield wipers. "Don't know. Like I said. We go and await a phone call."

"You promised there will be women," Toby said.

"And there will be."

"And weed."

"You don't need any more weed," Sam Frye said. "You were baked out of your mind when I picked you up. You need a clear head tonight. This storm will make whatever we have to do even harder. You just follow me. Do as I say and you'll be fine. I need you to keep your eyes open, keep awake, and keep the car running. That's it. You can handle it. Right?"

"I have a wedding this weekend," Toby said. "At the big casino. They want me to play all kinds of old-school music. Back from the eighties when you and Big Monte were young bucks. You and Big Monte like that stuff? N.W.A.? LL Cool J?"

"Naw," Sam Frye said. "We liked Metallica. Your dad ever play *Ride the Lightning* or *Kill 'Em All* for you? That's music. It was music with brains and substance."

"That stuff sucks, man," Toby said. "All the screeching and screaming. No heart and no soul . . . You and Big Monte. Y'all must've been something back in the day."

"Why do you call your father Big Monte?" Sam Frye said. "That shows disrespect."

"He was mean," Toby said, running his hand over his razor-short hair. "A drug addict."

"He once was a good man," Sam Frye said. "He provided for you and your mother. You think he liked wearing that uniform at the Rez and pouring drinks to gamblers? Telling jokes about teepees and wigwams and all that shit? He worked so you and your mother could have a life."

"He left my mother," Toby said. "For a white woman with big fake tits. She treated him like he was some kind of wild animal. A pet. And when he got sick, that woman left and went all the way back to California."

Sam Frye had nothing to say as they rolled farther into the county, passing the big billboards placed along Highway 45. DON'T MISS THE REBEL TRUCK STOP and THE HOLY BIBLE. INSPIRED/ABSOLUTE/FINAL. And one with Kermit the Frog. EATS FLIES. DATES A PIG. HOLLYWOOD STAR. The rain coming down harder now, and he saw a flash beyond the lights gathering around the truck stop, blooms of white and red neon. The outline of a woman, her curves outlined in neon, kicking her legs up and down.

"You promised we could go to the titty bar."

"That titty bar will come to us," Sam Frye said. "While we wait for the call."

"Amazing," the kid said. "You're kidding."

"Make the most of your time," Sam Frye said. "Be respectful of the girl they send. We could get the call at any moment. Finish up quick."

"I'm sixteen, Sam," Toby said, laughing. "I do everything fast."

"And no real names," Sam Frye said. "And no tall tales about the music business."

"What tall tales?"

"Big T," he said. "Famous Choctaw rapper."

"You'll have a girl, too?"

"I'm old," Sam Frye said. "Not dead. We both get rooms. When I come for you, leave the girl and follow me out. Say nothing. I'll tell you what you need to know on the way."

Sam Frye pulled off on the next exit, passing the red and blue glow from Vienna's Place and the sprawling pumps at the Rebel Truck Stop. His long black hair was chopped off straight at the shoulders and hanging loose across his ears and neck. Across the road he turned into the Golden Cherry Motel, a roadside wet dream from the 1950s. Sam Frye not surprised to see the cursive neon reading *Vacancy*. The swimming pool glowed in the darkness with a weird green shimmer.

"Same as Memphis?" Toby said.

"Same idea," Sam Frye said. "Different plan."

"I did what you said," the kid said, almost speaking to himself.

"And?"

"I liked it," he said. "Felt as natural as fucking."

"I know," Sam Frye said. "Your father would be very proud."

* * *

Wes Taggart finished his cheeseburger with extra cheese and pickles in less than two minutes in the conference room. He wiped his mouth with a handful of napkins and leaned back into the rolling office chair. Quinn and Reggie sat at the head of the table, Reggie not being sure this was the best idea, letting a prisoner like Taggart out of his cell and out of his handcuffs. But Quinn had told him he wasn't too worried about the situation. *If Taggart made a break for the door, how far do you think he'd get?*

"I'll tell you what," Taggart said. "Them folks at Sonic sure know how to make a cheeseburger. You boys want some fries? I don't think I can eat this whole bag. Lord have mercy."

He reached for his shake and started to slurp through the straw. Reggie looking over at Quinn and shaking his head. Quinn and Reggie were ex-Army and they both had a low tolerance for sloppy behavior. They'd both grown up—and later enforced—looking people in the eye, sitting up straight, and eating with proper manners at the table. It wasn't easy watching Taggart inhale a cheeseburger and mash a fistful of fries.

The rain had started a half hour ago, a mean storm with lightning and possible tornadoes rolling in from Arkansas. They were under a watch until midnight. Reggie stood and walked over to the door, arms crossed over his chest, almost daring Taggart to even try.

"The thing about it, Sheriff, is that I know I'm fucked five ways from Sunday," Taggart said. "Y'all are holding all the damn cards. I know you boys both saw me shoot some folks on Pritchard land. I know the Feds got some files and computers showing the gravy train we was running out of Tupelo. And even though I damn well know it's a lie, that friend of yours is gonna say it was me and J. B. Hood who done bashed his head in. I don't need some Memphis lawyer drawing me a diagram in the dirt. Even if I tell you a thousand damn times it was all J.B.'s doing. He was a hard, mean man, God rest his soul."

Quinn cocked his head, staring hard at Taggart. He watched the man's Adam's apple bob up and down while he swallowed his vanilla milk shake, taking a short break to reach into the cup with his index finger and fish out the cherry. He sucked on it with a big grin on his thin gray lips.

"You were talking about Vardaman," Quinn said.

"Was I, now?" Taggart asked. "Ain't that something."

Quinn took another long breath, having to slow down every bit of training he'd ever had. He spent a decade of his life taking on hostiles with as much speed and violence as necessary. Now he was having to sit across the table from this Grade A turd and try like hell to be civil. No doubt he and Hood had beaten Boom. No doubt they had meant to kill him. But the dumb son of a bitch also held a lot of answers that went well beyond Tibbehah County, understanding connections in play well before Quinn ever got out of the service. Quinn leaned his elbows flat across the table but kept staring at Taggart. Neither he nor Reggie Caruthers said a thing.

Reggie's radio squawked for a moment and he reached down to turn down the volume. The only sound now coming from the buzzing fluorescent lights overhead.

"Well now," Taggart said. "I might have seen a few things down in Biloxi."

Quinn kept quiet.

"Y'all know who Buster White is?"

Quinn nodded.

"Goddamn peckerwood godfather of the Gulf Coast," Taggart said. "Don't you believe them stories people say about him feeding folks to the gators. He's a good Christian man. Got grandbabies and them grandbabies got their own. Did you know he does an Easter egg roll down at the beach attended by a few hundred folks? He even hired me once to be the damn Easter bunny and dance around with the kiddos in the sunshine. Never sweated so much in my damn life."

Quinn held up his hand. "Skip the bullshit," he said. "Either you tell us about White and Vardaman or I'm gone. I should've been home two hours ago."

"Congratulations, by the way," Taggart said, leaning back into his office chair, licking the salt off his fingers. "I heard all about your wife from some of the other fellas here. I heard she was one fine little number. Small tits but birthing hips. Got her own little kid, too. How you liking be a daddy all of a sudden?"

Quinn didn't answer, taking a sip of cold coffee. Maggie had told him she'd be holding supper just in case he could get home. She had some kind of vegetarian tofu stir-fry she'd found online. Maggie hadn't been a big fan of the meals Quinn had been eating at the farm. Eggs and bacon. Venison with onions and peppers. Some fried catfish with whiskey on the side.

"It'll cost you," Taggart said.

"Figured it would, Wes," Quinn said.

Wes Taggart smiled. It wasn't pretty, as most of his teeth were yellowed and crooked. "Ain't you gonna ask what I want?"

Reggie walked up from the door and walked around the table, looking out the windows at the dispatch station. "Another goddamn cheeseburger?"

"'Fraid not, Sambo," Taggart said.

Reggie moved so fast, Quinn barely had time to make it over the desk and pull him off Taggart. Taggart flat on his back, smiling and laughing, the laughter turning into slow giggles as he curled up into a tight ball. Reggie backed away, knocking down a white grease board hanging on the wall. Cleotha's inspiration of the day written in red ink. DON'T LET NO MAN STEAL YOUR JOY.

"Sorry about that, Sheriff," Reggie said.

"About what?" Quinn said.

Quinn stepped back and Taggart lifted his head and stared dead-eyed at Quinn. "I bet you and your buddies up in Oxford sure would like to know how a man like J. K. Vardaman done beat the money folks in Jackson. Goddamn establishment machine sure didn't want a wild card like that old nut running this state. Went against his own people and not only triumphed but lived to see another goddamn day. It's a hell of a story. Inspirational as all get-out. Maybe better than some of them Bible tales or one of them *Left Behind* novels I read on the toilet."

"Vardaman and your people," Quinn said. "Sounds like a hell of a tall tale, Taggart."

Taggart grinned again. "Your fine little piece of tail got some supper on the stove for you?"

"Yep," he said. "And it's late. Raining like hell outside. And that high-dollar lawyer of yours ain't coming tonight. Or tomorrow."

"Funny how it works," Taggart said. "Everybody's all pals while the money's flowing. But you make one little mistake and everyone's running for the hills with their hands covering their peckers."

In the conference room, they could hear the sound of rain hammering the roof. In the few seconds of Taggart not running his mouth, a long, grumbling thunder shook the windows.

"I want a sit-down with you and the Feds," Taggart said. "I think those boys will go pretty damn far if I draw them a little diagram between Jackson, Biloxi, and Memphis. What I call a triangle of sin. Everybody done turned their backs on Vardaman, thought he was the goddamn oddball long shot in this election. All that talk about states' rights and a return to more decent times. He was a damn punch line on Jay Leno."

"Jay Leno retired," Reggie said.

"Y'all know what I'm talking about," Taggart said. "You heard all about the Watchmen Society and their plans for the state? Twirling those red bandannas every time Vardaman farts. Those people sure do love his style. You can scowl all you want at me, Deputy, but your black ass is gonna be back in the field picking cotton if these folks get their way. And you, Sheriff? Shit. They had plans for you since the start of the year. This crazy asshole wins the election and them state folks are going to be wiping their asses with the law book. *Turn back time.* You heard that shit? *Tick-motherfucking-tock.*"

"I've been dealing with y'all since I became sheriff," Quinn said. "And my uncle before that. Johnny Stagg. Bobby Campo. Buster White and Fannie Hathcock. Never really thought of any of them having some kind of political agenda. This all sounds like a tall tale to save your narrow ass."

Wes Taggart howled with laughter, rolling back in the office chair. Quinn looked up at Reggie, who was still close enough to reach out and choke the ever-living shit out of that wiry shitbird. A tattoo of a little cartoon devil decorated Taggart's left arm and read MADE IN HELL. Taggart noticed Quinn staring. "Hot Stuff," he said. "You recall that little son of a bitch? Or are you too damn young?"

"You got to give me something," Quinn said.

"Hell of a storm brewing outside," Taggart said, looking up at the ceiling. "I heard a tornado si-rene before y'all got me out of the cell. What we used to call a dang belly washer down in McComb."

"Come on, Reggie," Quinn said. "Supper's getting cold."

"I'm your only damn hope, Ranger," Taggart said. "I wouldn't say jack shit to the nasty woman who trucked my ass up here. Miss Virgil. But I'll tell you what. I don't just know where the bodies are buried. I sure as shit know who put them there."

* * *

"What the hell's that?" Bentley asked.

"Tornado alert," Caddy said, reaching for her iPhone on the bedside table, light shining hard into her eyes. She and Bentley had fallen asleep an hour or so ago, after watching a movie and heading on back to the bedroom. His hand fallen over her bare stomach as she dozed off. "Looks like one touched down in Lee County."

She got out of bed buck-ass naked and walked back to her bathroom to fill a cup of water. Jason was over at a friend's house and it gave her and Bentley a little more free time to be alone. Her son still didn't know they were dating, Caddy introducing him as a good friend from Jackson who knows his grandfather. There was little friendly about what they'd started doing when they got bored with the movie. Their clothes were twisted and fallen on the hardwood floor, rain tapping against the windowpanes.

"Don't get up," Bentley said. "An alert's not a big deal. We used to have them in Pocahontas all the time."

"We have them all the time here, too," Caddy said. "Did I ever tell you what happened to my last house?"

Bentley didn't answer, sliding his feet to the floor and starting to reach for his underwear and jeans. He was tall and lanky, a good solid body under those loose-fitting clothes he wore. A swimmer, a runner, who kept on trying to get Caddy to train with him for a marathon.

"Have you seen my boxers?" he asked. She could see his naked ass shining in the light from the living room.

"Where'd you take 'em off?" Caddy asked. She stood there, naked, sunburned across her chest and arms and down on her legs. Pale and white across her belly and over her breasts as she tipped the cup to her lips and drained it.

She liked the new place, moving in after Maggie and Quinn had gotten married. The old bungalow had been Maggie's grandmother's, only a few blocks from the Jericho Square, with a nice sitting porch and a big old oak to offer shade during the summer. Maggie had been in the middle of renovations when she'd moved out, the woman loving to take on projects herself, and half the kitchen was still torn up.

Bentley zipped up his jeans and walked over to Caddy, pulling her in and giving her a kiss on her mouth. "Damn," he said.

"You had enough?" Caddy asked.

"Yes, ma'am."

"How about you cut the 'yes, ma'am' stuff," she said. "Makes me feel older than I am."

Bentley laughed and Caddy slipped into a black kimono Maggie had left in the closet. Just like her sister-in-law to have a kimono decorated with dragons and Chinese symbols. The lights flickered on and off in the living room. The idea of a tornado rolling through town still scared the hell out of her. She'd lost everything in the last one, a good quarter of Jericho destroyed in a busted-ass path that ran from south of downtown to damn near up to Tupelo. The town still hadn't recovered.

The lights flickered again, more thunder booming outside, and then they stood there in complete darkness. She felt her way around the couch, seeing a bit thanks to a little light coming through the kitchen window. Caddy lit a couple of candles and set them on the table, brightening the small room just a little. Jason's football jersey had been left to dry over a kitchen chair, paperwork from The River piled up on another.

"Thanks," Bentley said.

"For what?"

"Inviting me over."

"I was bored," Caddy said. "Not much else to do in Jericho but get drunk. And I don't drink anymore."

"Sorry we didn't finish the movie."

"I'll show you the rest later," Caddy said. "You kept on falling asleep."

Bentley laughed again, leaning onto the kitchen counter, touching her face and grinning in a sleepy way. "Lots of hippie-dippie stuff," he said. "I guess all that was a long time ago."

"You should meet my Uncle Van," Caddy said. "Nobody's told him the seventies are over. Still wears bell-bottom jeans and smokes weed. He lives in his trailer in this little time capsule."

"Wasn't just the clothes," Bentley said. "Those people had kind of a crazy way of believing how things worked. Whoever made the movie seemed to have a real problem with authority, making it seem like every elected official was a crook."

"Aren't they?"

Bentley laughed again in the darkness. "Not all of 'em," Bentley said. "Some of us squares are trying to make a difference."

"The movie was one of my daddy's favorites," she said. "He trained with the same guy who taught hapkido to the main character. When Daddy was out in Hollywood, he and the actor who played the hero got to be good pals. Daddy was in some Western he made. They stayed friends pretty much his whole life."

"You don't think like that," Bentley said. "Do you? You don't think everyone with money is evil and wants to take advantage of the poor. Made it seem like the whole system was busted."

"Isn't it?" Caddy said.

"Come on, now."

"No," she said, the candlelight casting his handsome face in shadow. "You think we're all doing fine and dandy down in Mississippi? You think we don't have folks like Posner looking down their noses at Hispanics, blacks, Indians? I watch that movie and I think nothing has changed."

"When we first met, I told you we shouldn't talk politics."

"Or religion."

"I didn't say religion," Bentley said. "You know I'm a Christian. I believe in what you're doing here. I just don't like folks who go off on the fringe of things. That doesn't do anything but make the problems worse. It obscures all the good being done."

Caddy started to say something else but then thought better of it. Bentley was a good man who'd been brought up in a gilded world in Jackson. It would take some time, but she knew he had heart and ideals and would come around to the way things worked. Maybe it'd been too much to show him *Billy Jack* so soon. The Colson family watched the movie nearly every Thanksgiving after the parades, football games, and big supper. Those old action movies a big part of their family history.

"I don't think I've ever met anyone so mean in my life," Bentley said. "Tossing a sack of flour in a kid's face. Come on."

"He was trying to make him white."

"I did like that one girl," he said. "The one in those big boots and crazy glasses who told the asshole kid her name was Up. 'Up Yours.' She was beautiful. Had a nice little attitude."

"And you like a little attitude?"

"Yes, ma'am."

"Son of a bitch."

"Can I get a drink of water?" Bentley said, grinning. "Or you gonna just toss me back out in this weather?"

"I didn't plan on you staying."

"I know."

"But it is a long way home."

"Three hours."

"Don't want anything to happen to you."

She refilled her cup from the tap and passed it on to Bentley. Her phone started to ring, skittering across the kitchen table. Caddy picked up.

"Caddy?" a deep voice said. "It's Boom. I'm drunk as hell and sure could use a little help."

"Where are you?"

"Southern Star."

"OK," Caddy said. "Give me five minutes."

She ended the call.

Bentley turned to her. "What's up?"

"Nothing," she said. "Don't worry about it. Be right back."

The girls had arrived at nine as promised and were on their way by ten. Sam Frye bought a Coke for Toby outside at the machine, the weather still for a moment, just kind of hanging in there in pink and black swirls above the truck stop and the highway. It was real nice, gloomy and pleasant at the same time.

"Why'd you tell the girl you were my uncle?" Toby asked. Sam Frye handed him the Coke, standing back and amazed at the wonderful show nature was providing that night. The swimming pool was a light emerald green, ruffled by the wind.

"Made sense," Sam Frye said. "Two nice men. Old man and his nephew. The old man getting his nephew the first good ride of his life."

"Something that girl will never believe," Toby said. "No way she would think it was my first time any more than I would've believed it was her first. Did you see the body on her? She was little, compact and short. But strong, Sam. Boy, she really knew what she was doing."

"Don't fall in love with a whore," Sam Frye said. "If anyone asks, those girls will know us. They know we were here, passing through. Accounting for our time."

"When do we get the goddamn call?"

"It happens when it happens," Sam Frye said. "Jesus Christ, kid. Have you loaded your guns?"

"Sure," Toby said. "And the fucking car has plenty of gas."

"We won't be using that car," he said. "It stays here. Our car is waiting across the street at the truck stop."

"What the fuck you talking about?"

Sam finished his cigarette and ground it out under his pointy-toed black cowboy boot. He lifted his eyes and gestured, letting out a long stream of smoke.

"Only car I see is a cop car," Toby said. Sam leaned against the wall in his undershirt and underpants, nothing else on but his pair of boots.

"That's the one."

"You must be crazy."

"Shut up and follow me," Sam Frye said, moving toward the motel room and walking inside. He unzipped a black canvas bag and tossed the tan uniform with all the patches on the bed, pulling out a pair of spit-polished lace-up shoes. "I wear this."

"And what do I wear?"

"Doesn't matter," Sam Frye said. "You're the prisoner."

"The fucking what?"

Sam Frye pulled out a pair of handcuffs and tossed them on the bed. He looked at his Timex. The wind kicked up outside, blowing open the motel room door, a hard rain coming back in and hammering the parking lot. He walked over and closed the door with a soft click.

"I don't understand," Toby said.

Sam pulled off his T-shirt and slipped into the cop uniform shirt, pinning a star on his chest. He strapped on the gun belt and shook his head at the kid. "You don't have to," he said. "Just stand there and watch me. And keep this gun in your boot. When I say shoot, you shoot. OK?"

# TEN

Caddy parked her truck outside the Southern Star just as the storm really picked up, the big oak branches on the town square whipping about, a mean rain hammering the sidewalks of downtown Jericho. She had her radio set to the local country station, Merle and George Jones singing "Yesterday's Wine," one of her all-time favorites. She thought about her and Jamey Dixon listening to that song as they worked on the old barn at The River, both of them dusty and worn-out, feeling like they were really getting to the heart of something good. She could still see the thick scar on Jamey's shoulder where an inmate in Unit 23 had tried to kill him for not joining up with the Aryan Brotherhood. Damn, she missed that man.

The windshield wipers knocked back and forth as she waited for the reprieve in the rain that wasn't coming for a while. She got out of the truck and made a run for it, up to the metal awning outside the bar. The front door was open, spilling cold air out onto the sidewalk, a couple of men standing outside smoking cigarettes. They checked her out, taking sideways glances at her ass as she passed. One of them asking her, "Baby, where you been all my life?"

It was cool inside, damn-near cold, the light dim and neon-soaked, a dozen or so folks toughing out the storm with bottles of Bud and Coors and shots of Beam and Jose Cuervo. The bar had opened when she'd been up in Memphis, and most of the time since she'd been home, she'd had little use for it. Caddy Colson did her best to stay out of places like that. They called to her. She could smell the whiskey and cigarettes, the jukebox blasting in the corner, playing a song about voodoo queen Marie Laveau.

She spotted Boom at the end of the bar, his big head down resting on his huge left forearm.

Caddy shook her head and took a deep breath, hands in her jeans pockets, walking toward him.

"Caddy?" a woman asked behind her. Caddy turned and saw Tashi Coleman and that other girl she'd met at the Barn. What was her name again? Vanessa? Jessica? Something like that. A couple of Yankee girls trying to soak up some local culture down in Tibbehah County.

"Can we buy you a drink?" Tashi Coleman asked.

"I don't drink."

Tashi looked confused, and much younger than when they'd first met. She had her black hair pulled into a ponytail and she'd ditched the funny-looking glasses she had on the other day. She wore jeans and a sleeveless T-shirt, showing off a spindly little tattoo on her forearm. Authentic hipster shit.

"Want to join us?"

"I'm not staying."

"Did you hear about the tornado warning?" Tashi said, smiling. "The bartender said this is the safest place in the whole county with all this brick."

"He would say that," Caddy said. "I guess it's safe until the place falls in on you. Sorry. I've got to go."

"Maybe next week, then?" Tashi asked. "We need to talk."

Caddy pushed on past the shorter woman and headed on over to Boom, shoving his shoulder, trying to get him awake. Boom's muscles thick in her hands as she rocked him back and forth, a half-dozen shot glasses in front of him. The bartender, a man named Cooney who used to run a barbecue joint when she was in high school, smiled at her. "What's your poison?"

"You served him?"

"Sure," Cooney said. "Is that against the law?"

"You know who this is?"

"Yeah," he said. "I know Boom. He's an old friend of mine."

"If he was such a good friend, you wouldn't set those shots in front of him. How many has he had?"

"Oh, hell," he said. "I don't know."

"Idiot," Caddy said.

"Hey," Cooney said. "I thought your brother wore a badge. Not you."

"Go fuck yourself."

"Fine words, preacher."

Caddy leaned in and looked at Cooney's wide, pockmarked face and gray, thinning hair and said, "For the last damn time, I'm not a preacher. Now, how about you get around here and help me walk him out."

Cooney just laughed and wandered down the bar, shaking his head, leaving Caddy with Boom, who'd just come alive. He looked up at her and smiled and said, "Damn good to see you."

"Oh, Boom."

Caddy didn't weigh a third of what Boom Kimbrough did, but if she could get him on his feet, she might be able to offer a little support and help him back to her old truck. She could call Quinn, but that would only lead to more problems. Quinn's patience with Boom had thinned a little lately, never understanding how some folks could get weak sometimes. Quinn the Ranger. Quinn the damn crusading sheriff who woke before dawn and lived on black coffee and cigars.

"Can you stand?"

Boom's eyes were bloodshot and glassy. "Not really sure," he said. "Ain't tried it in a long while."

"I parked right outside," Caddy said. "We don't have far to walk."

"One foot in front of the other."

"That's it," Caddy said. "That's just right."

Boom shoved up onto his feet but lost his balance and reached fast for the bar, holding himself there, wavering, until he sat back down on the barstool. The two men she'd passed on the way in had come up on them, standing off a few feet and hovering, smirking at each other. They were having a time watching the show.

"Excuse us," Caddy said. "Y'all please step the hell back."

"I don't like this," Toby said. "They will have surveillance cameras. They'll see my face. Even if we get into the goddamn jail, kill that motherfucker, and get out, they will know who did it."

"Do you have priors?" Sam Frye asked.

"Off the Rez?"

"Yes," Sam Frye said, already knowing the answer. Already planning out every step after talking to two trusted friends who'd spent a few days at the jail.

"No," Toby said. "Shouldn't we wear masks or something?"

"Nothing will be left when we're gone," Sam Frye said. "They keep the monitors in with the dispatcher. We lock up the jailer, the dispatcher, or anyone else who gets in our way, and destroy the equipment. Every deputy in this county is out on a call. Look at that stop sign. See the way it's blowing? It looks like a damn toy."

"You don't give a shit," Toby said. "You don't have long to live and can be reckless. Not me. I have my whole life ahead of me. The little girl I was with tonight was some kind of mystic. She said she saw great things for me. Said she could feel my aura."

"Keep your head down," Sam Frye said. "When I unlock your cuffs, you reach down and grab your gun. I'll have a gun on me, too."

"Of course you'll have a fucking gun," Toby said. "Fucking Sam Frye. Big goddamn Indian. You're dressed as a damn cop. I'm the one they'll shoot first."

"The man we want is named Wes Taggart," Sam Frye said, driving the police cruiser around the town square, the rain pelting the windshield. "OK? Wes Taggart. We kill him and no one else."

"What if someone tries to kill us?"

"I hope it won't come to that."

"But it could."

Sam Frye lifted his eyes in the rearview mirror and didn't answer. He damn well knew the answer but didn't want any more trouble than was necessary. They were bad men hired to kill another bad man. You don't kill a police officer unless you have to. But this rain, this storm, was a blessing for all of them. He spotted the sheriff's office and the jail coming up on the right side. Sam found the burner phone and dialed in to their dispatch. He breathed as the phone rang and rang into the static.

His uniform and the vehicle would show they were coming from Lafayette County. All they had was a simple drop-off of a man wanted on a warrant in Tibbehah County. Just some friendly cooperation between the two counties.

He explained it all to the woman on the phone as he turned

behind the jail, the road running down below street level and stopping at a tall concertina fence.

"I don't know nothing about no prisoner transport," a woman said. "Where you coming from again?"

"I have the paperwork with me," Sam Frye said. "Let us in the sally port and I'll hand it all over."

The wind and rain shook the car, the wipers working a slow, steady rhythm.

"Son of a bitch," Toby said. "This is a terrible idea."

Sam Frye didn't answer. The patrol car idled by the wide chain-link gate. He noticed the lights flickering off in the jail yard but then flickering on again.

The gate started to roll open and Sam Frye drove inside.

Reggie peeked into the dispatch to let Cleotha know he was headed up to County Road 380 to check on a fallen tree. Cleotha sat at the control center wearing her headset, watching the computer screen, sipping on a jumbo sweet tea from Sonic. She waved Reggie away, telling someone that she didn't know a damn thing about some prisoner coming in from Lafayette County.

"What?" Reggie said.

"You heard about some man named David Allen Joy being brought over from Oxford?" Cleotha said. "Deputy said we got warrants on his ass for exposing himself to a gospel choir."

"Never heard of him."

"Man's insisting on it," Cleotha said, pointing to her screen. "He's waiting outside in the rain right now, said he got transport papers and all that mess."

Reggie slipped into his rain slicker, ball cap down in his eyes. He knew he'd hate like hell to have made this ride down to Tibbehah in

all this weather for nothing. He looked at Cleotha, who stared at him, aggravated as hell, with that tired look Cleotha liked to give, until he said, "OK. Send 'em in. Unlock the gate. I'll meet them outside and see what's up."

"If it ain't one goddamn thing," Cleotha said. "You know what I'm saying?"

Reggie didn't listen to the rest as he got buzzed into the main jail door, meeting a trusty named T. J. Burgess who'd been at the jail for the last two years. He couldn't last a day on the outside, getting arrested within hours of leaving the jail. It wasn't so much that he was a career criminal, he'd admitted to Quinn, he just didn't trust himself on the outside. He said he liked the routine of jail, knowing what time he was getting up, what time he was eating, and helping out with chores. T.J. was a good kid but had a serious mental defect.

"What we got?" T.J. asked. He was mopping the floor in the intake room, a slick checkerboard pattern of black and white linoleum tiles.

"Lafayette County's bringing in some man named Joy," Reggie said. "You heard anything about a man exposing himself to a gospel choir?"

"That's some sick shit, Reggie."

"Deputy, T.J.," he said. "Deputy. How many times I got to tell you?"

Reggie stood by the sally port, watching the man get out of his patrol car and walk around the side of the vehicle. The Lafayette deputy was a big man in a uniform, a ball cap down over his eyes, his wide, hatchet face in shadow. The prisoner was short and muscly, half hidden in a hoodie so you couldn't tell if he was Latino or black. He had his face buried down in his chest as he walked.

"What kind of man exposes himself to a choir?" T.J. said behind Reggie Caruthers. "Was it the whole choir? Or was it just one or two or three of 'em?"

"You missed a spot," Reggie said, pointing to the slick checkerboard floor. "Go on. Do your damn job."

"Yes, sir."

Reggie unlocked the side door and waited for the deputy to bring in the prisoner. He held the door and asked how the weather was looking on the drive over. The big deputy made kind of a grunting noise and pushed the man ahead, his hands cuffed behind his back. Reggie still not able to see his face as he worked, thinking it was odd they hadn't removed the hoodie.

Reggie picked up a clipboard to fill out the information. "Heard you got his paperwork with you?"

"Sure do," the big man said, turning and pulling out a big black revolver and pointing it at Reggie's chest. "How 'bout you walk me back to dispatch and no one gets hurt. I always hate blowing a hole straight through a man."

"Are you going to puke?" Caddy said.

"You gonna tell Quinn?"

"Doesn't exactly answer my question," Caddy said, driving with her left hand, taking Main Street on down to the turn to Sugar Ditch and Boom's house. Her radio was playing low, weather reports out of Tupelo. Sounded like the worst part of it had passed. A few more tornadoes had been seen over on the county line, well away from them.

"Quinn doesn't have to know," she said. "You always call me. Don't you ever try and do something stupid and drive."

"I just wanted one goddamn beer," Boom said. "And things kind of went south after that."

"That's the way it goes," Caddy said. "Did you call your sponsor?"

"Sure," he said. "But he's down at the beach with his momma. I guess I could've tried Mr. Varner, but I knew he was probably asleep."

"How'd you know I wasn't asleep?"

"'Cause you don't sleep, Caddy," he said. "And you told me the Bentley fella was in town. Where's he at anyway?"

Caddy didn't answer, peering into the darkness ahead, lightning cracking off down in the bottomland, just a good eight to ten feet shining ahead of them, the broken yellow line heading on out of town. She hit her high beams and looked for some kind of mile marker.

"Remember how you used to always drive me and Quinn?" he said. "You'd always show up at the end of Alma Jane's keg parties, telling us it was time to go. You always knew we'd get stranded because Quinn and Anna Lee had been drinking. And when they'd been drinking, they'd get into it. I'm really glad he didn't marry that woman. I don't think she's bad. Just not right for Quinn."

"You mean how she lured him into an adulterous affair?"

"Lured him?" Boom said. "Shit. You think that's how it worked?"

"How are you for money?" Caddy said.

"Fine."

"No, you're not," Caddy said. "You haven't worked since your accident."

"Accident?" Boom said. "Shit. Now who's the one not talking straight. Ain't a damn thing accidental about what happened to my ass. What happened to me was pure goddamn stupidity. I walked right into that shit."

"That's crap."

"No it ain't," Boom said. "I replayed this thing in my mind a thousand times. I didn't have to walk toward those men, seeing what I had coming to me. Both of them cocky motherfuckers standing there with baseball bats and my ignorant ass thinking I could take them both. I look like Luke Cage to you?"

"Who's Luke Cage?"

"A big, mean black man made out of steel."

"Is he bulletproof?"

"Oh, yeah," Boom said, sliding across the seat and into the window. "Damn. Watch those curves. Ain't no rush."

"Maybe I want to get home."

"To Bentley," Boom said, kind of laughing. "Bentley Vandeven. Now there's a goddamn name for him. Might be the whitest damn name I heard in my life."

"Are you jealous?"

"Oh, hell no," Boom said. "Just suspicious."

Caddy drove a while, taking the turn off the main highway, heading down the gravel road through the endless cotton fields, dark and stretching out forever beyond the forked creek. "What bothers you most about getting hit?"

"That I can't do shit."

"What do you mean?"

"One of those motherfuckers is dead," Boom said. "And the other one is under lock and key. I wish Quinn would've given me five minutes with the man. But you know it won't happen. So what I got?"

"That stuff will eat up your soul," Caddy said, both hands on the wheel, hitting a bad pothole and rocking the old truck. "Hate. Revenge. I'm not trying to preach. But hand it over to Jesus, Brother Boom. You know?"

"I wasn't raised like that," Boom said. "What's getting to me is the not doing."

"You can't live your life that way," Caddy said. "Revenge will eat you alive."

Boom kept quiet, knowing damn well Caddy Colson knew what she was talking about. Caddy stared straight ahead, seeing Boom's little shack, set back from the road and lit up with a string of Christmas lights.

"It'll be better when I'm back on the road," Boom said. "I feel like a million bucks behind the wheel, shiftin' them gears. Nothing but the long white line, leaving all this bullshit behind. Ain't that something? Ain't that purpose?"

"The woman and the deputy are locked up," Toby said. "And I smashed the ever-living fuck out of the consoles in the dispatch room. There's no video feed. I yanked out the whole damn hard drive and set it by the back door."

"You opened up the gate?"

"Of course I opened up the damn gate," Toby said. "First thing. I did like you told me."

"Wait in the car."

"I don't want to wait," Toby said. "I want to watch you kill this man."

Sam Frye and Toby stood in front of a small holding cell by the processing desk. The man they came to kill, Wes Taggart, sat in his bunk staring dead-eyed at the two men. He hadn't tried to stand or argue, just sat on the bunk, elbows on knees, waiting for them to get the whole thing done.

"Go," Sam Frye said. "Now."

He had added some real force to the words. The kid looked at him and turned toward the door back to the sally port. Sam Frye lifted his .357 off his belt and nodded to the man on the bunk.

"Don't move."

Sam Frye turned the key in the lock and opened the door. Taggart, a skinny, hard-looking white man, swallowed and kind of pursed his lips. "How's it hanging, Tonto?"

"On your knees."

"Why don't you just shoot me right here?"

"On your knees," Sam Frye said, slow and even.

Taggart stood up and walked a few feet. Sam could tell he was trying to judge the distance between him and the gun, thinking maybe, just maybe, he could wrestle it from Frye's hands and reverse his sorry situation.

"Who sent you?" Taggart said, getting to his knees. "Buster White? Or Ray? Or was it that redheaded cunt herself?"

Sam Frye didn't know any of those names or care to know any more than he'd been told. He heard the wind and the rain against the windows and the stolen patrol car turn over and then idle in the sally port. Sam Frye lifted the gun, wanting to make it a good, clean single shot. They would ditch the patrol car way down by the county line and pick up their car where they'd hidden it off a back road. The darkness, the rain, and the confusion would offer them the damn perfect cover.

"I used to like Indians," Taggart said. "Noble savages and all that kind of bullshit. But now? I think y'all deserved to get cornholed on this fucked-up land."

Sam lifted the gun toward Taggart's forehead and pulled the trigger. The lightning cracked and the lights sputtered inside the cells as he turned and made his way to the back door out of the jail.

**Tashi Coleman**
***Thin Air*** **podcast**
**Episode 4: THE TEACHER**

HUBIE PHILLIPS: It was the worst-kept secret in Jericho. Everyone in town knew I was gay but didn't seem to give a damn as long as I didn't make much of it. Folks joked with me, wanting to know when I was going to settle down with a nice lady or wanting me to help them pick out curtains or furniture because I had great style. Some even referred to me as the town queer behind my back. But let me tell you something. If they thought I was the only queer man in town, they were sadly mistaken. Maybe the only one who hadn't tried to hide it by getting married, having children, sneaking around on the side. Funny how people see only what they want. As long as I was funny, eccentric, and nonthreatening, everyone left me alone. I was an important part of the Tibbehah High faculty, a member of the chamber of commerce, and the president of our local film festival. The year Brandon died, I'd just put in to have Claude Jarman Jr. come to town. We were going to show *The Yearling* and *Intruder in the Dust*. Nobody seemed to give me much trouble until Brandon disappeared. That's when rumors started and I found out how many friends I actually had. Not just the ones who wanted to gay up their Christmas parties.

TASHI: What did they say about you?

HUBIE: Oh, you know. "Don't you think it's strange a grown man would spend that much time with a teenage boy? Why would a young boy want to go over to that man's house and say he was watching movies?" Let me tell you something, Brandon Taylor was one of the brightest young minds I'd ever met. His interest in film, books, and art could never even be fathomed by a man like Tim Taylor. Tim Taylor was the kind of man you'd see in an old Republic Western. The first cowboy to yell, "String 'em up."

TASHI: But that didn't come until he found the money?

HUBIE: Yes. But he'd found the money some months before. He was incensed by it. He called me up and called me all sorts of names. He blamed me for paying his son to perform unnatural acts. And I had to be smart with him, saying what he was insinuating wasn't unnatural if you knew the right way to do it. He threatened to beat me up. But of course he didn't. They dropped the money issue for then. But, of course, it came back up.

[A BELL RINGS. A MUFFLED BIT OF GREETINGS AND TALK, BRIGHT LAUGHTER FROM FAR OFF.]

TASHI: How much money did he find?

HUBIE: I can't say for sure. I never could get a straight answer from Brandon. But I had a feeling it was in the thousands, hundred-dollar bills rolled and wrapped with rubber bands, crammed in a shoe box and hidden in the top of his closet. I don't know how he got that kind of money.

NARRATOR: The money. No one in Brandon's family mentioned this to us, but Hubie Phillips said the money Tim Taylor found in his son's closet was a major point of contention in the Taylor family just before

Brandon died. How could a teenage boy from a modest family have thousands of dollars—in cash—hidden in his room?

> HUBIE: When I asked him, he said he'd been saving for a while. I figured he was lying. But I didn't push him. That was our relationship. We were friends. I wasn't a parental or authority figure.
>
> TASHI: What were you, then?
>
> HUBIE [SIGHING]: I think my home and my classroom was a haven. Brandon need a break from his parents and their pedestrian, straight-ahead life. He was a wonderful young photographer and I introduced him to all kinds of movies. I remember watching *The 400 Blows* with him. You know the Truffaut film?
>
> TASHI: Of course.
>
> HUBIE: Well, it was all new to Brandon. Truffaut. France. New Wave cinema. A revelation there was a world outside Tibbehah County, Mississippi. And he never had to be like his father. He never had to admit to himself that one day his youthful shell would crack away and he'd turn into a fat, bitter old fool like Tim Taylor. I wanted him gone. I had just started helping him research schools out of state. Good schools.
>
> TASHI: You miss teaching?
>
> HUBIE [LONG PAUSE]: Some. But I miss being someone. I'd spent a long time developing a reputation. After Brandon died, everything was destroyed.

NARRATOR: Hubie Phillips told us about the humiliation of being picked up at the high school and driven in a patrol car back to the sheriff's office. He spent two days in the jail without ever being charged. He told us of the humiliation of being asked personal questions by Sheriff Beckett about his love life and relationship with Brandon. On the third day, Phillips finally secured a lawyer in town and he was released.

> HUBIE: I thought I could resume my life at the high school. We all desperately wanted to find Brandon. I helped some with the search parties, brought food to the volunteers, and distributed fliers in three other counties.

NARRATOR: But two days before Brandon Taylor's body was found, Tim Taylor walked into Tibbehah High School, bypassed the main office, and marched right toward the yearbook lab.

> HUBIE: It was after lunch and we were all hanging out, looking at photos from earlier in the year. Many of them taken by Brandon. It was sort of a somber mood, but also hopeful, everyone so religious. Everyone had prayed as hard as they could that he'd be safe. And in rushed Tim Taylor in front of all my kids. He knocked a sixteen-year-old girl out of the way to get to me. He grabbed me by my shirt, ripping away my buttons, and dragged me down the hallway to the bathroom. Then he stuck a big black gun in my mouth. He demanded to know what I'd done with his son.
>
> TASHI: What did you say?
>
> HUBIE: Well, I couldn't talk. And once I could, he didn't want to listen to me. Coach Bud Mills pulled him off me. That seemed to mean something to Tim Taylor, as everyone in town worshipped the evil son of a bitch.

NARRATOR: As an aside, Tibbehah High School football coach Bud Mills actually did sexually abuse young boys, according to the acting sheriff, Lillie Virgil, who arrested him a couple of years ago for that and other crimes. Virgil, the first female sheriff in the state of Mississippi, was running for election at the time and her arrest of the beloved coach killed her chances. She withdrew, and the current sheriff, Quinn Colson, entered the race. Many in the community didn't believe what she alleged about Mills could be true. He didn't fit the stereotype. But let's get back to Hubie Phillips, who did.

At first, the threats against Hubie were small and impersonal. Heavy breathing on a late-night phone call, someone dumping FOR SALE signs in his yard. Other times, they were wild and up close. Twice someone shot into his living room. He was asked to give up his status as yearbook adviser. Members of the chamber of commerce thought it best for him to resign until things settled. And even his church shunned him. He sang in the choir and often practices and performances were scheduled without him being notified.

> HUBIE: It takes a lot of people to let a man know he doesn't really exist. Even after Sheriff Beckett ruled Brandon's death a suicide, folks blamed me. Even if he'd taken his own life, I was the one responsible. After all, who else could've exposed him to such regret and humiliation?

# ELEVEN

Ten days after Wes Taggart had been shot dead in the Tibbehah County Jail, Lillie Virgil stood in the open door to his cell and looked down at the stained floor. "Damn shame."

"It was a real mess, Lil," Quinn said. "I don't find much comfort in a man being shot while under my watch."

"Technically, he was under my watch," Lillie said. She glanced around the cell. The bloody sheets taken from the bed, a bare pillow and mattress left on the lower bunk. Quinn was told the state people were done taking pictures and he could use it again. Not many takers with the inmates he had now. Even after a lot of scrubbing, the concrete floors still held the stain.

"How long did the Marshals put you on leave?"

"Two weeks," Lillie said. "Paid. But still."

"I shouldn't have asked you to bring him here," Quinn said.

"You didn't ask a damn thing," Lillie said. "I brought him here because this was where the first charges were filed. It was up to you where they shipped his sorry ass next. I'm curious as hell about how and why this shitshow went down, but let's not pretend like either one of us is sad this turd's gotten taken off the board. You and I didn't cause this. Wes Taggart started the whole thing by throwing in with J. B. Hood and going after Boom."

Quinn nodded, wanting to tell her about Reggie and how he blamed himself. He'd come in to apologize to Quinn damn-near every day about screwing up, letting those two men inside the jail without getting confirmation. Quinn had told him that he would've done the same, no one expecting a couple of killers to roll up in a patrol car stolen from Lafayette County. They looked and acted the part. Everyone knows they got hit by some pros. Quinn had told him so.

"You think someone here snitched on him?"

"About what he said about Vardaman?" Quinn asked.

Lillie nodded.

"Nope," Quinn said. "I think they had this planned out the minute you snatched him up in Biloxi. He didn't start talking until his lawyer ditched him. Wes believed the Syndicate boys had already left him behind."

"Did he give you anything?" Lillie asked.

"Not really," Quinn said. "He only confirmed what we already know. I'd arranged for a meet between him and the Feds in Memphis. Jon Holliday had set it all up and Taggart had agreed to make some kind of bargain against jail time."

"But nothing you could work with until he got an official offer?"

Quinn nodded. "The boy may have been stupid, but he wasn't dumb. He wanted to see what kind of deal he could work with the Feds and I can't say I really blame him." Quinn lifted his chin toward Lillie. "Any chance you might stick around for a few days?"

"I shouldn't even be down here," she said. "But we can't have a prisoner killed under my watch. Or your watch. That's just plain disrespectful. What'd Boom say when he heard about Wes Taggart?"

Quinn shook his head. "I think it rattled him a bit," he said. "Boom was counting on evening things up with ole Wes somewhere down the road. When I told him, he wouldn't look me in the eye, just wandered off to the edge of the field and stared out at the cotton. Something's about to break in Boom. And this shooting didn't help a bit."

"Any idea about the shooter?" Lillie asked, both of them moving away from the cell and getting buzzed back through the gates to the sheriff's office. Walking and talking with Lillie in the hollowness of the concrete jail felt like old times. It was good to have her back, even it if was just now and again.

"Those boys beat the hell out of our camera system," Quinn said. "We didn't get much besides Reggie's description."

"A big Indian," Lillie said.

"And a rough-looking kid," Quinn said. "The one who was supposed to be a prisoner. Reggie didn't get much of a look at him. The kid had half his head covered in a hoodie and forced Reggie and Cleotha into a cell with a gun. Told them not to turn around or he'd shoot 'em in the back."

"When you sent me the sketch," Lillie said, smiling, walking back into the hall toward the offices, "I thought it was Jay Silverheels."

"Holliday's pretty sure they were sent up from the Rez."

"No shit," Lillie said. "You need a federal agent to draw you a map down to the casinos? Those folks joined up with our boys in Biloxi a long time ago. Ole Wes didn't stand a goddamn chance. He must've had some real nasty shit on those people and Vardaman."

"We'll never know."

"I wonder how many pole dancers will show up at the service?"

Lillie said. "Maybe they'll wear black G-strings while they mourn. Boy, that'd be a hell of a tribute. A little AC/DC and Aerosmith."

Quinn nodded, walking into his office, turning on the lights and slipping his .45 back onto his belt. He handed Lillie her Sig Sauer. "We both know the one person who could answer that question."

"Fannie Hathcock?" Lillie said. "Shit. That woman thinks you're cute. But these are her damn people. She may be the worst of 'em. She's not gonna ID these boys."

"Might as well try."

"How long has that woman been trying to get her claws into your Levi's?"

"Come on, Lillie."

"You know it's true." Lillie started to laugh. "Tell me I'm lying."

Skinner felt extremely blessed. As he drove the back roads of Tibbehah County, two fingers on the wheel of his red Dodge Ram 2500 that smelled of fresh leather right off the dealer's lot, he marveled at the beauty of his home in north Mississippi. A light fog lifted off of the pasturelands and rolling hills, looking almost like smoke drifting into the tall stretch of pines. Old barns sat crooked on land he'd known since he was a boy. Twisted creeks brought back happy memories of swimming holes and cane poles, drinking Coca-Cola from little green bottles and smoking rabbit tobacco. This was a land of values, faith, and history. He had his radio turned to a family station out of Tupelo, a morning show discussing how Chicago had become a lawless hell and how an Army chaplain was being court-martialed for speaking out against gays. Skinner shook his head as he drove, mad enough to spit, wondering how the America he'd known as a boy had all come to this. He'd no more set foot in Chicago than take a rocket to the moon. Those people were living like gosh-darn savages.

Tibbehah County was his home and he'd be damned if anyone would try and invade it.

Skinner's people had settled this land in the 1850s, driving out the red man, taking a few arrows for the effort, and had stood tall during the Civil War. Skinner was a proud member of the Sons of the Confederacy, having ancestors on both sides of his family who'd fought with honor. If some no-'count so-and-so wanted to come to Tibbehah County and remove the old boy in the kepi cap from the Jericho Square, he'd chain his old bones to the statue.

As he turned off onto County Road 433, rolling toward Vardaman's lodge, he had no doubt white Christians were under attack. That's how the whole idea for the Tibbehah Cross came about. The cross would become a beacon for every man, woman, and child moving through his little ole country county. They'd see the bigness, the majesty of Christ's power, light shining up into the heavens. And in the process, it would dim the glow on that den of iniquity outside the Rebel Truck Stop.

The radio show went to a commercial break, a man talking straight to other men about problems he had with low testosterone, finding vitality from a breakthrough pill boosting energy and stamina. Skinner rolled down the busted road filled with potholes, narrow, with no shoulders and a steep drop on either side, on up toward the Vardaman lodge. He had plenty to discuss with the senator about helping him get rid of the last vestiges of that old rascal Johnny T. Stagg. This was a long time coming, and the state legislator—soon to be governor—sure had to understand that. When Stagg had been running the show, taking over from Skinner when he'd suffered his first heart attack, there'd been compromises made. Stagg was a businessman who catered to truckers' needs, with an old-fashioned inkling those needs included not only a decent chicken-fried steak and a full tank of diesel but a primal release for some godless men.

He'd figured once Stagg and ole Larry Cobb got caught bleeding out the county till, they could take a backhoe to the old Booby Trap and shovel the remains into the county landfill. So many good men in Tibbehah County had gone into that place for the smell of liquor and the devil's grip of a woman's clawed hand. Skinner had no doubt at all Satan was real and that he walked in the form of a redheaded, big-busted woman named Fannie Hathcock, arriving through the sulfur and smoke.

The road twisted and curved through the rolling hills of Tibbehah County, the tires of his big truck rolling slow over crushed rock and dirt.

Skinner had his talk with Vardaman prepped and ready. The bed of his truck was filled with yard signs for the senator, VARDAMAN FOR OUR MISSISSIPPI VALUES, him never missing an opportunity to shake a hand and tell folks about the fella who was going to stand tall for their state.

"I've served you well, sir," Skinner would say. "And now I've come asking for a favor."

A man like J. K. Vardaman wouldn't take a request like that lightly. He'd take Skinner into his great room at the lodge under all the wild beasts Vardaman had shot and killed over the years: boars, African kudu, rhinos, and wildcats. The man once telling Skinner he'd been born with steel in his hands. God had given man dominion over the animals and nature. Skinner knew it, too, logging nearly a third of Tibbehah County, making money on the ancient tall oaks and knotty old cypress in the swamps.

Skinner had faith. But he also knew a man had to make compromises. And Senator Vardaman had brokered the peace between those gambling people down on the Coast, one of them who held the leash on that hellcat Fannie Hathcock.

"I want her gone, Senator," he'd say. "That woman's time has come. Not in my county. No way. No how. Not anymore."

And Vardaman, being a man of the world, might ask for a favor in return.

Skinner drove into the bright sunlight, his truck turning off the main road onto a long stretch of gravel up into the hills. He knew just the right offering. The great house made of stone and thick logs came into view, like some kind of medieval fortress. Skinner still thinking how the conversation would go that morning.

Skinner would nod, holding his tongue and being slow to speak, clutching his pearl white Stetson in his hands, and then say, "That ole boy Quinn Colson sure has been a thorn in your side, Senator. I might just know a way we can push him right out of the way."

"I brought you lunch," Maggie said.

"I had lunch," Quinn said. "But I appreciate it."

"Fried chicken from Miss Annie's?" Maggie asked. "Field peas and cabbage cooked with neck bones."

Sitting behind his desk, Quinn looked down at his watch. "OK. Maybe an early supper, then?"

"Works for me," Maggie said. "Might be the only chance to see me. The hospital has me working late the next two nights. I'm sorry for just barging in, Quinn. But I had to see you. We need to talk in a bad way."

He stood up and walked around the desk and reached around her waist. As he pulled her in and kissed her neck, Maggie felt a little tight, even rigid, against his side. She let him kiss her neck and smiled back but pushed against his chest with the flat of her hand, bracelets jingling on her wrist.

"You all right?"

Maggie had on her street clothes that morning, faded blue jeans and a gray V-neck tee, her reddish hair up in a bun, pale freckled face looking even more pale and serious. Her green eyes wandered around the office and to the old door with its frosted-glass pane adorned with a large black star. Quinn walked over and closed the door.

"Guess you didn't come to fool around."

She reached into her purse and dug out an envelope. She closed her eyes for a moment and passed it over Quinn's desk. He picked it up and pulled out a letter. "There've been others," Maggie said, looking a little rattled, playing with the bracelets on her wrist. Her mouth twisted into a little knot. "But not like this. I couldn't keep this from you."

> BRANDON DIDN'T DIE ALONE. LOOK AT THE FAR WEST CORNER OF WHAT USED TO BE THE PENNINGTON PROPERTY. THERE'S AN OPEN FIELD OF BRAMBLES AND PINE TREES. FIFTY FEET FROM THE SARTER CREEK YOU'LL FIND A FLAT STONE AS LARGE AS A TABLETOP. THEY BURIED HER TEN FEET DOWN.

"What the hell's this?"

"The letters started right before you and I met," Maggie said. "I didn't want to tell you because I figured you'd think I was crazy as hell. Getting letters from a dead kid. Most of them were kind and sweet, talking about how much he loved me."

"From Brandon Taylor?"

Maggie nodded and swallowed. "At first," she said. "They were definitely in his handwriting. I believed they were something lost in the mail. Like those stories about a family getting a lost letter from some GI who died in World War Two. I really treasured them. They were intimate and private. Like a special secret when we were kids."

"How many were there?"

"Two that I know Brandon wrote," she said. "These others, six of them, were different. Most of them were about finding his killer. Whoever wrote them kept on telling me to push you on this thing. And with everything between us, Rick and all his mess, I just couldn't risk it. We were planning a wedding and moving in together at the farm."

"Will you show them to me?"

Maggie nodded. "Of course," she said. "Quinn, I'm so damn sorry. I didn't mean to keep this from you."

Quinn read the letter again and set it aside on his desk. "Crazy folks sure love to stir up trouble," he said. "Cleotha hears from Jesus Christ Himself at least twice a day. Two months ago, Kenny got a call for a UFO sighting over Choctaw Lake. Turned out to be some kid flying a drone."

"The first letters were real," she said. "I know that much."

Quinn nodded, really feeling for Maggie, not wanting to make her feel crazy or that she couldn't share things with him. Looking at her right now, he was damn sure she believed whoever was playing with her mind. He reached out and grabbed her hand, holding it tight.

"This is some real sick stuff," Quinn said. "Messing with you. How many people do you think knew about you and Brandon?"

"Every story about his disappearance and death mentions me," she said, looking down at their hands in her lap and then looking back at Quinn. "Every website. Every Facebook page. I was one of the first people they reached out to when he was gone. You know his momma and daddy thought maybe he'd run away to be with me down in Mobile?"

"You told me," Quinn said. "Next time you get one of these letters, bring it to me. Promise me. Where'd they send this last one?"

"To the farm."

Quinn let go of her hand and shook his head. He walked over to the window and looked out on the jail yard at a few inmates playing basketball. In the parking lot, two trusties were washing and waxing his truck. Quinn looked back down at his watch again.

"Son of a bitch," Quinn said. "Damn, this is dirty."

"But what if it's true?" Maggie said.

"Someone's using you to get to me," Quinn said. "Don't you fall for it. None of it. You start getting letters from Brandon twenty years after his death? Now they want me to go dig up some field?"

Maggie walked over to him and took his hand. She lifted it and pressed it to her face. "Maybe it's nothing," she said. "But don't you want to find out?"

"You want me to go call up a judge for a warrant and find a backhoe to dig?" he said. "Right this very minute?"

"What could it hurt?"

"I don't like it," Quinn said. "We don't know a thing about who or where this is coming from. Damn crazy."

"So damn crazy it might be true," Maggie said. "I know you loved and respected your uncle. But Brandon deserved a lot better than this county gave him. Do you really believe your uncle did a solid and thorough investigation?"

Quinn didn't say anything. One of the inmates playing basketball jabbed a hard elbow into another man, turning and jumping to make a shot. The shot hit with a hard thud on the rim and bounced back onto the court, the inmates scrambling for the ball.

"OK."

"You promise?" Maggie asked.

"Looking for a body buried ten feet deep?" Quinn said. "I can't think of a better way to spend the afternoon."

"Maybe it's not crazy at all," Maggie said. "Maybe this person actually knows something."

"Guess we'll soon find out," Quinn said.

"I hear you loud and clear," Ray said, holding the cell to his ear. "But it might be a good idea to limit our conversations. Those Feds have had a big hard-on for me and the boys for a good long while and I find it's in my best interests they don't get satisfied and cornhole me till kingdom come."

"I promise this won't take long," Vardaman said. "Just hear me out."

Ray didn't answer, standing at the edge of the casino parking lot, looking out into the endless cotton fields. It still was several weeks until harvest, when those plants would explode into thick white bolls as big as your fist, giant tractors cutting them down at all hours, bright lights shining into the darkness. Farmers with mud on their boots coming into the casino to blow their damn load.

"There's been some concern from the good people in Jericho about the action out at Fannie Hathcock's place."

"OK," Ray said, setting his left hand in his pocket. Sweating like a damn pig in a black suit as the sun was going down across the river. Nearly a hundred fucking degrees today. "People have complained about that place since Johnny Stagg started selling titties and chicken-fried steak in the eighties."

"But this is different."

"How so?"

"The Hathcock woman ain't Johnny T. Stagg."

"Besides lacking a crooked peter," Ray said, "just what does that mean?"

There was a long pause and what sounded like Vardaman crunching candy or a breath mint with his teeth. After a moment, Vardaman said, "Folks have asked that I do everything in my power to shut the place down. We can make sure that woman answers to the law, forcing her. But I figured it was honorable for me to call you first. Let her leave town without a whole lot of mess."

Ray jangled the casino keys in his pocket. The sun heading down across the flat land looked like something out of an old biblical movie. Wide and dramatic, with insects sputtering and clicking deep into the cotton. Maybe Yul Brynner would appear at the far edge of his vision, a shadow before a big orange ball, head coated in a goddamn Egyptian headdress.

"Well, goddamn, Senator," Ray said. "I didn't know I was Fannie's daddy. She's a grown-ass woman. Talk to her."

"I don't speak to the hired help," Vardaman said. "And I sure don't really blame these people. They're simple, churchgoing folk. Jericho isn't Tunica. These people aren't Delta folks. This is the twenty-first century in the hill country. You can't operate some whorehouse on the edge of town like it's Dodge City."

"Have you considered Fannie Hathcock operates a hell of a lot more than just some highway titty bar?"

"That's y'all's business," Vardaman said. "Not mine. I don't really give a goddamn what that woman does for you and Buster White. I want her gone from north Mississippi. I plan on speaking about it at my rally in Jericho. A new day in Tibbehah County. Family, character, morals."

"This isn't about morals," Ray said, fishing out the cigarettes from his jacket pocket. "Is it? This is about that old cretin in the cowboy hat. *Skinner.* Just why do you give two shits about some Bible-thumping hick who wants women back in poodle skirts and saddle oxford shoes? Come on, now, Jimmy. How long have we known each other? I know just what you like. And how you operate."

"That was a long time back," Vardaman said. "No more leases. Or underhanded deals. I want that woman gone from my district. She causes too much trouble. She's dangerous as a copperhead snake."

"You never seemed to have trouble with those women before," Ray said. "I recall them being a great help to your dealmaking over the years."

"It's reckless as hell," Vardaman said. "You hear me? The goddamn party is over."

Ray lit the cigarette and blew out the smoke, the wind carrying it to the edge of the field, toward the sun. The big marquee for the casino flashing TONIGHT / COUNTRY PRIDE / CHARLEY PRIDE and FUNNY MAN JEFF DUNHAM COMING SOON / MENTALLY UNBALANCED TOUR. Ray had two hours to get the floor ready and make sure the doors opened on time, the bar stocked with booze, for when Charley Pride took the stage. "Kiss an Angel Good Mornin'." Fannie sure loved that song.

"Can I ask you something?" Ray said.

Vardaman didn't answer. A long, white-hot silence between them.

"Are you starting to believe the bullshit you're dishing out?"

The candy clicked in Vardaman's teeth and the line went dead. Ray sucked on the cigarette until it burned down to the filter tip and he tossed it out into the weeds.

# TWELVE

"I didn't think that old guy wanted to talk to us," Tashi Coleman said.

"He didn't," Jessica said, driving their Toyota rental way out in the great wilds of Tibbehah County, looking down at the GPS on her phone, searching for their next turn. As Jessica drove, Tashi flipped through the notes she'd collected the day before. "I called him personally five times before we left Brooklyn. One time he started yelling at me, calling me a goddamn Communist Mexican."

"Sweet man," Tashi said. "I guess it wouldn't have made a difference if he knew your parents were from Colombia."

"I doubt it," she said. "Once I mentioned the name Brandon Taylor, he got pissed. On the first call, he remembered the case. By the third call, he couldn't remember me calling and said he didn't know what the hell I was talking about. Actually, he said 'fuck,' which took me aback because I didn't think an old Southern man talked like that."

"And now?"

"I don't know what to make of it," Jessica said, finding the turn, a road called Turkey Trot Landing, with a sign pointing the way to a community called CARTHAGE. Tashi held on to the door handle as the Toyota cut hard, a plume of dust behind them. "When he called the motel, he said he'd be OK with taking a visit from two real lovely little girls."

"Ick."

"I know," Jessica said. "I know."

Tashi stared out the passenger window, the sun filtering through the oak branches overhead as they passed long stretches of pastureland dotted with black cows and a few horses. She saw goats, a miniature donkey or two. A hand-painted sign read FRESH EGGS & RABBITS FOR SALE. She wondered if this meant pets or meat.

"E. J. Royce," Jessica said. "When I asked if he went by his initials, he said sure or we could just call him Sweet Daddy."

"You bring your pepper spray?"

"Oh yes."

"How are you doing with all of this?" Tashi said, now on to the list of potential witnesses in the file, marking Royce's name with a check. "Settling down South in Tibbehah County, Mississippi?"

"To be honest, I think I'd go crazy without the Southern Star," she said. "They told me the place only opened up in '09. You couldn't buy beer in Jericho. But get this. Apparently, you could buy liquor. Isn't this town crazy?"

"Enjoy it while you can," Tashi said. "If we don't get somewhere fast on this story, we're going to have to pay for everything ourselves."

"We've done it before," Jessica said, glancing back down at her GPS, nothing on the screen but a long road heading into what looked like Nowheresville USA. Tashi turned back to the road, thinking about why the hell E. J. Royce would want to talk to them now. "Nobody said we do this for the money. That's not the life we wanted."

"At least we meet some nice people," Tashi said, smiling. "Right? You seemed to be doing just fine with those boys the other night. You were into a friendly game of pool when I left. If you don't mind me asking, which one did you choose?"

"The biggest and the dumbest of the bunch," she said. "When I asked what he did for a living, he said he worked a skidder."

"What the hell's that?"

"Some kind of logging equipment," Jessica said. "He tried to tell me as I was unbuckling his pants, but I really wasn't listening. Damn, he had a big buckle."

Tashi put her hands over her ears and laughed. "Oh, God. Oh, God."

"Don't you want to know about his tattoos?" she said. "His hunting club. And what happened to his momma?"

"Nope," Tashi said. "Not at all. There's our turn. It's Carthage. Right?"

"Just like Hannibal and his goddamn elephants," Jessica said. "And yet, we haven't had time to visit Burnt Oak. Blackjack. Driver's Flat. Sugar Ditch. You got to hand it to this county, they sure have some colorful names. It reminds me of something from an old Western. *The Bandits of Burnt Oak. Shoot-out in Blackjack.*"

They turned down another long dirt road and just drove for a while, the farms thinning out, becoming big parcels of woods and then acreage scraped clean of trees, with big ugly piles of burned stumps, the land eroded. Tashi stared out the window, seeing her reflection in the glass, her face turning into a grin. Damn, she was far away from home. Born and raised in Bloomfield Hills, Michigan. College at Michigan and then on to Columbia. Grad school and then the podcast. "How was he?"

"I promised to be diligent down here," Jessica said. "You know, I'm a damn good researcher. But I never promised to be celibate."

"Umm," Tashi said. "That's not an answer."

"Oh my God, he was so dumb," she said, laughing. "Didn't last five minutes and then he tells me he loves me."

"Ick."

"Yep."

"Is that it?" Tashi said. "That can't be it. Is that the old man's house?"

"Start recording," Jessica said, slowing and turning up a dirt hill. "We're here." At the top of the hill was a ramshackle dwelling slapped together with old boards, tin, and lots of plastic sheeting. A big, rangy hound appeared at the top of the drive, baying and moaning. A half dozen more dogs, looking of the same breed and type, joined the hound. They were all white with patches of black and brown, long, droopy ears, and long legs.

"Son of a bitch," Tashi said. "I'm not getting out. I hate dogs. A chihuahua bit me when I was a kid and I still have the scar."

A little old man with jug ears came out of the house, bald and slump-shouldered, wearing nothing but a pair of khaki shorts and rubber boots. He held a big stick and started swatting at the pack of dogs. "Go on, git," he said, yelling. "Git. You sorry-ass bastards."

Tashi let down her passenger window. "Mr. Royce?"

The old man smiled and licked his dry, cracked lips. His face covered in white whiskers. Skin chapped red, with a bulbous nose. Clear blue eyes. "Didn't I tell you little girls to call me Sweet Daddy? Y'all come on inside. These dogs won't hurt you a bit. They ain't nothin' but bark."

Tashi rolled up the window and turned to Jessica, who turned off the ignition. "OK. I'm not worried about the dogs," Tashi said. "But this old coot? Holy shit."

"Second-in-command under Sheriff Hamp Beckett."

"Jesus." Tashi nodded, took a deep breath, and opened the car door. "OK. OK." The old man saw the big microphone in her hand as she moved toward him. He stared at her for a few seconds and then broke into a big grin.

"Didn't think y'all would ever find me, did you?" he said. "Ain't it pretty out here?"

"Why are we out here again, Sheriff?" Reggie Caruthers asked.

"Not a bad question, Reggie," Quinn said. "Don't blame you asking. But if I told you, you'd think I might've gone insane."

"I heard you told the folks who owned this land you were looking for a body?" Reggie said, toeing at the dirt in the wide-open field. "And you might know right where to find it?"

"It's probably nothing," Quinn said. "And it's probably best we keep this whole matter between us. I made a promise to my wife. And being a married man, you know what that's all about."

"Oh, yes, sir," Reggie said. "I been married five years longer than you. And I don't lie to my woman about nothing. You know, she can tell anytime I'm not telling the truth. Like she can smell a lie on me. It's best just to play it straight and do what she asks. If you don't, you're just gonna catch hell for it later. Might not be right away, but a woman sure won't forget."

Quinn nodded, watching big Chucky Crenshaw unload his CAT backhoe off his trailer. Chucky was a solid citizen, always quick to assist the sheriff's office at a moment's notice. Earlier that year, Chucky, who weighed in at a little more than four hundred pounds, had helped Quinn subdue a suspect high on bath salts by sitting on him until they could cuff him. Chucky unhooked the chains from the backhoe tracks and hefted himself up into the seat, his XXXL MISSISSIPPI STATE shirt hanging down below his knees, the ball cap on his head about two sizes too small.

"Damn," Reggie said. "Where you think that man finds his clothes?"

Quinn leaned against the tailgate of his truck, the creek bed on the old Pennington property spread out in a Y, a big oak standing lone and proud in the middle of what used to be a cattle pasture. Before he'd called in Chucky, he'd found the creek, the oak, and the flat rock, just like the letter had described. Whoever had been pulling Maggie's leg had at least known a little about Tibbehah County and the Pennington family, although the letter had been postmarked Southaven.

Chucky backed the backhoe off the trailer and moved slow under the tree and toward the creek. It was a gray, overcast day, the creek running free after the rains from the week before, cottonwood trees, crooked and slanted, shadowing the slow-rolling water. Quinn walked over to the flat rock and pointed to Chucky, stepping back to let the man work. There had to be plenty of snakes around here. Quinn had spotted a copperhead sunning itself on a rock amid the ripples.

"How far down you think?" Reggie asked.

"I was told ten feet."

"Who said that?"

"I don't know," Quinn said. "Man, would you watch ole Chucky work. He could peel a damn grape with a backhoe."

"A true artist," Reggie said. "He the man to call if you got work and don't want your yard all tore up. He picked up that stone and set it aside like he was using his own hand. He still working down at Cobb's after ole Larry was put in jail?"

"Mmm-hmm," Quinn said. "He told me he liked to work for Tonya a hell of a lot better than her daddy. He said Larry was always trying to cheat him on his overtime, keeping him working sunup to sundown, sometimes making him come in on Sundays, and never giving him a nickel more."

Chucky dug down deep into the earth, pulling out big plugs of brown and then reddish sandy soil, turning the backhoe and setting down the dirt in a neat pile behind him. As Quinn had asked, he dug the hole ten feet down, working until Quinn and Reggie could get down there with shovels and poke around a bit.

"Heard Lillie got her ass chewed out at the Marshals'."

"She's on administrative leave," Quinn said. "I don't think she minded it too much. Lillie said she was glad to spend some time with her daughter up in Memphis. I think they were going to go up to Arkansas to camp and hike. What she did, shuffling the paperwork, might've gotten her fired."

Reggie nodded, something on his mind but not sure he wanted to say it. He and Quinn just stood there under the gray skies, shoulder to shoulder, watching the dirt pile up in a mound as neat as an ice cream scoop. Reggie finally said, "Damn, Sheriff. That night didn't have to go down like that. When Cleotha—"

Quinn held up his hand. "I don't want to hear that talk again. Those men knew what they were doing. They stole the cruiser from an auction yard. No telling where they got those uniforms. It was all a big lie. They played us. How were you to know?"

"Don't matter," Reggie said. "I should have never let them roll into the sally port without any notification. I heard you caught a little hell from the supervisors."

"Skinner made a point of asking if it all had actually happened," Quinn said. "Said he wants to start an inquiry on whether those killers were actually there."

"What's that old man talking about?" Reggie. "Goddamn. That's the craziest shit I ever heard. Those men weren't there. Shit, I seen them. One of them held a damn gun on me."

"He's trying to say I killed Wes Taggart because of Boom and then made up the whole thing. Skinner's wanted me gone since he took over for Stagg on the board of supervisors," Quinn said, walking back toward the hole. Chucky waved to him from the seat of the backhoe, his face covered in sweat, the little hat on his head down into his small brown eyes. "Grab us some shovels. Now comes the fun part."

"Never dug for a body before," Reggie said. "How long is this gonna take?"

Quinn remembered digging into the sand in Iraq, just outside an abandoned hospital. The Rangers were on a search and rescue for some captured soldiers and found a freshly dug pit. They used their entrenching tools and then their hands to dig into it, getting only about three feet down when the smell hit them. Battle-hard kids in his platoon had to walk away every so often to vomit, then come back and keep digging till they had pulled all the bodies out of the ground.

"It's probably nothing," Quinn said, reaching for the big shovel and heading for the hole. "Right? Would've been hard to keep something like this quiet."

"Did you bring what I asked for?" E. J. Royce asked, licking his old cracked lips.

Tashi didn't like it—in fact, she knew it broke some ethical rules—but the old man had insisted they bring a bottle of Fighting Cock whiskey and two packs of Lucky Strike cigarettes; Camels, if they didn't have his brand. Jessica pulled out the whiskey from the paper sack and handed it to the man, Royce craning his head to see if she had forgotten his smokes. She grabbed the two packs of Luckies and handed them over. He sliced the cellophane with a thumbnail and shuffled out a cigarette, plucking one in his mouth and lighting it with a Bic. He settled into a ratty old La-Z-Boy, kicking back, popping out the footrest, and saying, "Damn, now. Sure is nice to have a couple fine little ladies present."

"We were surprised to hear from you," Tashi said, taking a seat on the cleanest place in the room, which happened to be an overturned milk crate. Jessica just stood, holding the microphone while they spoke, a rangy old dog rubbing his butt against her leg. "What changed your mind?"

"Oh, hell," he said. "I don't know. I guess I figured you all were getting sold a bill of goods in Jericho. Hearing a lot of fucking dog shit in town about Hamp Beckett. I don't know if you girlies know it or not, but I was his top damn deputy. Fucking Deputy Goddamn Dawg from 1973, when he come into office, until 1993, when I done retired the first time. *Shit.* Where are my fucking manners? Y'all want to open up this bottle with me, sit down, and tell a few lies?"

"We're not into lies, Mr. Royce," Jessica said, her blue hair pinned back close to her head, dressed in jeans and borrowing Tashi's Doc Martens for the day. "We would like to know any facts you can offer."

"You said you retired in '93?" Tashi said. The wind popped the Visqueen sheeting outside his bare windows, the floor littered with fast-food sacks and empty packs of cigarettes. Old coffee cans overflowed with spent butts and the shells of sunflower seeds.

The old man grinned as he watched his dog stand up and place his paws on Jessica's chest. "Damn, old Cooter's nearly tall as you. Don't you turn your back on him, though. He can get romantic real fast. He ain't a true gentleman like me."

"You said '93," Tashi said, writing down the dates and a few questions on her mind. "Brandon Taylor disappeared in '97."

"Oh, I know. I know. I remember all that shit like it was yesterday," he said. "Hold up."

The old man snatched back the lever on the La-Z-Boy and sprang to his feet, walking into a little cove that served as a kitchen, an old farm sink sitting up on concrete blocks. He found a couple of dusty jelly jars and took them back to where they'd gathered, placing them onto a table fashioned from plywood set atop more blocks. "How about a drink?"

"No thank you," Tashi said. She leaned into where he sat, waiting for the old man to get to the damn point, but having the sinking feeling he was just lonely.

"Y'all met Miss Mary at the Fillin' Station," Royce said. "The old woman told me y'all was OK. That maybe you were getting some bad information about Sheriff Beckett and I could set y'all straight on the whole matter."

"Mary," Tashi said, crossing her legs, studying the old man's hollow face and crooked yellow teeth. "That's why you decided to see us?"

"Well," Royce said, face splitting with delight. "Didn't hurt I'd heard some fellas on the Square say y'all were a couple damn New York hellcats, pretty as could be."

Tashi looked over to Jessica, Jessica looking like she just might puke. But both of them having to take it, sit there and watch this old creeper drool over them, sucking on a Lucky Strike, as he unscrewed the top of the whiskey. He poured it out in all three dusty glasses.

"You heard Hamp was a crook?" Royce said. "Didn't you?"

Tashi didn't answer, studying the blank page of her notebook, tapping her pen on it.

"Maybe heard it from his own flesh and blood?"

Again, nothing from Tashi or Jessica, both of them trained to let those long, sweet silences sit and hang there, knowing a source, especially a lonely old bastard like E. J. Royce, would just fill the silence.

"Well," he said, finally. "It's all a fucking lie. Sheriff Beckett was two-time lawman of the year in the state of Mississippi. Never a more true or honest fella ever walked in Tibbehah County. That sack of shit Johnny Stagg did his dead-level fucking best to besmirch his name. And then his smartass nephew had to come back to town with head hanging low, like Hamp done something he shoulda been ashamed of. That man—listen to me now—never took a fucking bribe. He never stopped bird-dogging the bad guys. Hell, he was cut from the same cloth as Wyatt Earp and Matt Dillon. I can see him now, standing nearly six foot five, shoulders wide as an ax handle, and keeping that ole .44 on his hip. He was ready, ladies. Always cocked and ready."

"Ready for what?" Tashi asked.

Royce reached down for the glass of whiskey and quickly drained it. He looked up with shiny eyes and smiled. "Go on, now, take a drink. I ain't doing this shit alone. Y'all brought the whiskey. You want me to talk, then we's gonna have a little party."

Tashi took a deep breath and swallowed. "What do you know about Brandon Taylor?"

Royce widened his eyes and gestured around the room, offering his bounty of booze and cigarettes. Tashi ground her teeth and reached for the glass, looking to Jessica, who just stood by with the mic and shook her head. Jessica, unlike Tashi, had some limits. She looked like she wanted to body-slam the old man and get the hell out of there. The room smelling of kerosene and cigarette butts.

The dog moved over toward Royce and settled down by the chair, Royce lighting up another cigarette and pouring himself another drink.

"I was working for a pest service then," he said. "I was doing exterminator work on all kind of critters. Damn fire ants to opossums and snakes. How's the whiskey? Smooth? Ain't it?"

Tashi hadn't tried a drop. She nodded.

"When that boy got lost, Hamp called me in like he did from time to time," he said. "I was kind of what you might call an honorary deputy at that point. I helped him with some interviews, checking on some things, walking them Big Woods for days trying to find out where the boy might've gone."

"On the phone," Tashi said, "you said you were there when they found the body."

Royce tugged on the whiskey and looked her right in the eye. "Yes, ma'am," he said. "Won't forget that long as I live. Damn animals got to him. Coyotes. They was just moving into Tibbehah County back then. We ain't never had no coyotes when I was a boy. What those creatures did to that kid? Lord. I just prayed his momma never saw him like that. But I guess y'all read all about that mess in the report."

"There was no report," Jessica said.

"What'd you say, doll?"

"I said there was no report," she said. "Everything has been lost."

Royce started to laugh, and then the laugh developed into a coughing fit. He stubbed out the cigarette and poured himself a third shot, closing one eye and studying Tashi's nearly full glass.

"Lost, huh. That sounds like Quinn Colson's doin'."

"What does?" Tashi said.

"How about you come on over here a little closer and I'll tell you all about it."

"I'm quite comfortable here."

"You'd be a lot more comfortable in my lap," he said. "You or the blue heeler over there. Don't you girls worry. I don't bite. I'm no more harmful than your ole grandpa. If you don't like whiskey, I got some butterscotch hard candy in my pant pocket. Come on, now, don't y'all be shy."

"Why'd you mention Quinn Colson?"

"How long you girls been in town?"

"A few weeks."

"And I guess y'all been fooled by that young man," he said. "'Cause he's tall and handsome and pretends to stand on the right side of the fence. A goddamn war hero, is probably what he told you. Trying to get your panties hotter than a damn skillet."

Tashi shook her head. "He never said a word about his military record."

Royce snorted. "That kid was a damn wild card from the word go. Not a bit different from his no-'count daddy, who lied to anyone who'd hear him out about how he did all Burt Reynolds's stunts and was fucking thick as thieves with Clint Eastwood. One time he showed me this hat he got, said it belonged to James Arness and the man gave it to him before he died. I'm a trained lawman. I never believed that shit for a second."

"What's any of this have to do with Brandon Taylor?"

The old man drew on a cigarette pinched between his thumb and forefinger and smiled, letting out a big cloud of smoke. "Well now, then," he said. "We're getting down to the meat in the bone. I'd say it has to do with about all of it. Hamp Beckett was as fine a man who ever walked this earth. But he had one goddamn blind spot. And that was his sister's boy. He'd sell out me, anyone else he knew, trying to look out for Quinn. That kid should be in goddamn jail, you ask me."

"For what?"

The old man started to laugh again and the laughing only led to another coughing fit. "Dang," he said. "Mary said y'all were some hot-shit reporters from up North. Don't tell me the media is as goddamn stupid as they are corrupt. Y'all want to know what happened to the Taylor boy, you might start looking at our current sheriff. Those two liked to hunt the same ground, following the same buck. And maybe the same girl. Didn't he just marry a woman named Maggie Powers? Wadn't she sweet on that Taylor boy? Damn, girls."

Tashi hadn't written a word, watching the old man talk and smoke, holding court on his tattered easy chair. She couldn't see anything in him but hate and determination, the cigarette burning down to a nub in his fingers.

"Oh, hell," he said. "I said too much. Where's my fucking manners?"

"Go on."

"No, ma'am," he said. "I ain't saying another goddamn word.

Unless ole blue dog over there wants to suck some of the hard candy I got in my pocket."

Jessica looked at the old man and extended her middle finger as she walked from the room. The old door hanging off its hinges when it flew open. Two dogs wandered into the house.

"We're done," Tashi said.

"Sure do appreciate the whiskey," he said, licking his lips again. "Y'all come on back anytime. You hear?"

Quinn and Reggie dug around the hole for about twenty minutes until they first spotted the edge of the blue tarp. Reggie flicked at the edge of the tattered material with the blade and said, "Oh, hell."

Quinn kept digging more around the hole until he found a portion of the tarp that was frayed and worn. He got to his haunches and started working with his hand, reaching into what felt like a pocket of nothing until he found the first thick bone.

"What is it?" Reggie said, looking like he wanted to get the hell out of that hole. A short ladder leaned against the freshly dug earth. "You found something, Sheriff? Didn't you? Oh, goddamn."

"Reggie, call up Ophelia Bundren at the funeral home," he said. "Tell her to get down here right this second. Pick her up, if you have to. Let's go ahead and tape this hole off. Tell Chucky we're good."

"We got a body?"

"We got something," Quinn said, standing up and wiping his hands across the thighs of his jeans. "I don't want us messing around here anymore until we get some pictures and work on the removal."

Reggie moved over to the ladder, putting one hand on a rung and turning back. "You and Ophelia Bundren straight now?" he asked. "I heard the woman threw a steak knife at you a couple years ago when y'all were dating."

"We're straight," Quinn said. "She sent me and Maggie a set of steak knives for our wedding."

"That doesn't sound like you're straight."

"Tell her we might have a crime scene here," he said. "Like it or not, she's the county coroner and we'll need her to exhume whatever we got."

"I think I'm gonna be sick," Reggie said. "What'd you touch?"

"Bones."

Reggie put a hand to his mouth, his eyes watering.

"Be sick up top," Quinn said. "We got some work to do down here and not a lot of daylight left."

# THIRTEEN

It had been a week since they found the body on the Penningtons' land. Caddy sat up in the football bleachers with her momma and Maggie, talking about damn well anything but the Brandon Taylor case. This was the first game, a bright and clear Saturday morning, and Jean had brought donuts and coffee. Jason's team was down by a touchdown just into the second quarter and Caddy was a little annoyed they'd moved her son from quarterback to halfback, not giving him the ball but twice.

"They better check the birth certificates on those Booneville boys," Jean Colson said. "I passed one before the game and he stood nearly tall as me. Had a little mustache and a neck as thick as a bull's."

"Some kids grow up quicker than others," Caddy said. "Maybe they feed them more over in Booneville."

"Must be all the beef and sweet potatoes," her momma said. "Getting all those hormones they shoot into the cattle. This boy didn't have some milk mustache. It was damn-near as thick as Sam Elliott's."

Maggie laughed. Caddy shook her head, knowing her mom was prone to exaggeration. It was damn hot that morning, the three of them finding some shade under the canopy of a pop-up tent another family had brought. Jean shared her donuts and coffee, but Caddy was too nervous to take a bite, watching Jason, waiting for those six-foot kids to knock him in the head.

"Sorry Quinn had to work," Jean said.

"He's gonna try and get here by halftime," Maggie said. "It's been a week."

Caddy didn't say a word, knowing a great deal about those bones they'd found. It hadn't made the papers yet, but Quinn said Ophelia Bundren could tell the remains were those of a young woman. They'd worked for forty hours straight tagging evidence down by the creek, not finding much but bones, a blue tarp, and tattered bits of old clothing. One high-heeled shoe and an empty snakeskin purse. Everyone in town was talking about it.

"I'll be surprised if Brandon even gets in the game," Maggie said. She was wearing mirrored sunglasses and a Bo-Keys T-shirt with the sleeves cut off. Her pale skin almost pink from the bright sun, her reddish hair pulled back in a ponytail. She was a thin girl, a little too skinny, and Caddy wished like hell she'd try just one donut. One donut wouldn't ruin whatever health kick she'd been on, wanting to eat nothing but vegetables and no animal products at all. No damn eggs. No damn butter. How could a person live like that?

"It'll come," Caddy said, watching the boys trot off the field. The defense taking over, Jason sometimes filling in as outside linebacker. "This is Jason's third year on the team. They can watch football all they want. But until they do it, it's tough to understand."

"I just don't want his brains scrambled."

"They're just kids," Caddy said. "Not the pros."

"Even soccer players can get hurt."

"The worst Jason's been hurt is a pulled muscle," Caddy said, clapping as Jason went back onto the field, lining up against the tight end, the Booneville quarterback stepping back in shotgun formation. "It's fine."

"Has Quinn told you about the woman they found?" Maggie asked.

Caddy eyed her mother and gave her a knowing look before turning back to the field. The Booneville quarterback got the ball and ran the opposite direction of Jason, looking downfield for his receiver. Jason rushed toward the quarterback's turned back. That kid was so fast it looked as if he was flying.

"We don't talk about work," Jean said. "Quinn doesn't like to talk about work."

"But that girl—"

"Come on," Caddy said, getting to her feet, yelling, "Go, Jason."

"That's Quinn's business," Jean said.

Jason reached out his hand just as the quarterback let the ball go, grabbing the boy's jersey and pulling him down. The ball sailed twenty yards down the field and out of bounds, Jason and the quarterback falling into a heap.

"Can I ask y'all something?" Maggie said, pretending to watch the game. Her son milled about on the sidelines while Jason gathered with the defense, ten minutes left until the half. Those goddamn boys from Booneville huddling up like they were playing for Ole Miss.

"Can you hold on?" Caddy said, yelling, *"Come on, now. Come on!"*

Third down and long. That Booneville quarterback taller than Jason, those boys on the line rough-and-tumble country boys, ready to knock Jason and the rest of the Tibbehah Junior Wildcats up into the stands. The ball was hiked and the quarterback dropped straight back, Jason rushing hard and fast toward him.

"I just want to know one thing," Maggie said.

"Shh," Caddy said.

The boy pumped the ball and saw his man downfield. Just as he was about to throw, Jason jumped on his back and knocked him down fast and hard into the grass. The football flew free, two of the Wildcats chasing the spinning ball. A whole mess of boys falling on it, Caddy on her feet trying to see what the hell happened. She was yelling with excitement.

"Did Quinn ever hunt on the Hawkins land?" Maggie asked. "When we were kids?"

Caddy didn't answer, watching the referees pulling the boys from the pile, looking down into the mess of arms and legs, trying to find the ball. She stood with her hand on her mouth.

"Did he?" Maggie asked.

The referee jumped up and pointed in the opposite direction. The Junior Wildcats had recovered. Jason pumped his fist and ran toward the sideline with the other boys, his coach reaching out and hugging him. The team exploding into celebration.

"Why don't you ask Quinn?" Jean said. Always trying to be the damn peacemaker among them.

"I did," Maggie said.

"And?" Caddy asked, taking a seat, looking back at the clock, as Jason grabbed some water on the sidelines, ready to head back into the game.

"He said he didn't remember," Maggie said. "He said he hunted all over the county."

"That's about right," Jean said. "Fishing, hunting, his ass always on a four-wheeler, chasing rabbits and squirrels with Boom. He wasn't happy unless he was sleeping under the stars, living like it was a hundred years ago."

"And deer, too?" Maggie said.

"When the season was on."

"Maybe on the Hawkins land?"

Caddy took a deep breath, feeling the blood rush to her face. She tried to recall a Bible verse that would slow down where she was headed. The most accessible being, *Fools give full vent to their rage, but the wise bring calm in the end.* Proverbs.

"Let's just watch the game," Jean said. "Y'all two just sit."

As much as Caddy learned about herself, praying and teaching, helping others, she couldn't hold some things back. She swallowed, trying to keep it down, trying to keep her eyes on a child she loved so much, but then saw Maggie turning with her mirrored sunglasses and waiting for an answer.

Caddy gritted her teeth. Damn this woman for asking such a question. "Quinn isn't Rick Wilcox."

Maggie didn't respond, Caddy not really being able to see her face behind the sunglasses, and turned back to watch the game. As soon as she'd said it, she was sorry for bringing up Maggie's sorry, two-bit ex-husband, playing basketball and writing cheesy country songs from his cell at Parchman. Maggie was damn lucky to have Quinn and should know it.

"OK," Maggie said, standing. "I understand."

Maggie walked from the long row of seats and headed down the bleachers. Jean Colson sat still beside Caddy, her mother in her gold T-shirt reading MY GRANDSONS ARE NUMBER 12 AND 33. JUNIOR WILDCAT PRIDE. Her mother stole a quick glance and then shook her head a bit, a typical look of Jean Colson disapproval. "Was that really necessary?"

"Yes," Caddy said. "Damn straight."

"That woman has been through a lot."

Caddy nodded. "Haven't we all?"

Fannie Hathcock had asked for Quinn personal.

"Can't you send Dave?" Quinn said, on his cell to Cleotha at dispatch.

"Dave's real fond of Fannie. Said she reminded him of a young Maureen O'Hara. Thinks she's charming as hell. Besides, what kind of trouble can they be having on a Saturday morning? While they're closed?"

"She said this was personal shit," Cleotha said. "I told her I'd tell you what she said. But I didn't make no promises, neither."

"Did she say what kind of personal shit?"

"No, Sheriff," Cleotha said. "Figure why it was personal. You want me to call her back?"

"Nope," Quinn said. "I'll stop by."

Quinn U-turned on Main Street, just north of the Square, and headed back toward Jericho Road and Highway 45. As he stopped on the Square, he texted Maggie he'd be running late. He was supposed to be at the stadium a half hour ago but had to work a wreck out on 281. An overturned 18-wheeler heavy-weighted with concrete culverts had flipped on its side. Maggie might be mad, but she'd understand, always knowing being the county sheriff wasn't like being an insurance salesman. Just like he knew working at a hospital wasn't like selling Mary Kay.

He pulled into Vienna's Place five minutes later and parked his truck in the nearly empty lot. The morning light was harsh against the tin walls painted a bright pink. The sign outside said WE FIRED THE UGLY ONE, COME ON IN. The front door was closed and sealed off with an iron grate. The parking lot bare except for Fannie's white Lexus, a beat-up white Kia, and a red Ford Ranger parked between the strip club and the truck stop. Quinn thought he saw a man inside, but the light reflecting hard off the truck's windshield obscured his view.

Quinn was about to dial Fannie's direct line when the door opened and then the iron grate. An Asian woman with bright pink hair and dressed in a black nightie motioned to Quinn with her finger. She looked as if she'd stepped out of a Japanese anime movie. He followed the pink-haired girl into the big open building, and she trailed off toward a back door. Quinn spotted Fannie Hathcock, smoking a cigarillo, in a little grouping of easy chairs in front of a skinny young girl with black hair and her face in her hands. A halo of smoke, greenish red in the neon, hovered above the two.

Quinn nodded to Fannie.

"Hope this wasn't your day off," she said.

Quinn shook his head.

"Good," Fannie said. "Come on over here and sit down, Sheriff. This is my employee, Miss Dixie Nightingale."

"Come on, now," Quinn said, standing above them both. "You think I'm going to put that name in a report?"

"I don't care what you put in your report," Fannie said. "She didn't do a damn thing wrong. This girl's afraid to leave the premises on account of her mean motherfucker boyfriend waiting outside to snatch up her nightly earnings. Isn't that right, Dixie?"

The girl lifted her face from her hands, her fingernails painted a bright purple. She didn't look a day over eighteen, probably right out of high school. Stripping being one of the few jobs where lack of experience was a plus.

"Thought you usually adjusted men's attitudes with your claw hammer," Quinn said.

"Not worth shit against a .44," Fannie said. "Dixie said her boyfriend threatened to shoot her, me, and anyone else damn well in the way of him getting his cut."

Quinn nodded down at the girl. She was tall and thin, with spindly white legs poking out of her frayed jeans shorts. A red shirt was tied up above her stomach, showing off the black ink of a tattooed revolver, the barrel aimed down into her panties.

"You from here?"

The girl shook her head. "Grenada."

"Who's your boyfriend?"

"Bradley Wayne Guthrie."

"And what's your name?"

"They call me Miss Dixie Nightingale."

"What's your momma call you?"

"My name's Dana Ray."

"OK, Dana Ray," Quinn said. "Does your boyfriend drive the little red Ford Ranger parked outside?"

"Yes, sir."

"And he owns a .44 pistol."

"Yes, sir."

"And how long has he been sitting there?"

"All fucking morning," Fannie said, blowing a stream of smoke from her mouth. "For the last hour. I tossed his ass out after midnight. He was yelling and screaming and calling me an evil cunt. I mean, really, Quinn. Do you think I like hearing that shit?"

"Should have called us then."

"He left," Fannie said. "Little son of a bitch peeling out onto the highway, flipping me the bird from his open window. But when Dixie tried to leave this morning, there he was, standing outside his little red truck, screaming he deserved some kind of goddamn apology."

Quinn looked at the girl, the hair too black to be real against her china white skin. Her false eyelashes highlighted bloodshot eyes. "You want to file charges?"

"I don't want him to stomp my ass."

"You have somewhere to go?"

Dana Ray nodded.

"And a way to get there?"

"I'm parked right out by Miss Fannie," she said. "I just don't want no trouble and I want Bradley Wayne to leave me the hell alone. He may have paid for my tits, but I paid his sorry ass back a long time ago. I don't owe that man nothing."

"OK, then," Quinn said. "I'll walk you out."

"What'd I tell you," Fannie said.

"You said the sheriff was a real gentleman," Dana Ray—Miss Dixie Nightingale—said. "You said he didn't care who you were or what you did, he'd make sure to look out for what's right."

Fannie looked up at Quinn and gave him a big ole Hollywood smile. Quinn kept his hands on his hips and motioned to the door with his chin. "Ready?"

The girl said she had to get her bag and ran back toward the dressing room. Quinn turned his eyes back to Fannie, who was waving away the smoke with the back of her hand, a self-satisfied expression on her face.

"You could've gotten one of your bouncers to toss his ass."

"And get shot?"

"Midnight Man?" Quinn said. "Nobody messes with him."

"He had the day off."

"Come on, now."

"Are you saying I called you for another purpose?"

"I don't know," Quinn said. "You have something you want to tell me about Wes Taggart and Big Daddy White down on the Coast?"

Fannie stared through all the smoke and neon and winked. "Always good to see you, Quinn. A goddamn true-ass Southern gentleman."

Dana Ray appeared back in the strip club with a duffel bag over her shoulder. He walked with her toward the front door, held open wide by the Asian woman with the pink hair. "Come again," the woman said, her voice straight out of the piney woods.

The sun was white hot when they hit the blacktop. Across the lot, the driver's side of the little red truck jacked open and the sawed-off little creep walked toward them. He wore a sleeveless work shirt over a white undershirt. Quinn spotted the butt of a handgun.

"Oh, God. Oh, God. Oh, God!"

"Get in my truck," Quinn said, reaching for his .45. "This won't take long."

"Who the fuck are you?" Bradley Wayne said.

"Damn, Bradley Wayne," Quinn said. "Sorry about your lack of schooling. This silver star on my chest give you any indication?"

Skinner stared down into the sanctuary as E. J. Royce ambled up the skinny staircase behind the choir loft to the baptism room of Jericho First Baptist. Royce didn't say a word as he walked over to the big porcelain tub to fire up a cigarette. The man having no class, no sense of propriety, acting the way he did, thumbing his nose at convention and at Christ Almighty Himself. "Hell of a place for a meeting," E. J. Royce said. "Smells like an old woman's coot."

"You shouldn't smoke in here."

"Why?" Royce said, grinning. "You gonna tell the pastor?"

"Put it out."

"Whatever you say, Mr. Skinner," Royce said. "I aims to please."

"Let's get this done and over with."

"Didn't figure you brought me here to save my soul," Royce said, spewing smoke from his nostrils and then tossing the cigarette into the empty baptism bathtub. "I figured you had me come here because the good Reverend Traylor lets you do as you please. You really have your own key?"

"I'm a church deacon."

"Goddamn," Royce said. "Ain't that something? So this is where a man gets born again."

Skinner gripped his Stetson tighter in his hands, nearly crushing the crown. His eyes began to water from the cloud of smoke, mixing with all those good church smells of old hymnals and burnt candles and such. During the Christmas season, they'd fill the tank with a tower of poinsettias, the prettiest dang thing he'd seen in his life.

"Maybe you should try it, Royce."

"Oh, hell," Royce said. "I been saved so many fucking times, I can't even recall. This tank's a mite better than Sarter Creek, where they damn near drowned me when I was a kid. All that 'Shall We Gather at the River?' bullshit. The last time I got saved was by my whore wife who done run off with the mailman."

"Don't know about all that," Skinner said. "Where I come from, a man's only saved once."

Skinner heard a creak out in the sanctuary, stopped for a moment, and lifted his finger to his lips. He walked from shadow into the light, over where the choir usually stood and the pulpit. He didn't see anything and turned back to Royce, as much as it pained him to be in the profane man's presence. But every man had a place in God's toolkit. God love him, Royce had his place just as much as Skinner.

"What'd those New York women say?"

"What'd you mean what'd they say?" Royce said. "I was the one doing the talking."

"And you told them?"

"Damn, Skinner," Royce said. "We done worked all this shit already. They run out on me the first time. But I said my piece the second go-round. And they sure as shit listened. You trying to screw me over what I'm owed?"

"No, sir," Skinner said, swallowing, stepping back from the sunlight filling the sanctuary from the skylights and filtering through the stained-glass windows. "I don't doubt you do as you're told. You've always been a faithful servant to this county."

"Servant?" Royce said. "Christ Almighty. Where's the fucking money?"

Skinner reached into the square pocket of his short-sleeved dress shirt and pulled out a wad of hundred-dollar bills. He counted out the cash, lifting his eyes to Royce halfway through, the rangy old man licking his lips. "Wait until five minutes after I leave," Skinner said. "And then you can go, too."

"Wouldn't want no one to see us together," Royce said. "It'd really make those other Baptists shit their drawers."

Skinner took a long breath and turned toward the skinny little staircase, his tall frame having to bend down to get through the low opening. As he left, he heard the pop of a match and looked back to see the bright flame against Royce's whiskered old face.

Royce winked at him and began to laugh.

"How dumb would you have to be not to know you're the sheriff?" Maggie asked. "It says it right there on your sleeve."

"I ran Bradley Wayne Guthrie's record after I arrested him," Quinn said. "Not too bright. The .44 he carried in his saggy-ass pants was stolen from a chicken hauler over in Yalobusha County. He had warrants on him in Lafayette and Union counties for check fraud and stealing propane. Looks like his only means of income was what Dana Ray brought home in her panties every night from Vienna's."

"I hate that place," Maggie said. "I wish y'all would just tear it down."

They sat across from each other in a booth at the El Dorado Mexican restaurant, Brandon beside Maggie still dressed in his football pants and cleats. Under his pads, he'd worn a T-shirt adorned with a T. rex trying to pick up a hamburger with its short arms. THE STRUGGLE IS REAL.

"That place, in some form or another, has been around for more than twenty years," Quinn said. "I don't think they'll ever get rid of it. No matter what the supervisors say, it just brings in too much money to the county."

"Can't you shut it down?" Maggie asked.

"All I can do is enforce the laws," Quinn said. "Dancers have to answer to a certain dress code or else Fannie loses her liquor license. Sometimes we check to make sure the dancers have on their G-strings."

"What's a G-string?" Brandon asked, his blond hair wild and his face flushed from being outside in the sun all morning.

"It's underwear about as wide as dental floss," Maggie said.

"Ouch," Brandon said.

"You got that right," Maggie said.

Brandon made a face and dug into the chips, Quinn thinking back on the lie E. J. Royce had repeated about the standards at the El Dorado, a rat jumping out and scurrying back to the kitchen. Had to have been some bad blood between him and Javier, Royce claiming Javier had brought the Cartel to Tibbehah County some years ago. There had been some activity, but it didn't have a damn thing to do with Javier, a hardworking good man who kept his restaurant running on the town square back when everything else left. The Cartel had come to town at the invitation of Quinn's childhood buddy Donnie Varner. Donnie, now in prison, wouldn't make the same mistake again.

Javier brought them big plates of food, carne asada for Quinn, a veggie burrito for Maggie, and a plate of beef tacos for Brandon. Just as Quinn began to eat, he watched Tashi Coleman walk in the restaurant and head toward their table. He had a stack of notes from Cleotha to call Tashi back, but it had been a busy morning. Steam floated up off the tortillas, a roasted jalapeño at the edge of his refried beans.

"Shit," Quinn said.

Brandon looked up with a grin. He loved to hear Quinn cuss

because he so seldom did. Quinn left that to the bad guys and Lillie Virgil, Lillie being a master at the art of cussing.

"I left you five messages at the sheriff's office," Tashi Coleman said. "When I drove by, I saw your truck and decided to take a chance."

"Maggie," Quinn said. "You know Tashi Coleman?"

Maggie nodded. She'd done two interviews with Coleman since the crew had come down from New York. Maggie said she actually kind of liked the women and greatly admired what they were trying to do. Quinn didn't ask her much more about it, letting it be Maggie's personal deal, doing what she could about Brandon Taylor's death.

"I wouldn't bother you if this wasn't important."

"We still don't have an ID on the body," Quinn said. "State sometimes takes months. I'll call you when I hear something."

"Finding that body at the Pennington property brings up a lot of questions."

"And I'll answer them when or if I know more."

"How in the world did you even know it was there?"

Quinn looked over at Maggie and then pointed to the empty spot beside him. "Have you eaten?" Quinn said. "Javier has carnitas with chile verde today. It's hard to beat."

"Can we speak in private?" Tashi said. "Just for a moment?"

"Will you be recording it?"

"We always record what we do," she said. "But not here. With your family. I'm not here to make trouble, Sheriff Colson."

Quinn turned to Maggie and she shrugged. Quinn knew she wanted him to help these women. This whole Brandon Taylor thing was causing some friction in the Colson household. Tashi Coleman had asked Maggie about him and Brandon having a falling-out in high school, which surprised him. The truth was Quinn barely knew the kid.

Quinn slid out of the booth. "Ask Javier for some tinfoil and some hot sauce."

"Sorry about your lunch," Tashi said. "This won't take long."

Quinn followed her out of the El Dorado to where she'd parked a little Toyota. Her friend Jessica sat on the hood and handed Tashi the big microphone they carried around everywhere they went in Jericho.

"Go ahead."

"Did you guys win?" Tashi asked, smiling. She sat down beside Jessica on the hood of the car. Everyone was all smiles and friendly.

"Brandon's team got beat forty-three to thirteen," Quinn said.

"How old is Brandon?" Jessica said.

"I don't mean to be rude," Quinn said, "but my carne asada's getting cold."

Tashi crossed her arms over her chest, looking a little nervous behind the thick black glasses, biting her upper lip. "OK," she said. "How did you know where to dig?"

"It's an open investigation."

"Could the body be from the time Brandon went missing?"

"We don't know."

"How old's the body?" Tashi said. "And when was the victim killed?"

"Body was of a young woman," Quinn said. "We can't be sure yet how long it was down there."

"Are we talking the Civil War or modern times?"

"I can't talk about all that now," he said. "You need to understand why we keep an open investigation closed to the public. It's not on account of being secretive."

Tashi held the mic in her hand. It was an odd-looking thing, about as big as a softball and covered with fuzz. Jessica stood up by the curb, arms wrapped around her waist, her blue hair looking washed out and dark at the roots. Quinn smiled at them, waiting for them to get what they needed so he could finish his damn lunch.

"Is that it?" Quinn asked.

"You're a big hunter. Right?"

"Easier to tell you who doesn't hunt around here than who does."

"And you've been hunting since you were Brandon's age?"

"Younger," Quinn said. Jessica pulled the blue hair from her eyes and stared at Quinn as he stood close to their car. She wasn't worried. She looked hungry and eager. Quinn tried to count all the piercings in her left ear but quit at eight.

"Did you ever hunt on the land where you found the body?" Tashi asked.

"Nope."

"Never?" Jessica asked. "You got in trouble for hunting on private land before. Right? Even back when you were a little kid."

Quinn nodded, believing he knew where they were headed with this. The time back in the Big Woods when he was lost, at only ten years old. Something he never liked to discuss except with Caddy, because she was the only other person alive who knew the truth. "I didn't pay much attention to boundaries as a kid," Quinn said. "And, yes. Sometimes it got me in trouble. Everything about that time was in the papers. I don't really have too much to add."

"This isn't about you," Jessica said, speaking up quick. "This is about Brandon."

"We heard you'd been run off that land a week before Brandon went missing," Tashi said.

Quinn shrugged. "I don't recall that."

"And it was Brandon Taylor who had turned you in."

"No, ma'am."

"We have a source who said you and Brandon got into a nasty fight over a deer stand," Tashi said. "Or maybe your relationship with Maggie?"

Quinn shook his head. "I barely knew Brandon, let alone Maggie, back then. I only had one girlfriend in high school."

"Maggie told us you'd met when she'd come down for the summers."

"We met," Quinn said. "But she was a lot younger. Just what are y'all trying to say?"

"Our source says there had been reports of some wild shooting out on the Hawkins property," Tashi said. "And after Brandon Taylor was found dead, your uncle made sure the state investigators never heard about it."

Quinn just stood there and shook his head, aware of the microphone and knowing how more denials might sound on tape.

"Our source is pretty solid," Jessica said. "They put you there on the land. And they were present during a cover-up."

Quinn was glad they didn't know more about when he'd been lost years before. Some things were truly best left buried. "Miss Coleman," Quinn said. "I'm going to bet your source is a man named E. J. Royce. And if I'm correct, I'd hope you put your investigative skills to work and look at that man's record. He should've never served in law enforcement in this county. He's an embarrassment to the profession."

"He showed us his accommodations," Jessica said. "He said he was your uncle's best friend and was your uncle's very first hire at the department."

"My uncle had a big heart," Quinn said. "He often looked after people who took advantage of him. He took in stray dogs and took care of folks in the county who didn't have enough to eat. Sometimes he bought coats for poor kids . . . I better get going."

"Did you ever shoot at Brandon?" Jessica asked. "Even if it was just to scare him?"

"Nope."

"Were you jealous of his relationship with Maggie Powers?" Tashi asked.

Quinn placed his hands on his hips and shook his head. He turned to look inside the plate-glass window of the El Dorado and saw the back of Brandon's head and Maggie laughing at something the boy had said. He hadn't eaten since five that morning and that was just a tall cup of hot coffee and a cold biscuit.

"I appreciate what y'all are trying to do," Quinn said. "Come back to see me when you have better sources."

"So you deny it all?" Tashi said. "We need to be clear on this. It's why we're here."

"Yes, ma'am," he said. "Every damn word. My family appreciates what y'all are doing. I know the Taylor family does, too. But some bad folks are playing with your good intentions. This county has a way of messing with your head. Stick around a while longer and you'll see exactly what I mean."

"We plan on it, Sheriff." Jessica nodded at Quinn. "We're not going anywhere."

# FOURTEEN

It was mid-September when Quinn and Lillie arrived at the annual Good Ole Boy, a big gathering of every swindler, huckster, and elected official in north Mississippi. Quinn parked his big green truck on a far hill under a pecan tree, both of them walking down a winding gravel road to Old Man Skinner's work barn. Skinner had been hosting the big event, which kicked off the fall elections, ever since Johnny Stagg went to jail. It was early night and the air smelled of barbecue chicken and woodsmoke, summer edging toward fall. A large bonfire blazed in an open field. Gray-headed men in plaid shirts and jeans with fancy-ass pockets warmed their hands by the flames. There was a lot of laughter and backslapping, everyone wanting to be seen and heard.

"I can't believe you talked me into coming with you to Bullshit City," Lillie said. "I hated this thing when I worked for the sheriff's office and hate it even more now."

"Don't you want to hear how Mississippi is about to become the next Utopia of the South?"

"Sure," Lillie said. "But after you make the rounds and we get to eat some of that good chicken, let's get the fuck out of here. Only reason I come here is for the goddamn chicken."

"Sheriff has to be looking ahead," Quinn said. "Election next year. My uncle always said it never hurt to shake a few hands."

"Just disinfect when you get home," Lillie said. "I should've worn a hazmat suit instead of my good jeans. *Goddamn.* Would you look at Ole Man Skinner over by the fire, grinning like a fucking idiot, eating up this shit like it was vanilla ice cream. Does he really think he looks good in that old Stetson? He reminds me of the goddamn Crypt-Keeper."

"After these rumors have been swirling around Jericho about me," Quinn said, "I figured it's best for me to show my face. Confront anyone who wants to whisper behind my back."

"Those girls from New York still convinced you're the spawn of Satan?"

"They believe I have something to hide."

"Lord help us," Lillie said. "If they're letting it all ride on the word of E. J. Royce, then what the fuck has the world come to? If those women stick around long enough, they'll figure it all out. Right now, everything must seem like a conspiracy. You hunting on private property—you and Hamp. You marrying Maggie. That damn, poor Taylor kid found with a fucking hole in his head. Now those old bones buried by the creek. Sometimes bad shit happens. You can't force a fucking answer to every goddamn thing."

"That's pretty much what I told them," Quinn said. "And they haven't come around since."

"They still bugging Maggie?"

Quinn nodded, moving through the hundreds of folks who'd

gathered for the free barbecue, coleslaw, baked beans, white bread, and iced tea. It had also been moonshine and whiskey when Stagg ran things. Quinn couldn't help notice the gathering wasn't what it had been when he'd first come back to Tibbehah and been elected sheriff. Stagg was a Grade A turd, the crookedest man ever to hold an office in north Mississippi, but the son of a bitch sure knew how to throw a party. Now Skinner ran the show like a church picnic, as if it'd been all his idea.

"Just be glad you're not with Caddy," Quinn said.

"Where's Caddy?"

"She agreed to attend a fund-raiser with Bentley Vandeven down in Jackson."

"Jackson?" Lillie said. "Christ Almighty. Your sister sure must want that new building out at The River pretty damn bad to be fucking that frat boy."

"Come on, Lil," Quinn said.

"Come on?" Lillie said. "The kid's got the personality of a damn dildo."

Across the grayed heads and baying laughter, Quinn spotted men in black ball caps, wearing black Watchmen T-shirts, and strolling about the Good Ole Boy as if on security detail. Quinn saw the short, stubby guy from the Neshoba County Fair with his arms crossed by the chicken spit. He tried to give Quinn a hard stare, but it was hard to look tough once you'd been grabbed by your nose and brought to your knees. Lillie saw the men before Quinn even mentioned it.

"Who the fuck are these assholes?" she asked.

"They travel with Vardaman."

"Like fan boys?"

"Pretty much."

Lillie lifted her chin over by the fire, Skinner shaking hands and posing for cell phone pictures with Vardaman. "If they make trouble, I bet a few of 'em have jumped bail," she said. "I know that look. Goddamn chicken fuckers."

"They know their place," Quinn said. "We had a talking-to at the Neshoba County Fair."

Lillie wasn't listening, watching Vardaman standing tall by the blazing fire. "Speaking of Satan . . ."

"His people say I make him feel uncomfortable."

"Hot damn," Lillie said, grinning. "I guess we are here for a reason. Let's walk over to the fire so I can warm up my ass."

"Where'd you go?" Bentley said. "They love you in there. Twenty people must've come up to me in the last half hour wanting to know who the hell you are. You're like Cinderella in cowboy boots."

"You tell them I'm just a redneck girl you found up in Tibbehah County?"

"Nope," Bentley said. "But I did tell them about The River and all the good work you're doing. Folks are ready to write you a check on the spot."

"That's not why I came here," Caddy said. "For money."

They stood together at the edge of the horse barn. But to call it a horse barn would be doing it a disservice. Bentley's family had constructed the place, about twenty miles outside of Jackson, from polished stone and thick wooden beams like some kind of damn palace, larger than an airplane hangar inside, where they had a country band and an open bar. White café lights hung from the entrance down toward the pasture, where several horses milled about. Caddy wondered if her father had worked with any of these animals. Jason Colson had slipped back into Mississippi from California years ago without telling his own family and was more a part of Bentley's childhood than he had ever been of hers. After spending some time back in Tibbehah a couple of years ago, he'd left again. Neither she nor Quinn had heard from him since.

"Wouldn't it be nice to get the outreach building finished?" Bentley said. "You said yourself you couldn't afford to put a roof on it yet."

"That will come," Caddy said.

"Why wait?" he said, smiling, looking handsome in a navy linen suit, white dress shirt open at the throat. Caddy had bought a new outfit at Belk's in Oxford for the occasion, a simple blue shirtdress, little suede boots, and a small brown leather purse. She wanted to look nice but sure didn't want to look like country come to town. Caddy had done her best to dial back on the makeup, just a few pieces of jewelry. She wondered if Bentley had told his mother what Caddy used to do before she'd gotten clean and straight with her family and God. It wouldn't be the most pleasant of conversations. *Momma, my new girlfriend used to work the pole up in Memphis.*

"Let me ask you something," Caddy said. "What was my father like when he was here? The first time. Was he a mess?"

"Your father is one of the finest men I've ever known," Bentley said. "I would trade every man in the stables for one Jason Colson. I told you about my dad, what he was like before he fell apart. Your dad was there the whole damn time, looking out for me, getting me to ride, teaching me to shoot skeet. I remember the last intervention with my father, it was your dad who got me away from the house, all that yelling and crying. We rode horses all day. Did you know he has this trick horse named Hooper? He can damn well do anything, including drink Coors beer."

"Oh, yes," Caddy said, holding her purse against her thigh. "I know Hooper. Big Jason left him with Quinn when he blew town."

"You're kidding me," he said. "Why didn't you tell me? I'd sure love to see that horse."

Caddy shrugged. The music and laughter filtered out from the stables, the band starting into a nice rendition of Dolly and Kenny's "Islands in the Stream." She and her mother had always talked about how Kenny Rogers had gotten a rough shake of it lately. "The Gambler." "Lucille." "Coward of the County." Those were some damn fine songs. If he hadn't gone and had all that plastic surgery, he'd be up there with the all-time country music legends.

"Quinn isn't great about having visitors to his farm," Caddy said. "I think he's worried about me. And I don't have the best luck with men. They either make a damn mess of my life or get themselves killed."

Bentley smiled and leaned over and kissed Caddy on the mouth. "I don't plan on doing either one."

Caddy smiled back at him, touching his smooth, handsome face, still wondering what the hell she was doing with a boy six years younger than her. She was even more surprised at what a great time she'd been having. Bentley's mother had done some nice work with the caterer, having three open bars, a huge table piled high with steak, shrimp, lamb shanks, and sushi. There must've been five or six hundred people there, paying five hundred dollars a ticket to mingle with the high rollers from the foundation.

"Your mother is kind to me."

Bentley laughed. "Of course she is," he said. "You're Jason Colson's kid."

"I still can't believe what you said," Caddy said. "Your mom is so sweet. Elegant and smart. Why the hell would she consort with a man like Jason Colson?"

Bentley took her hand, squeezing it. "Women do love cowboys."

"My dad was never a cowboy," Caddy said. "He just played one on TV when they needed someone shot or to fall off a building."

"Come on," Bentley said, steering her back toward the stable entrance, the band switching into "Jolene," the singer really hitting those high notes. "Give me five minutes and you'll have that roof paid for. Wouldn't be a bad thing. Would it?"

"I'm not here for that," Caddy said.

"Then why are you here?" Bentley said, whispering into her ear, already knowing the answer. His arm, wrapped around her waist, pulled her in closer.

Vardaman saw Quinn before Skinner did, the old man's back turned, talking about some potential companies visiting the industrial park and who they'd selected to be grand marshal for this year's sweet potato festival. Vardaman nodded at Quinn, his eyes not leaving him as he walked close, causing Old Man Skinner to turn his stiff neck around and stare at Quinn and Lillie. Vardaman held out his hand by the fire, Quinn getting close enough to feel the heat on the cool September night. Skinner stepped back, blank-faced, not offering any bit of recognition of him or Lillie.

Against his better judgment, Quinn shook the man's hand, noting again how unusually small it was. Vardaman's eyes burned bright with energy, roving over Quinn's face, trying to get a read on why he was there, whether he was going to make trouble or just eat some barbecue chicken. His face a doughy mask of deeply tanned skin with hooded eyes, the silver hair swept up off his large forehead.

"Glad to see you, Sheriff," Vardaman said. "I can't tell you how much I appreciate Mr. Skinner's hospitality."

"Oh, just burning some old brush and cookin' chicken," Skinner said, his jowly face closely shaved, looking red and chapped in the firelight. "It's all about tradition. Can't disappoint half the gosh-darn state."

Quinn turned to Vardaman and introduced Lillie. Lillie gave a cursory nod as Vardaman asked if she was his wife. Lillie started to laugh.

"Damn," Lillie said. "You're much funnier in person, Senator."

Vardaman smiled.

Lillie said, "Taller, too."

Quinn watched three of the Watchmen gather by the bonfire, exchanging looks with Old Man Skinner. They were definitely all familiar with one another. Skinner looked uneasy, stepping back, nearly tripping over a stray piece of firewood onto his ass. Quinn had to reach out and grab the old man's forearm to keep him upright, his Stetson nearly falling off his old bald head. Skinner found his footing, his face flushed with embarrassment.

"Can I ask you something, Sheriff?" Vardaman said.

Quinn nodded.

"You mind if we talk confidentially?"

"You mean away from my wife?" Quinn said.

Lillie scowled at Quinn, squinting, but seeing the humor, too.

"You don't mind, honey?"

"Oh, fuck no," Lillie said. "I'll just go talk to the ladies about how they dish out that juicy peach pie."

Skinner had composed himself, his Stetson still crooked on his head, stepping up to their little circle. "Lillie Virgil," Skinner said, watching her backside as it disappeared out of the firelight. "Used to work around here. Now she's a dad-gum Marshal. Ain't that something? The world's gone PC on us."

"Best shot in the state," Quinn said, standing wide-legged with his hands on his hips. "Lillie was a star member of the Ole Miss Rifle Team and a great law enforcement officer here and up in Memphis. I wouldn't knock her, Skinner. You of all people should know better."

"How 'bout we take a walk, Sheriff," Vardaman said, handing Skinner his red Solo cup. "You don't mind. Do you?"

They moved away from the fire and the barn, the loose gathering of Watchmen standing their ground, watching Quinn, with their guns on their hips and their knives at the small of their backs. They all wore polos or T-shirts with the Watchmen logo and their sunglasses perched above the bills of their caps. The sawed-off man Quinn had grabbed turned his head and spit in the fire.

"Skinner's a tough ole nut," Vardaman said. "He thinks he's running everything himself but doesn't understand we're all the same. You don't serve at his pleasure. You're an elected official same as us."

"He knows," Quinn said, moving into the shadow of some tall oaks toward Jericho Road, more cars heading into the party. Headlights shining through a thicket of pines, moving toward the barn. "He just doesn't care."

"Well," Vardaman said. "We don't need to communicate through Skinner anymore. There's not a reason in the world why you and I can't be friends."

"There's a few reasons," Quinn said. "Want me to list them?"

Vardaman kept walking. He was wearing a red-checked shirt with fancy jeans and distressed brown loafers. His hair looked freshly cut, brushed back from his bronzed face. He was nearly Quinn's height, maybe an inch or two shorter, but walked tall and straight like a man wanting to be noticed. "Don't worry about all that business before," he said. "At the summer rally."

"I don't."

"I think you know what Tibbehah County means to me," he said. "It ain't just some little old postage stamp in the state. This place has become my home, where I hunt and fish, and have become part of the people and the whole fabric. I do everything I can for this county, passing legislation, bringing in industry. I want you and me to be able to communicate about your needs down here. Things are changing. Problems you've had in the past with sin and vice won't be around much longer."

"Since when do you tell the Syndicate what to do?"

Vardaman stopped and stared at Quinn. "I have no idea what you mean."

"Your people sent two men to my jail to murder a man in federal custody," Quinn said. "And then you come back to Tibbehah wanting to talk about old-time values and turning back the clock in Mississippi?"

"Don't we all want the same thing?" Vardaman said. "When you first came back to Jericho, it was overrun with meth dealers and crooks. Now folks are shopping on the town square, opening coffee shops, little boutiques. It's like it used to be."

"I think you see a South that never existed," Quinn said. "We don't want the same things."

"Funny to hear a military man talk like you, Sheriff Colson," Vardaman said, still grinning. "We do believe in the same thing. Duty to God and country, putting America above all else. You want to split hairs with me on the way things get done."

"Next time you come to Jericho, get your goddamn permits straight."

"We all have to make compromises," Vardaman said. "Haven't you figured that out yet, Sheriff?"

Quinn looked at Vardaman, half in the light from the barn and half in the shadow of the woods. The man looking eager, nostrils flared, waiting for Quinn to accept that he'd won.

Quinn just looked at the man in his fancy jeans, with their spangled pockets and brass snaps, and said, "Bullshit."

Skinner stayed out on his property long after the Good Ole Boy had ended. Vardaman had parked his tour bus along Jericho Road, the side splashed with a good picture of himself looking tough and determined to all the passing cars and trucks. STAND YOUR GROUND, MISSISSIPPI. Skinner spent most of the last hour picking up red Solo cups, disappointed to smell all the liquor brought to the event, paper plates filled with chicken bones and congealed beans, and discarded business cards and church fans with candidates' names on them. There had been some fine stump speeches but none better than Jimmy Vardaman's, nearly as good as his namesake, a distant cousin who'd been governor of Mississippi at the start of the twentieth century, back when all was right with the world.

"Can I get you some pie?" Skinner asked.

Vardaman sat in an Adirondack chair out by the fire. Holding a Solo cup in his hands, he leaned back in comfort and took a long sip, before turning down the offer of pie.

"We got plenty," Skinner said. "My wife made a lemon icebox pie that would break your heart. She saved a thick slice for you in the freezer."

"Sit down, Skinner," Vardaman said. "Enjoy this first cool evening by the fire. You can feel fall blowing in. How about a whiskey? The tour bus is filled with some wonderful ole stuff."

"No thank you," Skinner said, taking a seat on a log, his old knees raising up toward his chest, feeling the changing of the seasons down in his joints. "We sure do appreciate you coming here, Senator. And for everything you do for our little ole backwoods county. You're a true Mississippian through and through."

Vardaman studied Skinner in the firelight, his longish face and swept-back gray hair looking almost damn-near royal. Skinner couldn't have been more damn proud to have a man like this rooting for Tibbehah County.

"I tried talking some sense into your sheriff."

"And?" Skinner asked.

"Just like you said," Vardaman said. "He just wants to make trouble for us, poke right at the working man who supports him, pays his salary, and feeds his family. He's not gonna stop until he makes a damn mess of things happening a long time back."

"Don't you worry," Skinner said. "Don't you worry about nothin', sir. I got that all taken care of. Everyone's done something in their past to be ashamed of. *But if we confess our sins, He is faithful and just and will forgive us our sins and purify us of all unrighteousness.*"

"Amen to that," Vardaman said, toasting Skinner with his cup of whiskey.

"That's what's been done. Right?" Skinner asked, removing his hat, playing with the brim in his hand. "You've asked for forgiveness and now walk with our Lord a new man?"

"Absolutely, sir," Vardaman said. "No doubt. I sure do appreciate your support. Now, would you mind walking back to my bus and filling up this cup? It's a damn lovely night under the stars."

"For what?" Skinner asked, studying the man through the smoke.

"Watching the fire," he said. "Don't you just love the smell of smoke?"

**Tashi Coleman**
***Thin Air* podcast**
**Episode 5: THE SHERIFF**

NARRATOR: The one thing you'll constantly hear about the late Sheriff Hamp Beckett is that he was a good man.

> WOMAN'S VOICE [BACKGROUND NOISE OF BUSY DINER]: I never met a man who stood taller than Sheriff Beckett. He was like John Wayne and Buford Pusser in one. People were afraid to break the law when he was in office. Folks would see his patrol car rolling down the road and wave. We all knew we had someone to look out for us. The way he wore that old cowboy hat and rancher coat, he looked just like he'd stepped out of the Wild West.

NARRATOR: And the one thing you won't hear anyone say is Sheriff Beckett had often been accused of bribery, physical force against prisoners, and being the enforcer for the county kingpin, a man named Johnny Stagg, who would later go to federal prison for his crimes.

> MAN'S VOICE [BACKGROUND NOISE OF CICADAS BUZZING OUTSIDE]: That was all a bunch of gosh-dang malarkey. Sheriff Beckett knew this place would return to a hell on this earth, the lawlessness after the Indian days or right after the Civil War. He knew Tibbehah County had a wild streak a mile wide and he had to be tougher than most. Maybe we did get a little rough with the

prisoners sometimes. But let me tell you something, we never did nothing to anyone who didn't deserve it. This place would've been up there with Phenix City, Alabama, if Hamp Beckett hadn't taken care of us. All the nonsense about him throwing in with Johnny Stagg is a dang lie. Beckett hated Stagg and did everything in his power to get rid of him.

NARRATOR: But Beckett never could. Thirteen years after he ruled Brandon Taylor's death a suicide, Sheriff Hamp Beckett took his own life while still in office. He shot himself in the kitchen of his family farmhouse, a plate of pork chops and Cajun rice on the stove, the report says. Foul play suspected. None ever proven.

MARY WATKINS: He just couldn't live with what this place had become. Stagg had gotten too powerful. And after those folks had moved up to Hell Creek, the ones who followed that devil, Gowrie, he lost all control. A lot of folks started dying because of those drugs and Johnny Stagg did his dead-level best to make sure Hamp couldn't make any trouble. He was old then, just hit sixty-seven, thinking on retirement, which never would have suited him. I saw his hands start to shake many times when I waited on him. Or when we were together in the off hours. He was a sick man. And he was humiliated. That's why he killed himself.

NARRATOR: Hamp Beckett had been in the U.S. Army during the Korean War. Twice awarded the Purple Heart and once the Bronze Star. He credited the military for shaping his life, leading him to a disciplined, moral path. Later, he'd try to instill those same beliefs in his nephew, Quinn Colson. Beckett and his wife, Halley, never had children, often looking out for Quinn and his sister, Caddy, as if they were their own.

QUINN COLSON: My uncle put a .22 in my hand on my sixth birthday. We shot cans and bottles. He taught me how to fish and to hunt. Some of my best memories were walking into the woods with that man. He seemed to stand taller than the rest. He just kind of showed you how to act by the way he treated his own family and even those he had to arrest. I never wanted to be like my father, but I wanted to be like my Uncle Hamp. Whatever is whispered about him now doesn't tell the whole story. Something awful happened to him, but Hamp Beckett was once a damn good man.

# FIFTEEN

Tashi knew approaching Maggie Colson at the hospital again would be a major fuckup. She had to wait until she was off, away from Quinn, and not so guarded about talking. Making a run for Quinn at the El Dorado had been her biggest mistake since coming to Mississippi. She should have tried to validate what she'd learned, talk to Quinn when she had everything in order and not just some working theories. But with the money running out, her people in New York desperate for progress, and the need to push, she'd gone too far too fast. She and Jessica decided the best thing to do was to get Maggie back with the program, make her feel as important and part of the team as when they'd first met. Everything they wanted to know Maggie had answered. Every little detail about the summers of 1996 and 1997 came from her strong recollections. The magical summers full of endless nights, flickering fireflies, and kids making out behind the old stadium and down at Choctaw Lake. A wild, tangled teenage romance.

And now, if there was a connection to Quinn, she'd be their best bet.

It was Wednesday, weeks since they'd gone to Quinn with more questions about his time poaching on the Hawkins land and the fight they'd heard about from E. J. Royce. She decided to go at it alone, leaving Jessica at the county courthouse searching more records from the mid-1990s, Jessica already knowing the clerk's favorite brand of cigarettes and love for Little Debbie snack cakes. Maggie Colson was their best bet, but she'd grown distant, evading phone calls, refusing to talk when they ran into her in town. Maggie wouldn't even look her in the eye the last time she and Jessica had shown up at the hospital.

Tashi followed a long, winding road up to a little hamlet called Fate and then off onto County Road 380, deep into some newly planted loblolly pine (she'd learned about the local trees online to add color to the podcast), and into some cattle pastures and wide expanses of farmland. The locals called the place the old Beckett homestead even though the homesteaders and the last Beckett had died off. Quinn Colson had lived in the house for nearly a decade now, the same house where his uncle had taken his own life. Maggie and her son moved in after they married in June.

She knocked on the screen door, the main door open wide into a long, wide hallway, country music loud and coming deep from inside the home. Tashi didn't know the song, something about *Satin sheets to lie on, satin pillows to cry on . . .*

Tashi knocked again, the recorder strapped over her shoulder and microphone in hand almost becoming an extension of herself. The music grew softer and Maggie appeared down the hall with a basket of laundry in her arms. She didn't look pleased to see Tashi. Maggie put down the basket and came to the screen door, not opening it, only looking through the mesh at Tashi. "We're done," she said. "I've tried to be polite. But y'all don't seem to understand. I can't believe you'd accuse Quinn of something so horrible."

"I didn't accuse him of anything," Tashi said. "We heard some details and we went right to him. That's what we do. We investigate."

"Quinn and I didn't even know each other back then."

"Not at all?"

"We were friendly, but we weren't friends," Maggie said. "Y'all are trying to make it like Quinn had some kind of secret thing for me. He had a girlfriend named Anna Lee Amsden. They were in love and damn near got married right out of high school. Why don't you talk to her? I wasn't but just some knobby-kneed kid to him."

"Are you sure?"

"You bet," Maggie said, ready to close off the conversation and slam the solid-wood door. "Sorry you drove all this way."

"Can I come inside?" Tashi said. "Just for a minute? I know you're angry. But if you would just answer a few questions, maybe we can clear this part up and we can move on. Your husband won't work with us anymore. You know why we're here, Maggie. The only thing that's important is finding out what happened to Brandon Taylor. That's it. And in doing so, we're going to piss some people off. I'm sorry. It's just part of the process."

Maggie hung there behind the screen door, not bothering to open the latch. Her eyes an intense green, her mouth a tight little knot. "I'm busy, Tashi," she said. "I've got four days' laundry to finish in the next few hours while I study for certification in geriatrics and still pick up my Brandon at school. How about I call you later?"

"You never call us back," Tashi said. "Every time we try and talk, you say you're busy."

"What more do we need to discuss?" she said. "You want me to tell you Quinn had the hots for me when we were kids and took some shots at Brandon? That's truly the craziest damn thing I've heard in my life."

"Some people swear it happened."

"Who?" Maggie said. She asked the question with contempt, like she already knew who.

"I really can't say," Tashi said. "Not yet. We've got a lot of questions about what kind of kid Quinn was and what his Uncle Hamp did to shield him. It may not be anything. But it's something we can't ignore. To us, he looks like a person of interest."

Maggie shook her head, forearm resting against the doorframe, as Tashi shifted the recorder strap on her shoulder. "I wish y'all all the luck," Maggie said. "But we're done. I don't want to talk about this anymore."

"Why not?" Tashi said, making sure to get the question on the record if Maggie was really going to cut them off. "You told us Brandon's death has haunted you all of your adult life. Isn't that right? Why quit on him now?"

"I'm not quitting," she said. "But don't you dare try and run down my husband. Y'all have no idea of the people who are whispering into your ear. Did you take a second to pause and look at the record of that man, E. J. Royce?"

"He was second-in-command to Sheriff Beckett for more than twenty-five years," Tashi said. "He may be a reprehensible human, but we never found any marks on his professional record."

"And why would you?" Maggie said. "You two can't even find the records on one of the biggest mysteries in this whole county. Why would they keep around the records on a warped old racist like E. J. Royce? Why don't you ask Quinn about that man and what he did back in 1977 to some black soldier who wandered into Tibbehah County at the wrong time?"

"Some say Quinn was pretty wild," Tashi said, trying to stay on the question, not wander into some ancient history. "Two of his former teachers called him a juvenile delinquent. He once stole a county vehicle and nearly destroyed it in a chase along Highway 45."

"He and Boom Kimbrough took a volunteer fire truck for a joyride," Maggie said. "They weren't but sixteen. It was stupid, but they were just kids."

"That's a felony," Tashi said. "Right? And the charges were dropped a week later."

Maggie started to pull the door closed, still watching Tashi from behind the screen. "Y'all two think you're smart," she said. "You don't know a damn thing about my husband. Why don't you check his record when he was in the Army?"

"We know who he became," Tashi said. "We just want to know who he used to be."

"Quinn's always been the same person," Maggie said. "You need to spend some time checking up on E. J. Royce. It didn't take me long to learn he's the nastiest racist old fool in this county. He has enough dirty secrets and lies to fill up a million of your podcasts. Whatever he's saying about Quinn is a goddamn lie."

"I don't like Royce any better than you do," Tashi said. "Being in his presence makes me sick to my stomach. But I've learned details and leads can come from unlikely sources. Like you said, you didn't know Quinn then. And you really can't know what he was capable of doing."

"Rumor is not fact," Maggie said. "Lies will never become truth. Y'all are no damn better than Sheriff Beckett, looking for an easy answer to something really horrible."

"Did Quinn and Brandon ever argue over the Hawkins land?"

"That never happened."

"Who is the girl they found?" Tashi asked. "Has he even mentioned her to you? A woman wrapped in a blue tarp buried on the Pennington property."

"God," she said. "You people are like damn scavengers." Maggie

Colson slammed the door so hard the windows shook, leaving Tashi alone on the front porch.

She pressed stop on her recording and walked back to her car.

"Royce," Quinn said, calling out at the man's back. "Stop right there."

"Goddamn it," Royce said, turning around in the parking lot of the Piggly Wiggly. His brown-and-yellow-striped dress shirt ruffling loose and open around his undershirt. "Can't a white man buy him some damn groceries without being harassed? My dogs ain't et in two days and I ain't et in one. The church quit delivering meals to me on account of me patting the backside of Mrs. Sorrows. Didn't mean a damn thing by it. Hell, the woman must weigh two-fifty. I was just trying to thank her for being so kindly. Fat women love to get attention."

"I heard it wasn't her backside you patted."

"That woman's so big it's hard to tell the front from the back."

Royce lifted a bag of Butcher's Best dog food and tossed it into the bed of his truck. Quinn could smell the rank whiskey on his breath from six feet away. He had on an old white undershirt, stained down the front, and a pair of threadbare jeans. The MAGA hat crooked on his head as he stared at Quinn through a pair of dirty eyeglasses. Maggie had just called Quinn, told him Tashi Coleman had shown up at their farm, asking more questions about what Royce had whispered in their ear.

"You told those two reporters from New York I took shots at Brandon Taylor out at the Hawkins place. Where in the world did you come up with a lie like that?"

"What the hell are you talking about, boy?"

"You're a terrible liar," Quinn said. "Always have been."

Royce leaned against the grocery cart, a light wind rippling all the plastic bags. He rubbed the white whiskers on his chin, smelling of booze and body odor. His fetid breath like an old ashtray. "I guess we'll have to agree to disagree," Royce said. "I recall your uncle covering for your ass one too many times."

"I never denied my uncle looked out for me," Quinn said. "And kept me out of a lot of trouble. But to say I had some kind of run-in with Brandon Taylor? I barely knew the kid."

"Funny how the mind works," Royce said. "It's etched in my memory right clear."

"You son of a bitch."

"Don't you take that tone with me, Sheriff," Royce said, grinning. "Those New York women sure took a shine to this old man, took a seat at my knee like I was their papaw, wanting to know things ole Hamp kept off the books. This is just a set of alternative facts, son."

Quinn wanted very much to grab the man's skinny neck and wring the hell out of it. But Quinn knew knocking some sense into E. J. Royce in the Piggly Wiggly parking lot wouldn't look good to a lot of people. Even though the old man deserved it. You couldn't knock good sense into a stupid man.

"I don't want to take sides in this matter," Royce said, holding up the palms of his hands. "I don't want to get involved in some kind of personal pissin' match between you and your wife. I seen pictures of her when we were looking for that Taylor kid. You know, she sent him some pictures of her in a baby blue bikini down at Panama City Beach. Goddamn. Hard to erase something like that from my mind. Boys that age can do some crazy things with their hormones and peckers going crazier than a divining rod."

Royce popped a cigarette into his mouth and lit it with a match. He coughed and coughed, using the cart to steady himself, smiling through the smoke. E. J. Royce had been waiting for years for this. Ever since Quinn and Lillie learned he'd thrown in with a psychopath named Chains LeDoux and the Born Losers to lynch a man in the seventies, Royce had wanted to turn things on Quinn. Quinn just studied the old man's face like you'd watch an animal at the zoo.

"Someone paying you, Royce?" Quinn said. "That's a lot of groceries."

"I get my monthly check," he said. "Just what are you trying to say?"

"You never had an original idea in your life," Quinn said. "Trying to tie me into Brandon Taylor's death didn't come from you. It's too creative for your warped mind."

"I didn't say you did or didn't," Royce said. "I just said your Uncle Hamp never told them state people about running you off that hunting land."

"I never once saw Brandon Taylor out hunting anywhere," Quinn said. "And I sure as hell didn't take a shot at the kid."

"Like I said, funny how the mind works," Royce said. "Different set of facts. I guess we see the events in two different ways. Maybe it's best to let them women decide on what happened to the Taylor boy. I'm just trying to do my best to help them ladies out."

Quinn looked into the open window of Royce's truck and saw a brand-new black baseball cap emblazoned with a Watchmen Society patch. He looked back at Royce and shook his head. "Vardaman will eat your old ass up."

"That man's got vision, Quinn Colson," Royce said. "What the fuck do you got?"

Quinn watched Royce load the backseat of his truck with bags of canned goods, raw hamburger meat, and cartons of cigarettes before climbing behind the wheel. The old man ashed the cigarette out the open window, cranked the ignition, and peeled out of the lot.

He could arrest Royce for speeding, reckless driving. But it was best to let him go, let the line out and see under what stump or stone the man would go hide.

Quinn reached for his cell and called Reggie Caruthers. "Reggie?" Quinn said. "I need you to watch someone for me. Yep. Just let me know where he goes."

Caddy watched Boom work under the hood of her ancient GMC truck, peeking out every few moments to complain about the condition of the engine. She'd driven over to Boom's place an hour before, bringing him a plate of catfish, fries, and hush puppies from Pap's Place for lunch. The last time they talked, she knew Boom had been drying out, not eating much, on a black coffee and cigarettes diet. And she knew some catfish and a little honest work never hurt anyone.

"These are the worst-looking spark plugs I've ever seen," Boom said. "These hadn't been changed in ten years. How long you had this truck?"

"Eight years."

"You ever changed them in that time?"

"She's never let me down before."

"You call your truck a woman?"

"Why not?" Caddy said. "Jason named her Big Bertha."

"She'd be an ugly woman," Boom said. "All these scratches and dents. Busted-ass windshield. Tires balder than Ole Man Skinner's head. You got maybe five hundred more miles at the most."

"Scars add character," Caddy said. "Scars tell a story."

"Sometimes they're just a goddamn mess."

"Can you get me a deal at J.T.'s?"

"Better ask your Uncle Van," Boom said, coming back from under the hood, wiping his prosthetic hand with a dirty blue rag. "He and J.T. play in that gospel group with Diane Tull. What do they call themselves?"

"The Revelators."

"Yeah," Boom said. "Right. I like that name. Diane Tull sounds just like Jessi Colter."

His prosthetic hand had been specifically fitted by the VA for his job, holding a variety of tools while he worked. At the moment, he had a crescent wrench fitted snug into its base. He removed the wrench and plugged in a screwdriver, going back in for more. It was early afternoon, a little after one, and the sun was high and hot over the cotton fields, the stalks growing brown and brittle, October and harvest coming soon. You could hear the wind in the dry leaves, rustling like paper, the radio going inside the cab of the truck. Boom had tuned to a station out of Tupelo. Classic country all the time. He and Quinn had a severe hatred for most modern country, Boom calling Jason Aldean the Anti-Hank.

"How'd it go down in Jackson?" Boom asked.

The radio station played Waylon singing "Rainy Day Woman," one of Caddy's favorites. The old music reminding her of good times on the front porch with her Uncle Hamp and Aunt Halley.

"Fine."

"Just 'fine'?"

"Maybe better than that," Caddy said. She and Boom kept few secrets from each other. She maybe trusted him more than her own brother. Boom knew what it was like to be in the goddamn black hole that could eat you alive. And he was the kind of person who never leveled a judgment against you.

"OK, then," Boom said. "No drama?"

"No drama."

"All those rich folks treat you right?"

"I was surprised, but I liked them," Caddy said. "They can't help they have money. Most of them seem to want to do some good with it. They wanted to know all about The River and the work we do in

Tibbehah County. I told them about folks who volunteered their time and talents."

"Time and talents?" Boom said. "Sounds like I'm not getting paid."

"I brought you catfish."

"You looking at a whole tune-up," Boom said. "Front and rear brakes. Only thing I can't do is the tires. The tires is on you."

"I can handle the tires."

Caddy watched him work, sitting on the small porch of his cabin. He had a pair of old rusted porch chairs and a glider that used to belong to his grandmother. Caddy rocked back and forth in the glider drinking some Mountain Dew, looking out at the long dirt road running straight and long through the Sugar Ditch bottomland. She thought about Boom staying down here for so long, hiding from town when he got back, healing up after Iraq, taking that job at the county barn and then hitting the road, driving trucks. He got beaten down right where he was standing now. J. B. Hood and Wes Taggart coming onto his land, his world, thinking he'd been the one tipping off those Pritchard boys after they jacked one of their drug shipments.

"You mind if I ask you a question?" Caddy said.

"Never stopped you before."

It was Kitty Wells now, "How Far Is Heaven." The song saying... *let's go tonight. She just wanted her daddy to hold her tight.* Miss Kitty sure knew what country music was all about.

"Can you ever let it go?"

"About you not changing your damn spark plugs?"

"Wes Taggart."

"Taggart?" Boom asked, reaching back into the engine and returning with a rubber belt. A cigarette hung loose from his mouth. "No, ma'am. Can't do it."

"But you know he's dead?" she said. "Holding on to that hate will eat away at you."

"What about scars adding character?"

"The kind of stuff you're feeling is deeper than scars," she said. "We both talked about that."

"Belts," Boom said. "And hoses, too. Did you know your heater hose has been leaking like hell?"

"I knew something was leaking," she said. "But Big Bertha has been running and I didn't ask any questions."

"Maybe you should have," he said. "Just because shit's running don't mean it's correct."

"I know."

Caddy walked up to the truck and stood side by side with Boom. She watched as the big man loosened the strap of the prosthetic and set it with a thud on a bench he'd pulled out for the work. He used a towel to dry the wet nub of his arm. Caddy smiled at him. "How are you doing, Boom?"

"Fine and dandy," Boom said.

"Come on," Caddy said. "I know you."

"You want to check my house?" Boom said. "I tossed out all the liquor last night. Two full bottles of whiskey. Poured both out into the ditch."

"You're going cold turkey."

"Why not?" Boom said. "Gonna try and wrangle those snakes in my head without Jim Beam helping. See how it works."

"Can we pray?" she said. "Can I least do that for you?"

"I would, Caddy," Boom said, turning his back to get back to work. "But every time I close my eyes, I see those bats flying down on my head. I'd just as soon skip that part."

# SIXTEEN

Thanks for trusting me," Maggie said. "I know this is crazy as hell."

"You and I decided to get married four months after we met," Quinn said. "I'd say we're a long way past just trust."

"No more secrets," she said. "I promise."

"I know," Quinn said, sitting at the wheel of a Jeep Cherokee Lillie Virgil used to drive. They'd removed the sheriff's office paint and stickers at the county barn and now it was an extra vehicle to use when Quinn didn't want to announce his presence. They were about twenty miles from the Tennessee state line, heading up to the Flying J Truck Stop in Olive Branch. He'd called ahead to the DeSoto County Sheriff's Office and they agreed to have a nearby unit on standby. *Just in case.*

"How'd you see past all my damn baggage and bad mistakes?" Maggie said. "That crazy son of a bitch Rick Wilcox would've scared off most sane people."

"I'm not sane," Quinn said. "I also liked your pretty freckled face and your cute little ass."

"Now, that's true love."

Quinn reached across the shifter and squeezed Maggie's leg. She looked nervous as hell that morning, no makeup on her sun-flushed skin, playing with the bracelets on her wrist the whole drive north. Her reddish hair pulled back into a ponytail, wearing a sleeveless David Bowie tee with ragged jeans and sandals. *The Best of Lee Hazlewood* in the CD player, "The Night Before."

A new letter had arrived two days ago, again signed FOB—Friend of Brandon—promising EXPLOSIVE DETAILS and SHOCKING REVELATIONS. Quinn had told Maggie he didn't know if they were dealing with a confidential informant or a writer for the *National Enquirer.* The only thing he'd asked is she not make a move without him, with the questionable suicide, the old body found, and Tashi Coleman stalking her around Tibbehah County.

"I've been having dreams about my father lately," Maggie said. "They are so damn real I sometimes feel he's still alive. Daddy was the first one to tell me about Brandon, waking me up at five a.m. before school and saying he'd been found. He asked me what he could do for me and I asked him to drive me up to Jericho. That man canceled a big run he had that week to Dallas, unhooked his trailer and we hopped in his semi, The Blue Mule. I felt safe in that truck, riding so high up, Daddy listening to Jerry Reed and Ray Stevens. I woke up this morning humming 'Everything Is Beautiful.'"

"As long as it wasn't 'The Streak.'"

"You don't like Ray Stevens?"

"Of course I like Ray Stevens," Quinn said. "Sometimes I forget how little time we've spent together and how little we know each other. We both have a lot of catching up to do . . . *Do I like Ray Stevens?* . . ."

"I never questioned what we've got," Maggie said, reaching down and placing her hand over his, her short nails painted black and a tiny tattoo on her inner wrist. "Ever."

"Don't give this meet too much thought," Quinn said. "There are a lot of cranks out there. Some folks just wake up in the morning devising ways to mess with people's minds. I don't know how this person got those old letters, but that doesn't mean they're sane. It might mean they're dangerous as hell."

"You can't go in with me."

"I know," Quinn said. "But I won't be far. You go in the restaurant, take a seat, and I'll be out here watching. If this person asks you to go outside with them or if they say they have something for you in their vehicle . . ."

"I'm not stupid, Quinn," Maggie said. "Like you said, I doubt they'll even show. Whoever this is probably just wants some money. Why the hell else would they reach out to me now, after all these years? Doesn't make a damn bit of sense."

"Well," Quinn said. "It's nice being together. First day in a while we're not on the wrong ends of a shift. You on night or me on days or the other way around."

As Quinn turned off Highway 78, he spotted a big sign raised high above the road reading T-BONE STEAK, BAKED POTATO, SALAD & A DRINK. ONLY $11.99.

"It's your lucky day, Maggie Colson," Quinn said. "A day off and a T-bone steak."

"If only I ate meat."

"You heard from Tashi Coleman again?"

"Not since she showed up at the farm," Maggie said. "I think I made it pretty damn clear she wasn't welcome."

Quinn turned right into the truck stop parking lot, driving around back of the restaurant, near the trucker entrance by the diesel pumps. He parked out of sight and switched off the ignition, arriving a half hour earlier than the letter asked. "I wish you'd kept that gun in your purse."

"No thank you."

"Not much to it," Quinn said. "Just aim and squeeze the trigger."

"I know how to shoot," she said. "I prefer healing people, not bloodying them up."

"I prefer not bloodying them up, either," Quinn said. "But that's their call."

Quinn turned on the radio while they sat there in the parking lot waiting for the time Maggie would step into the truck stop and meet someone who promised probably a lot more than they could deliver. He and Maggie didn't speak for a while, Hazlewood now singing, "Cold Hard Times."

"Did you love him?" Quinn asked. "Brandon?"

"Very much," Maggie said.

"Maggie Colson is done," Tashi said, driving with Jessica out County Road 150, map in hand because the GPS stopped working south of the Big Black River. "We might as well mark her off the source list. When I asked her about knowing her husband when they were teenagers, she literally slammed the door in my face."

"Ouch," Jessica said. "We never accused the sheriff of any wrongdoing, we're only asking a few sensible questions. I mean, Jesus. This is one fucked-up county. Everyone is one degree of separation. Like a goddamn Greek tragedy."

"I told her we weren't blaming him," Tashi said, the windows down in the rental, her drinking the last bit of a Diet Coke. "But she saw us as taking sides, E. J. Royce over her husband. E. J. Royce is super-gross. He looked at me like he was imagining me naked, smiling with those crooked yellow teeth, licking his lips. But what if he's right? He was there. We can't just ignore it."

"Did you tell her we came to town with no theories or ideas of what happened?" Jessica asked, blue hair scattering across her face. "As far as we knew, Brandon really did shoot himself and all this work would go nowhere. At least we know he wasn't conflicted about being gay. Maggie was quite clear on that detail."

"How do you think the sheriff's gonna like hearing about his wife losing her virginity?"

"He seems like a grown-up," Jessica said, looking down at the map spread against her thigh. "The story isn't tacky or sordid. Sounded nice really, driving out to Choctaw Lake, taking her cotton panties off in the back of a pickup under the stars."

"'Shameless' playing on the radio," Tashi said.

"That's right," Jessica said. "It's going to be a bitch getting the rights to that song. But we have to have it, don't we? Garth Brooks is super-nineties."

Tashi nodded but was already taken in by the strange structure up on a grassy hill and through a thicket of trees. The old Tibbehah School stood just as the woman back at the clerk's office had told them. Tashi slowed the car onto a gravel road sprouted with weeds. They drove as far as they could until the weeds got higher than the hood, small trees poking up through the gravel.

"You have to be fucking kidding me," Jessica said.

"This can't be right."

"This is where they said," Jessica said, opening her door and reaching into the backseat for her backpack and laptop. "I mean, why the hell not? They said all of the old boxes and file cabinets were taken out here in 2001. With any luck, we might find something."

"Not exactly climate-controlled."

"Nothing is climate-controlled in Mississippi," Jessica said, walking up the hill through the weeds and little trees to the abandoned brick school. Windows covered with plywood spray-painted with pictures of penises and satanic symbols. Words sprayed in streaky paint letters: CHRIST FORGIVES. LOVE YOU FOREVER, PATTI. STAY IN DRUGS/ DON'T DO SCHOOL. SUCK IT PUSSIES. 21-17.

"They'd have been better off burning everything," Jessica said, heading up to what had probably been an entrance, the wide expanse of sun-curled and faded plywood in the shape of a door. They'd brought along a crowbar, but the closer they got, they knew they wouldn't need it. A large section had been torn back, the sunlight shining into a hallway.

"That doesn't smell pleasant," Tashi said.

"Nope," Jessica said. "It sure doesn't. How about you go first? You brought the flashlight."

Tashi didn't answer, only stepped inside out of the sunlight and moved into the brick structure over a spreading puddle and what had been a long hallway. Lockers collapsed down the expanse, busted boards and pieces of the ceiling fallen into heaps on the old linoleum.

"Did she say where they put the file cabinets?"

"Nope," Jessica said. "More like a tip. I heard they might have this kind of thing. God. Smells like a dead animal in here."

"Seems like the perfect place to get murdered," Tashi said, laughing, flicking on the flashlight with her thumb. "Right?"

They walked the hallways, stepping over fallen bricks and soggy insulation, more lockers, and broken glass. It looked like a few people had started small fires, empty bottles of cheap booze and cigarette butts everywhere. Shoes, boots, some old clothing, underwear. More graffiti along the inside walls, Tashi reading it aloud for the recording as they continued to wander. ARM THE TEACHERS and EVERYONE IS DEAD.

"Here," Jessica said, calling out. "In here."

Tashi followed her voice to another classroom, this one filled with dozens of four-drawer filing cabinets. Some neatly aligned against a far wall, others toppled onto the floor, the contents scattered into dirty puddles from the leaky roof. Tashi waved the flashlight over all the cabinets and loose papers, not knowing where in the hell they should begin.

Jessica, being Jessica, had already started, rifling through the top drawer of the first upright cabinet. A swath of daylight cut into the center of the dark room like a white-hot laser. Kudzu had started to crawl and grow between the broken slats of plywood over the windows. Water continued to drip from above. "Jail records from 1982," she said. "That's something. I'll take this first row and you take the next. Let me know when you hit the nineties."

Tashi turned off the flashlight, her eyes adjusting to the dim light, and reached down to an upright cabinet, her foot nearly stepping on what she thought was a big black rubber hose. And then the hose moved and raised up its thick, squat head. The snake's skin a dark color, the air smelling of a musky scent. "Holy shit. Holy shit. Holy shit!"

"What?" Jessica said, walking up. She gripped Tashi by the arm and pushed her back behind her. Jessica picked up a fallen piece of wood and went straight for the snake, clubbing it with a rage Tashi didn't know Jessica had. She finally stepped back, blue hair scattered, face and long, bare arms glistening with sweat. Jessica's eyes were wide. "Damn," she said. "Glad you saw it coming. It was a big one."

"Oh my God," Tashi said. "Did you really kill it? You did. You killed a fucking snake."

"Yeah?" Jessica said, breathing heavy, looking as if she'd surprised herself. "I guess I did. I killed the bastard. OK. Now let's get back to work."

"Were you recording?" Tashi asked.

"We're always recording."

* * *

Quinn moved the Cherokee out front where he could watch Maggie seated at a booth in the truck stop, studying the menu, not even contemplating that fine T-bone steak deal. He'd shifted Lee Hazlewood out for some Tyler Childers, listening to the new song, "Honky Tonk Flame," spotting the DeSoto County SO marked unit cruise the pumps and then roll toward a nearby strip mall. Quinn let down the window and started up a cigar, watching the front door and the back, getting a decent view of the wide entrance feeding into the restaurant. Maggie still alone, sitting behind the fogged glass, waiting for some crazy person who probably wouldn't have the guts to show. If she felt in the least uncomfortable, she'd hit the call button on her cell. But if not, she'd sit there and listen to what this person had to offer.

Quinn could call DeSoto dispatch and run into the restaurant. He could make the arrest and hand whoever this was to the locals.

Most folks have a little more time to unwind, unpack the wedding gifts, set up shop in their house and get into a new routine. Quinn had maybe two months before Tashi Coleman had showed up, making shit tough for Maggie, bringing up some hard memories for her, making her walk back into the woods with them, trying to figure out what happened back in the fall of '97. More than anything, Quinn just wanted those women gone and his wife back. They'd been trying like hell to keep little Brandon away from all this mess, but two nights ago, after Tashi had showed up at the farm, he'd wandered in, listened to talk about the body, the placement of the gun, all the craziness that followed. Little Brandon wanted to know why they were whispering about him and why did he shoot that gun?

Quinn could see a waitress walking up to Maggie, the women talking to each other for a bit and then the waitress walking away. His cell phone started to ring.

Quinn picked up.

"They're gone," Maggie said. "But they left me a key to the lockers. Let's see what this bullshit is about."

Quinn spotted Maggie over by the candy aisle and the novelty T-shirts. BLACK SMOKE DON'T MEAN IT'S BROKE. I LOVE THE SMELL OF DIESEL IN THE MORNING. JESUS CHRIST, THE #1 SAVIOR. Maggie tilted her head toward the trucker entrance facing the diesel pumps. They passed through the snack cakes, the hot dogs turning on heated rollers, black coffee stagnant and burnt in clear pots, action movie DVDs and audio tapes of Westerns and erotic thrillers. They wandered into a break room with a half-dozen truckers lounging about in easy chairs, half awake, watching flickering images on a corner TV set. Judge Judy, with her glasses down her nose, taking two women to task for trying to get out of paying for a parrot.

Maggie headed back toward the bathrooms and showers to a row of metal lockers, nodding toward one and turning the key. She pulled out a single photograph, a four-by-six picture of her and Brandon Taylor. The two sat together on a couch, but a decent distance apart, Brandon laughing, Maggie cutting her eyes over at him, a dubious look on her face. She had much longer hair then, nearly down to her waist, but the same turned-up nose and spread of freckles, eyes so green they almost didn't seem real.

"I don't remember taking this," Maggie said.

"Anything else in there?"

Maggie reached into the locker and pulled out a small silver chain, a silver heart pendant rocking between her fingers. She held it up to the light, tilting her head to study the inscription. Her face reddened as she dropped it back inside like it were hot.

"How close?" Quinn said.

"Real close," Maggie said. "Brandon gave it to me the first summer we met. I gave it back to him the next summer when we broke up. We'd had a silly fight. Just stupid. About me flirting with another boy on the Square. We made up, but I never saw him again. God, I'd forgotten all about it."

"Maybe we can get some prints off the necklace or the photo," Quinn said. "I'll talk to the manager here about pulling some security footage and talk to that waitress. Just what did she tell you?"

"She said I sure had pretty hair," Maggie said. "And then asked if I was Maggie Powers."

"Not Maggie Colson?"

"Nope," she said. "The waitress said the man who'd left this said I'd have real pretty hair."

"I'm not going to sugarcoat it, Mags," Quinn said. "That's creepy as hell."

"Goddamn, this pisses me off."

"Someone's definitely messing with your head," Quinn said. "Don't let 'em in."

Maggie nodded, letting out a long breath and placing the flat of her hand against her forehead. "Promise me you'll get this fucker, Quinn," she said. "I'm not fifteen anymore."

"Damn," Jessica said. "We're going to need our own box for all of Quinn Colson's records. Disturbing the peace. Reckless driving. Assault. Another assault. Minor in possession of alcohol. More reckless driving. Can you even go a hundred on these back roads?"

"Funny how all this went away."

"Well," Jessica said. "He was a minor. Most of the driving offenses happened when he was sixteen and seventeen. Some kind of junior varsity Burt Reynolds tearing up the hills of Tibbehah County. I don't know if this really tells us a whole hell of a lot other than Quinn was a wild kid, joined the Army, and got his shit straight. Good background material. Definitely tells us Sheriff Beckett was no stranger to cutting breaks for family."

Tashi flipped through more files, most of the offenses on notecards, alphabetized when they were lucky. But some of the file cabinets had been toppled and the cards had been scattered. They'd uprighted the cabinets and sorted the cards back in order, doing a great service for Tibbehah County's pristine recordkeeping system. She looked down at her watch—nearly six o'clock—and it was already getting dark. They'd either need to go grab dinner and some more flashlights or just come back in the morning. It scared her to leave all this tonight now that people knew what they wanted to find. All of this could disappear tomorrow. This place was a find, a stroke of luck, on account of Jessica being so damn chatty with the clerk. Sometimes it helped having blue hair. No one could play funny and inoffensive like Jessica Torres.

"Remember the time you talked the bartender at Dutch Kills into opening that bottle of really expensive bourbon?" Tashi said. "What was that stuff called again?"

"Twenty-three-year-old Pappy Van Winkle," Jessica said, heaving another file cabinet off the floor. "Bottle probably cost six hundred bucks."

"And we never got a tab."

"'Twern't nothing."

"I was impressed," Tashi said. "You always get people to do things like that. People open up to you, trust you, more than me. People are so damn guarded when I talk to them."

"Please," Jessica said. "First off, people love to confide in you. You have a wholesome face. And the only reason we drank the good booze that night is because I showed him my tits."

"Bullshit."

"Well, not there in the bar. But the night before. We hooked up. He was a decent lay, but a much better bartender."

Tashi started to laugh, rifling through more files, getting pretty good at it. The cards themselves had been well done, typed out in bold black ink, names, dates, and offenses clearly marked. If the stack was in order, she could get dozens done within a few minutes, looking for either *Colson* or *Taylor.* Only finding *Colson* so far. She kept flipping through. *Caldwell*, *Carmody*, *Chase*, *Clemons* . . . More *Colson, Quinn*. She picked up a card and started to read it, finding an envelope stapled to the back. Opening the envelope, she pulled out two neatly typed pages, an arrest report with a narrative attached.

"Holy fucking shit."

Jessica peeked up from the other side of the cabinet, resting her forearms on top, staring at Tashi. The thought suddenly coming to her how ridiculous it was to have gone from their dorm at Columbia to a shithole apartment in Williamsburg to an abandoned schoolhouse in Mississippi in only two years. Tashi flattened the sheet of paper out on top of the cabinet, Jessica now moving behind her and reading over her shoulder. "What?" Jessica said. "You need more light?"

"Shh."

Jessica turned on the light on her cell phone, chin resting on Tashi's shoulder blade.

"Holy fucking shit," Jessica said.

"I know," Tashi said. "Right?"

"Illegal trespassing," Jessica said. "On acreage belonging to the Hawkins family."

"Did you see the date?" Tashi said.

"October 1997," Jessica said. "Less than a month before Brandon Taylor disappears."

# SEVENTEEN

It was now the fourth of October, a Thursday morning, and the exotic dancer Dana Ray had finally had enough of Bradley Wayne's shit, shooting him in the right thigh with his own .44 pistol. Quinn sat with Reggie in his F-150 in the rain, drinking coffee and watching the EMTs load Bradley Wayne into an ambulance. Dana Ray had been arrested and taken to jail by their new deputy, Celia Jackson. Quinn cracked the window as the ambulance drove off onto Jericho Road toward the hospital, hoping to hell Maggie wouldn't be the one to have to deal with Bradley Wayne's sorry ass next.

"That woman says she didn't mean to shoot him in the leg," Reggie said, typing up the report on the laptop.

"I know," Quinn said, lighting up the back half of his Liga Privada. "She meant to shoot him in the pecker."

"Did she really say that?"

"Yep."

"You want me to put it in the report?" Reggie asked, looking over at Quinn, eyes wide.

"No, sir," Quinn said, blowing smoke out the window, watching the working girls at Vienna's Place gather under the long expanse of its sloping tin roof. All ten of them were wearing black negligees, some covering themselves with black silk robes. In their thigh-high boots with the tall acrylic heels, they looked like a conspiracy of ravens.

"Never a dull moment in Tibbehah," Reggie said. "This morning Deputy Cullison and I chased two brothers from Yalobusha County down County Road 191. They'd stolen six toilets from Robbie Neece's work shed. The boy driving hit a pothole and damn near threw the commode into our windshield."

"Where'd y'all catch them?"

"Highway patrol stopped them on the county line," Reggie said, typing as he talked. One of the working girls at Fannie's caught Quinn's eye, opening her robe wide to show off her sparkling bra and panty set. She blew Quinn a kiss. "Mr. Neece sure was pissed about his commodes. Two of them got busted. Those damn brothers had been working for him on the new houses he'd been building up by the high school."

Quinn watched two more girls wave. A new girl turned her butt to him and smacked it. Quinn hit the light bar on his truck with the siren and the black-clad ladies all stepped inside out of the rain. He continued to smoke, putting down the cigar for a moment, smoke curling up from the ashtray as the windshield wipers rocked back and forth. Fannie had added something new to Vienna's sign. SUPPORT SINGLE MOTHERS.

"Any luck with those women from New York leaving town?" Reggie said, not looking up, the laptop screen shining on his face.

"They have every right to be here," Quinn said. "I just don't like them stopping by unannounced pretty much every other day. They don't seem to understand forensics takes some time, especially in Mississippi. They think I'm hiding what I know about the body we found. And some other things, too."

"What they were saying," Reggie said, "sounded like a lot of bullshit to me. I'm sorry they're making things tough on you and your family."

"What they said is all true," Quinn said. "I did all those things. I used to get into fights. I stole a county vehicle. Sometimes I trespassed on people's land. I may have poached a little bit when I was a kid. What my uncle did may not have been legal, but I'm thankful for it. He knew I didn't have a lot of guidance back at home with Jason out in L.A."

"What's the damn point of it?"

"You hadn't heard?" Quinn said, lifting the cigar to his lips.

"No, sir."

"E. J. Royce told those women I'd been shooting at the Taylor boy before they found him dead," Quinn said. "Royce said my Uncle Hamp covered it up when the kid went missing. Like he covered up a lot of things. Those women just happened to find about dozen or so times I was arrested but never prosecuted. One time I'd crossed over on the Hawkins land. I didn't even know it. My uncle did his best to keep me clean, on track."

"And that gives some kind of credibility to a man like Royce?" Reggie said. "*Please.* That man is plain-out wicked. You won't even believe what he told me the first time he saw me in uniform."

"I bet I would," Quinn said.

"Yes, sir," Reggie said. "Just like that. Racist old peckerhead. But what you did or didn't do back then doesn't mean a damn now. I wouldn't even speak to those ladies next time they come by the office. If they make any trouble, I'd throw their asses in jail."

"Can't do that," Quinn said. "Protecting their right to question me is kind of the reason we risked our ass in the Army all those years. I saw them last week and answered all their questions. I verified everything they said and denied the rumors and flat-out lies. It's all part of my job. But what they're doing to Maggie? That's a whole other deal."

Reggie closed the laptop. He reached for his mic and told Cleotha he was headed to Tibbehah General to keep an eye on Bradley Wayne Guthrie while they extracted the bullet. Reggie put down the mic and looked over at Quinn, hand on the door and ready to get back to his own cruiser.

"How's Maggie doing?" he asked.

"Not too good," Quinn said. "She's pretty much a nervous wreck."

"You told me about what y'all saw at the truck stop up in Olive Branch," Reggie said. "Anything come of that?"

"I pulled the surveillance at the Flying J and interviewed the waitress," Quinn said. "I got a still from the video, but it's tough to see a damn thing. The necklace Maggie found and the photograph didn't have any prints. Not a one."

"Some weird shit."

"Yes, sir."

"What do you want to do with Bradley Wayne?" Reggie asked.

"When he comes to, charge him with agg assault," Quinn said.

"And what are you going to do with Miss Dana Ray?"

"Maybe give her a lesson about improving her aim."

"I don't think this is a good idea," Skinner said, standing in the rain at the clearing along Highway 45. The dirt work just starting for the Tibbehah Cross, backhoes digging into the side of a sloping hill of orange clay. "We really shouldn't be seen together."

"I left fifteen messages with your secretary, Miss Ida," E. J. Royce said. "I don't mean to be all sensitive, but I have to say it sounds like a big ole brush-off to me. So this morning down at the pool hall, I heard y'all had broken ground on some civic project and I said to myself, 'E.J., I'll bet that's why ole Skinner ain't called you back. Maybe you should go visit him in person and get right down to the ole nitty-gritty.'"

Skinner leaned against his brand-new Dodge 2500, fire engine red, bought and paid for by the county. Some people took notice it had both a sunroof and deluxe leather package. But he'd been working on and off for Tibbehah County most of his life and figured it cut an impressive image when meeting with important folks around the state. Success brought on success. The rain tapped at the brim of his pearl white Stetson as he watched the bulldozers scrape away the hill, leveling out the earth where the new cross would stand tall and proud.

"What're y'all putting in?" Royce asked. "Some kind of service road to get to the steak and titties faster?"

"No, sir," Skinner said, leaning against the hood of his truck. "We are not. Don't you read the newspaper, Royce?"

"These days only thing a newspaper is good for is wiping your damn ass," Royce said. "That business turned to shit about twenty years ago. Now it's nothing but stories about Hollywood elites and fake news from the goddamn liberal machine. How's a white man supposed to know what the fuck's going on in the world? Sometimes I wish I could punch Betty Jo Mize right in her fucking nose. The things that woman writes."

Skinner felt his face flush, rain sliding off his hat and down the slick surface of his cowboy duster. "I'd appreciate you not using vulgar language in my presence."

"Oh, I forgot, Skinner," Royce said. "You're the fucking Moral Majority of Tibbehah County. You and Anita Goddamn Bryant. Damn,

I used to daydream about squeezing that woman's big old fat titties like a pair of Florida grapefruits."

"Enough," Skinner said, raising his voice, slapping his hand on the hood of his big new truck. "None of that gutter talk. Not here. You bring a dust cloud of deception and immorality everywhere you go. Here I was, standing out here in the rain, thinking on this morning's meditation—*I have made you a light for the Gentiles, that you may bring salvation to the ends of the earth*—and then you appear, talking filthy about squeezing a woman's breasts like grapefruits."

"And what's wrong with that?" Royce said. "Don't tell me you don't like titties, neither."

"I hope this cross will become a beacon of light in the darkness," Skinner said. "I'm told folks will be able to see its light for nearly two miles, beyond the hills and turns of this here highway."

"Hallelujah, Brother Skinner," Royce said, turning his head to spit. "Hallelujah."

"Don't you dare mock my faith," Skinner said, feeling the heat in his face begin to cool. "What do you have when things get black as midnight up at your little shack in Carthage? Or when the final trumpet blows?"

"I got me some old dogs to keep me warm, dirty movies on some VHS tapes, and some Fighting Cock whiskey," Royce said, grinning and scratching at his neck. "But I have to say my groceries have gotten a mite low since the last time we met. Hard keeping me and them dogs fed on a state pension. Two of my checks done bounced at the Piggly Wiggly last week and they posted them on the manager's window like I'm some kind of fucking criminal."

"You can't help it," Skinner said, seeing the whole cross taking shape there on the hill and in the rain. The majesty of the whole thing nearly made him weep. "You spew out profanities as easily as some men breathe. Did you ever consider some good, God-fearin' folks find that kind of behavior reprehensible? It's why I don't care to be seen in your presence."

"Yeah," Royce said. "You might just lose your job handing out the collection plate for Pastor Traylor at First Baptist. Now, that'd be a damn shame. Some of the old women might stop wearing their good panties to Sunday service."

"I have business to tend to," Skinner said, wiping the rainwater off his hands on his trousers. "Just tell me what you want."

Royce just grinned, his gold glasses fogged up and dotted with moisture. His bald head bare and slick, age spots dotted along his scalp. His loose skin hung off his skeletal face as if it was made of melting wax. He licked his lips, his breath smelling like charred ash, and kept on smiling.

"How much?" Skinner asked.

Royce named a figure.

"Mr. Royce, I think you're out of your cotton-pickin' mind."

Royce started to laugh. "Maybe," he said. "But if you don't like this here deal, I'd be glad to explain to some folks how the goddamn Watchmen wanted me to railroad Sheriff Colson. I imagine a lot of folks would pay a quarter to read all about it."

"I don't really know how much your word is really worth," Skinner said. "Against mine."

"Sure would be embarrassing for the senator at this time," Royce said, rubbing a hand over his mouth as if to hide his big grin. "The Watchmen skulking about Tibbehah County like some boogerwoods G.I. Joes. Maybe when you take that man's peter out of your mouth, you might give me a straight answer."

Skinner felt the heat grow from his face and swell into his chest. He ground his back teeth against each other, the sounds of the earthmovers silent and still, almost muffled, as the rain started to fall hard again. Water rolled from his hat brim and collected in a muddy puddle at his feet.

"You know where to find me," Royce said, winking. "Don't make me have to ask twice."

Fannie watched Ray stand at the hotel window and light up a cigarette, blowing smoke as cool and clean as Melvyn Douglas used to do in those old black-and-white movies. He had his suit jacket off, neatly folded over a chair in the sitting area, dressed down to his baby blue silk shirt, boxers, and navy blue dress socks. He'd greeted her at the door like that, Ray already warning her that he sure needed her in a bad way. But Fannie had told him on the phone to hold his damn horses a bit, she needed to tell him a hell of a story. One of her sweet young things had tried to shoot her boyfriend right in the pecker.

"How's she doing?" Ray said, ashing his cigarette by the drinks cart.

"I sent a lawyer for her," Fannie said. "And spoke to the sheriff. But I was damn glad not to be there when the shit went down. If I'd seen that son of a bitch try and grab one of my girls, I'd have shot him myself. And you know me, Ray. I sure as shit don't miss."

"You want a drink?"

"Of course."

"Something to eat?"

Fannie shook her head, walking over to him and running her hand inside his silk shirt and feeling his hairy chest, a gold Saint Christopher medal around his neck.

"Maybe later," she said. "God, it's horrible out there. Rained the whole way from Tibbehah County. Nothing but Louisiana pissing all over us."

Fannie turned to the drinks cart and poured herself a tall scotch. Normally she wasn't a scotch gal, but, goddamn, Ray always had the best fucking whiskey. Smooth as silk, hot, sliding down the back of her throat. It was hard not to enjoy it. She sat down in a cushy chair and took a sip as she crossed her long legs, Ray watching her as she moved. Rain hitting the window glass, quiet and cool in the room.

He'd already spread back the sheets on the king-sized bed. She smiled up at Ray, but there was a coolness in his face, looking a bit ashen and worried.

"Go on," Fannie said. "Say it."

"Buster wants you gone," Ray said. "He's made some kind of fucking cockamamie agreement with the local yokels. He'll find a place for you. But he's taking away north Mississippi. He said he'd find work for you elsewhere."

"Let me guess," Fannie said. "A casino greeter down in Biloxi? Someone to tug the peckers of old men on golf weekends? Laugh at their bad jokes, pat their bald heads, and make them feel twenty years younger?"

"Yeah," Ray said, blowing out some smoke. "Something like that. I won't dip dog shit in powdered sugar. But I told him hell no. I told him if he wants to get you gone, I'm out, too. He made a goddamn deal with you to run things. I'm too fucking old and tired for his crap, going back on his word. Buster understands what I bring to his goddamn buffet. I can take my people and my business elsewhere. I'll head back to New Orleans. Those folks love me down there. It won't change a damn thing for me."

"Appreciate it, Ray," Fannie said. "You are a real gent. But I don't like it. I don't like having a chaperone."

Ray's face softened. He walked to the drinks cart and uncorked the scotch, studying the label and nodding his approval. He looked handsome yet funny in the long silk shirt and the boxers, navy blue socks hiked up to his skinny knees. "I'm glad to do this for you," he said. "I'm glad to be of some use."

"That's not what this has ever been about."

Ray nodded. "I know."

"I took off my panties when I got to Batesville," Fannie said, taking a little sip. "I couldn't wait."

"You're bluffing." Ray laughed a little. "I see it on your face. I've always been able to tell when you're lying to me."

Fannie raised her eyebrows and undid the ties on her wrap dress, a classic Diane von Furstenberg in a bluish cheetah print. She kicked off her black suede heels and opened up her dress. She had on a black lace bra with a front latch and absolutely nothing else down below. She widened her knees and leaned back into the plushy chair, a grin on her lips. "Take off those goddamn silly socks."

Ray took off his socks so fast Fannie thought he was going to trip right on his face. Within a few seconds, he was down to nothing but his silk boxers, pulling her up to her feet and peeling the dress off her shoulders. She could feel his lips and mustache against her neck as he told her how damn beautiful she was, reaching down and rubbing her between her legs. She led him back through French doors and onto the bed, where he scrambled out of his boxers and lay on top of her, saying the damn nicest things to her. There was no preamble or foreplay, just getting on down to business. He smelled like good cigarettes and cheap aftershave.

"Can we at least play some music?"

"There will be music later."

"Oh, my hair."

"I'll get you a place at the salon."

"Ray."

Ray's eyes were closed as he worked in a steady rhythm over her, Fannie reaching around his waist with her legs and hooking her feet at the ankles, locking him in place. Feeling all his energy and heat. She'd never felt him being so damn forceful with her, riding her like Bill Shoemaker on Silky Sullivan, heading on toward the finish line. "Ray," she said. "Slow down, Ray. We have all night."

His back felt hot. Ray had never been a man who had trouble rising to the occasion, but it seemed like he was having a hard time getting there. His Saint Christopher medal swung over her like a pendulum. Fannie felt for him and pushed him onto his back, his head on the pillow, telling him just to be cool and relax, don't push anything, she'd do all the work. And Fannie screwed Ray so hard, she about drove him down into the thick mattress. Now it was Fannie's time, feeling she was nearly there, about to break apart, riding him slow but hard as hell, screwing him down into the bed like a pile driver. His eyes had grown wide and his breath shortened as she was nearly there. His face drained of color and he looked as if he might be in some kind of pain, like he would break apart. A roiling deep down in his throat.

"OK, Ray," Fannie said. "OK."

He made a chirp, something like *eek*, his eyes fluttering and skin going pale, his entire body going slack. Fannie was out of breath, her business unfinished, as Ray lay still and silent beneath her. She leaned down and kissed his forehead, noticing his eyes were still wide open, the same grand bemused grin on his face. "Ray?"

She grabbed his chin and shook it from side to side. "Ray. Fuck, Ray. Listen to me."

Fannie felt a coldness spread down her neck and shoulders as she pulled away and off him, falling and tripping onto the floor into a tangle of sheets, leaving Ray lifeless and still on the grand bed.

"Oh, God. Oh, God."

Fannie reached for the phone and dialed the front desk, already moving over to the floor where she'd dropped her wrap dress and purse. Ray's cell phone on the nightstand kept buzzing and buzzing as she slid back into the dress and reached for her soft suede shoes, heading toward the door.

She'd never felt more alone in her whole damn life.

"Goddamn, Quinn," Lillie said, eyeing the target at the far end of the range. "You arrest any more strippers and you'll have to get a brass pole for the exercise yard."

"I didn't charge the stripper," Quinn said. "Only her boyfriend, for aggravated assault. I'm keeping her for a few hours until she calms down. Nobody will look at what happened as anything other than self-defense."

Lillie had come down from Memphis an hour ago and wanted to shake Quinn loose from the sheriff's office and do a little target practice. The rain had all but stopped, slowing into a gentle patter out at the range and shoot house, near the abandoned town of Burnt Oak. "How's the dickhead boyfriend?"

"He'll live," Quinn said, loading twelve rounds into his lever-action Winchester, a classic cowboy gun that held .45 ammo. He picked up his cigar to watch Lillie take her next shot with her trusty .308.

"Damn shame," Lillie said, squeezing off her shot, knocking down a small metal plate, the sound like a little bell ringing.

Quinn had secured the property not long after becoming sheriff, giving the department five acres to work on their marksmanship and tactical skills. A few years ago, he'd even had a small shoot house built to work out different scenarios for going to work in close quarters. The hills looked lush and green after the rains, a narrow shot of about two hundred and fifty yards cleared up into the woods.

"We've got this indoor range up in Memphis," Lillie said. "But there's nothing like being outside and firing your weapon. How about I take out those two turkeys and that metal chicken on the right side?"

"Be my guest."

Lillie pinged the chicken, knocking down the targets and jacking a new round into her rifle time after time. Quinn had met few who could shoot like Lillie Virgil. Her whole being seemed to take on a stillness and calm when she went to work. There was no one better on overwatch when you headed in to deal with bad guys.

"Been thinking on your situation," Lillie said, now aiming at an old skillet dangling from a tree. "How about you let me reason with E. J. Royce? The son of a bitch nearly pisses his pants when he sees me coming."

"Not worth your time," Quinn said.

Lillie squeezed off a third shot, the skillet twirling, the sound of the quick ping filling the air. Quinn lifted the cigar again and watched Lillie standing there, arms outstretched, her muscles tight and flexed as she held the gun and sought her next mark. He blew out the smoke, Lillie scanning over the many targets on the grassy knoll, the smell of woodsmoke coming from far off in the hills.

"I don't like how things went down with our ole buddy Wes," Lillie said. She aimed for a tricky one on the far edge of the hill, the whole two-fifty away from where they stood. "Not one goddamn bit."

She fired the last round toward a tall target, dropping it as fast and hard as a bad man sneaking through the woods. Lillie slowly lowered the gun and set it onto a carrying case on a wooden table. Quinn set his cigar on the rim of an old coffee can. Someone earlier had been spitting sunflower seed shells into it, the insides half filled with rainwater and shells.

"Be nice if we could find the guys," Quinn said.

"How'd it go at the Rez?" Lillie asked.

"'Bout like you would expect," Quinn said. "No one seemed to know our guys. And they just laughed at the composites I brought.

Can't really blame them. Nobody got a good look at them. And the cameras weren't any help with everything busted up."

"Maybe y'all should think about updating the jail from 1873," Lillie said. "Wasn't that when it was built?"

"Nineteen twenty-three," Quinn said. "But we could do better with the tech. If the supervisors could find a way it would benefit them to have a new camera system with an online feed, then it would get done."

Quinn cocked his Winchester and lifted it to his shoulder, aiming for another metal turkey.

"I miss working with you, Quinn," Lillie said. "But I ain't gonna lie. I don't miss this county and the bullshit one damn bit."

Quinn closed his left eye and looked down the scope with his right. He fired and knocked the turkey down on the hill. He levered the gun again.

"Driving down," Lillie said, "I had a few ideas."

"You want to head back to the Rez with me?" Quinn said, taking aim again, this time back on the skillet. "Maybe introduce them to some of that Lillie Virgil charm?"

He fired and another high-pitched ping filled the woods of Burnt Oak, Mississippi. The skillet twirling like a top.

"Nope," Lillie said. "I figured we might take a run at Curtis Creekmore."

Quinn reached for his cigar and took a puff, a quiet settling over the range. "Is he out?"

"Curtis got out last year," Lillie said. "Living over in Yalobusha County, outside Coffeeville. Dealing in the same ole shit he was doing over here in Tibbehah."

"He have a warrant?" Quinn said, setting down the cigar again.

"Yep."

"Might make him more willing to talk about his buddies down in Biloxi and Tunica."

Lillie smiled, placing her right hand in her jeans pocket. Her whole face lighting up with the thrill of going after a real-life shitbird together. Just like the old days. When she smiled, the dimples deepened in her cheeks.

"I don't think Curtis is in any rush to get back to Parchman," Lillie said. "He might just be willing to tell us what he knows about Wes Taggart and why his sorry ole ass was so important to the Syndicate boys. Might even have some names."

Quinn nodded. "Do I have time to take one more shot?"

Lillie smiled again. "Be my guest, Ranger. Need you sharp."

# EIGHTEEN

"Sorry I'm late," Bentley said. "Please tell me we're winning. We're winning, right?"

"Winona took the lead right before halftime," Caddy said. "They picked off a pass and ran it back with ten seconds to go. What kind of coach takes it to the air with a little bit of time left? Come on. These kids aren't old enough for complicated plays like that. They barely ran that one at practice and then all of a sudden the coach wants to roll the dice."

"Only three things can happen when you pass," Bentley said. "And two of them are bad. Just ask Ole Miss. They're leading the SEC in turnovers. I think I'm skipping going to the Grove on Saturday. I'd just as soon watch us lose at home."

"Really?" Caddy said, watching the boys take the field for the third quarter. It was a rare Thursday night game, the bright lights shining down on the patchy field. All the kids were splattered in mud, Caddy knowing Jason's white pants would be hell to clean tomorrow. "I told Jason and Brandon we'd be going. Quinn and Maggie were fine with it. Isn't that right, Momma?"

Jean Colson nodded, scooting over in the aluminum bleachers, patting a place between her and Caddy for Bentley. He was dressed in a red Ole Miss polo, khakis, and expensive-looking suede boots with zips down each ankle. Her mother had already told him twice how handsome he looked. Bentley couldn't quit smiling as he offered Jean popcorn from his little paper bag. Always the gentleman.

"It's awfully nice of y'all to include Brandon," Jean said. "I don't think he's ever been to an Ole Miss game before. Of course Quinn always pulls for Auburn. He took a few classes there when he was at Benning. I don't know who Maggie pulls for. Do you, Caddy?"

"Maggie doesn't like football," Caddy said. "She almost didn't let Brandon play, says it's too dangerous. Maybe she should quit marrying men who find pleasure in a damn war zone."

Bentley and Jean didn't respond, knowing better than to get in the middle of her spat with her sister-in-law. Caddy had been cold and a little distant with Maggie since Maggie asked her about Quinn hunting the Hawkins land, still pissed off as hell Quinn's own wife would listen to such trash talk. Down along the high school track, a ragtag group of cheerleaders, little girls in street clothes, worked on some really mean-spirited cheers about the mommas of the Winona players. *U-G-L-Y. You ain't got no alibi . . .*

"When did cheerleaders get so nasty?" Jean asked.

"Momma, they've been doing that cheer forever," Caddy said. "Don't you remember me doing the same one?"

"Did I ever tell you how much Elvis liked cheerleaders?" Jean said, reaching for some of Bentley's popcorn. "He used to like the girls he was dating to dress up in those short skirts. This was after he and Pricilla got divorced, of course. Tight sweaters and pom-poms. They'd put on little routines for him down in the TV room. One night, we were watching *The Carol Burnett Show* . . ."

"Shh, Momma," Caddy said. "Can we please just watch? Bentley doesn't need to hear all about how you and Daddy used to go up to Graceland to shoot guns and ride horses."

Bentley said he didn't mind. In fact, he'd love to hear all about it. He said he had Elvis on SiriusXM Radio and loved listening to *The George Klein Show*, George always having great stories about his time with the Memphis Mafia. It had started to mist a little, the raindrops little specks in the hot white stadium lights.

"Shh," Caddy said, holding up her hand, watching the quarterback pitch Jason the ball. Jason got around the end fast but got hit two yards off the line, spinning off a tackler and trying to find some daylight before three Winona boys brought him down.

Caddy saw Boom on the sidelines, walking without a cane or any assistance, shaking his head and yelling at the referees. She wasn't sure what he was mad about, but Boom was mighty pissed off. He said something to the head coach and then yelled at the referee out on the field. One of the other assistants walked over and placed a hand on Boom's good arm, telling him to calm down a bit, walk back to the bench. Boom shook him off, stumbling a little on his way over to the bench and kicking at a water bottle.

"Everything OK down there?" Bentley asked.

"Don't know," Caddy said, standing up to watch Boom, her hand over her mouth. Something was definitely off-center, not only with Boom's walk but his focus. Boom wasn't the kind of man to take Little League sports so seriously, always kidding around, providing positive encouragement for the kids. He limped on back to the sidelines, yelling something at the ref, who seemed to pay him no mind.

Caddy looked across Bentley at her mother. Jean caught her eye and nodded. Yep. Boom was drunk.

"Should I do something?" she asked her mother.

Jean shook her head. "I wouldn't go down on that field right now for nothing in this world."

Boom stayed put for a moment, but then, unable to take it anymore, walked back to the sideline, stepped onto the field, and yelled back at the referee as Tibbehah was about to punt. The referee answered and pointed to the head coach, the coach turning to Boom. Three assistants now reaching for Boom's massive body, wrapping him around the waist, holding his good arm, trying to coax him back off the field to the sidelines.

"What's he so mad about?" Jean asked.

"Jason should've had first down," Bentley said. "Can't say I blame Boom. That referee spotted the ball two yards back."

"I'll get Boom," Caddy said. "It's just a game."

"I wouldn't do that," Jean said.

Caddy headed down the bleacher steps and to the exit onto the field. Four coaches and Kenny from the sheriff's office had already started to walk Boom toward the field gate. Caddy met them at the exit. "Let me give you a ride home."

"Nah," Boom said. "I'm good."

Caddy nodded to Kenny and Kenny backed off, Boom heading out the gate ahead of her toward his truck. "Come on," she said. "This game is done anyway. Give me your keys. I'll get you home."

"Winona must be paying that ref," Boom said. "Did you see that shit?"

"Let me have your keys."

"I said I'm good."

"Boom," Caddy said. "Don't do this. You and I both know it's a hell of a trip back."

Caddy reached out her hand, but Boom turned away from her and jumped into his beat-up old truck. He cranked the engine and sped out, the pipes growling, with only one working headlight. As she watched him go, a trailer chain dragged behind his tailgate, throwing sparks up into the darkness.

Quinn and Lillie found Curtis Creekmore hunched over a workbench, cigarette bobbing out of the corner of his mouth, as he worked on the engine of a Stihl chain saw. A small radio sat beside him playing David Allan Coe singing how *Mona Lisa lost her smile*. The dingy little shop cluttered with used pressure washers, weed whackers, and dozens of old, dirty chain saws hanging from the ceiling, tagged like meat in a butcher shop. He looked up and grinned with crooked yellow teeth and said, "Well, goddamn, if it ain't Johnny and Jane Law."

"Curtis," Quinn said. "You're a long way from Jericho."

"Guess not far enough, Sheriff," Curtis said. "What can I do you for? Deputy Virgil? *My, my, my.* Ain't never seen you in no street clothes before. You don't look half bad when you're cleaned up. Almost look like a woman."

"And you look about the same, Curtis," Lillie said. "Like you just stepped out of one of those *Lord of the Ring*s movies. One of those fellas with pointy ears, yellow eyes, and fucked-up teeth. Is that a new tattoo?"

"Yes, ma'am," Curtis said, pushing away from his workbench and examining his skinny bicep. "Ain't it pretty? That's my ole cat Mr. Whiskers. God rest his soul."

"Is he wearing a cowboy hat?" Lillie asked.

"Sure is," Curtis said. "And smoking a corncob pipe. Just the way I always saw him in my mind's eye. He was a damn good little pussy. Got this one down in Jericho before y'all kicked my ass over to

Parchman this last time. Rerun is a true *artiste*. Man can ink up anything you bring him. I was all tore up when Mr. Whiskers got kilt. Got run over by the damn UPS truck. Damn near killed the motherfucker driving. I can still see him standing there, in those little brown shorts, telling me I'm the one responsible for not keeping my animals put up. You know better than anyone, Deputy Virgil, how a pussy sure do love to roam."

"I'm a U.S. Marshal now, dickhead," Lillie said. "And you got two outstanding warrants out on your sorry ass. You haven't shown up for your last three court appearances."

"I haven't?" Curtis said, cigarette still screwed into the corner of his mouth, eyes squinty from the smoke. "Don't know nothing about that."

"Fella that owns this shop knows you're a felon?" Quinn said.

"He damn well better," Curtis said. "Used to be my dang brother-in-law."

"You hadn't been out of jail two weeks when you got busted stealing a trailer full of work tools."

"That was a misunderstanding."

"Maybe you should've shown up in court, then," Quinn said. "Told your side of the story."

"That fella said I could borrow them anytime I liked," Curtis said. "Me and him drinking buddies at the Southern Star. Must've had Jäger on the brain the night he offered 'em because now he's acting like me and him never even met."

*The Essential David Allan Coe* kept on playing. "Need a Little Time Off for Bad Behavior." *Looks like I've been too good for too long . . .* The air hazy under the fluorescent lights, the windows dark and covered with thick metal bars. Curtis had on an Under Armour hoodie and paint-splattered jeans tucked into his mud boots. His sallow face and thin graying beard shadowed under a ball cap, sunglasses resting on the bill.

"I know folks sure do miss you in Tibbehah," Lillie said. "Maybe you can get that girlfriend of yours to bring you more Popeyes fried chicken."

"I ain't seeing her no more," Curtis said. "Said I wasn't willing to spiritually grow with her, whatever the fuck that means. Some real Oprah shit going on. I guess that's what you get when you date a black woman. Did y'all really drive all this way to come and give ole Curtis a hard time? If I knew this was the way my night was gonna turn out, I would've packed my toothbrush and a few pairs of underwear."

Quinn looked to Lillie and Lillie nodded back. Curtis's hair grew long and stringy down the back of his skinny neck in an epic mullet. His hands down at his sides as he stayed on his metal stool. Quinn couldn't see a gun anywhere, although Curtis was the type to pick up a chain saw, let her rip, and clear a path for the nearest door.

"The last time we busted your ass, you had a thick roll of hundred-dollar bills in your pocket," Lillie said. "You'd just gotten back from a long weekend down on the Coast. Said you'd hit the big time playing blackjack."

"That's right."

"You were big-time," Quinn said. "That work shed of yours looked like the inside of King Tut's tomb. Fifteen pickup trucks, a tractor trailer. Rolexes, gold chains, diamond rings. Forty guns. You've really taken a step down."

"You got a hell of a memory, Sheriff," Curtis said, grinning. "I might've dabbled from time to time helping folks sell a few things. I didn't know being a goddamn businessman was a fucking crime until y'all busted in my shop like Navy SEALs on Bin Laden's ass, making me damn near shit my drawers."

"Being a fence isn't a vocation," Lillie said. "It's more of an affliction."

"Yeah?" Curtis said. "Well, I don't do that no more. Go on ahead and look around. Not many high-dollar items here. I'm just a simple man, doing a simple job."

"Just the way God and Mr. Whiskers intended."

Curtis dropped the smile and stood up, not impressive at maybe five-six, one-twenty, with a sunken chest and hard round belly. "I'd appreciate you not joking about something so personal. You're just being flat-out mean, Miss Virgil."

"You still keep in touch with Buster White and his people?" Quinn asked.

"Y'all were always trying to tie me into some big criminal conspiracy," Curtis said, ashing his cigarette. "How many times I got to tell you? I don't know no one named Buster White and there ain't no such thing as the fucking Syndicate or Dixie Mafia or whatever the fuck y'all want to call it this week. I may have bent the law a time or two, but I did my goddamn time. And you coming over to me won't be nothing more than a fucking field day when I talk to my people at Morgan and Morgan."

"What a shame," Lillie said. "If you did know something, I might forget I ran into you down here in Coffeeville. Let nature take its course in y'all's confederacy of thieves."

Curtis swallowed and tilted his chin up to Lillie. "Goddamn, I can't talk about that shit. I'd just as soon not end up dead like that motherfucker Wes Taggart."

"So you do know these people?" Quinn asked.

"I got a TV," he said. "I seen the news outta Memphis and Tupelo. Everybody knows some bad folks busted in your jail and took ole Wes's ass out."

Lillie nodded. She walked through the smoke up close to Curtis, tapping his sternum with her finger, making him take two steps back, his butt knocking into a metal shelf loaded with machine parts. "I figured you might be smarter than that," Lillie said. "Maybe interested in some kind of trade?"

"Just what are you talking about?" Curtis said.

Lillie turned her head to Quinn. Quinn stood close by, hands on his hips, nodding back at Lillie.

"Oh, I don't know," Lillie said. "How does a head start sound to you?"

Caddy headed back from the parking lot, through the admission gate and straight to the bathrooms behind the bleachers. She needed to clear her head before going back to her momma and Bentley, composing herself before she went back to the stands, with all those nosy goddamn folks sitting around them. She walked up to one of the sinks set against the concrete wall and turned on the faucet, staring at herself in the mirror, the PA system outside playing the Migos for their hype music. *Walk it, like I talk it . . .* Caddy knowing damn well what it was like to be Boom, sliding off the rails and rolling into that fuzzy fucking abyss, trying to find the walls as the earth kept on tilting on you.

She reached down and splashed some water on her face. Glad to see a different face there without all the blonde hair and makeup from years before. Just a plain, thin face and straight, freckled nose, elfin ears, and a few more lines under her eyes. She still had the nasty scar on her temple, a thin white line running into her sun-bleached hair where a man at a club had had too damn much to drink and knocked her off the stage with a bottle of Bud Light. She touched the scar with her fingers, still feeling the blow twelve years later.

"Hello?" a woman asked.

Caddy turned off the faucet, looked in the mirror again, and saw Tashi Coleman coming in from outside. She wasn't carrying the microphone this time, just a purse thrown over her shoulder, some kind of T-shirt with a flowered Mexican skull—Day of the Dead. Her long black hair worn loose and stringy down her back.

"Not right now, Tashi," Caddy said. "OK?"

"I just need you for a moment."

"That's always what you say. *Just a moment.* But you always want much more, don't you? You want me to break down and tell you my brother was a teenage sociopath and my uncle was just another corrupt redneck sheriff. I know we have to amuse the shit out of you down here, Tashi Coleman. But today, I don't have time to entertain."

"I saw what happened out there," Tashi said. "I'm sorry."

"So what?" Caddy said. "Boom got drunk. Nobody cried. Nobody got hurt. Not even the makings of a country song. Just another night in Tibbehah County. How about we don't make such a damn big deal of it? It's nobody's business but his own."

"I don't care about that," Tashi said. "I just had two very important questions about the time Brandon Taylor died. If you could just answer those, I swear to God I will leave you alone for good. We think we might know whose body they found last month out at the Penningtons' place."

"Oh yeah?" Caddy said. "Did Quinn shoot her, too?"

"We never said Quinn shot Brandon," Tashi said. "It was just an anomaly, a question. We know for a fact Sheriff Beckett continued to dismiss charges against your brother. Jessica and I found dozens of arrests for Quinn when he was in high school. A few of them with Boom Kimbrough. Most of them were pretty minor. But a couple were pretty serious. Your brother was arrested for assault and then the charge just went away."

"Sure," Caddy said. "But if you took the time to find out how it went down, you'll understand that preacher had it coming."

"He assaulted a minister?"

"You had to be there," Caddy said. "It was just a youth pastor with a smart mouth. Are we done here? I don't have anything to add. And I don't give a damn to be on your little hipster radio show. But I do want you to leave my brother the fuck alone. He's done nothing but try his best to clean up this messed-up county. Did you know he walked away from the U.S. Army to make a difference in his own backyard? He figured Tibbehah wasn't a hell of a lot different from the shit he was seeing over in Afghanistan. Corrupt chieftains, drug dealers, crimes against children and women. Who really gives a shit if he used to raise hell as a kid? Let's move on to the next episode."

"Did you know Quinn got charged with poaching on the Hawkins land in '97?"

"So what?" Caddy said.

"It's a pretty big deal," Tashi said. "Your brother has denied it, but we've found the reports. He's lying to us."

"Or maybe he just forgot," Caddy said. "I'm sure you know Quinn hunted a lot of land without permission. Is that why you came to see me? You wanted to tell me about some bullshit that happened twenty years ago?"

"There's more."

"Of course there is." Caddy dried her hands on some paper towels and was about to push past Tashi to the door when Tashi asked her about Ansley Cuthbert. The name came out of nowhere and stopped her cold.

"What about her?" Caddy asked.

"She was a friend of Brandon Taylor," Tashi said. "Right? Maybe his best friend. She disappeared a few months after Brandon."

Caddy closed her eyes and shook her head, not knowing if she was about to scream or start laughing. "You think Ansley Cuthbert is dead?"

"We can't find any family," Tashi said. "We've tried our best to track them down. We think maybe they moved to Houston a few years ago? She had a stepmother who's still alive but no one at her last known address. It doesn't look like anyone has seen Ansley since high school. We found a missing persons report. And we know she dropped out before graduation—"

Caddy held up the flat of her hand. "You want to talk to Ansley Cuthbert?"

Tashi nodded. "Very much so."

"Would that make you leave Quinn the hell alone?"

"She disappeared right after Brandon and now a young woman's body has been found. You don't think that has to mean something?"

"I know Ansley Cuthbert," Caddy said, folding her arms over her chest. "We were in the same class and got to be pretty damn good friends up in Memphis. That girl was wild as hell. I can promise you one thing. She sure as shit didn't die back in '97 if she was up in Memphis partying with me fifteen years ago. We worked at the same clubs, dated some of the same men, were pretty much inseparable until I decided to get my ass clean."

Tashi looked disappointed her theory was being shot to shit but interested at the same time. Her chin tilted upward, the fluorescent lights overhead reflected off her chunky glasses, old-school sneakers on her feet. "Can you help us find her?"

"I haven't seen Ansley Cuthbert for almost ten years."

"That's a lot more recently than most," Tashi said. "If you could maybe tell us where to look or anyone who might have kept in touch."

"Did you try the Memphis phone book?" Caddy said. "Y'all are *some* damn reporters."

"We called every person we could find with that name in the South."

"Could still be in Memphis."

"Where did you two work?"

"Oh," Caddy said. "A real fine place right near the airport. Ever heard of a gentleman's club called Dixie Belles? She used to put on a hell of a show to Led Zeppelin's 'Black Dog.' Knee-high fur boots, black leather bikini, and a damn bullwhip. I don't know where Ansley's gone, but ten to one she's still in the life."

"Will you help us?"

"Like I said," Caddy said. "Will you leave Quinn alone?"

"All depends," Tashi said, shuffling her black Chuck Taylor sneakers, trying to look tough. "On what she has to say."

"Don't y'all dare use my damn name," Curtis Creekmore said. "I don't want to be listed as no CI, neither. I don't want you even thinking about putting my ass on the stand because I swear to Holy Christ I will deny every damn word I'm about to tell you. What we talk about in Coffeeville damn well stays in Coffeeville. Just between me, y'all, and these here chain saws. We got a deal or not?"

Quinn looked to Lillie and she shrugged. "I guess so," she said.

"What the hell you mean you guess so, woman? You said y'all would leave my ass in peace and let me tend to my damn business if I sent you in the right direction about Wes Taggart. And I promise you one goddang thing, what happened to Wes was a long time coming. That motherfucker has been wiping his ass all over north Mississippi since him and J. B. Hood took over at Sutpen's. If I live to be a million years old, I'll never understand what made Mr. White take a chance on those shit-for-brains. I figured on things going much worse than they did. Them Fed boys shut down their shop, but Buster White is still eating that prime rib and shrimp dinner down on the Gulf Coast, sunbathing with half-nekkid women and hanging out with superstars like Donny and fucking Marie. So what the hell does that tell you?"

"Donny and Marie?" Lillie said. "Are you fucking kidding me?"

"What did Wes tell you, Sheriff?" Creekmore said. "I know that boy couldn't keep his mouth shut. He'd do anything to save his own ass."

"Ironic," Lillie said. "Ain't it?"

Creekmore stared at Lillie, reaching for another cigarette from a pack on the workbench. He set fire to the American Spirit with a Zippo adorned with the Playboy bunny head. The air filled with more smoke as Creekmore snapped shut the lighter. "White used to be an honest crook," he said. "He didn't give a damn about nothin' but making money. Long as you shared your business with him, everything was cool. Long as you didn't cross him, everything was cool. Me and him used to be friends. I made him a lot of money and he cut me in on a lot of action. But since I got back from Parchman, the man ain't the same no more. He's not thinking about business. Gulfport and Biloxi ain't enough for his fat ass. He's looking to run the whole damn state."

"He pretty much does," Quinn said.

"As a crook," Creekmore said. "Now he wants everything. I used to go down to his casino and get treated better than fucking Sammy Hagar. That man rolled out the red carpet for me. I got a suite, a big ole mess of chips, and vouchers for their seafood buffet. But last time I seen him, he didn't have no time for Curt Creekmore. *No sir.* He was too busy entertaining some big ole swinging dicks from Jackson. Men who wore navy blue sport coats and fancy-ass ties and looked down on a fella like me like I was someone to put another coat of wax on the Hummer. White done expanded his vision. That's why Wes got kilt. He knew where a lot of money was going."

Quinn knew where he was headed but needed Creekmore to say

it. Creekmore ashed his cigarette into a metal bucket filled with sand. He looked up at Quinn and nodded. "What all do you know about this ole boy Vardaman? The one who's gonna make the state of Mississippi great again. Turning back the clock to the good ole days of plantations and dark folks working the field."

"Plenty," Quinn said.

"I don't think no one saw that come-from-behind victory back there in the primary," Creekmore said. "Running this state ain't about nothing but money. And that was a war chest the fancy Jackson folks were never gonna open for a redneck like Jimmy Vardaman. Buster White wined and dined and got their rocks off with top Southern cooze. But no one could right things for Vardaman. That boy is stone-cold crazy and them folks all know it. All this nonsense with the fucking Watchmen Society. Only Buster White would bankroll a son of a bitch like that. The old guard in Jackson never wanted crazy come to town. You never know when crazy'll turn on you. But Buster was just licking his chops to take a dump in the governor's mansion and ole Wes Taggart was his go-between."

"You know who did it?" Lillie asked. "Who were those boys?"

Creekmore held up his hand in the smoke and shook his head. "Oh, hell. I said too damn much."

"Actually," Lillie said. "You haven't said enough. It's not too late to drive you up to the Memphis drunk tank. I think they'd just love that long silky hair. They'd turn you into a regular Billy Ray Cyrus, working on your achy breaky ass."

"Damn, Lillie Virgil," Creekmore said. "Y'all got to do some damn things on your own."

"The men who came to the jail looked Native American," Quinn said. "Closest we have to that is the Choctaw Nation. I went down to the Rez and showed their picture around. No one seemed to recognize them."

"Oh, yeah?" Creekmore sucked on the cigarette, burning it down to a nub. "Maybe I know who those fellas are."

Quinn shook his head. "You gonna tell us?"

"Nope," Creekmore said. "I value my life too damn much. And if I were you, I'd keep the fuck away from those boys. If they can break into a goddamn jail to git you, where exactly is a man safe?"

**Tashi Coleman**
***Thin Air* podcast**
**Episode 6: QUINN COLSON**

NARRATOR: In one way or another, everything kept on coming back to the sheriff. Both the old one and the new one. Hamp Beckett and his nephew, Quinn Colson. The more time we spent in Tibbehah County, the more we met people who compared the two. Both U.S. Army vets, Beckett served in the Korean War and Colson in both Iraq and Afghanistan. Beckett earned two Purple Hearts and a Bronze Star. Colson earned three Purple Hearts and a Silver Star as a U.S. Army Ranger. But Colson didn't want to talk about that time with our producer, Jessica. We couldn't tell if it was out of privacy or modesty, but that part of his life was off-limits.

> QUINN COLSON: I joined up right out of high school. I thought of it more of a vocation than anything. This was a year or so before 9/11.
>
> JESSICA: I understand you didn't have much choice in your decision.
>
> QUINN COLSON [LAUGHING]: True. My uncle pretty much gave me an ultimatum. At first, I thought I might play college ball like every other kid in Mississippi. But after my senior year, I was told the Army was my best option. Best thing could've happened to me.
>
> JESSICA: How so?
>
> QUINN COLSON: I needed a heavy dose of discipline.

> The Army gave that to me. And being a Ranger only solidified it.
>
> JESSICA: Did you see much action?
>
> QUINN COLSON: Mmm-hmm.
>
> JESSICA: Could you tell me a little about that? When did you first see fighting?
>
> QUINN COLSON: I'm sorry. But what exactly does that have to do with Brandon Taylor?

NARRATOR: Even though he wouldn't talk about it, Colson's Army record was easy to access. Like he said, he joined the Army in 1999. He went through basic training at Fort Benning, Georgia, a base he'd return to many times as a member of the elite B Company, Third Battalion, 75th Regiment. We learned a Ranger doesn't just volunteer once but three times. A Ranger must join the Army, sign up for Airborne School, and then go through the rigorous Ranger Indoctrination Program. That's where the Ranger motto, *Sua Sponte*, comes from: Of their own accord. Rangers are known as those in the Army who lead the way, as they often have to clear the most heavily fortified areas in a war zone.

Colson was one of the first into Iraq, securing the Haditha Dam, a highly important target early in the war that the Iraqis threatened to destroy.

> QUINN COLSON: Getting the tab was one of the proudest days of my life. They really put you through hell. It's not just physical. It's mental, too. We start off at Benning and end up down in the swamps of Florida. If you're lucky enough to make it to that point, you haven't slept for days. You do everything you can to keep your mind sharp, focused, on the maneuvers and mission.
>
> JESSICA: Will you tell us about the Silver Star?

QUINN COLSON: I was only doing what I was trained to do.

JESSICA: And what's that?

QUINN COLSON: Neutralize the enemy.

NARRATOR: A newspaper account in the *Army Times* offered a brief narrative of Sergeant Quinn Colson in Afghanistan in 2006. His company was on a nighttime mission in Nangarhar Province when they came under heavy fire immediately after being inserted by helicopter. Sergeant Colson exposed himself to "rigorous gunfire" as he scaled to the highest elevation to knock out enemy targets. The firefight lasted eight hours, until sunup, and Colson protected the lives of his entire company as he called in air strikes.

JESSICA: How many people have you killed?

QUINN COLSON: Over there or in Mississippi?

NARRATOR: Since returning to his home in Jericho, Mississippi, in 2010, Colson has killed several people. One firefight between himself and his deputies and a crew of escaped convicts left four people dead—including the chief and assistant chief of the Jericho Police Department. An inquest into the shooting determined Colson and his chief deputy, Lillie Virgil, killed the police officers—not the convicts—but also determined that the police officers tried to kill Colson first. Colson and Virgil were exonerated, but the violent action and whiff of scandal caused him to lose his second election. The man who won, Rusty Wise, was shot and killed while deer hunting just a few weeks after taking office. Sitting in the deer stand with him and also shot in the ambush—Quinn Colson. Despite a gunshot wound, Colson managed to survive a couple of days alone in the woods and kill his armed attackers. It's significant, because Colson is known around here for once surviving a week lost in the woods when he was just ten years old. News stations from Memphis covered his disappearance, much as they would Brandon Taylor's just seven years later. The difference is Quinn Colson lived through it. He's lived through a lot.

We found several other justified shootings with known criminals, drug dealers, and bank robbers—the usual law enforcement stuff. Too many to focus on in this podcast. One was particularly interesting. Colson was involved in a shoot-out earlier this year with a man named Rick Wilcox, a Marine veteran turned interstate bank robber. While trying to rob a local gentleman's club, Wilcox and his crew killed five bikers paid to protect it. And when Colson arrived on scene, they destroyed his truck with a grenade launcher. Colson and Virgil took Wilcox alive this time. We'd probably tell you about this incident anyway, as it made the national news, but what makes it even more interesting is this: Rick Wilcox had a young son named Brandon, named to honor an old friend of his ex-wife. You know her as Maggie Powers Colson.

So, it's been less than a decade since Quinn Colson came home from two wars. In that time, his sheriff's office has racked up an unusually high body count for a county of this size and attracted statewide attention for their arrests. Not everyone sees this as a good thing.

> PASTOR TIM TRAYLOR: Are we better off with Quinn Colson as our sheriff? I guess it depends on who you ask. I will say Tibbehah County was a lot more quiet under Sheriff Beckett. Sheriff Beckett was a man who liked to keep the peace. It seems like Sheriff Colson is always on a search and destroy mission. That's just what I'm hearing. But who am I to say?

# NINETEEN

"Why do you have to use so much profanity?" Sam Frye asked, driving straight up Highway 45 from the Rez in the dark and the rain. Both hands on the wheel, wipers tick-tocking across the windshield. He had his black hair pulled into a ponytail, his flat black eyes looking up into the rearview mirror to behind them. "Can't you make your music without all those *motherfuckers*, *bitches*, and all that business?"

"'Cause we hard, man," Toby said. "You want those rhymes to drop on your head like a goddamn atom bomb. Why don't you like it? *Damn, it feels good to be a motherfucking Native. You talkin' that shit, we the wrong ones to play with. My tribe and your tribe. Your race and mine. Mississippi Choctaw 'bout to take it to the pines.*"

"Is that your crew?"

"Nah, man," Toby said. "It's Big Savage. He was born in Oklahoma but came back to Mississippi to keep shit real. That's good stuff, man. Big Savage. His last video got like a half-million views on

YouTube. Last time I seen him, he got himself a big ole black-ass Cadillac, spinning rims. Whole inside of that ride shines with electric blue light."

"That's what you see for yourself?" Sam Frye said, eyes on the broken yellow line ahead of him in the slanting rain. "Living large with Cadillacs and rolls of cash?"

"You know it," Toby said. "Shit, man. Beats the fuck out of killing folks for a living. You do this shit long enough and tables gonna turn on your ass. Someone is going to be waiting for us. Like tonight. Rolling the fuck back up in Tibbehah County? You got to be some kind of crazy."

"Not crazy," Sam Frye said. "Tonight, I wait in the car and you go inside and take care of business."

"I don't like it," Toby said. "Shit, man. I heard the sheriff here came down to the Rez, flashing a picture of me at the jail around the casino floor. Chief Robbie saw it. He had to warn the whole fucking tribe to shut their damn mouth."

"I saw the picture," Sam Frye said. "It looked nothing like you or me. Just a blurry photograph and a sketch of what they thought you looked like. But it was nothing. Don't worry about Chief Robbie. He knows what we were sent to do. None of our people will sell us out. That business is all over."

"What's up with the Chief, man?" Toby said, sinking down in his seat, an Oakland Raiders cap with a flat bill down in his eyes. "Why he have us killing these folks up in the damn boogerwoods? What the hell they done to him? Or the tribe?"

"Why does it matter?" Sam Frye said. "If the Chief wants something done, we are the men he sends. This is his decision. It's a high honor."

"And we get paid?"

"We do."

"Hope this shit don't take long," Toby said. "Me and my boys got a party over in Greenville tomorrow night. We sold out this motherfucking club by the railroad station, big-ass old warehouse, moonshine and black women twerking their big asses and all that countrified shit. You'd like it. You should go."

"No thanks."

"How 'bout we stop off at the titty bar on the way back?" Toby said. "I know the little girl I tore up last time would be real glad to see me. Wouldn't mind a little time with her in the champagne room. Let her take my dog out for a little walk."

"Not tonight," Sam Frye said. "Tonight, we drive you far out in the country. We will stay to back unpaved roads where there is little light and no one to see us come or go. You will be the one who'll go into this house and kill the man. Are you ready? Is that something you can do on your own?"

"I've done it before," Toby said.

"Yes," Sam Frye said. "But he was a man you knew and you wanted him dead. This man is nothing. I don't even know what he looks like. Or even his name."

"Then how will you know it's even him?"

"Because there's no one else," Sam Frye said. "He's an old man. He lives alone."

"Why send us?"

Sam Frye shrugged, taking the last exit before the Tibbehah County line, trying to stay away from the big truck stop by the strip club a few miles down. He slowed into a small BP gas station, only four pumps and a little cinder-block store offering bait, tackle, and barbecue. Cajun boiled peanuts and ammo. He killed the lights and headed on inside to pay cash to fill up the tank. It was a wet, slick night and he didn't want to stop again after they'd finished their business. A slick plastic sign popped in the wind reading BUD LIGHT WELCOMES HUNTERS.

When he got back to the car, he saw Toby fingering rounds into a .357 Magnum.

"You found the gun."

"You told me it was under my seat."

"Sometimes you look exactly like your father."

"No thanks," Toby said. "That's not why I do this."

"Not for the tribe?"

"For the goddamn money," Toby Williams said. "The music I make is to honor the history of the tribe. What we're doing here is nothing to be proud of, Sam. We're just taking out the trash for Chief Robbie. Where the fuck is the honor in that?"

E. J. Royce was drunker than a goddamn skunk.

He'd been watching a *Gunsmoke* marathon on the Western Channel since the sun went down and the rain rolled in, trying to get a good look at Miss Kitty. There was something about the way the woman wore those fancy ole-timey dresses and those big hats with ostrich feathers that flat out did it for him. Royce had his pants around his knees waiting for his old parts to spring to life, a box of Kleenex and jar of Vaseline handy, the mood usually hitting him when Miss Kitty stepped on or off a stagecoach. Or when she gave one of those coy side eyes to old Matt Dillon. But at the damn moment, he was forced to watch some cock-and-bull story about Chester heading out of Dodge to go fishing and some captured Injun being brought into the general store by the local agent. The agent had a rope tied around the savage, the man being led around like a dog as he was being forced back to the Cheyenne Rez. That dumb-ass daughter of the store owner getting one look at that big-muscled savage and falling for him even though he doesn't speak a word of English. Royce kept on trying to place the fella playing the Indian agent. Was it Strother Martin?

Damn, where the fuck was Miss Kitty? Hair done up just right, little mole on the side of her mouth. Royce bet she smelled like dusting powder and perfume and would give him a good talking-to. Make him understand manners, a napkin in his lap and how a man should use a knife and fork at the table.

*Nothing.* Royce hitched up his britches and walked back to the table, where he'd set the rest of the Fighting Cock. He found a quarter bottle and three cigarettes left. He lit up a cigarette and poured a good portion of the whiskey in a jelly jar before fanning out the match. The TV now showing the white girl meeting up with the Indian, who'd shook loose of the agent somehow out back of the barn. The damn Indian couldn't say jack shit in English but the word *help*. The white girl told him he needed to go or her daddy was gonna shoot his dick clean off.

It was raining outside, turning the long drive to the main road into a muddy goddamn river. Royce's dogs kept on scratching at his door to let them in, but he'd be goddamned if he'd let those hounds come in and shake their wet coats all over his sofa and chairs. He walked over to a window covered in Visqueen as the lightning flashed across the sky, power dimming and then coming back on. A thin line of electricity running two miles from the other nearest house. If he lost power, it might take those lazy assholes at the co-op three fucking days to fix it, leaving him to live out on the land like goddamn Jeremiah Johnson. The dogs kept scratching.

Royce reached down and picked up his boot off the ground and tossed it at the door. "Shut the hell up."

He headed back for his La-Z-Boy, settling in with a jelly jar full of whiskey. All the racket with the storm and the dogs making him lose the last few minutes of *Gunsmoke*. Still no Miss Kitty, just that white girl and the Indian, the dumb girl now packing up some vittles for him and filling up a canteen full of water. But here comes Chester, riding high and tall on his horse, headed to his fishing hole and coming across the white girl's farm just as she's about to play cornhole with the Indian. If he knew Chester, that boy was about to shoot the ole Injun right in the pecker.

Royce tossed back the rest of the whiskey in the jelly jar. Still had some supper left over on the stove from the Quick Stop, a spicy chicken wing and a whole Styrofoam carton of baked beans and turnip greens. He was about to set down with it when Miss Kitty in that white dress filled him with a sharp, crooked pain.

*Blam!*

Yep, Chester shot that damn Indian, knocking his ass right onto the ground, the white girl springing up and running for him, madder than hell. Chester shocked as could be this white girl knew the boy. *He trusted me and you tried to kill him.*

How could she blame Chester? He thought the Injun was trying to steal a horse. Now she wanted Chester to save his red ass.

What the fuck was the world coming to? He couldn't even watch fucking *Gunsmoke* without being force-fed a goddamn politically correct message. Damn Chester and the Cheyenne now lighting out for the hills before the white girl's daddy came for this red man's pecker. Something about Chester keeping a goddamn promise.

*I'm a friend,* Chester said. A friend. *I got to get that bullet out of you.*

What a bunch of horseshit. He heard thunder and the howls of the dogs. More scratching at the door, the Visqueen in the windows popping and fluttering with the storm.

As the lightning cracked again, he saw something outside that gave him more of a jolt than seeing Miss Kitty's ole red-haired crotch waffle.

"Shit," Royce said, getting to his feet. "Son of a damn bitch. Who's out there? Is that you, Colson?"

Royce had seen a man. The dogs making a big racket now, howling and barking.

"Who the fuck is out there?"

Royce looked for his gun but couldn't find it under the mounds of clothes and old magazines, empty bottles and cigarette cartons. His heart fluttered in his old chest like a wind-up toy. Where the hell did he put his goddamn shotgun? What the fuck was going on outside? He found his pay-as-you-go phone over by the nearly empty bottle of booze and dialed in to the sheriff's office.

"I seen an Indian out there in the rain."

"Mr. Royce, you been drinking again?"

"I know what I saw, some ole Indian sneaking out my property, probably looking to steal a horse. But he ain't gonna find no white girl to save his ass. No, ma'am. I ain't like ole Chester. Ole E. J. Royce shoots to kill if he could find his goddamn weapon."

"We done told you to quit calling, Mr. Royce," the smart-mouth black woman said. "Last time you told me the MS-13 gang was selling drugs down at the Gas & Go in Blackjack. Other time, it was some black girl selling cookies for the Girl Scouts."

"Call the sheriff," Royce said. "Call the goddamn sheriff and tell him what E. J. Royce done seen."

Quinn and Lillie rolled back into Tibbehah County at 2100, heading straight for the sheriff's office, when he got the call from Cleotha, hearing a lot of talk about E. J. Royce's crazy ass. The rain had gotten worse. Quinn slowed his truck, high beams on, as he got off at the first exit, taking the back way into town.

"He said what?" Lillie said.

"Royce said he was under attack by Indians."

"That I'd love to see," Lillie said. "Maybe if he's that damn drunk, he'll tell us the truth about why he's spreading around all that bullshit about you."

"I don't have time for Royce," Quinn said. "You need to get back to Memphis. And I need to get on back home. I'll send a deputy out for a welfare check."

"But Indians," Lillie said. "He said Indians."

"What did you expect?" Quinn said. "Royce never heard about Native Americans. I had to dial it down a good bit last time I saw him at the Piggly Wiggly. I'd just as soon not be in that man's presence. I will never understand how my uncle put up with him."

"I think he felt sorry for him," Lillie said. "Hamp could be charitable to a damn fault. How about we roll on that way and see what we can find? I sure wouldn't mind a few minutes with Royce. I'd love to know who's aiming to make your family look bad."

"We know."

"Skinner, for one," Lillie said. "I bet he'd throw a fucking parade if you got voted out of office. Between all the trouble you caused for him with the supervisors and you going after Vardaman, that's plenty of damn motivation. I've got to be honest with you, Quinn. I'm surprised as hell they hadn't come gunning for you a lot sooner."

Quinn slowed down on the country road, turning on his ticker, slowly stopping in the rain before deciding to take a hard turn north and head on up to Carthage and the wilds of Tibbehah County, where old E. J. Royce lived like he hadn't moved on to a new century.

"Did you ask him about those remains you found?"

"I didn't," Quinn said. "But Dave Cullison went and talked to him. Royce pled ignorance on the matter."

"He's good at that," Lillie said. "What'd you hear back from the state folks?"

"It was a woman's body," Quinn said. "Ophelia Bundren thinks the remains had been buried at least twenty years ago."

"Maybe at the time Brandon Taylor went missing?"

"Maybe," Quinn said. "Bones were pretty busted up. And we still don't have a cause of death. Body was buried nearly ten feet deep."

"With a location passed on by a Brandon Taylor freak who remains unknown to this day," Lillie said. "You got to wonder why the fuck would all this shit start spilling out right now. Brandon Taylor's been dead a hell of a long time and his ass ain't coming back. Who's making trouble? And why?"

"I didn't tell you something," Quinn said, steering around the winding road, headlights still on high, shining up into the tree branches and along the slick pavement. "Maggie and I tried to make contact with whoever was writing those letters."

"And how the hell did that go?" Lillie asked.

"Nothing came of it," Quinn said. "I think I spooked whoever wanted to meet with Maggie."

"When was this?"

"Three weeks back," Quinn said. "This person asked Maggie to meet them at the Flying J up in Olive Branch and not to tell anyone, especially not me. After we found the woman's body, we agreed not to keep any more secrets. Nobody knows anything about this wild card."

"No one showed?"

"Someone showed," Quinn said. "Some man had a waitress pass along a locker key to Maggie. That's how we got the old picture and the necklace. I took a look at the truck stop video, processed the evidence for prints, but didn't get a damn thing. DeSoto County reached out to Memphis TV stations with the video still, asking for tips."

"I have to be honest, too," Lillie said. "I wouldn't put it past your uncle to have muddied the water around the Taylor case. Hamp was a good man and tried to do the right thing. But Lord knows, he failed plenty of times."

Quinn turned onto the road to Carthage, passing through the little grouping of a Dollar General, two gas stations, and a metal shed for deer processing. The dash of his truck glowed in the darkness, a slow rain drumming onto the windshield and cab of the truck. The road snaked through fields and forests, coming up into a thicket of pine trees, skinny cottonwoods along a creek bed. The creek was roiling hard in Quinn's headlights, a muddy slice of water snaking down a rocky drive from up toward Royce's place.

"If you feel the need to slap the taste out his mouth, don't do it," Lillie said. "Just give me the nod and I'll do it for you."

Royce found his shotgun and slung open his front door into the rain. Wind chimes made of old coffee cans and spent bullet casings tinkled like bells on his front porch. He'd pulled on a pair of old boots and a stained work shirt that smelled like the inside of a chicken house. Holding the gun, he nearly got knocked off his feet by the dogs, one of them almost his height as she stood on her hind legs and put her paws on his shoulders. Royce shooed them away, clutching the old J. C. Higgins shotgun loaded with buckshot and salt.

"Who the fuck's out there?" Royce said, yelling into the blackness and rain, stepping out onto the soft ground by his shack. "Better show yourself or you're gonna be picking rock salt out of your asshole in jail, boy. Come on out."

He couldn't see nothing without his glasses, his eyes filling with water. Royce kept the shotgun up in his arms, scanning the cleared land and the edge of the woods. There weren't many places to hide. Behind his truck, maybe, or beyond to his work shed. As he took one step in front of the other, slow and easy, everything looked fuzzy and distorted like some old black-and-white movie. He got to thinking maybe he didn't see nothing at all. Maybe that crazy mix of the Fighting Cock and watching that old episode of *Gunsmoke* had messed up his goddamn mind. His dogs trailed behind him as he passed by the old truck, peeking under the chassis, and then heading out to the shed where he kept his mower and some old tools.

A damn river of mud and shit was eroding his red clay hill, running over his drive and down to the main road. He could feel the wetness soaking into his leather boots as he got to the little tin shed and cut on the lights. The wind whipped the old lamp to and fro, Royce having to squint into the darkness past the heaps of junk he'd collected over the years. Used-up mower blades, empty oil cartons, and busted-up furniture.

He couldn't see nothing and walked on out of the shed, favoring his left leg, the arthritis kicking up in his right, that leg dragging behind him as he got back to the porch. Royce saw the goddamn door was wide open and those dogs were nowhere to be found, probably already ate up his leftover chicken and greens, maybe getting to some of the homemade jerky old Tom Roberts had given him for Christmas. Fucking dogs. Ain't got a lick of sense or no goddamn manners.

Royce left the door open and called out for his hounds, hearing some shuffling in the kitchen. He lay the shotgun on the La-Z-Boy and hobbled on back there in the dark, the power having gone out while he had been outside. There was a breaker box above the commode that maybe he could fiddle with, but he knew he was probably shit out of luck. No more dinner. No more *Gunsmoke*. No more Miss Kitty, with her pretty red hair and high-dollar crotch waffle.

"Git," Royce said, calling out. "Y'all hear me? Git outta there. Leave my supper alone."

Then he heard the dogs outside, baying and barking, tracking some kind of animal out into the woods. He stood there in the kitchen, listening, reaching around the table for his supper, when he looked up and saw the shadow of a man before him.

"If you come to rob me, I don't got shit but the television," Royce said to the shadow. "And it's busted most of the time."

The shadow didn't talk back, Royce now knowing he had seen the man outside his window.

"You that black-eyed Indian?" Royce said. "The same one who shot up the jail?"

The figure didn't move or speak. Royce could hear the tapping of water off the man's jacket, nothing really but a form in front of him.

"Well, goddamn son of a bitch," Royce said. "Go on and get it over with. I should've known I wasn't never getting no payday. Ole E. J. Royce never gets what's coming to him."

The man lifted his hand and Royce could clearly see the gun. The man stepped forward, Royce seeing it was a goddamn Indian but also a fucking kid. Royce smiled, hacking out a laugh, the boy wearing a silly-ass hat like some kind of black man would wear. That boy didn't look like nothing but a cheap filling station thief.

"Don't go on and get stupid, boy," Royce said. "That pistol in your hand ain't no fucking toy."

And the damn Indian shot him. Royce fell back, slamming onto the kitchen table and scattering the baked beans and greens, the pint of Fighting Cock shattering on the floor. Royce held on to his chest, feeling blood and so much pain he couldn't even mouth the words for mercy. And then the second shot came and it was all over.

Quinn stopped at Royce's old blue mailbox and knocked his truck into four-wheel drive, turning up onto the eroding gravel road and heading toward the old shack on top of the hill. Lillie popped some chewing gum as she watched the truck's bright lights wash over Royce's place, saying even dogs deserved better shelter.

"Doesn't look like he's here," Lillie said.

"He's here," Quinn said. "There's his truck."

Quinn slowed and stopped close to the front door of the shack, a group of a half-dozen Walker hounds coming out to greet them as he got out. Lillie followed, pulling on the hood of a black slicker, the truck's headlights shining up onto the porch and into the darkness. Quinn reached down for his radio mic and called in the location to Cleotha and hit the light bars to make sure the old man didn't come out shooting.

Lillie pulled the Sig Sauer off her belt and headed up for the porch.

"I thought you said to take it easy," Quinn said.

"This is easy," Lillie said.

Quinn carried the old Winchester lever-action he'd brought with him to the range. He called out to Royce, seeing the shoddy aluminum storm door was wide open, battering against the wall. He called out again. The door kept hammering against the siding.

The dogs started to bark—rapid, high barks—as if they were on the trail of something. Lillie nodded to Quinn and followed the barking around the back of the property. The storm had passed, but thunder rolled in the distance as he walked up onto the porch and into the house. Another dog headed out to greet him, wagging its tail.

Quinn reached for a small flashlight he kept on his belt and shone it around the inside of the shack, the place smelling like a damp ashtray, wet dogs, and kerosene. He aimed the light over an easy chair and old couch, mounds of clothes and trash scattered around the floor. Quinn had been in the shack before and never knew how a human being could live in such filth. As he turned back to a far window, the electricity cut on, the overhead lights brightening the room, the television flashing on as Royce's satellite worked to regain the signal. Matt Dillon appeared as a drawing that morphed into the man as he reached for his six-shooter and shot toward the screen. The volume turned up high for Royce's deaf ears, filling the silence. *James Arness as Matt Dillon. Dennis Weaver as Chester. Milburn Stone as Doc. And Amanda Blake as Miss Kitty.*

He heard a snuffling and rooting around in the kitchen, Quinn seeing the backs of two dogs hunkered over something that had fallen on the floor. There was the smacking, lapping sounds of dogs eating. As he passed by the kitchen table, he saw a man's legs and a pair of muddy boots, the cracked linoleum floor splattered with blood.

Another gunshot cracked. Quinn looked back to the TV but it wasn't *Gunsmoke*. Two more quick shots from a handgun.

Quinn ran outside and back around Royce's house, Lillie standing by a stretch of apple trees, her arms stretched out with the Sig.

"He had a gun," Lillie said.

Quinn nodded, scanning the woods line, searching for the shooter as he reached for his radio. Rain pelted Quinn's back as Lillie wandered up close to him.

"Royce is dead," Quinn said.

"This boy wouldn't stop," Lillie said. "When I yelled out to him, he turned and raised his gun. I hit him, Quinn. He couldn't have gone far."

Quinn reached down for a hat on the ground, a flat-billed Oakland Raiders baseball cap. "Could it be one of our guys?"

"Looked like a Native kid to me," Lillie said. "Just like Royce said. I guess even liars tell the truth once in a while."

"We better get this secured fast," Quinn said. "Royce's dogs were already getting to him, making a mess of the crime scene."

"Dogs," Lillie said, shaking her head. "They'll damn near eat anything."

* * *

Sam Frye sat in the idling car, looking out into the rain, when he spotted Toby stumbling from the woods. The boy holding his stomach, falling down to his knees. Sam ran out and grabbed the boy, helping him into the backseat, finding an old towel to hold to the gunshot.

"Cops," Toby said. "They came from fucking nowhere, Sam."

"Don't talk," he said. "I'll get help. Just breathe and lay back. I know many back roads to the Rez. Hold tight. We'll get you fixed up, son. You hear me?"

Toby didn't answer and Sam looked back in the rearview, seeing the boy curled into a ball with the pain. He turned on his high beams, taking a wide turn down south, trying to get out of Tibbehah County as fast as they'd come. There was a good doctor at the Rez, an old friend, who never asked questions with wounds like this. If they didn't have any more trouble, he could get Toby there in thirty minutes.

"You with me?" Sam Frye said. "Hold that towel tight. Keep all that blood in."

"Goddamn, it hurts," Toby said. "Damn, Sam. Holy fucking shit."

"Hold on," Sam Frye said, high beams soon hitting the county line sign. "I've been shot many times. It hurts like a bastard. But you grit your teeth, do what you need to do to stop that bleeding. Just breathe. You can breathe, right? Breathe with me, son."

"Damn, they got me good. I feel like my whole goddamn stomach got shot out. Fucking shit, man."

"This isn't the life for you," Sam Frye said. "We get you home, get you healed, and I don't want you to mess with this stuff. You say you like to make music? Make your music. Go party. Drink, smoke some weed. Go meet some nice girls. And bad ones, too. But this life? What me and your father got into is no way to live. You were right. Get out before it eats you whole. Once you head down this path, there is nowhere else to go. Nothing else for you to do. You understand? Do you understand me?"

Toby didn't answer, and somewhere miles and miles from the Rez, on a long, dark country road, Sam Frye pulled off into a clearing. It was still raining as he cut on the overhead light and turned toward the backseat. Toby stared, wide-eyed and open-mouthed, the front of his shirt covered in blood, as his loose fingers held a red-stained towel.

"They didn't get you," Sam Frye said. "You were never caught. You did real good. Now it's time to take you home. We're going home, son."

Sam Frye turned off the overhead light and knocked the sedan into drive, slowly heading up onto the back road, driving that steady speed limit, and checking his rearview until he could see the bright casino lights miles away. A billboard ahead promising THE FIRST JACKPOT YOU'LL WIN IS BY WALKING THROUGH OUR DOORS!

# TWENTY

It had been five days since E. J. Royce got himself killed when Caddy headed up to Memphis with Tashi Coleman. She wanted to shut down all the bullshit, the questions, and innuendo around her brother. Those girls from New York not having a damn clue on how Tibbehah County worked, listening to anyone who'd run their mouths. If she could find Ansley Cuthbert maybe she could not only help them out, but also stop all the lies about Quinn. They roamed up Highway 45 to Tupelo and then cut up to Memphis on 78, passing the exits to Holly Springs and Red Banks. Caddy had made the trip so many times, she felt she could drive it blind.

"I saw two girls on the Square yesterday with blue hair," Caddy said. "I think your friend Jessica is making a style contribution to Jericho."

"She's made a lot of friends," Tashi said, driving her small blue rental with Caddy beside her. "That girl is good at getting people to talk, open up. She just has a way of getting sources to trust her."

"I know you didn't ask but I'm going to say it anyway," Caddy said. "Quinn and Lillie didn't have a damn thing to do with that old man's death. Royce was one of the biggest crooks in the county, no telling what he found himself trapped in."

"Did you hear about his dogs?" Tashi said, turning on her headlights, the sky darkening as they got close to the Tennessee line. Not really answering Caddy but not challenging her on it, either.

"Yes, ma'am," Caddy said. "Everyone heard that detail about the dogs. Betty Jo Mize said it was too awful to print in her family newspaper. I think she worded it that the body had been ravaged by animals."

"That made it seem like wild animals or vultures, not his own dogs," Tashi said. "God. How could his own dogs do something like that?"

Caddy told her that if it was all the same, she'd rather not talk about it. The whole thing making her sick to her stomach, saying she always knew there was something the matter with Royce. "When I was a kid, his eyes would just kind of linger on you. He was a deputy and worked for my uncle so I believed he was important. But what kind of man stares like that at a young girl, telling her how she's filling out and that she has a nice figure?"

Tashi didn't say anything, listening as she drove, heading past Olive Branch and that big Ford dealership, a supersized Walmart, and a grouping of the regular suspects of Starbucks, Applebee's, and an O'Charley's.

"When we were kids, we had to drive up to Memphis to go shopping," Caddy said. "It always seemed like the center of our Southern universe."

"Just how long did you live in Memphis?" Tashi asked.

"Too damn long," Caddy said. "About four years."

"Why'd you leave home?"

"You've been there," Caddy said. "Does Tibbehah seem like the kind of place a woman in her twenties would want to live?"

"Oh, I don't know," Tashi said, both hands gripping the wheel, intently staring at the rainy highway ahead through those thick black glasses. "I think Jericho is a pretty charming little town. With the Square and all those little restaurants and shops. I get a little tired of Brooklyn's preciousness. Jericho is real to me. Real South. Real America."

"Maybe too real at times," Caddy said. "There wasn't much on the Square when I left. Nearly every business was boarded up. Most of the buildings had fallen in on themselves. Vines and weeds growing through the busted glass. Looked like the A-bomb had hit the town. It was either be a checkout girl at the Piggly Wiggly or marry some loser and be trapped forever."

"What about college?"

"Ha," Caddy said. "Not everyone can go to college. You either get a scholarship or your family has money. My family's not poor, but they didn't have the money to send me or Quinn to school. My daddy rarely paid child support. And my momma worked when she could, receptionist-type jobs at the high school or some doctor's office. It was tough. The way you see Jericho now isn't the way it was. When the recession hit, we barely even knew it."

"Was Memphis better?" Tashi asked.

"For a while," Caddy said. "When I was clean. But you can't do the kind of work I was doing sober."

"As a dancer?"

Caddy laughed, sort of snorting through her nose. This girl really was on her best behavior, really wanting to find Ansley Cuthbert by calling Caddy a dancer. There wasn't a thing about dancing in her whole show, although back then she might have argued it. She used to have a canned answer about song selection, acrobatics, and connecting with her customer. In truth, all she did was show her tits and grind her hips for more than minimum wage.

"Is that not right?" Tashi asked.

"No, ma'am," Caddy said. "I was anything but a dancer. Do you want to see where I worked?"

"Was that where Ansley worked, too?" Tashi asked, heading over the Tennessee state line. THE VOLUNTEER STATE WELCOMES YOU.

"She got me my first job," Caddy said. "She was stripping first. I met her out in Memphis at some club, drinking and partying like you do when you're that age. Right? Ansley always seemed to have money. The best clothes. Hair and nails done, lots of jewelry. And boys. Damn, Ansley Cuthbert was the queen bee. When you met her out, she'd have a minimum of six, eight boys buzzing around her."

Caddy looked out at the dark, rainy landscape, the trucking companies, garages, liquor stores, pool halls, and cut-rate motels. This was always the crossover, the river of grit, before you got into Memphis proper. It was still early, but girls were working the big truck stop by Shelby Drive. Across the street was a Best Western that used to rent out rooms by the hour, one of the closest motels to Dixie Belles, a regular for businessmen who didn't want to take their girls back to the Peabody or the Madison downtown. There was a barbecue restaurant in the lobby and Jacuzzis in every room. Sometimes she'd fly so goddamn high she didn't realize or give a damn where she was headed, only that the money was right and she got paid up front. Those four years never seemed real to her, nothing but images from a fuzzy dream, anesthetized to pain and feeling nothing but indifference. Shots of Goldschläger, big glasses of Jack Daniel's, lots of blow on little compact mirrors, Ecstasy, enough weed to choke a goat, and finally stuff you shot into your veins, pushing the plunger to unclog your fucking head and feel even less. There used to be a Western-wear shop on the corner behind the Wendy's where she'd buy getups for her stage show, belt buckles and big hats, fancy boots and spurs. Now the shop was gone, only a big ceramic red boot out by the highway.

"Tell me where to turn."

Everything was the same but different. Across the highway from an old farmhouse where she used to shoot up was a sprawling intermodal facility, slapping Conex containers onto 18-wheelers or loading them onto trains. Giant cranes, lit up in the dark, lifted those big containers from a stacked maze of hundreds and put them onto the right track and the hell out of Memphis. In the light and the rain, the whole setup looked like a kid's toy room, an Erector Set with train tracks.

"Here," Caddy said.

Tashi turned west on Winchester, past the old Americana Club, which used to be the Eagle's Nest, where her mother said Elvis had his very first gig. When Caddy worked here it was a Mexican club, full of undocumented workers and Norteño bands playing long into the night. Caddy recalled going there one night after hours and watching a man bleed out in the parking lot from stab wounds. Holding his hand until the paramedics came, long after he died. She had prayed to him in English. He didn't understand a damn word.

"Dixie Belles?"

"That's it," Caddy said. "See that place? It's one place that hasn't changed."

The building looked like a neon wedding cake, four times the size of Vienna's back in Jericho, with eight stages and two VIP rooms. The sign outside boasted a nationally known porn star who said she had sex with the president of the United States. Tashi slowed in the parking lot. A muscular man with a shaved head stood under the portico by a long black limousine. Just being back here shortened her breath, made her sweat a little, the neon glow shining onto her face.

She closed her eyes, her pulse racing. She could do this. She could do this.

"Why'd you quit?"

"Are you kidding?" Caddy said, taking a deep breath. "Come on inside. I'll show you exactly how it used to be."

"We don't have to," Tashi said. "I can stop recording."

Caddy reached for her door handle. "Quit trying to be empathic and come on," she said. "Keep that mic out of sight. Some girls might get a little paranoid."

"You always take your dog to work with you?" Fannie Hathcock asked Quinn.

"Depends," Quinn said.

"On what?"

"On whether Hondo feels like work," Quinn said, reaching down to scratch the cattle dog's head. "Sometimes he just feels like sleeping on the front porch. Older he gets, the lazier he gets."

Quinn was working late, taking over for Reggie, who had a sick wife at home and two young kids. Fannie had wandered in unannounced, knocking on his half-open door, dressed in a tight-fitting black dress with a plunging neckline and lacy straps. Her silver ruby locket hung down between her large breasts as she leaned against the doorframe. She looked worn out, with tired, reddened eyes.

"You just coming from a party?" Quinn said, pushing back from writing a report on his laptop and looking up at Fannie. The visit was a surprise and a rare occasion.

"A funeral," Fannie said. "In New Orleans. I just got back and heard about all the action the other night. I know you say you didn't shoot that Royce fella in the head. But I couldn't blame you, Sheriff. The man was bad for business. He was the kind of creepy old coot who'd show up with a dozen roses from the Piggly Wiggly to hand out to some teenage girls."

"You won't have to worry about that anymore," Quinn said.

"I heard y'all shot who did it," Fannie said. "Maybe the same fella who killed Wes Taggart?"

Quinn shrugged but didn't say anything about the hat they'd found or that they believed there was a second shooter who had escaped Royce's place, the older man in the video footage from the jail.

"A shame you shot him," Fannie said. "If you ever find him, tell him he's got free lap dances all night long. Royce and Wes Taggart. A goddamn two-for-one special."

Quinn kicked up his boots, watching Fannie stroll toward the open seat in front of his desk, his door still cracked open in case anyone wanted to walk in. You didn't have closed-door meetings with a woman like Fannie Hathcock if you wanted to keep your job. He wished Hondo could've been a witness to whatever she came to discuss. Setting his boots at the edge of his desk, he said, "What's on your mind, Fannie?"

Fannie sat down, resting her elbow on her knee, her hand cupping her face, looking up at him with those tired eyes. "How's Bradley Wayne?"

"Fine, last time I checked," Quinn said. "Calmed down a lot since that first day. I think he's about to bail out, finally."

"I appreciate what you did for Dana Ray," Fannie said. "It's why I always ask for you special. You seem to have a soft place for the working girls. I don't think I've met a stripper yet who didn't have bad taste in men. I guess it goes with the job. But, goddamn, when I was working the pole, I was a little more careful where my money went. You have to tip the damn house, the bouncer, the DJ. I'd be damned if some lazy peckerhead would be getting my earnings."

"You could have called," Quinn said. "Cleotha would have been happy to give you an inmate report. Jail records are also available online, twenty-four hours, and up-to-date."

"You don't like me," Fannie said. "Do you?"

"I like you fine, Miss Hathcock."

"Christ," she said. "Don't call me that. Some simpleminded folks make more of it than it is. Men seem to resent a bossy woman, seem to think it means I got something tucked between my legs."

Quinn smiled. "I never thought that, Fannie. Ever."

"Good."

Fannie sat up straight, both hands on her knees now, jutting out her sizable chest in the tight velvet dress. In the bright light of the sheriff's office it looked as if she'd been crying, mascara muddied around the corner of her eyes. He didn't say a word. The window open in his office, letting in the cool night air.

"When someone close to you dies," Fannie said, "you kind of take stock in your life, think on things you might want to do better. I hate we haven't been better friends since I came to town. I blame most of it on Lillie Virgil, who did truly have some kind of hard-on for me. That woman looks at me like I'm dog shit on the bottom of her shoe."

"Is that it?" Quinn said. "You want to be better friends?"

Fannie lifted her eyes and tilted her head. She was a pretty woman, striking as hell, with all that red hair and wide-set eyes and full red lips. Some might have said she was a little too voluptuous but not Quinn. Fannie Hathcock distributed what she had into all the right places. "I think you and I share a similar problem."

Quinn didn't answer, shutting his laptop and reaching for his mug of coffee at the edge of his desk. He let her finish, fill in the long pauses, with whatever she came to discuss.

"Ole Man Skinner chaps my ass," Fannie said. "He doesn't like either of us. And he's done everything he can to run us both out of town."

"How's that working for him?" Quinn said.

"Don't laugh," Fannie said. "I'm goddamn serious. You and I both know who he's friends with and what the man is capable of doing. All this horseshit about family values and turning back the clock to sucking your momma's titty in Mayberry is crap. They don't want morality, whatever that is. What they want is complete control. And Skinner and Vardaman won't have it with us around."

Quinn nodded. "You coming to me with a plan?"

"No," Fannie said, whispering now and leaning into the desk, her violet eyes big and serious. They were co-conspirators now. She placed a hand on his desk and looked back at the open door. "I came to you with a warning."

Quinn nodded. He didn't touch his coffee, listening to what the truck stop madam had to offer.

"You know a punk kid named Bentley Vandeven from Jackson?"

"I do."

"I heard he's gotten real close to your sister," Fannie said, now smoothing out the dress over her full thighs. "You do know who his people are and what they do?"

Quinn nodded.

"And it doesn't give you pause? A spoiled little shithead like him singing hymns at some busted-ass church in Tibbehah County? Men like that don't change their ways. They don't have a fucking calling. You might ask yourself, who the fuck is this son of a bitch sniffing around my sister? And what the hell does he need up in Tibbehah County?"

"I know he's connected," Quinn said. "And I know he's rich. My father used to shoe horses for his family."

"Goddamn you, Quinn Colson," Fannie said, standing up. "You don't know the fucking half of it. Why don't you check up on Vandeven's daddy and see whose golden apple he's been polishing for a while. I wouldn't want my sister within a thousand goddamn feet of those people."

* * *

"Wow," Tashi Coleman said. "Just wow."

Tashi and Caddy were now at a dive bar on Madison Avenue in midtown Memphis called the Lamplighter. They'd spent more than two hours at the strip club. All that smoke and cherry-scented perfume had been a little much for Tashi. She needed a drink in a bad way. They sat at a tattered booth across from the old jukebox playing some classic soul. Syl Johnson, Ann Peebles, Otis Clay. Above the jukebox was a velvet painting of Elvis Presley as a toreador fighting a bull.

Caddy sipped on a Coca-Cola while Tashi downed a Pabst Blue Ribbon. They'd gotten a tip at Dixie Belles that Ansley Cuthbert used to tend bar here and still hung out on occasion. So far no one seemed to know her. Caddy and Tashi decided to stick around for a few more songs, Tashi ordering a second beer and a shot, asking Caddy if she wouldn't mind driving them back to Tibbehah County. The jukebox now playing "Take Me to the River."

"Haven't you ever been in a strip club before?" Caddy Colson asked, which might sound like a strange question coming from a woman known for her rural outreach ministry. Caddy wore her hair in a short pixie cut, dressed in a neat little cowboy shirt and with a simple silver cross around her neck. She looked like she should be teaching Sunday school and probably did.

"Of course I've seen strippers," Tashi said, turning up the bottle of Pabst, feeling more at home and safe here than at the club. This place reminded her of plenty of dive bars she frequented back in Brooklyn with Jessica and their friends. A place where you kept quarters handy for the old jukebox and kicked back with a game of darts or foosball. The light was dim from a few vintage lamps and beer signs. There were shabby chairs and a threadbare sofa, a short little bar toward the back where they sold bottles of cheap beer and made burgers and grilled cheese sandwiches.

"But not a strip club like that," Caddy said, smiling at Tashi.

"No," Tashi said. "I guess not. I guess I've been to more like burlesque shows my friends were in. They'd dress up in retro lingerie and do routines to Billie Holiday or the Beastie Boys. Dixie Belles was a little more explicit. That show with those two girls in the canary cage . . ."

"It wasn't a show," Caddy said. "It was an anatomy lesson. Maybe I'm nostalgic, but I remember working the pole more in my day."

Tashi smiled. "Did you have any favorites?"

Caddy played with the straw in her glass of Coke, looking up and shrugging. "Oh, I don't know. I guess I really responded to G N' R. Anytime I took the stage, the DJ had me on a rotation of 'Sweet Child O' Mine' and 'November Rain.' Oh, I did have this great routine to 'Welcome to the Jungle.' Oh, God. I found this leopard-print bikini and this necklace made out of bones that just made the men go crazy. That was something I only did on a hot night, when I knew the money was there. It was something kind of special."

"Sounds like you didn't hate it," Tashi said. "At the time."

"Are you recording me?" Caddy asked. "Because it's a little difficult to explain."

Tashi nodded, the microphone right there in plain view on the table. She carried it with her so much people forgot it was even on. Caddy looked like she might have changed her mind about talking about this stuff, her face changing a little bit in the bar light, looking over at a life-sized cutout of Vampirella, the sexy bloodsucking heroine. Tashi had seen one of the films at the Spectacle on cult movie night.

"Hold that thought."

"What is it?"

Caddy Colson was already up out of her chair and headed to the bar. A dark-headed woman in her thirties leaned over it to talk to the bartender. The girl had on old Levi's and a man's white tank top, showing off a sleeve tattoo on her left arm. Her black hair tied up in a red bandanna like Rosie the Riveter. When she saw Caddy, she jumped up in excitement and wrapped her arms around her in a big embrace. Tashi stayed at the table, drinking her beer, still trying to come down from being in that club for the last hour. The bad music, the horrible smell of air fresheners and disinfectant, the live sex acts she'd watched performed on stage, would stay with her for a while. She reached for the shot of Jack Daniel's and tossed it back. God, she hoped this story was headed somewhere.

Caddy waved her over. Tashi met the two women at the bar. The girl with the sleeve tat a little glassy-eyed and giggly. She cut a glance over at Caddy and then back at Tashi. "Did you really think I was dead? Now, that's funny."

Bentley had been coming to the same steakhouse in Jackson since he was a kid. His dad used to take him in the dank, smoky building and set him up at the bar, ordering a Roy Rogers and a Macallan neat, making a joke to the bartender about who got the scotch. Everyone there seemed to know his dad, bringing him a second drink without asking, not ever needing to know how he liked his filet cooked. Before they added flat-screens to the restaurant walls, next to all the pictures of athletes, politicos, and country stars, Bentley used to just sit there alone and observe. Gray-headed men huddled over small tables, cigarettes burning in ashtrays, conferring in private. His dad often disappeared back behind the bar and through the swinging doors to the kitchen. Where did he go? Bentley didn't know and only asked once, his dad winking at him behind the wheel of the big black Mercedes he always kept. "Tasting the soup," he said.

The steakhouse had been there ever since he could remember, a small stand-alone building toward the county line, anonymous and tucked away among all the gas stations, motels, and strip malls. Sitting at the bar now, he made small talk with a waitress, feeling bad for her having to wear a tight black T-shirt and black jogging shorts, old men eyeing her as she held trays loaded down with bloody steaks and fat baked potatoes. Her tee so tight it looked like it was about to bust.

"Where's your dad?" she asked.

"He's coming."

"He sure is funny."

"Oh, yes," Bentley said. "This is his second home."

"How about another?" she asked, pointing at his glass.

Bentley looked up and grinned. "Twist my arm."

The waitress brought him another full glass of Maker's Mark, writing her phone number and a smiley face in the corner of the napkin. Bentley could never tell if the girls here really liked him or only cared about his family. Either way, he couldn't call. He had too much trouble as it was and planned to get good and stinking drunk tonight. He'd leave his car here and Uber it back to his apartment. He was supposed to be back in Tibbehah County, doing whatever it was he was supposed to be doing for his foundation, by noon tomorrow. A new grant. Finish that all-purpose building for Caddy.

He sipped his bourbon, studying his face behind the bar—delicate yet handsome, is what his mother would say. He lifted the drink and toasted no one in particular. A pro football game played on all six screens in the room as he sat there alone, a bowl of mixed nuts in front of him instead of dinner, waiting to be ushered back to taste the fucking soup.

The goddamn thing of it all was he never intended to get in so far. He figured he really might be doing some good up there, his family always looking to give away money, as that was the best way to get your picture in the society rags. And, damn, if his mother didn't love hosting a party. Her acceptance and appreciation of Caddy Colson was real. Caddy Colson was exactly the kind of tragic case she just ached for. His daddy, on the other hand . . . His daddy had other ideas.

Bentley took a sip, lifting his eyes again beyond his shaggy-haired reflection and over at the flat-screen, watching the Titans taking on the Texans. He really could give two shits about pro football, those spoiled rich assholes trying to knock one another's goddamn heads off. Once those boys left Ole Miss, he was done with them and on to the next season.

"Are you gonna eat?" the waitress asked, back now, even more flirty, standing close, resting her bare arm on the bar. She even did a nice little hair flip, playing a little with the ends.

"Waiting."

"OK," she said. "You tell me if you need anything at all."

Damn. Caddy. He liked her. He really did. Bentley had gotten into north Mississippi politics on his dad's urging back when Stagg ran the show. There was even a time when he thought he had a true partner in Jason Colson. The entire point of him being up there was to work as a go-between for Stagg and his daddy's friends. But when Jason bailed again—no wonder his kids hated him—he was left to comfort Caddy, check in with her, spend some time at the waystation she called The River, and keep tabs on the new people, Skinner and that nasty bitch, Fannie Hathcock. How damn stupid had Bentley gotten to believe he was now doing some good, drinking the holy water Kool-Aid Caddy Colson served at her Sunday service? What in the world would his pals at Jackson Prep and Ole Miss think about him now? Maybe his daddy had been right. After the party at their horse barn when his dad met Caddy, he told Bentley, "Why don't you learn from your mother? You can sleep with country trash, but don't bring 'em back to where you live."

The story he told Caddy about his dad and rehab had been partly true. His mother wanted to hold an intervention. The only problem was no one wanted to come and tell his daddy how to do his business. It wasn't an all-out lie, more of a way to assimilate with whatever Caddy had been through. He was a little jealous of her strength, that she'd undergone an actual trial by fire and had walked out stronger and even more faithful to God. That was a hell of a thing, something that, as a faltering believer, he truly admired. Caddy Colson had guts. And she was so goddamn beautiful. She wasn't some spray-tanned honey from the Delta. Caddy Colson was the first true woman he'd ever been with.

Bentley felt a solid clasp on his shoulder and looked up to see the manager of the steakhouse. A short, squat Greek man who'd been there for years and years, a brother-in-law to the owner. Bentley left his bourbon and followed the man behind the bar and through the swinging doors of the kitchen, the steaks hissing and burning on the grill, black men in all white tending to hot bread and making salads. None of them looked up from what they were doing, knowing never to make eye contact with those headed into the back room.

The door was open and the manager spread his arms wide to welcome him in. The room nothing too fancy—wood-paneled walls, a long bookcase filled with footballs from bowl games and trophies from celebrity golf tournaments. A few pictures of pro wrestlers and a lot with the steakhouse owner and a big-titted blonde woman fishing and playing golf. A half-dozen men sat at a long table in red leather swivel chairs. It could've been any conference room in corporate America.

Although his father wasn't there, Bentley knew all the men. And at the head of the table, J. K. Vardaman stood and offered him a seat at the end. There were no handshakes. Another waitress in a tight top and jogging shorts appeared to take new drink orders. Vardaman, tanned and silver-headed, placed reading glasses at the end of his nose and looked down at a legal pad. "Let's cut the bullshit, gentlemen, and get right down to business. How about one of you boys go shut that goddamn door."

The old men looked to Bentley. He got up and closed the door with a sharp click.

"God, I haven't seen you for how long?" Ansley Cuthbert said, turning up a cold Pabst, looking like a Southern version of Amy Winehouse, with her stiff-teased hair up in the red bandanna and with sharp-drawn eye makeup. "Five years? Ten years? I wanted to find you so many times, Caddy, but I knew what you had been doing back home and didn't want to make any trouble. I wasn't so sure you wanted to hear from me."

Tashi didn't say a word, sitting beside Caddy Colson in a worn-out booth under a blazing PABST BLUE RIBBON neon sign, wondering if any of the audio would be worth a crap so close to the jukebox. She'd watched Ansley Cuthbert load a pocket full of quarters to play nothing but Johnny Cash and Elvis. *Get rhythm when you get the blues . . .*

"More like ten," Caddy said. "And you can come see me anytime. I'm not embarrassed by my past. You know how Jericho can be. Everyone knows it anyway. What does it even matter?"

"How's your kid?" Ansley asked. "A son. Right?"

"Jason," Caddy said. "He's eleven."

"And you're a preacher now?" Ansley said.

"Never," Caddy said. "I run a nonprofit out toward Sugar Ditch that helps low-income families with meals, healthcare, and spiritual growth."

"Damn, girl," Ansley said. "Look at you. Me? I'm still slinging cocktails five nights a week at a new place over by Overton Square. They call me a master mixologist, whatever the hell that is. I work part-time at Goner Records and volunteer some at the Pink Palace. I guess that's something. Better than the old days. Oh, God. I'm sorry. I shouldn't talk about back then, should I? I'm so sorry."

Caddy shook her head as she placed her hand on Ansley's leg and told her there were no secrets between them. Tashi studied the long curl of tattoos on Ansley's left arm, trying to decipher their meaning. The tattoos were well done, all in black ink. Stars, a Buddha, a black rose, Escher's twirling staircase. And a year. 1997? Did she see that? Ansley caught Tashi staring, moved her arm off the table, and turned to her with a smile.

"I heard y'all were in Tibbehah," Ansley said, leaning forward, gripping her left elbow with her right hand, covering up the tattoo. "That Brandon Taylor thing is a real sad story. Do y'all really think someone killed him?"

"We think there is a strong possibility," Tashi said. "Did you hear the sheriff's office dug up a body of a young woman on the same land where Brandon used to hunt?"

"No kidding?" Ansley said, nodded, taking a long sip of beer, closing her eyes for a moment and then opening them again. "That sure is something. Do you have a picture of Jason, Caddy? God, I'd love to see him."

"I wonder if you might talk to me outside?" Tashi asked. "It's hard to hear over Johnny Cash."

"You don't like Johnny Cash?" Ansley asked, with a little bit of an edge.

"No, I love him," Tashi said. "But we need to talk."

"About what?"

"Brandon Taylor," Tashi said. "That's why we're here. I know you were close friends."

"Sure, I knew him," Ansley said. "So what? Did you track me down for that, Caddy? Shit. I thought we were friends. When did I ever talk to you about Brandon? That was a long time ago. And private. Christ Almighty."

"You told me he was your boyfriend," Caddy said. "You said you loved him and that his dying about busted you in two."

"Bullshit." Ansley crawled out of the booth, knocking her beer over and not bothering to pick it up. "I don't give a damn about that crazy-ass kid."

Hands on her hips, Ansley looked down into the booth at Caddy and Tashi sitting side by side. Some of the spilled beer poured into Tashi's lap, but she didn't look away from Ansley Cuthbert. That woman knew a hell of a lot more than she was saying.

"I'm sorry," Caddy said. "I wouldn't have said anything if I didn't think this was important."

"Who else did you tell about me?" Ansley asked, arms crossed over her chest.

"No one," Caddy said.

"Do you promise?"

"Of course, Ansley," Caddy said. "Listen, you can trust this woman. She's been told a pack of lies about Quinn and Brandon having some fight over hunting land. I need you to explain that time to her. No one knew Brandon better."

"Quinn and Brandon?" Ansley said. "God. Where'd she hear shit like that? Those two didn't exactly run in the same circles. Did Quinn even know Brandon? Quinn was a lot older."

"Right," Caddy said. "Can you just sit back down and talk? All you need to do is set a few things straight. That's all. I promise."

Ansley closed her eyes, took in a deep breath, and shook her head as if deciding something. "I can't," Ansley said. "I can't do it. I talk to you and they'll know where to find me. I've kept free of this shit for too many years. *Goddamn it.* Why the hell did you have to bring Tashi Coleman up to Memphis? That's not how it was supposed to work."

That stopped Tashi cold, looking at Caddy in the booth and back at Ansley Cuthbert. "How was it supposed to work, Ansley? Were you the one who first reached out to us? You can talk to me. On or off the record. I'll keep your whereabouts safe. I promise."

"'I promise, I promise,'" Ansley said, mocking her. "God. Is there any more foul a statement? Everyone lies. Everyone promises you something. And then you're left with a big steaming pile of dog shit at your front door. Not this time, girls. I'm fucking out of here. And don't you dare try and find me. I don't want a goddamn thing to do with those people."

"What people?" Tashi asked. But Ansley was already out the door.

"Sorry," Caddy said.

"Will she come around?"

"Ansley Cuthbert?" Caddy said. "Oh, hell, you never know. That girl has always been a wild card."

# TWENTY-ONE

Quinn wasn't exactly sure how they ended up in bed, but there they were, he and Maggie, twisted under a white sheet trying to catch their breath. The topic of conversation hadn't been all that sexy, Quinn leaving the late shift that morning, carrying the news of the forensics on the girl they found out at the Pennington property. Maggie had dropped off Brandon at school, still dressed in sweatpants and a T-shirt, drinking coffee on the porch when he got back to the farmhouse. He sat on the porch with her and laid out all of it. The girl was a teen or in her early twenties, buried at least twenty years ago, maybe more, the state folks saying she died from a massive blow to the head, several broken bones. They said her skull had been cracked in a dozen places, leaving them with a probable cause of death.

Maggie, as Quinn knew she would, said the girl was now definitely connected to Brandon. The letter, the location, now the time. Quinn didn't disagree, going back in the house for a cup of coffee, joining her on the porch swing to talk about forensics and horrible ways to die. It was a beautiful morning, bright blue and a little chilly, the leaves on the oaks and pecans just starting to turn.

"Any idea who she was?"

"Nope."

"Any chance you'll find out?"

"We're checking through missing persons reports from back then," Quinn said. "If we get a possible match, there's always dental records to compare. But that's on down the line. Maybe some DNA. Still finding out about that."

"Damn," Maggie said. "Just damn."

Hondo came running up from the barn and headed up the steps, tongue lolling from his mouth, panting hard. Maggie said he'd been in the pasture earlier in the morning herding cows and rolling in cow shit with even more enthusiasm. Quinn wasn't mad, just glad the old boy was still trying to keep up with his work. He had a lot more gray around his eyes and muzzle. Still a strong and tough dog. Quinn scratched his pointy ears.

"I wanted to tell you first," Quinn said.

"Thank you."

"And I'm sorry."

"For what?" Maggie said.

"You know what? I don't really know. I guess I'm just sorry all this has come back on you. I know you didn't come back to Tibbehah County to get into all this mess. Especially with what you went through with Rick."

"Me?" she asked. "He blew up *your* truck."

"Yeah," Quinn said. "You're right. I sure did love that truck."

Maggie nodded, kicking the swing back and forth. She looked pretty sitting there, even in sweats and a sleeveless tee, holding a ceramic mug. Staring out at the cow pasture beyond the road and the barbed wire, she turned to Quinn and said, "Want me to put on a record?"

Quinn smiled, looking at his watch. "Sure," he said. "I'd like very much for you to put on a record."

He watched her walk shoeless back into the house, heard the click and whir of the turntable and then Lee Hazlewood and Nancy Sinatra, the second album they did together. *Nancy & Lee Again*. "Big Red Balloon." Maggie returned, leaning against the doorframe, looking down at Quinn with his mug in hand, and said, "Are we gonna screw or what?"

"Hoping that's what you were thinking."

"Isn't that what Lee and Nancy always means?"

"It sure does," Quinn said, standing and placing the coffee mug on the porch ledge. "God bless 'em."

He left Hondo outside with his muddy paws and stinky coat and closed the front door, placing his hands under Maggie's shirt and on her bare hipbones, kissing her hard on the mouth. Sweatpants, soft and worn, falling low over her waist. Nancy singing *You ain't nothing but an old fool*. Maggie jumped up into his arms, wrapping her legs around his waist. Quinn held on tight, walking her up the stairs to the bedroom. Quinn knowing this was a temporary escape from all of it, but taking what he could get.

A half hour later, they lay there in the tangle of sheets, looking up at the spinning ceiling fan. Maggie, bare-chested, had her arm across her forehead, as Quinn worked to catch his breath. The world flickering back to normal speed.

"That's one way to start a day," Quinn said.

"It's always been like that," she said. "Hasn't it?"

"Yes, ma'am," Quinn said, then turning toward Maggie, her head on the pillow, staring at him with wide green eyes. "Are you sure you're OK?"

"I'm fine," Maggie said, unblinking, reaching for his hand. "Just fine. How about some breakfast?"

Tashi and Jessica had spent the last four days at the offices of the *Tibbehah County Monitor*, relegated to a back storeroom with light wood paneling and faded green carpet, relying on Betty Jo Mize, the newspaper's owner and managing editor, to bring them clip files. Betty Jo was a nice woman, somewhere between sixty and eighty, with a lot of teased brown hair and half-glasses she kept on a chain around her neck. She'd slip them up to her nose with her left hand when double-checking something, the right hand usually busy with an extra-long cigarette. Tashi wondered about the safety of a lit cigarette in a big room stacked floor to ceiling with paper files and oversized ledgers of past editions.

"Glad to meet some young reporters who understand everything isn't on the internet," Betty Jo said. "Computers have done nothing but make the world even dumber. I swear to God, I don't think some folks can wipe their ass without first Googling how to do it."

"Is this all you could find on Quinn Colson?" Tashi asked.

"I only have clips from when he was a boy," Betty Jo said, ashing her cigarette into an empty coffee mug, looking over Tashi's shoulder, staring down at her notes. "There might be a few items from when he was in the Army. I'm pretty sure we ran a photo of him and Miss Jean when he became a Ranger. Maybe some small items about him getting injured over there in Iraq."

Tashi thanked her and pulled out the hand-cut newspaper clippings from a small manila envelope. They were musty and brittle in her hands, the back room smelling like that library smell of old books and ancient paper. The clippings went back to 1990, one headline so large she had to unfold it several times across the desk. It read

COUNTRY BOY DID SURVIVE. A story from the Associated Press and a column by Betty Jo Mize, looking pretty much the same in the photo from almost thirty years ago as she did now. Same glasses around her neck. Same hairstyle. Only the extra-long cigarette was missing.

"How's it coming?" Tashi asked Jessica after Betty Jo had left them alone.

"This is the fourth box on Hamp Beckett," Jessica said. "Reading up on some big Wild West shoot-out at a pizza parlor on the Square. This was '79. A guy shot two employees and one deputy while trying to rob the place. Looks like Sheriff Beckett and E. J. Royce took care of the rest. Another one from the early nineties about a big pot bust out in the county with that guy Heath Pritchard I told you about. It says here it was one of the biggest marijuana hauls in Mississippi history."

"We have plenty on Quinn Colson," Tashi said. "I think with the interviews we have and some of these stories, we can juxtapose what happened to him in 1990 with what later happened to Brandon Taylor. I just love the idea of the Big Woods as a dark, mythological place, almost something out of a fable. Two boys walk in but only one walks out. That kind of thing."

They'd first come to Betty Jo Mize to find out what they could about Ansley Cuthbert, trying to figure out her connection to Brandon. They'd already learned from Brandon's sister and mother that he and Ansley had been close that last year, Ansley most likely taking over from Maggie Powers, something about a returned necklace. Ansley, the new girl in town that his mother thought was a little fast for the boy. The only clippings they could find showed Ansley with Brandon at some kind of high school journalism awards at Ole Miss. Hubie Phillips was being honored, too. The kids and Phillips looked so young. That world so long ago. Tashi was still a toddler in Michigan when all this was going on.

"Why are y'all so interested in Quinn Colson?" Betty Jo Mize said, reappearing in the back room, taking a seat at a long wooden desk stacked high with newspaper ledgers going back a hundred years. She let out a long stream of smoke that floated up into a ceiling fan.

"We're very thorough," Jessica said, speaking from a far back corner, her blue head craned over a big file of more clips. "We want to know more about the town and how it related to Brandon. The story is more than just Brandon."

"I heard y'all thought Quinn Colson might have something to do with the Taylor boy killing himself," Betty Jo said. Her eyes squinting in the smoke, a noncommittal look on her face. "Right?"

"We're checking out our sources," Jessica said, sounding a little annoyed.

"How long is this radio show of yours?"

"It's a podcast," Tashi said. "Probably eight to ten episodes."

"And how long is each episode?"

"About an hour," Tashi said. "But we're not confined by time. It can run short or long."

"And both of you work for this media group up there in New York City," Betty Jo said. "Do y'all get paid for all your work down here? Like a regular newspaper?"

"We do," Tashi said. "But if we don't make sense of what happened to Brandon Taylor, we're going to have to leave soon. It's a good story on its own, but, at this point, we need some kind of twist, some sense of the unexpected, that no one ever found out."

"Isn't that what we all want?" Betty Jo said, pulling on her cigarette, burning it back down to a more normal size. "A real, solid, twisty tale. Since y'all have gotten here, the sheriff has found a dead body buried out on the Pennington land and E. J. Royce finally went and got himself shot. Although, to be clear and honest with both of y'all, I'm shocked that didn't happen sooner. E. J. Royce would've tried the patience of Job."

Tashi nodded, smiling back at the woman but wanting to get back to work, filling in those last little bits about Quinn Colson's time in the woods. She'd already started to really doubt everything she'd heard about the man. The massive search party in 1990, the big press conferences with his uncle, the idea that Quinn would never be found, and then the boy emerging from the woods a week later without a scratch. Quinn already great media fodder even as a kid, talking about how he hunted and fished his way through being lost, making shelters in the fashion of Choctaw Indians with tree branches.

"Did y'all ever think maybe the Taylor boy just got lost in those woods and got so confused and turned around that he killed himself?" Betty Jo said. "Sometimes things like that happen. Not everything can be explained. Nicest fella I ever knew in my life was a man named Barney Ellard. He was the pharmacist here for more than twenty years. Married, three kids. Never saw the man without a smile on his face. Collected these little Peanuts figurines—you know, Snoopy and Charlie Brown and all. They'd say things like 'Psychiatric Help 5¢' with Lucy sitting in the little booth. Well, one morning he didn't come to work. His wife found him back at home running a garden hose into the windows of his Buick Riviera. Of course we didn't write about what he did. You don't write anything about suicide, such an awful personal matter."

Tashi figured she wouldn't get any more done with Betty Jo hanging out and pushed the clips to the side. She was hungry anyway, and figured she would walk across the Square to the Fillin' Station diner for two of those premade biscuits and a cup of coffee. For all the jokes back in New York about biscuits and grits, she was actually starting to really like them both.

"Are you wanting to see my file on Quinn's father, Jason?" Betty Jo said. "That might take some time. Somewhere I have a box with nothing but pictures of him doing tricks here in Tibbehah or when he'd done stunts on one of those Burt Reynolds movies. He never forgot me, always telling those publicists to send me a press pack from *Hooper* or *Smokey and the Bandit*, too. Lord, now *his* father, Quinn's grandfather, is a whole 'nother thing. You ladies know the picture *Thunder Road* with Robert Mitchum?"

"We're good with just Quinn and Sheriff Beckett."

"Not that it's any of my business," Betty Jo said, placing two fingers to her cheek, "but y'all are wasting your time looking into Sheriff Colson. Some people believe by spreading around their own stink they can taint everyone as bad as themselves. That was E. J. Royce. And that's the kind of people he worked with. Now, I'm just an old newspaper lady in some country town. You young ladies haven't asked me for one thing besides looking at some musty clips. But if I were you, I'd be looking back to E. J. Royce, asking why he was telling such god-awful lies and how he ended up tying his own noose."

"Sheriff said he caught someone robbing him."

"Is that what he said?" Betty Jo said. "Sure is interesting. Did either of you gals notice the description of that *robber* looked just like one of those fellas who broke into the jail and killed that prisoner?"

"We asked him about it," Jessica said, popping her head up. "But Sheriff Colson wouldn't answer our questions."

"Y'all do know being a reporter is a hell of a lot more than what people tell you," she said, letting out a steady stream of smoke from her mouth. "It's making good sense of the puzzle pieces you're given. Nobody's gonna figure it out for you."

Tashi nodded, stood up, swung her purse on her shoulder, and told Miss Mize and Jessica she would be right back. The morning light was white hot over the Square, a group of old men sitting in the gazebo drinking coffee from Styrofoam cups, a city worker pruning the big oaks buckling the walkway, and a man selling frozen catfish and sweet potatoes from the back of a beaten old truck.

She almost missed the two men sitting in a newer truck, maroon with a tinted windshield, the windows down as they eyed Tashi making her way across the Square.

She was used to men staring at her. She was a younger woman and in shape, and men weren't exactly subtle. But these guys looked like they wanted her to know she was being watched. They had short beards, sunglasses, and dark baseball caps with some type of gold symbol on them.

Tashi looked away as if she hadn't noticed, walking faster toward the diner, as the men started their truck and pulled out in the opposite direction.

"Nobody's looking at you," Buster White said. "Nobody's staring. Quit being so goddamn paranoid. Christ Almighty. Take your coat and tie off, Senator. I'll get you a swimsuit. We can drink and smoke like we used to. You aren't in front of the cameras. Come as you are to the party."

"I'll be in my room when you're ready."

Vardaman sat next to Buster White in White's personal cabana, a little enclosure by the swimming pool that looked like something out of ancient Greece, with fancy Doric columns and a blue awning overhead. White had been out there all morning, big belly slathered in baby oil, with two cocktail waitresses lying beside him on their stomachs with their bikini tops untied, sleeping off hangovers. Sometimes Buster would toss a glass of ice water on their backs just to give the men at the pool a real show.

"Is that any better?" Buster White said. "Whether you have a room here or you're by the pool, what's the damn difference? At least here we are wide open and pretty much naked to the world. I sweep those rooms every damn day, but you better start to understand the Feds.

Did you know they have goddamn cameras smaller than a chipmunk's butthole?"

"Why didn't you return my calls?"

"I hate phones."

"What about my personal messages?"

"I don't know those fucking people," Buster said. "That goddamn frat boy Bentley? *Shit.* Listen. What do you want? A club sandwich and a Bloody Mary? You see the bartender over there? That girl with the amazing tatas? She makes the best damn Bloody Mary you'll have outside New Orleans. Puts a whole salad in there, with pickles, olives, and peppers. Come on, now, put on a suit, oil up your old hide, and unwind. Tonight, we got Johnny Fucking Mathis playing. How do you like that? *Chances are . . .*"

"How was the funeral?" Vardaman said.

"Lovely," Buster White said. "I paid a colored band a thousand dollars to play 'When the Saints Go Marchin' In.' Ray's wife just loved it, smiling and laughing, tears running down her face, all that joy and sorrow for a man who would've put his dick in a light socket."

"I came to talk to you about that light socket."

"Ha," Buster White said, grinning and reaching up to the waitress for his Bloody Mary, watching her ass switch and sway as she walked off. "Fannie giving you some trouble? Don't worry. I'll talk to her. She's going through a time. She was so torn up at the service but had to hold it all in on account of Ray's family. But I'm pretty sure Ray's wife knew who she was. They had some kind of open deal going on. One look at Fannie and his wife couldn't really blame the son of a bitch. I don't care how old she is."

Vardaman was sweating in his dark blue suit, long red tie barely unknotted, Buster noticing the guy still had on some kind of makeup. You could see it around his ears and where his forehead met the big sweep of silver hair. He was seated sideways on the lounge, the two waitresses on the other side of him still knocked out. Vardaman rested his elbows on his knees, hands clasped, Buster really hoping the guy hadn't gone full-tilt nuts and wanted him to pray with him. He looked nervous, a little jittery.

"I told Skinner he can shut down Vienna's Place," Vardaman said. "What you do with Fannie Hathcock is your problem. I've been doing business in Tibbehah County for a long while. It's unseemly as hell to have that titty bar right off the road. I want it gone. Take it over to Calhoun County or somewhere in Alabama. I don't give a damn. But it's over."

"And you think because Ray's dead, I'll do it?"

"You don't like that goddamn bitch any better than me."

"Don't fool yourself," Buster said, sipping the Bloody Mary through a straw. "What I like or don't like doesn't have a damn thing to do with business. You don't ever stick your dick down the throat of the golden goose. You just might choke the bitch."

Buster White was losing his mind with this spray-tanned, holier-than-thou jackoff. He'd put up with him for too damn long. Working with him on account of Stagg and then Ray and then with his Ole Miss crotch sniffers over in Jackson. If it weren't for Buster, this fucking guy would still be trying to pass legislation to turn 45 into Jefferson Davis Highway or skimming off the top of every two-bit road and bridge project instead of picking out goddamn drapes for the governor's mansion.

"This isn't about Fannie," Buster said. "You made some kind of deal with Skinner. For what?"

"She'll be shut down before the election," Vardaman said. "I'll hold a press conference with the highway patrol. I can't imagine what all she's running out of that claptrap."

"Jimmy," Buster said. "You won't wipe your goddamn ass without me telling you the direction. Got me? Now tell me. What is Skinner doing for you?"

"Nothing."

"You are one tricky-dicky fuck," Buster said. "Surrounding yourself with these Bible-thumping hicks. Those goddamn Watchmen militia fuckwads. You got their vote. But don't you forget who backed you when those white-haired cocksuckers in Jackson wouldn't give you the time of day."

"I better get going."

"Sure thing," Buster White said, grinning behind his Wayfarers. "Is that all you came for?"

One of the waitresses started to stir, reaching up behind to expertly tie her bikini top purely by touch. A fucking magic trick. Buster White was amazed how she pulled it off. Vardaman was sweating like a pig now, makeup melting down his face.

"Johnny Mathis?" Buster said, beaming, slapping the waitress's butt with his hand. The woman scowled at him and turned her head the other way.

"No thank you," Vardaman said, wiping away the sweat with the back of his hand. "Some other time. I can't give up now. We're so damn close."

"I know what you want," Buster White said. "I've known it for a long time. But I'm not going to kill the goddamn sheriff of some jerkwater town. That would bring so much fucking heat on me I just might melt. Thank you very much."

"But Fannie—"

Buster White stood, stretching his bad back, patting his big stomach and looking to the big, cool swimming pool. "OK, Senator," he said. "Whatever makes you happy. I'll talk to her about new arrangements."

# TWENTY-TWO

Two days after getting the forensics on the girl, Quinn met Caddy and Tashi Coleman over at the Fillin' Station diner. It was late for the breakfast crowd. Most of the six a.m. boys were off on their tractors, at their job sites, or on their runs up over to Tupelo or Memphis. Quinn nodded to his sister and Tashi as he walked in the door, taking off his sheriff's ball cap and setting it on a hook by the door. Mary winked at him from behind the cash register, bringing him a hot cup of coffee before he even reached the booth.

"Not every day I get a message saying *Get your ass over here*," Quinn said.

"Needed an attention grabber," Caddy said. "Don't you ever call people back?"

"Been a little busy," Quinn said. "I guess y'all have seen the news."

Tashi nodded, lifting her coffee to her lips, staring at him over the rim of the cup. Caddy waved over to Miss Mary that they were ready.

All of them giving the woman their orders as Miss Mary refilled Tashi's cup, not writing any of it down. Miss Mary was a pro at her job.

"Do you have an ID yet?" Tashi asked.

"Takes a little longer than that," Quinn said. "State folks are looking for a match with dental records of some missing persons cases. Like you probably know, the woman was in her late teens or early twenties. And she died at least twenty years ago."

"And she'd been shot in the head."

"I can't say how she died," Quinn said. "But there was some serious trauma to the head."

"But not shot?" Tashi asked.

Quinn looked over at his sister, annoyed as hell she'd roped him into this meeting with all he had going on. He'd just had to do a stand-up with local media about the body that morning and then answer a bunch of questions about whether this was tied to Brandon Taylor's death and whether the department had officially reopened the investigation. Quinn just answered coyly that he wasn't sure it had ever been officially closed.

"You did real good on TV," Caddy said. "Tashi and I were watching you from over at the motel. You stood up straight, looked right in the camera, and didn't stutter once."

"Glad it worked out for y'all," Quinn said. "Is this a friendly breakfast meeting or is there something on your mind?"

"Given I'm meeting you here with Tashi and I called you direct after seeing you on the news, you might deduce we're here regarding Brandon Taylor."

"Guess this is as good a time as any," Quinn said. "I haven't eaten breakfast yet and can chew while you ask me things I can't answer."

"What did I tell you?" Caddy said, glancing over at Tashi, shrugging. "He can't even imagine that we're not coming to him with questions, we are coming to him with some information. But if he wants to be pigheaded about it, I guess we don't have to share any of it."

"Hold up," Quinn said, putting up the flat of his hand. "Hold up. Would you please, in God's name, speak English and explain to me exactly when you became a part of all this? From where I've been sitting, you don't have a damn thing to do with this, Caddy. This is none of your business."

Tashi looked uncomfortable. She bit her lip and nodded, waiting for Quinn to finish. "Your sister has been a huge help to us," she said. "Since she'd been in school with Brandon and she knew a lot of the same people."

"Oh, hell, Caddy," Quinn said. "Are you helping them with damn Ansley Cuthbert? You really don't need to be dragged back into all that mess. I may not be moving fast enough to your liking, but both of y'all need to step back and let us do the work. We occasionally *do* close a few cases."

Quinn looked up from the table and spotted Luther Varner wandering in the front door and setting his SEMPER FI ball cap next to Quinn's. The tall, lumbering old man taking a seat at the counter, making some small talk with Mary. He heard laughter as Mary made her way back to their booth and refilled all their coffees. "Won't be but a minute," she said.

"Well?" Quinn said. "Did you find her?"

"Yes and no," Caddy said.

"Hell."

"Caddy helped me find her last week," Tashi said. "And I tried to interview her, but she walked out on us. She said she was scared and didn't want to talk. I'm pretty sure she's the one who reached out to us in the first place. She told me I should've never sought her out, it wasn't supposed to work that way. She freaked out."

Quinn nodded and leaned back in the booth. The front door to the Fillin' Station opened again and he spotted Chucky Crenshaw walking in with Kenny, Kenny on his day off and dressed in head-to-toe camo. They nodded toward Quinn and started talking to Miss Mary. A bell rang up by the kitchen window. Quinn hoped it was their food, so he could get something to eat and get on with his day.

"Now you want me to press her?" Quinn said. "Bring her in as a potential witness?"

Caddy nodded. "Only one thing," she said. "We can't seem to find her. Tashi tracked down the apartment where she lived and some potential phone numbers. But she hasn't lived in the apartment for more than six months and all those numbers have been disconnected. I checked the bar and record store in Cooper-Young where she worked and they haven't seen her since we have. She hadn't shown up for a few days. I think she's hiding, Quinn."

Miss Mary laid down the Southern Man platter for Quinn—two eggs, two strips of bacon, grits, and a biscuit. Caddy got a scrambled egg with sausage and Tashi just got white toast with butter and jelly. Some people were just strange that way.

"I'll contact Memphis police."

"You may want to do more than that," Caddy said.

Quinn didn't answer. He'd learned long ago not to open his mouth when his sister wanted to explain something to him. Like it or not, she was going to complete the objective. Quinn cut into his eggs and took a bite. Three homicides in the last few weeks and she wanted him to drop everything for Tashi Coleman.

"I think she's the one," Caddy said.

Quinn looked up, chewing, watching the serious look on Caddy's sunburned face. Her hair had been sun-bleached nearly white over the summer.

"She's the one who was sending those letters to Maggie."

"How do you know about the letters?"

"Maggie told me," Caddy said. "Ansley Cuthbert knows about all this. And she's scared to death. If that girl y'all dug up had something to do with Brandon Taylor, she'll know."

"I'm worried about Ansley," Tashi said. "What if she's in trouble? Or someone is after her? She made it clear to us she didn't want any part of this."

Quinn picked up a piece of bacon, looking at the young woman, waiting for her to get to the point of what had really been bothering her. Tashi's black hair pulled tight and tied in a ponytail at the back of her head. She didn't have on any makeup and seemed even younger than when they'd first met, almost like a teenage kid.

"Some people have been following me and Jessica," she said. "They were watching me on the Square two days ago. Last night they were parked outside the Traveler's Rest Motel."

"Why didn't you call the sheriff's office?"

"We did," she said. "A patrol car came right after they left. Didn't you hear about it?"

Quinn shook his head, taking a sip of coffee, exchanging a glance with Caddy. He didn't like Caddy getting involved in sheriff's office business. He already had to deal with Maggie's personal ties to the story, but now Caddy, too. Some days it just wasn't worth getting up in the morning. He drank some more coffee, thinking. "OK," he said. "Did you see the men following you?"

Tashi nodded. "They had hats and sunglasses. One of them had a beard. They were driving a dark red truck. I tried to tell the deputy who came out last night about the make. But I'm not really sure."

"OK," Quinn said. "Were they white or black? Young or old? Did you see anything that might make IDing them any easier?"

"The guy driving had a beard," she said. "He was white. Younger. All I could really see was some kind of gold symbol on his hat."

"What color was the hat?"

"Black," she said. "The gold symbol looked almost like a pocket watch."

Fannie thought she might be hallucinating as she watched Skinner stroll on into Vienna's Place, craning his neck and turning about with delight as he studied the inside of the titty bar. He seemed downright amused by the stages, the brass poles, the bar, and the crow's nest high in the rafters by her glass office. Skinner kept on his Stetson hat, dressed today in his uniform of short-sleeved plaid shirt, pocket laden with pencils and pens, and old man khakis with farm-and-ranch boots to show he was truly a man of the people. One of his most often repeated turns of phrase at those horrendous supervisor meetings was *I'm not no better than no one else*. But everyone knew Skinner believed he was better than everyone. Always talking about his close and personal connection with Jesus Christ as if he had the Man from Galilee on speed dial.

"Skinner," Fannie said. She'd been checking on the liquor supply behind the bar and in the storeroom, and they were running low on cheap champagne and good whiskey. She'd need Midnight Man to make a run over to Tupelo sometime later tonight.

"This is quite a place," Skinner said. "Sometimes I forget what a marvel we have in Tibbehah County. Just what do the women do up there, up there in that crow's nest?"

"That's my office," Fannie said.

"What about those platforms?" Skinner said. "Is that where your girls take the customers? Just like hens fluttering their wings, finding a place to roost."

"No," Fannie said, dressed down today in black slacks and a pink velvet top. "It's where I watch out for my dancers and all the desperate suckers down on the floor."

"Now, that's something," Skinner said, taking his eyes off the walkway and back down to Fannie behind the bar. "Y'all sure have it planned out. Yes, ma'am. Let me ask something, if you don't mind."

"Sure," Fannie said. "Ask away, Supervisor."

"What does a young woman get for getting nekkid here," Skinner said. "I mean, is it really worth a young lady's dignity to expose herself like that?"

"Depends on how many private dances she gives."

"And what's entailed in a private dance?"

"You know the answer," Fannie said. "Or do you just like to hear the details? You want to know how those young ladies crawl up in a man's lap and grind his pecker until he shoots the moon or just can't take it anymore?"

"That's some direct talk."

"I'm a direct woman," Fannie said. "Now, what in the fuck do you want?"

"Do you always have to be so profane, Miss Hathcock?"

Fannie didn't answer, letting the silence speak for itself, reaching for her cigarillos, that bald-headed dickbrain always making her smoke. She lit one up with her gold Dunhill lighter.

"I think me and you have always been civil to each other even if we didn't see eye to eye," Skinner said. "We had some colorful exchanges of words at the supervisors' meetings. But that's how it had to be. No different than that old cartoon with the sheepdog and the wolf, knowing things between them are different when they punch the clock."

"You're a lot older than me," Fannie said. "I haven't a goddamn clue what you're talking about."

"I'm going to kind of miss this in a small way," Skinner said. "It sure has been an education."

"Come again?" Fannie asked, feeling a cold prick against the back of her neck. She stared at the tall, potbellied son of a bitch as he continued to take inventory of her bar, smiling at himself in the mirror from beyond her shoulder. Son of a goddamn bitch.

"I'm going to make the motion to outlaw nekkid dancing, or whatever you call it, to the supervisors next week," Skinner said. "Oh, don't you worry. We'll have to hold some meetings, maybe do a study or two, but you know how it will all shake out. The kind of business you're offering off Highway 45 ain't welcome here no more. Ole Johnny Stagg wanted to give those truckers a real show a long time back. But this is the dawning of a new age, back to old family values. This kind of thing wouldn't have been considered back in my day. They would've taken a woman of your ilk out to the town square and burned her at the stake."

Fannie blew out some smoke, ashing her cigarillo and thumping it with her thumb and middle finger. She waited until the smoke dissipated before she spoke, carefully thinking, choosing her words as direct and hard as she meant them.

"That won't sit well with some people."

Skinner laughed, sucking at a tooth, a remnant from his fat-daddy lunch over at the El Dorado Mexican restaurant, where he held court most days. He patted his stomach, busting and prominent.

"They'll cut you into a million pieces if you go against them."

"Oh, I don't think so, Miss Fannie. I think you need to talk to your wrangler and understand the new terms of this here lease. I'm on solid authority your time here is finished, and it couldn't come soon enough. Have you stepped outside these darkened doors lately and looked out to what we're building on the hill?"

"The cross?" she said. "Are you fucking kidding me?"

Skinner closed his eyes as if someone had squirted lemon into his pale blue eyes. "Why must you say things like that? Like nails on a chalkboard."

"So sorry to injure your old virgin ears, Skinner," Fannie said. "But I honestly don't give a good goddamn. I don't know if you ate a bad chimichanga this afternoon and got the shits or if the senility in your ancient brain is showing itself. Either way, I have work to do this afternoon and don't have time for bullshit or idle threats. If you'd made the effort to read the sign on the door, we don't open until four o'clock."

"Sorry to trouble you," Skinner said. "But I figured it was best to tell you in person. I'd tell your girls to get what they can in tips, they're gonna have to get themselves right or head on up to Memphis or down to New Orleans."

Fannie wrapped her right hand under her breasts and clasped her left elbow, holding her cigarillo high, nails manicured to a bright red and damn-near perfect. She tilted her head to study Skinner's repulsive old fucked-up face. He walked close enough that she could hear his raspy, excited breathing.

"You do know there is an over-the-counter cure for halitosis?"

"Night-night, Miss Fannie," Skinner said, placing the hat back on his sun-spotted bald head. "Nice knowing you."

"They wouldn't deal with you," Fannie said. "They would never deal with someone so very, very small."

"I promised to deliver on something you never could," Skinner said, winking. "Loyalty is one hell of a thing, Miss Hath-cock."

"How bad is it?" Boom asked.

"It's been worse," Caddy said. "In fact, most of the time it's much worse."

"Can you get through the week?" Boom asked.

"We can get through the end of the month, but the holidays are looking rough," Caddy said. "And you know that's the toughest time. Something will come in. It always does."

"The power of prayer?"

Caddy nodded, looking over at the empty skeleton of the new outreach building, the first stage of construction eating up a good bit of The River's budget, Caddy always robbing Peter to pay Paul but now not finding a new Peter right for the job. They sat on the tailgate of Boom's old truck, Boom just hauling over a bed of canned goods donated by the Piggly Wiggly. The local manager was always generous on the scratch-and-dent side of the business.

"What happened to those folks in Jackson?" Boom said. "I thought they were going to pay for the construction."

"That was the idea," Caddy said. "Bentley said they should have everything in order by Christmas. But you know that's a long stretch of time. We can't let folks go hungry just because I moved on this too quick."

"I'll be back on the road in a few weeks," Boom said. "I get these damn pins taken out of my leg and I should be good to go. Lots of outfits up in Memphis who'll hire me."

"Don't move too fast," Caddy said, leaning back on her arms, hands flat on the bed. "Take care of you."

"Been taking care of myself too damn much," Boom said. "I go from sitting at my house to getting a ride over to rehab three times a week. I ain't gonna lie to you. Ain't nothing for me to do but sit around and watch television and drink. Drank me a whole damn bottle of Jack Daniel's last night. Only thing that kills those damn snakes in my head."

Caddy nodded, both of them sharing the ugly addiction, although Caddy hadn't a drink or pill in more than three years. She'd come down hard when Jamey Dixon got killed, acting like she was tough and doubling down here at The River, until one night she found herself rolling up in the backwoods for a few pills, a little weed, one little hit from a pint of Aristocrat vodka to keep those demons in check.

The next thing she knew, she'd left Jason and Tibbehah County and was back somewhere in Memphis, Quinn kicking in the door to an apartment with an ax handle in his hand and taking her home.

"The kids' league banned me for the rest of the season."

"I know."

"I want to apologize to Jason," Boom said. "He don't need that bullshit in his world."

"Not necessary," Caddy said, patting Boom's huge thigh. "That boy's seen ten times worse from me or his grandmother at Thanksgiving. One year she got so damn loaded she performed the 'American Trilogy' on top of the kitchen table."

Boom grinned, shook his head, feeling the rough edges of his beard. "Everything's gonna be better when I get a truck back, jamming those gears and hitting the highway. Get the hell out of my little shack. Damn, Caddy. I think I'm losing my mind."

Caddy wanted to tell him about riding up to Memphis with Tashi Coleman, riding past those shitty little motels and pool halls, spending some time back in the belly of the beast, Dixie Belles, to find out where they could track down Ansley Cuthbert. She didn't think much of it that night, while she was doing it, watching the whole thing like it was a movie playing back in her head. But since then, it had brought her full awake at three in the morning, gasping for breath, sweating, turning on the nightlight to make sure she was safe in bed, heading into Jason's room to pat the covers, make sure her son was still with her. No. Boom didn't need to know all that. He had too much of a burden on him now, a damn good man who'd lost his way and his purpose. Something in sad supply in Tibbehah.

"You think I should tell Bentley the truth?" Caddy said. "That we're flat-ass broke?"

"What harm could it do?" Boom said, cutting his handsome dark eyes at Caddy. "That boy's crazy about you. Ain't nothing gonna change that fact."

"You know, I believe there is a reason for all this," Caddy said. "My relapse? What happened to me, it was for a reason. I got weak again, I didn't value what I'd been given. God showed me what it was like to lose it all, again. And because of that, I'm twice as strong as I used to be. I needed Jamey Dixon at first, and when he was gone, I was left with me and didn't think I was enough. Now, this is all me."

"That ain't a reason not to ask for help."

"One thing I've learned running this ministry is everyone hates to beg," Caddy said. "I've prayed and prayed on it. Something will happen. And something good will happen for you."

Sometimes Fannie liked Vienna's best right before the front doors opened for the long night. There was a quiet kind of pregame excitement to the place, dimming the lights, switching on the neon and flashing lights, all the liquor bottles filled and in order. The easy chairs in the VIP room had been rubbed down with Armor All, carpets vacuumed, and the wooden floors swept. Sometimes she played a little music to get the girls in the right mood, some of them in back suiting up for the night, others already ready for their shift, slumped in chairs around the stages, taking selfies to draw in their best customers or playing Candy Crush on their iPhones. Tonight, she just couldn't help herself as she poured herself a third cocktail, Debby Boone singing "You Light Up My Life," one of Ray's favorites, feeling a little raw and emotional, more on edge since that walking dildo Skinner paid her a visit.

Midnight Man worked slow and silent behind the bar, plugging in fresh kegs in between slicing lemons and oranges for the cocktails.

The small bottles of champagne looked pretty as a picture behind the glass door of the refrigerators.

"The problem with that old liver-spotted son of a bitch is his dick is broken. Probably hasn't worked for years. Makes him hate anyone who can find pleasure in this shitty little cold planet. He doesn't drink, doesn't smoke, drives around high and mighty in that Ram truck, looking down on people who don't belong to his particular club of goody-goody assholes, that rotten little smile on his face, acting like he knows something more than the average person. What do you think he sees, Midnight Man, that you and I don't see?"

Midnight Man looked up from cutting lemons at the bar, Fannie's head held in the cradle of her hand. Her steady drink of gin with grenadine and extra cherries before her, cigarillos smoldering in the tray. Debby Boone singing her goddamn heart out.

"It's bullshit. True and authentic bullshit, my friend. Do you know what he told me? He said he could offer my people—my fucking people!—something I couldn't. What the hell does that mean? You were here long before me, barbecuing the whole hog for Johnny Stagg, listening in and knowing every dirty, rotten goddamn deal in north Mississippi. What the fuck could that bastard offer someone like Buster White? You and I both know, the only thing our people care about is money. Money is goddamn everything. Anyone who tries to go and lay some Dr. Phil shit on your ass doesn't understand their asshole from their elbow. Power? Sex? Where is that shit if you don't have the money? I learned that a long, long time ago, watching boys leave dollar bills at the edge of the stage, making eyes at me, until they emptied their wallets. You'll never know the true heart of a man until he shudders in your hand, eyes goddamn crossing, whispering he loves you as he lays down his last hundred bucks for companionship and understanding during an Aerosmith song. You know Aerosmith, right? You know them?"

Midnight Man shook his head, eyes down on his work, loading the plastic buckets with fruit for the highballs and Old Fashioneds the rich boys like to drink. Those rich boys from Oxford and Starkville coming in with fat wallets and hard-ons that made them walk nearly sideways.

"Make me another."

"You good, Miss Fannie," Midnight Man said. "It ain't even four o'clock."

"You know what my grandmother used to tell me? The original Vienna who ran that cathouse down in New Orleans? She used to say *Man may work from sun to sun, but a whore's work sure is fun*. That woman sure was something. Did you know I didn't even know she'd been a whore until the second time I'd been busted, my worthless stepfather coming after me with his belt, trying to whip the fear of Jesus into me even though he's the one who parked the devil there. Son of a bitch. That's how it is. Isn't it? Skinner and that rancid bastard were nothing like Ray. Ray had class. A gentleman. God. Where is my drink?"

"I'm sorry, Miss Fannie," he said. "Mr. Ray was a nice man."

"A drink," she said. "Now. Extra damn cherries."

Fannie reached for the cigarillo and relit the end, watching the smoke curl and float up over the floor. Debby Boone now gone silent, the whole floor quiet and dead, worse than a funeral, worse than Ray's service with that horrid fat wife of his doing the second line around the muffulettas and po' boys stacked not twenty feet from the casket. What in the fuck was happening?

"They gonna close us down?" Midnight Man said, his deep, muffled voice somewhere between a whisper and a grunt.

Fannie didn't answer, thinking back now on what Ray had taught her. Don't be emotional about a threat. Be tactical, look at a way to seek out the problem and neuter the son of a bitch. Skinner didn't get uppity until Vardaman started his run for things, suddenly making Tibbehah County more than Dogpatch, Arkansas. It was some kind of damn poker chip into the governor's mansion. Skinner had been shining the man's boots for far too long. But she'd seen the way Vardaman looked at him, as if he was some local yokel joke, until this year.

What could Skinner deliver that Fannie couldn't? The only thing Buster White figured Fannie couldn't do is get rid of Quinn Colson's ass, sending in the goddamn Hee Haw boys, pickin' and a-grinnin', to run roughshod over the county. And see how that damn thing worked out, more bullets and blood flying than a Saturday night in Dodge City.

Fannie took a long pull of her drink, winking at Midnight Man for making it just right. That was it, wasn't it? Skinner had promised Vardaman something he needed more than anything and couldn't get himself. Fannie turned around as music started up, a new DJ taking the roost, hitting the first notes of Harry Styles . . . one of her new Latina chicks from Houston warming up on the pole, spinning and spinning, stretching her arms and legs, lifting her eyes to the stage lights, bringing Fannie back to everything she'd been doing for Vardaman and Stagg before that. Girls, girls, girls. That spray-tanned fuckwad couldn't get enough of 'em. And now some teenage girl's remains found out in the county, only a few miles from Vardaman's place, a couple of two-bit Nancy Drews skulking about, asking questions about some shit that went down back in 1997 when the Booby Trap was the flavor of the month and Stagg was the main pimp for all of Vardaman's people.

Fannie started to smile, nodding to herself, leaning across the bar and kissing Midnight Man on his sweating bald head. "That's it," she said. "That is fucking it. Vardaman is about to shit his damn drawers.

What'd you ever hear about his parties out at the Cracker Barrel ranch, back in the day?"

"When we talking?" Midnight Man asked.

"Oh, twenty years back," Fannie said. "What exactly did Johnny Stagg have on the menu?"

**Tashi Coleman**
***Thin Air* podcast**
**Episode 7: MAGGIE**

NARRATOR: Since we arrived in Mississippi, we always knew that Maggie Powers, now Maggie Colson, was the heart of the Brandon Taylor investigation. Once the teenage girlfriend of Brandon, and later the wife of someone we believed to be a possible suspect in his killing. She was key to both the modern world of Tibbehah County and memories of Brandon's final summer. We made many mistakes during the telling of this story, most notably being led astray by false rumors of her husband's involvement, but were always grateful for her insight into and memories of Brandon. She knew him over two summers, 1996 and 1997. When they weren't together, they corresponded. He sent her mix tapes full of Garth Brooks, Alan Jackson, and George Strait. They talked about one day running away and getting married. He gave her a silver locket after they were intimate. In the fall of last year, Maggie Colson took us to Choctaw Lake, where they'd spend many long nights together. It was a warm day, the sun gold across the water.

> TASHI: What did you think had happened to him?
>
> MAGGIE: I guess, at first, I blamed myself. My God, I was only fifteen. He was the only boy I'd been with and then I heard he'd killed himself. I had all kinds of religious guilt at the time. Did I do something wrong? Had we sinned? It was all so confusing. I couldn't share anything with my mother. My father was a straight-

and-narrow Baptist truck driver, he didn't want to talk about feelings and guilt. I just swallowed it up whole.

[WALKING ON GRAVEL. BIRD SOUNDS. A WOODPECKER KNOCKING ON A TREE. A BOAT MOTOR FAR OFF ON THE LAKE.]

TASHI: But you said you never believed it. That you thought there had to be more?

MAGGIE: We exchanged a lot of letters. I went through them piece by piece, like some kind of jigsaw puzzle. And there was no sadness or guilt. He wrote me only about our future and finally seeing him again that summer. He was excited. We even talked about maybe meeting up during spring break in Gulf Shores.

TASHI: When did he start to mention the money?

MAGGIE: That fall. Maybe a month since I'd seen him last. And before we kind of broke up. He said he'd gotten his truck fixed and there wasn't anything to stop him doing what he wanted to do. He railed a lot against his dad, his dad always wanting Brandon to be like him and do the things he thought were important. The SEC football obsession and gun collection. Brandon said this thing he had going would make him independent. He could live his own life.

TASHI: Did he ever tell you what that was?

MAGGIE: Not really. But I had the feeling it wasn't good. He wrote about it like he'd been stealing something. Or doing something dishonest for the right reasons. I wasn't worried about it then. But reading back what he said later, I wish I could've warned him. There was something dangerous and reckless about the whole thing. I couldn't get a feel for it other than he'd come into a lot of money. Or at least started to brag about it.

[MORE CRUNCHING OF GRAVEL. WIND THROUGH TREES. GENTLE ROLLING OF A CREEK RUNNING OVER ROCKS.]

TASHI: This is the place?

MAGGIE: It is. This is where we came when we wanted to be alone and not seen. When I first came back, after my grandmother died, I drove out here and stayed for a long time. I put on a Garth Brooks CD and said a little prayer for Brandon. That crazy kid will always be fifteen, lying on his back, looking up at the stars, coming up with the craziest ideas. We were going to get married. Move out to Nashville or L.A., where he could work on his music and photography and maybe be in movies. None of it I believed. I just loved to hear him talk. He always had some kind of thing working.

TASHI: And that's what killed him?

MAGGIE: None of us know what will come from this. I'm not so sure that I believe in a heaven and a hell. But I believe in a right or wrong, that arrogant people can't just decide who lives or dies, making an example of a kid like Brandon Taylor. I loved him. I really did. What happened in this county ripped my damn heart out of my chest and made me grow up real quick. I don't like the words *revenge* or *retribution*. Everyone gets busted up in the world. That's just part of the deal. I just want people to know Brandon as he lived and breathed and why he was killed. This whole thing destroyed his family, nearly destroyed me. The truth is all we can hope for. You can't hide in a pocket of lies like some kind of animal. Karma is real, and I do believe it'll come back on you like a ton of bricks.

TASHI: You sound like you believe that there will be some justice?

MAGGIE: That crazy kid deserves it.

[SOUNDS OF CRYING. A LONG MOMENT OF SILENCE.]

TASHI: Are we going to play it?

MAGGIE: Sure. OK. Damn straight.

[THE FIRST CHORDS OF GARTH BROOKS'S "SHAMELESS" ACCOMPANY THE SOUNDS OF THE RIPPLING CREEK, SOUNDING TINNY AND SMALL IN THE VAST WOODS DOWN BY THE LAKE.]

TASHI: Memories?

MAGGIE: So damn many.

# TWENTY-THREE

I'm sorry," Tashi Coleman said. "I shouldn't have trusted E. J. Royce."

"No," Quinn said. "You shouldn't have."

"Why would he make something up like that?" she said. "He was damn specific about the details. You and Brandon Taylor mortal enemies, fighting over land to hunt?"

Quinn didn't answer, both of them sitting in his truck outside Hubie Phillips's house on St. Nick Drive in east Memphis. Mr. Phillips wasn't home and they'd decided to wait a while to see if he'd show up, Phillips being the one and only connection between Brandon Taylor and Ansley Cuthbert. He and Tashi had spent a good deal of the afternoon trying to track down Ansley without any luck, even using some information Lillie Virgil had provided. The best Quinn could tell, the girl had just skipped town.

"Betty Jo Mize had a lot of nice things to say about you," Tashi said, sitting still in the shotgun seat, typing fast on her iPhone while she spoke. "She said Jericho was a ghost town before you came back, eaten up by corruption and greed. I heard a lot about you and that man Johnny Stagg and how everything started to get better a few years ago."

"You don't know me," Quinn said. "Like you said, you only know what the records say, what I used to do when I was a kid. I guess if I'd been in your position, I might have been inclined to listen. I may have crossed on the Hawkins land once or twice. I really don't remember."

"Caddy and Ansley Cuthbert set us straight," Tashi said. "We were being used. We've been being used in one way or another since before we came to town. I don't even know what Ansley wants out of this. I mean, does she know what happened to Brandon? And if she does know, why the hell won't she tell us? I think whoever was working Royce took advantage of us not understanding Southerners, not knowing how the wheels turned beneath all those smiles and the hospitality. You must think we're pretty dumb."

"To quote the late, great Burt Reynolds," Quinn said. "Exactly how dumb you are largely depends on what part of the country you're standing in."

"So noted," Tashi said. "Is it really true your father was his stunt double? I heard that from a lot of people, but we haven't been able to confirm it yet."

"My father lied about a lot of things," he said. "But seldom about his days in Hollywood. It's true. Give or take a lie or two. I know he worked on *Smokey and the Bandit*, one and two, and *Hooper*. He did a lot of stunts with a deaf, half-Cherokee woman named Kitty O'Neil. I always thought I'd meet her one day and maybe get the whole story."

"Do you mind if I ask you a few questions about your dad?"

"I'd rather not," Quinn said. "It's the one thing I'd rather not discuss."

"Just like your sister," Tashi said. "She said you both haven't heard from him for a couple of years. Do you know where he ended up?"

"Nope."

"Do you want to know?"

"Not really," Quinn said, looking at his watch. The shadows starting to fall earlier and earlier, even at five o'clock. Hubie Phillips had decorated his door with jack-o'-lanterns and witches, orange and purple tinsel. "I'd rather just stick to Mr. Phillips. Maybe he'll be a little more forthcoming with me. I took a few of his classes. I liked him. He used to tell me I had more potential than I believed. He was that kind of teacher, always getting us to see beyond Tibbehah County."

"If he wanted his students to move away, I wonder why he stayed?" Tashi said, putting her phone down and staring at Quinn.

Quinn shrugged, watching the narrow little street, all small saltbox houses built end to end at another time, after another war, a little sliver of Memphis that hadn't changed in a long while. They could be sitting right there at the start of the 1950s, roofs topped with hundreds of TV antennas.

"Can you tell me the story of how you and Maggie met? The last time."

"Why?" Quinn said, leaning back in the driver's seat, ball cap over his half-shut eyes. "I thought you knew all that."

Tashi reached into her satchel and pulled out the microphone, setting it on the console between them. Quinn looked down at the fuzzy mic and turned his head to Tashi.

"Would be nice to hear your side of the story," Tashi said. "Maggie already told us hers. She said she knew right away you were going to be together. Did you feel the same way?"

"I did."

"And?"

"I knew straight off," Quinn said. "Once we worked out some unpleasant details, we just got right to it. I asked her to marry me on our second real date."

"You only knew her for a few months," Tashi said. "That's bold."

"Long as I needed," Quinn said. "I wasn't about to let her go. Maggie is something special."

Quinn looked in his rearview, spotting a gray compact car slowing behind them, idling and then parking along the street. Hubie Phillips got out, opened up his trunk, and grabbed some plastic bags, seeming a little confused and hesitant as Quinn got out of the truck and met him in the driveway.

"Mr. Phillips."

Hubie Phillips smiled. "Quinn Colson," he said. "Didn't I warn you about staying in Tibbehah County?"

"Yes, sir," Quinn said. "Only about a hundred times. You know Miss Coleman."

The smile faded as he nodded, holding several bags in each hand, trying to reach for the keys in his pocket. "Come on inside," he said. "Is there something I can do for y'all?"

Caddy had been waiting for more than an hour for Bentley at a Huddle House down in West Point. West Point was about halfway for them both, Bentley saying he couldn't make it all the way to Jericho today but they needed to talk. He said he'd heard about the trouble at The River. The shelves were bare and the freezers cleared out, running damn-near empty, and they'd be flat-ass broke by Christmas. Caddy tried to argue the point, not wanting to take another dime, but Bentley said keeping The River going was in all their best interests, especially for the folks who really needed them.

That was this morning. She'd driven straight south to the little glass-box diner off Highway 45, drinking coffee with a little cream and a lot of sugar and watching the cars pass by. A jukebox in the corner pumped out some classic George Jones and Tammy Wynette,

"Golden Ring." Caddy wondering just what Bentley had in mind for The River. He knew a little bit about the operating expenses but not everything. If they could just keep their doors open until Christmas, they could make it. Christmas was the best time for donations, and most of their grants would kick in at the beginning of next year. The last thing Caddy wanted was for Bentley to think she was using him or had been impressed with his family and money down in Pocahontas. If this deal, whatever it was, was to work out between them, they needed to have their own lives. The whole point for Caddy and for those she served was to never be dependent on anyone. That's a surefire recipe for screwing up a person's self-worth.

She spotted Bentley's SUV pulling into the empty lot and watched him walk toward the diner. Caddy liked watching him move. He was a tallish, goofy guy with shaggy hair and nice blue eyes. The kind of a man who had good manners, said "yes, ma'am" and "yes, sir," and held the door for her when they went out. Although that didn't happen often in Jericho, Caddy not quite ready to step all the way into public.

"Is that Tammy Wynette?" he asked.

Caddy nodded as Bentley sat down at the booth.

"Did you know she was from Mississippi?" he asked.

"Tremont," Caddy said. "Right up the road from Jericho. Some real country music royalty around here."

"My mother said her music always made her cry," Bentley said. "And your dad used to tell her she'd been a dear friend of his. He said her manager had been a real son of a bitch."

The waitress refilled Caddy's coffee as Bentley asked for a burger, French fries, and a Coke. Caddy reached for a folder she'd brought in with her and spread it out on the table. She'd highlighted some of the money coming in and circled the deficits in red ink. "This was really sweet of you," Caddy said. "I know you're busy as hell. But you were right. I'm not even sure we can keep on the lights into next week. The folks at the co-op board have been a lot more patient than they should have been. We're two months behind. If we could just keep the lights on, maybe hit the operation budget for November, I think we can do it."

Bentley smiled, reaching out for Caddy's hand on all the bills, receipts, and the running list of high-priority items: canned goods, diapers, baby formula, shampoo, soap, razors, shaving cream . . . She looked up from all the paper into Bentley's eyes. He didn't look like he'd shaved that morning, sporting a nice-looking dark shadow on his jaw. "I'm sorry," she said. "I just got right down to business."

Bentley leaned back into the booth and held out the palms of his hands. "Please," he said, reaching into his sport coat for a leather-bound checkbook. "It's not a big deal. How much do you need for the rest of the year?"

"I don't need for the rest of the year."

"But if you did?"

"Bentley," Caddy said, shaking her head. "Please."

"I'm serious," he said, scribbling on a check, lifting his eyes. "I'm going to write in a figure on a foundation check. If it's too much, I'm sorry. Just put it in savings. It's not a gift. OK? An investment. Besides, if we left y'all high and dry for the winter, my mother just might have my ass. She says hello, by the way. She was really taken with you. Said you're very easy to talk with. That's high praise. Did I tell you what she used to call my girlfriend at Ole Miss?"

Caddy shook her head, drinking a little coffee. It was bitter and needed more sugar. How the hell her brother drank this stuff all damn day and night was beyond her. Quinn's blood type was dark roast.

"OK?" he said.

He slid the check across the table. She looked down at the number, squinting to make sure she saw it right. There looked to be a few extra zeros in the figure. She looked back up, shaking her head, a rock forming in her throat. "Too much."

"Did you meet those assholes in Jackson?" he said. "They spent more than that on their damn party. I won't even tell you how much my father paid for that group out of Nashville. You'd think we were all insane."

"I don't know what to do."

"Don't think of yourself," Bentley said. "Think of how many people you can help."

Caddy closed her eyes for a moment and opened them, nodding, picking up the check, the paper feeling thick and heavy in her hand as she folded it and placed it in her purse. The waitress returning with Bentley's cheeseburger, asking if he needed any ketchup.

"No, ma'am," Bentley said. "Appreciate it."

The check in her purse felt like a damn boulder had been lifted off her back. She breathed a little easier, already running down what she needed to do once she got back to Tibbehah. First order of business was to pay the electric and propane and then maybe ride on up to Costco past Olive Branch for some much-needed supplies. Maybe even pay the contractors to finish dozer work behind the new outbuilding. This was too much. But exactly what she needed.

"Just promise you won't put on any role-playing exercises," Bentley said, holding the burger with both hands and taking a large bite.

"Like Delores Taylor in *Billy Jack*?" she said. "Sure. I can imagine getting Skinner and the supervisors out to The River to explain ethnic diversity and other words those old boys can't spell."

Bentley finished chewing, looking at the waitress to bring him more Coke. Charlie Rich now on the jukebox, *My baby makes me proud* . . . "Behind Closed Doors." The album so damn familiar as it was only second to anything Elvis Presley recorded in the Colson household. She saw Jean standing in the kitchen, washing dishes and humming the song.

"I had another reason for seeing you."

Caddy reached under the table and pinched his knee. She was smiling so big Caddy felt her face might just freeze that way. She should really slow this down, make some sense of it. Six years' difference.

"I don't know any other way to say this but to say it," Bentley said, putting down his cheeseburger and leaning into the table. "Your brother needs to watch his back," he said. "He's in some danger and needs to know about it."

Caddy stopped smiling, a tense feeling spreading across her neck and shoulders, looking up at Bentley. She started to speak but stopped herself, her breath caught.

"Please don't ask me to explain how or why I know this," he said. "But I do. Quinn's making trouble for some important people. He understands better than anyone how just lies and rumors can muck up the water."

Caddy swallowed.

"People I know," Bentley said. "I know people."

"What people?"

"Come on, Caddy," he said. "Jesus. Don't make me sit here and spell it out. I like you. I like you a whole hell of a lot. Does it matter how any of this started? All that matters now is I'm pretty sure I'm in love with you. I don't care about Daddy or his damn friends or the age difference. I want you, Caddy."

"Hold on," Caddy said, sitting up straight, blood pulsing in her temple. "How this all started? What in the hell does that mean? Did you come up to Tibbehah County to spy on me?"

Bentley didn't say anything for a long while, his eyes dropping like he just might tear up. When he finally did speak, he reached out for her hand again. "I'll tell you," Bentley said. "I'll tell you every dirty little detail. But please, please know one thing. I love you. One doesn't have a thing to do with the other."

Caddy pulled back her hand, setting it in her lap, listening.

"E.J. Royce is dead?" Hubie Phillips asked.

"Yes, sir."

"What a shame," Mr. Phillips said. "I didn't see it in the news."

"Tibbehah County sometimes doesn't make the Memphis news."

"Unless there's a shoot-out with some bank robbers out at the Booby Trap," he said, smiling.

"Yes, sir," Quinn said. "That made national news. Only it's called Vienna's Place after Johnny Stagg went to jail. Really classed the place up."

Quinn, Tashi, and Mr. Phillips sat in his living room, with its dark wood paneling and blue shag carpet, a thousand pictures on the wall of Phillips's time back in Tibbehah, his aging mother at church, his students working on the yearbook, down at Choctaw Lake waterskiing. And several awards from his time as a teacher, both in Jericho and later in Memphis. A sliver of light split the room from a pair of thick baby blue drapes, the air smelling musty and pent up, like the inside of an old trunk. Mr. Phillips sat with his legs crossed in a hard wooden chair as he spoke, looking much older than Quinn recalled, with thin white skin and receding white hair. He had on a neat blue button-down shirt with faded jeans and white sneakers without socks.

"We're having a hard time finding Ansley Cuthbert," Quinn said. "We were hoping you kept in touch with her."

"Ansley?" he said. "Oh, Lord, no. I haven't heard from her since I left Jericho. Does she have something to do with Brandon Taylor? Now, that little girl was trouble. So fast."

Quinn kept on looking around the room, the endless pictures and framed movie posters: *Intruder in the Dust*, *O Brother, Where Art Thou?* and *Cookie's Fortune*.

"I got that *Cookie's Fortune* poster signed by Robert Altman himself," he said. "I think I would've gone crazy a long time ago without movies. Next week, I'm taking one of those TCM cruises down the Caribbean. I went a few years ago, back when Robert Osborne was still alive. I met Eva Marie Saint and Ruta Lee. She was in *Seven Brides for Seven Brothers*."

"I remember you used to talk to me a lot about Westerns," Quinn said. "I think you were the first person to tell me to watch *Red River*."

"God, I love that movie."

"And *She Wore a Yellow Ribbon*."

"John Ford," Mr. Phillips said. "I pegged you for a John Ford man right off. I think about people like that. Who are their directors. I don't know you well, Miss Coleman, but I think you'd really like W. S. Van Dyke. *Penthouse*, *Manhattan Melodrama*. Ole One Take Woody, is what they called him. Some of my favorite films are from the Depression. So much realism. Cynical but with hope. Like your stories."

"So you're not sure where we can find Ansley Cuthbert?" Tashi said, reminding Quinn of Lillie. Enough with the small talk, getting right to the point.

"I haven't seen her for twenty years," Mr. Phillips said. "I do remember she and Brandon were very close. It was obvious they were boyfriend and girlfriend, always spending a lot of time in the darkroom. Hours and hours. He took a lot of pictures but never printed many photographs. I knew what they were doing in there but didn't want to make any trouble for them. Kids will be kids. All those hormones. I remember you, Quinn. What was your girlfriend's name?"

"Anna Lee Amsden."

"Anna Lee," Mr. Phillips said. "Of course, of course. She was lovely. She had that whole icy blonde Hitchcock thing. No wonder you were crazy about her."

"Icy blonde," Quinn said. "That's about right."

"I do have something for you," Mr. Phillips said, standing and disappearing to a back room. He returned with a small filing box and set it down on the coffee table. "When I first heard from Jessica about the podcast, I went through my files. I kept the last few batches of photos Brandon left at the lab. When he died, I couldn't imagine throwing them away. I can't see any way in the world they would help you. Lots of pictures of the woods, artsy stuff. But here you go. Have at it."

Quinn nodded and offered his hand. Mr. Phillips shook it, the bones in Phillips's hand seeming thin and brittle, light, in Quinn's fingers. "Appreciate it, sir."

"I will warn you, Quinn," Mr. Phillips said. "I said some horrible things about your uncle and Deputy Royce. I told them all about those first days after Brandon disappeared and the way they treated me. Even though they're both dead now, I still don't know if I forgive them."

"They had no right," Quinn said. "I'm sorry."

"Brandon did not kill himself," Mr. Phillips said, still holding on to Quinn's hand. "I know it like I know my own name. Maybe Ansley Cuthbert can help you. Lord, I hope so. Funny how the mind works. I recall how she and Brandon came to class one day, hand in hand. She had this little silver necklace. A locket? Or maybe a heart? She kept on playing with it, running the chain through her fingers. You could tell how much it meant to her. I think they were very much in love."

Quinn picked up the box and tucked it under his arm. Tashi stood and looked up at Quinn. "We found her," Tashi said. "And spoke to her. But since then it looks like she left Memphis."

"I just pray she doesn't head back to Tibbehah County," Mr. Phillips said, walking them both toward the door. "No offense, Quinn, but I can't imagine why anyone would stick around there. I did a long time for family, history and all. Why'd you come back?"

"That's a long story, Mr. Phillips," Quinn said. "I guess I got offered a job."

"Town sheriff," Mr. Phillips said. "What did I say? John Ford. Have you seen *My Darling Clementine*?"

"Maybe a hundred times."

"I knew you had," Mr. Phillips said, opening the front door, afternoon light spilling into the entryway. The welcome mat read GOD BLESS THIS HOME. "It's good to see you, Quinn. Keep up the good fight. You are absolutely nothing like your uncle. He kept a boot on each side of the times, straddling Southern history. So many people down there don't want to see anything change, only looking backward to what we've been. Or an idea of what they thought we'd been. *Gone with the Wind*? Lovely Technicolor and costumes and all, but an absolute steaming bucket of ahistorical crap. Keep moving ahead, both of you. Mississippi needs you. God love you for answering the damn call."

The high-rise tower and bar at the Choctaw casino had always reminded Fannie of an enormous pecker. The long, cylindrical luxury wing with golden windows was topped with a large, bulbous rotating lounge that had to have come from some pretty unsophisticated minds, some on the Rez saying it was a monument to Chief Robbie's true skill set. Fannie figured that was about right. He didn't have much upstairs, so God would've had to have blessed him in more obvious ways. She looked up at the tower in the casino parking lot and crushed her cigarillo under her new Sergio Rossi suede boots and headed toward the grand entrance, the inner workings of the casino familiar as hell from the old days, the beeping, whirring, and mind-numbing bullshit of it all.

The Chief knew to expect her, told her to come straight to the floor and he'd come down and meet her at the bar. The casino floor looked a little shopworn from when she'd been working down here. Back then, the casino had just opened, with fresh paint and carpet, every bit of it new to the touch. Now it looked like the interior of an old Chevy truck about to be traded in by its redneck owner. The floor was threadbare and worn out, the baseboards scuffed and dirty, brass railings needing a good polishing. She looked around at the hundreds of slot machines, blackjack tables, and roulette wheels. The games all worked by folks from the tribe, that being Chief Robbie's big claim to fame for his people. He brought the money back to Mississippi. Or at least that's what his press agent said.

Fannie had gone all out for the meeting. Not only the Rossi boots but a Burberry long-sleeved silk dress hitting her about mid-thigh. She'd dabbed a little Chanel Gardenia between her tits and put on her finest pair of black lace panties in case she had the opportunity to uncross her legs in the right company. The Chief had tried for the jackpot before but never gotten it. When she'd worked the girls at the Rez, she hadn't been a bit turned on by a grown man who spent his leisure time wrestling alligators.

"You're a very bold woman," Chief Robbie said.

Fannie turned around. Chief Robbie himself, live and in person, standing there in his Canadian tuxedo of denim on denim with a large chunk of turquoise around his neck and on his wrists. His long black hair combed straight back off his flat Native face and tied into a ponytail. The man's shirt must've had five pearl buttons undone to make the point he still pumped a little iron. He looked like Engelbert Humperdinck had fucked the hell out of Pocahontas. The real one, with the hatchet face, not the hot Disney chick with the long legs and nice tatas.

"There was a time when I would've had you arrested on sight," Chief Robbie said, hands on his hips, staring right through her with his coal black eyes.

"Really?" Fannie said. "I'm glad those times are long gone."

Chief Robbie sniffed at the air, looking like one of the good Indians from the Westerns, maybe getting down to one knee and running his fingers over the worn carpet. *Two salesmen from Slapout, Alabama. Walked toward the seafood buffet.*

"What would you like to drink?"

"I can get it."

"Not here," he said. "I'll have drinks brought to us. Follow me."

She told the Chief about her special drink, the exact relationship of the grenadine to the gin to make a Dirty Shirley, and followed him toward what used to be their signature steakhouse but had now been sealed off with Visqueen sheeting and drop cloths for painting. He opened a door marked WET PAINT and led her into a big, empty room, where she kept aware of her nice new boots and the splatters of white paint throughout. Her heels made slapping sounds on the plastic as Robbie made his way to a large round table with a half-dozen stiff-backed metal chairs around it. He waved his hand toward a chair and sat at the opposite end. Fannie feeling silly, since likely nobody else would be joining them.

Ceiling fans worked above, lightly lifting the sheets of plastic, making it feel like waves were running beneath the floor. A woman in a tuxedo shirt and a string tie walked in and set two drinks on the round table. A pink gin for Fannie and what looked to be a neat whiskey for Robbie, although she wasn't sure he actually ever drank. This looked to be some kind of ceremonial deal.

"Whatever happened to those motorcycle people you had working for you?"

"There was some trouble," she said. "And they just kind of scattered. Why?"

"Just wondering who you can trust now," he said. "I heard about your predicament with Mr. White."

Fannie raised her eyebrows, not liking so small of a word for such a big-ass problem. A predicament was shitting your pants while at church. Losing control of the entire north Mississippi corridor was a flaming, full-tilt fucking problem. She stirred the cocktail with a swizzle stick. Chief Robbie didn't touch the glass. He stared at her from across the table as if he were still pissed from four years ago. Christ Almighty. Let it go, man.

"Were you surprised?"

"No," Chief Robbie said. "I had asked for Mr. White to get rid of you a long time ago. I think you're a wild card. Not to be trusted. Instead, he handed you half the state."

Fannie took a sip of her drink. Too much goddamn grenadine. She liked the Shirley dirty, not syrupy sweet. "Buster White is a prehistoric slab of whale shit," she said. "You were right. He shouldn't trust me. Any more than I trust him. Or you. Can we all just admit we're each in this business for ourselves, only sticking together when it's beneficial?"

"How's your drink, Miss Hathcock?" the Chief asked, folding his massive arms over his chest.

"It tastes like Rainbow Brite took a squat in my glass," she answered. "It makes my teeth ache."

"I know who I am and what we do," the Chief said. "I work for no one. I never have. But being nice, making friends, is never a bad thing in this state. You made nice with Ray and that got you a seat at the table."

"I got my own fucking seat."

"You played nice with Buster White and you got yourself a start-up strip club after running a chicken-choking business from double-wides."

"I got my own fucking club," she said. "The most profitable in the Mid-South."

"Is that before or after Buster White's money wash?"

"You know I control more than all the titties in north Mississippi," Fannie said. "Ask Marquis Sledge up in Memphis if he gives a shit about Buster White. Besides, I never heard you complain about the way I ran my cooze."

"Never was a problem, Fannie," he said. "Until you up and decided you'd rather be chief. The girl you used nearly destroyed my life. My second wife left me. I nearly got voted out as chief. Dirty, dirty business."

Fannie laughed, spilling a little of her drink, licking the wetness off the back of her hand, using the cocktail napkin to sop it up. She leaned back and crossed her legs, thinking what a big goddamn waste it was to wear a pair of hundred-dollar panties.

"I am a chief now. I don't need Buster," she said. "You don't need him, either. But you still need me."

"And why is that?"

"Because I'll be working our incoming governor like the joystick of a claw machine."

Chief Robbie shook his head, not believing a word she was saying. "Go into business with you? Maybe with Ray. Ray was a very good man. Honorable."

"Thank you."

"The compliment was not intended for you," Chief Robbie said. "You weren't his wife. Or family."

Fannie just smiled, the expression cold and frozen on her face, waiting for him to grow more curious. But he just sat there in the empty white room, the plastic drop cloths undulating, a blank look on his thick, heavy-browed face. The ceiling fans rocked and creaked overhead.

"White doesn't run Vardaman," she said. "Nobody runs Vardaman. Yet."

"And how do you plan on doing it?"

"The hellhounds are coming for his ass," she said. "And I'm the only person who knows how to stop 'em."

# TWENTY-FOUR

The T-shirts. Holy fuck. All the damn T-shirts. Tashi Coleman couldn't help but see everyone at the Vardaman rally as a walking billboard for their own personal agenda. I'LL KEEP MY GUNS, Y'ALL KEEP THE CHANGE . . . PRO-LIFE, PRO-GUN, AND PRO-GOD . . . YOU AIN'T ENTITLED TO NOTHIN'. And the one that brought an audible gasp from Jessica as they walked up into the high seats at the BancorpSouth Arena in Tupelo. JOURNALIST. ROPE. TREE. SOME ASSEMBLY REQUIRED.

"Did I just see that?" Jessica said. "Did we just enter a parallel dimension?"

"Keep walking," Tashi said. "We're not here to judge. Only observe. By the way, are you getting all this?"

"You mean the radio guys raffling off the AR-15, the youth chorus singing a song called 'Mississippi Matters,' or those two women getting into a fight over who was going to get their daddy's four-wheeler when he died? I mean, the last one was hard to pass up. Did you see me just kind of hang there by their car, acting like I was checking my iPhone? The one woman said she'd choke that bitch if she even thought about getting on Daddy's Yamaha."

"Nicely done."

"Vardaman isn't going to speak to us."

"Nope."

"So why are we here?"

"Local color," Tashi said, taking a seat and looking far down onto the arena floor, a large stage set up at the end draped in American and Mississippi flags. Mississippi still featuring the stars and bars of the old Confederate flag. One of the episodes would focus entirely on Tibbehah County history, a major battle fought for control of the railroad supply chain across the state. "This story has always been about more than just Brandon Taylor. Those photos Hubie Phillips found just gave us a reason."

"And why would a kid be taking pictures of Vardaman's hunting lodge?" Jessica said, scrolling the scanned photos on her phone. "You can clearly see it's the same structure. The roof is a different color and there's that massive addition. But it's the same house. No doubt in my mind. Yeah, this is a big help."

"Not that we needed a reason to stick around Mississippi," Jessica said. "I see Cirque du Soleil will be here next week. We've can cover that, too. And, later on, Disney On Ice: World of Enchantment. Featuring Elsa the Ice Queen. Fuck Times Square and Broadway."

An old man in overalls with a bushy white beard held up a sign reading DEPLORABLE LIVES MATTER. A woman seated next to them wearing an American flag vest over her frilly blue shirt had a sign that said GOD BLESS MISSISSIPPI. Down on the arena floor, a college-aged boy had dressed up like an elderly Confederate colonel, with white hair and a fake beard and a giant red-sequin hat. He pretended to walk with the assistance of a cane but would occasionally dance a little jig in case someone got confused about his real age.

"The interview we got with Betty Jo Mize about the New South being dead?" Tashi asked. "That comes right before this rally. This is exactly what she warned us about."

"I feel like I've taken some peyote," Jessica said. "Or need some."

A contemporary Christian band on stage sang a song about opening the eyes of your heart to Christ. Most people didn't seem to be listening, talking and laughing, deaf to the words, or taking selfies with their phones. The band finally finished up two songs later and another local politician gave an introduction to "Mississippi's next governor." Vardaman took the stage, with his hands raised, to lots of applause, yelling, and whistling. Someone in the rafters had an air horn. A song called "Take Back Our Country" played on the PA system. *Don't tread on me. Don't you tread on me . . .*

"What's this shit?" Jessica said.

"Sounds like the theme to *Monday Night Football*," Tashi said. "With even dumber lyrics."

Vardaman thanked the crowd too many times, arms and palms outstretched wide, in front of the dueling national and state flags. Tashi noted he looked like a study in humility, closing his eyes, nodding his head. So very thankful for each and every person there. He was silver-haired and spray-tanned, in a navy blue suit and a long blood red tie. People screamed and yelled his name. Too many American and Confederate flags flapping to count.

"This election, I need y'all's prayers, support, and friendship more than you know," Vardaman said. "This is our time. We don't recognize our state anymore. The traditions we find important don't matter to my opponent. What are we without our history and tradition? This is a fight to restore our culture. Modern times, radical ideas, and political correctness have created uncertainty and instability in our society. We unite in our shared history and our faith and for our children. Things must return to the way they were. This is a battle for opposing visions of our state. We're all here to take it back. Faith, family, and values. Those aren't just words, friends . . . Our way of life must be restored. We will not compromise."

Off-the-charts applause as Tashi scanned the people seated down on the floor and then over to a side exit where several Watchmen stood. There were maybe a dozen of them, in the black hats, black T-shirts, and military-style gear. All of them had guns on their hips. Another half dozen flanking the stage as Vardaman spoke.

"None of y'all asked for any handouts," he said. "Y'all aren't those kind of people. Am I right? We all pulled ourselves up by our bootstraps to feed our families. We are all hardworkin', tough-talkin', God-fearin' rednecks. And we owe it to our children, and our children's children, to stand our Southern ground. Too many good men, good people, fought and died for what was taken away from us. So much blood spilled not more than five miles from where we stand."

Huge, gushing, thunderous applause and lots of rebel yells. Jessica cut her eyes to Tashi. She'd seen the Watchmen, too. Jessica shook her head, leaned into Tashi, and said, "We're not getting anywhere near him."

"What are they going to do?" Tashi said. "Shoot us?"

"Maybe," Jessica said into her ear. "Yeah. That's a distinct possibility."

"I'm going to ask him," Tashi said. "I'm headed right down after the speech to put the microphone in front of his face and ask him about those pictures of his hunt lodge."

"And then what?" Jessica asked. "So Brandon Taylor was on his land. What do we ask as a follow-up question?"

"I just want to see his reaction," Tashi said. "See how he handles it."

"What if he doesn't react at all?" she said. "What if he acts like he has absolutely no fucking clue?"

Tashi didn't answer, transfixed by everything she was hearing. The crowd standing on their feet, yelling and screaming to take back their country, their Mississippi. Fists raised and flags waving. "I'm still working on that part."

"Do you recognize anything from these pictures?" Quinn asked, spreading the photos Hubie Phillips had given them out on the Taylor family kitchen table.

Both Rhonda and Shaina Taylor sat with him. Shaina held a little lapdog, a white Shih Tzu, that went for Quinn's throat the moment he walked in the door. Rhonda Taylor had on pink sweatpants with PINK written across her backside. Her daughter, Shaina, was ready for work, dressed in blue jeans and a white blouse, a blue Dollar General vest with her name tag attached hung over a nearby chair. Her styled blonde hair falling over her shoulders. The women looked so much alike it was a little strange sitting with them both at the same table.

"Where'd you get these?" Shaina asked.

"I can't say," Quinn said. "But I was hoping y'all might make some sense of them."

The women picked up the black-and-white photos at random, as if selecting pieces for a jigsaw puzzle. Most of the photos were obvious, teenagers doing teenager business at high school. Most of the faces Quinn had IDed on his own. One of the photos featured Caddy decorating the halls before some football game, standing on a ladder and taping up a banner. WILDCAT PRIDE! Another one showed Hubie Phillips sitting on top of his desk, surrounded by a dozen or so kids from the yearbook staff. He wore a big smile, hands thrown up in mock exasperation. Others were stark shots of the woods in the winter, dead leaves in the mud, animal tracks and twisting trails leading into darkness. A dead deer covered in frost. They could've been about anywhere in Tibbehah County. Quinn wasn't sure if they meant much to Brandon beyond the quality of light and composition.

"What's this?" Rhonda Taylor said, looking down at a photo of the Vardaman compound, then up to where Quinn stood.

"A big place in the north part of the county," Quinn said. "I don't think it had been there long back then. You know it?"

Rhonda Taylor snatched the half-glasses hanging from around her neck and pursed her lips as she studied it. "Can't say I do. Shaina?"

Shaina held it up to the light coming from the kitchen window. She nodded as she studied it and then leveled her eyes on Quinn, a curious look on her face. "That's the Vardaman place, ain't it?"

Quinn nodded.

"What was Brandon doing out there?"

"I don't know," Quinn said. "Was hoping y'all might tell me."

"Then why didn't you just ask that straight off," Rhonda Taylor said, scooting back the little wooden chair and waddling into the kitchen. She poured out the rest of a green smoothie shake into a tall glass. "Why'd you make us look at them football games and test shots for Most Beautiful and Most Athletic. Might've saved us some time, Sheriff."

Quinn placed his hands on his hips and nodded to the women. "Brandon ever tell you about hiking out there?"

"Never," Rhonda Taylor said, stirring the smoothie with the handle of a wooden fork.

"I've seen it," Shaina said. "But not for a long time after Brandon died. We went up there during Christmas. The Vardamans were having some kind of party and he had the place all lit up like a winter wonderland. I remember he brought in some company from over in

Georgia to make fake snow. Kids at school were talking about it, but we couldn't get in. Got stopped right there at the big gate. It was only for rich folks. People who wouldn't consort with us. We had to turn around and go home. But I saw it. And then I passed by there a few years ago, just driving on the back roads, thinking on things with Brandon."

"Why there?"

"Well," Shaina said. "That place isn't far from where they found him. Right? If you went as the crow flies and not by any map."

Quinn nodded. He didn't want to lead her. But she was right.

"Y'all thinking that man knows something about Brandon?" Rhonda Taylor asked.

Quinn looked down at his boots and back up at the Taylors. "I don't know," Quinn said. "But I'm betting he's never been asked."

Rhonda Taylor sat down, leaving her smoothie on the counter. She reached across the table and grabbed Shaina's hand, squeezing her fingers, as she started to cry. "Thank you," she said. "That's all we ever wanted. Someone to ask about him. We sure do appreciate this, Sheriff."

Caddy and Jean were at the high school track, walking laps around and around, as they tried to do at least three times a week. Jean had already lost a ton of weight, laying off the carbs and sweet tea, still not doing so good with her weekly box of chardonnay. The whole thing getting to be a bone of contention with them both. Caddy knew her momma drank too much. And Jean Colson straight out didn't give a damn and told her so.

"Has he called?" Jean asked, wearing a blue velour tracksuit with a GRACELAND baseball hat and sunglasses. "Maybe he didn't mean what he said. Maybe Bentley's just worried about Quinn on his own."

"We talked it through," Caddy said. "I asked him a lot of questions at the Huddle House."

"How'd y'all end it?" Jean asked, rounding the bend of their fourth lap out of eight. For an older woman in her sixties, she had set a pretty nice pace.

"I told Bentley the Huddle House was the perfect place for country trash to break up," she said. "I told him it'd make a hell of a story for his prep school buddies down in Jackson. Hope they all don't choke on their scotch laughing."

"You didn't," Jean said.

"Damn right, I did, Momma," Caddy said. "There wasn't a reason in this world for the boy to be sniffing around The River other than wanting to get into my business and Quinn's business. Only reason I let my guard down was on account of him knowing Daddy. And, in hindsight, that should've been a warning more than anything."

"Jason Colson can be charming," Jean said. "It's a side of your father you never saw."

"Hard to see any side of a man who was never around," Caddy said. "Please don't go and be making excuses for Daddy now, too. I just don't think I can stand it. I told Bentley he was a two-faced son of a bitch and to never call on me ever again. I took the damn check and ripped it in a million pieces, scattering it right there in his French fries and ketchup."

"I wish you'd heard him out," Jean said. "You and your brother have quick tempers. Quinn likes to fight and you like to dog-cuss folks. I saw the way Bentley treated you, the way he looked at you when you couldn't see him. I don't know why he came down to The River. I figured it was all about his family foundation. But I know he loved you, Caddy. Don't be thinking of anything otherwise because that will eat you damn-near whole and we all can't go there again."

Caddy quit walking, red-faced and out of breath, but not on account of the exercise. Her mother always, always knew how to say the wrong thing at the wrong time and go right for the soft spot in her. It was a talent most mothers had with their daughters.

"You don't want to go there again?" Caddy said. "I sure would hate to disappoint you, Momma, if I went off the rails again and ended up in a black ditch like those times before. I sure don't want to be an inconvenience around the holidays. Don't say things like that. And don't you dare make excuses for Bentley Vandeven. You want me to be real honest with you, daughter to mother? I let my guard down because he was handsome, had good hair and nice teeth, and seemed to have eyes for me. I hadn't been with a man I cared about since Jamey died. And it felt real good to have that again. I should've known it was all bullshit. A man six years younger than me wanting to get into my pants."

"Caddy."

Caddy was so damn mad she wanted to spit. She turned her head and did spit, on the track, and kept on walking, following the same lane, Jean walking up beside her, pumping her arms, staring straight ahead through her sunglasses. The bleachers were empty, the aluminum seats glinting in the sun.

"Caddy."

"I don't want to talk about it, Momma."

"You said he warned you about Quinn?" Jean Colson said. "Just what did he mean?"

"I told Quinn about it."

"Now tell me."

"Bentley said some friends of his dad had been talking," she said. "He said they'd do anything they could to get rid of that cocky son of a bitch up in Tibbehah County. They called out Quinn personal."

"Why?" she said.

"Bentley swore up and down he didn't know," Caddy said. "But he believed it had something to do with the man shot dead at the jail. And maybe something to do with Brandon Taylor."

"Brandon Taylor?" Jean said. "What on earth?"

"Nobody in this county wants to talk about unpleasant things," Caddy said. "It doesn't matter if we have schools that can't pay the light bill or buy books or even if half of Mississippi is going hungry, we're supposed to smile and talk about hospitality. When Brandon Taylor was found, y'all told us kids not to talk about it. Like it was some kind of nasty disease needing to be contained. Everybody just wants those kinds of things to disappear without ever trying to find what went wrong. Maybe that's why we can't do a damn thing to get better."

Jean kept walking, silent for several minutes. Caddy pretty sure Jean was about to deliver the Sermon on the Mount or pass along a bit of wisdom Elvis told the Memphis Mafia. Still pumping her arms, Jean turned full onto Caddy and said, "But did you really have to tear up that check?"

Quinn had already left the sheriff's office for home when Tashi Coleman called, rambling and out of breath, scared, asking if he could stop by the Traveler's Rest Motel. As he drove, the sky broke purple and black, scattered wild clouds over the rolling hills toward the north part of Tibbehah.

"Slow down," Quinn said. "Who and what happened?"

"Those damn Watchmen people," Tashi said. "They followed us all the way from Tupelo. We didn't see them until we stopped off at this Chick-fil-A and they were there, watching us in the parking lot. They followed us all the way back to Jericho. I can see them right now from across the street."

"Why were they following you?"

"I tried to talk to Vardaman at his rally," Tashi said. "They pushed

Jessica down and stole our equipment. We filed charges in Tupelo. But they're not quitting."

"What are they driving?"

"Black Chevy Tahoe," she said. "It has a cracked windshield, one side kind of scraped up. I see two of them. But there may be more."

"Roger that," Quinn said, making a U-turn on Highway 9, ten minutes from the farm. Hondo was riding shotgun. Quinn rubbed his neck and told him supper was going to have to wait.

Quinn saw the Tahoe down the old Tupelo Highway, parked sideways in front of a defunct Texaco station right across from the Traveler's Rest. Quinn knew the motel, had stayed there when he'd first come back home from Fort Benning, the sign outside still offering COLOR TV, WI-FI & FREE FISHING IN OUR BASS POND. It wasn't much, but would do until they decided to bring a Ritz-Carlton to Tibbehah County.

Quinn radioed Reggie, who was coming up in the opposite direction, Kenny and Dave Cullison on standby if there was any trouble. He didn't expect any. If the Neshoba County Fair was any indication, these guys would fold pretty easy, wanting to intimidate more than engage. He slowed about a hundred meters from the Tahoe, turning on his blue lights as he parked, Reggie rolling in behind the Tahoe. Quinn prepared for any quick action, watching the two men seated in the front seat. Neither of them moving, staring straight ahead and trying to look tough.

Quinn approached the driver's side as he would any traffic stop, the window slowly rolling down. Reggie approached from the back.

"What's the problem, Officer?" the driver asked, smirking. A little bit of tobacco under his front lip.

Quinn hadn't seen the man before. This guy was beefy, with a goatee and black glasses, some kind of black do-rag on his head labeled AMERICAN SNIPER. He wore a thick, braided silver chain around his neck like a dog collar. There was another guy in the passenger seat, a lot older, with a short white beard and reddened, chapped skin. He turned to give his best hard, tough look at Quinn. Both wore black military gear, tactical vests, and cargo pants.

As he turned in the passenger seat, Quinn spotted a gun under the older man's windbreaker.

"You fellas lost?" Quinn said. "Long ride from Tupelo."

"We ain't from Tupelo," the old man said. "I wouldn't be from Tupelo for all the money in the world. Hellhole of bullshit upon this earth."

"License and registration."

"How you gonna ticket a man when he's parked?" the driver said, snorting. "Y'all in the damn KGB? This is America, last time I checked."

Quinn glanced over at Reggie, nodding slightly. These guys were a couple of Grade A shitbirds, itching to make some kind of trouble for the sheriff's office.

"Can't a man take a drive without being harassed?" the old man said. "That's what this is. Pure and old-fashioned harassment."

Quinn looked at the older man, with his yellowed teeth and saggy jowls. He could smell his sour breath from outside the vehicle. His nose bulbous, broken veins across his cheeks, like a professional drinker. "You have a permit for that weapon?"

"Bet your damn ass," the old man said. The driver stayed silent.

Quinn stared down into the car, keeping a safe distance between himself and the open window. Reggie had already pulled his sidearm, standing there behind the Tahoe, waiting for Quinn to give an order. The driver looked into his rearview mirror and shook his head. "Y'all really taking the affirmative action thing serious," he said. "How many white men would kill to have that job?"

"How about you just quit talking for a while," Quinn said. "Let your brain catch up with your mouth."

"We got a dang lawyer," he said. "Whole damn team of 'em."

"Damn straight," the older man said. His skin was pinkish, his small eyes bright blue and beady like a pig's. "Goddamn right."

"Both of you, step out of the vehicle," Quinn said, motioning for Reggie to take the older man on the passenger side. He didn't like the look of either of them, both of them shifty and nervous, not exactly the types to think something through.

"In all my life, I ain't never been treated like some kind of criminal," the driver said, crawling out. "A white man has rights in Mississippi."

"License and registration."

Quinn watched the driver reach for his wallet, slow and easy. The man's stubby fat little hands shaking a bit as he handed over the cards. Quinn gave them a quick glance, asking the driver to move toward the front of the vehicle, Reggie doing the same with the passenger, keeping the two in the headlights of Quinn's truck. It was nearly dark, sky going orange and purple now, with black shadows down the highway.

Quinn spotted Tashi Coleman standing out by the motel registration desk, watching them. Her arms hugging her waist as if she was cold, wanting both men to see her and know she wasn't afraid.

"What's your name?" Quinn asked the older man. Already knowing the driver was Joseph Gibson. Ugliest damn driver's license pic he'd ever seen. The man looked like he had a live wire switched up his ass as the photo had been taken, hair sticking up and eyes bugging out of his beefy head.

"Norm Southwell."

"Concealed permit, Mr. Southwell?"

Southwell reached for his wallet and handed Quinn a card.

"This is a hunting license."

"What's the damn difference?"

"Plenty," Quinn said. "Keeping that automatic under your jacket is a felony. You didn't announce it when I came up on the vehicle. Please place your hands on the truck."

"You're full of damn shit," Southwell said, mouthing off but doing what he was told. "I know why you're here. I'll have you know those two girls come to harass Senator Vardaman at his rally. They didn't have no right to push their way through permitted folks and start asking a bunch of crazy-ass questions. That rally was a private event for the senator's fans and friends. They weren't on no list. And we got one of those fucking free speech zones or whatever you call that shit over by the bathroom. They want to run their Yankee mouths and pop a squat, they can go to it. They nearly knocked the senator's teeth out with that big microphone of theirs. We videoed the whole dang thing."

Quinn nodded, pulling the man's gun from an inside pocket of his jacket. A fully loaded Ruger SR9 with a nitride finish.

"You're crazy," Norm Southwell said. "You know what kind of shit you're gonna stir up?"

Quinn kicked the old man's legs wider, his military pants wrinkled and sagging off his bony ass, the crack of his butt showing. The back of his neck thick with white unshaven hair. He had on unlaced military boots and a sheathed knife on his belt. The man was mumbling something unintelligible under his breath as Quinn took the knife, turning for a short moment to spit down on Quinn's polished boots.

"You can't arrest him," the younger, fatter man said. "He didn't do nothing wrong. You don't need no carry permit in Mississippi. That's right. That sure is right. Governor done signed it and everything. You hear me?"

"He had it in his waistband," Quinn said. "Not in a holster and not in plain sight. You need a concealed carry permit to do that. It's the law. You want to stick around and bail him out in the morning? Glad to find you a comfortable place to sleep at the sheriff's office."

Joseph Gibson glared at Quinn, still wearing his sunglasses at dusk, standing there like he was about to do something he wasn't. Quinn stared right back at him. He knew the type, a man with no mission in life who found comfort in the well-oiled machinery of a gun. People like that just kind of wandered, pissed off at the world, convincing themselves of any lies filling their ears. All the damn gear and weaponry Gibson bought online would never make a soldier out of him. A good soldier fought with training and purpose, not with costumes and props.

"I dealt with folks like you when I came home," Quinn said. Reggie cuffed the old man, Southwell, and pushed him toward the back of his patrol car. The man cussing up a storm, spit flying from his mouth, his face turning a deep shade of purple. Reggie grinned while he placed him inside, Southwell's hands cuffed tight behind his back. "Only difference is y'all used to hide in the woods. Now you've crawled on out into the daylight."

"You'll be sorry."

"Already am," Quinn said.

Reggie drove out of the parking lot, saluting Quinn from behind the wheel, heading onto Tupelo Road back toward town. Quinn stood in front of his truck until Gibson pulled out in the Tahoe and headed east, hopefully out of town. He crossed the back highway in the coming darkness, finding Tashi Coleman standing by a Coke machine, her hands in the pockets of her hoodie.

"What happened?"

"You were right to call."

"They took our gear," she said. "Our recorder. Our microphone. Jessica's camera and her phone. They couldn't get mine. I wouldn't hand it over. I dared them to touch me."

"They said you nearly busted Senator Vardaman in the mouth."

"You believe that?"

"Nope."

"They'll come back," she said. "They won't stop us from asking questions."

"And I'll be here to stop them," Quinn said, sticking a dollar in the Coke machine and getting two bottles back. Hell of a deal. He offered one to Tashi.

"I'm so damn mad I can't even think."

"Where's Jessica?"

"Upstairs."

"How about we all have a talk?" he asked. "Did y'all get to eat?"

"No," she said. "We drove off from the drive-through when we saw them. We haven't eaten all day."

Tashi looked up at Quinn, Quinn noticing the girl couldn't be more than five foot two. Her hands still plunged deep in her hoodie pockets, her small, lean face drained of all color. She took the Coke as they headed back into the U-shaped motel, its doors facing what used to be the pool. Years ago, someone had filled it all in, but you could still see where it had been, the ground soft and sunken. Back in high school, kids used to come here after the prom, the night manager not giving a damn if they were underage.

"We have to find Ansley," she said.

"Working on it."

"Work harder."

"I have a friend," Quinn said as they got to Tashi's motel room door, fluorescent corridor lights sputtering on for the night. "She's damn good at tracking folks down."

# TWENTY-FIVE

Thirty-six hours later, Lillie Virgil walked into Quinn's office, pulled up a wooden chair, and took a seat. She lifted her suede boots up onto his desk, folded her hands in her lap, and said, "You can't rely on me and the U.S. Marshals Service for all your needs, Sheriff," she said. "Just because this woman may or may not be a witness in a high-profile case isn't a concern for us. She's neither a felon nor an escaped convict. I'm not inclined to go out and find Ansley Cuthbert for you unless I've got a court order. And I don't see that coming for a long while."

"You remember her?" Quinn said, looking over his desk at Lillie.

"Of course I remember Ansley Cuthbert," Lillie said. "Wilder than a march hare. That girl ruined many a good Baptist at Tibbehah High. Remember when she posed in a bikini for the FFA Calendar? Standing in the mud by her boyfriend's Jeep? That was a pretty big controversy in Jericho. More teenage boys were wankin' to Ansley than to posters of damn Tiffani Amber Thiessen."

"Yep," Quinn said. "Tripled sales that year. I heard they went out and bought a brand-new tractor."

"And what's this shit about some dickless paramilitary assholes giving y'all trouble?" she asked. "When I couldn't reach you, I called Reggie and he said two men had been stalking those reporters from New York. I hope you busted their ass good. You can't come in to Tibbehah County and put your feet up on the furniture. Am I right?"

Quinn nodded to Lillie's boots at the edge of the desk. She didn't pay him any mind, leaning back in the hard wooden chair like she'd had a hell of a day. "So let me get this shit straight. Y'all went up to Memphis trying to find Ansley Goddamn Cuthbert and ran into Mr. Phillips, who, by the way, is a hell of a sweet man. How's he doing anyway?"

"Fine."

"And Mr. Phillips knew something about Ansley which made that crazy-ass girl a top-shelf priority? Because I can't for the life of me think of one damn reason Ansley Cuthbert could be of any help to y'all on Brandon Taylor."

"She was his girlfriend at the time," Quinn said. "Mr. Phillips and Rhonda Taylor both say they were very close before he disappeared. Caddy and that girl Tashi Coleman tracked her down at a Memphis bar a couple weeks ago. She wouldn't talk, but said some things that made Caddy think she's the one who sent Maggie all those letters about Brandon and about the girl's body on the Pennington land. If that letter was from Ansley, then she likely knows who that girl was and how she died. When I went back to find her and ask her about it, she'd blown town."

"I know," Lillie said. "I got your damn voicemail. We've already been over every inch of this crap. You know I do have a shitload of trouble on my desk? I had to drive over to Atlanta to pick up some man who'd killed two folks over a set of tires in south Memphis. And let me tell you something, that son of a bitch didn't want to go quietly."

Quinn reached into his humidor for a fresh Liga Privada, setting fire to it with his battered Zippo. He smiled at Lillie Virgil through the smoke. "I figured that's why you missed the service for ole E. J. Royce," he said. "You were too busy."

"Yeah, that's the reason," Lillie said. "I hate I had to shoot the kid who killed him. I knocked that hat right off his head but he kept running. All that blood we found? No way he made it."

"He had help," Quinn said. "I guarantee those boys drove straight back to the Rez and are hiding out now."

"Couple of button men," Fannie said. "I'd rather find out who mashed that goddamn button."

"Can't ask Royce."

"Nope," Lillie said, shaking her head. "Did y'all have enough of the bastard to bury? Looks like his hounds got most of the prime cuts."

"We had plenty."

"A shame," Lillie said. "I hope none of those dogs ended up with worms."

Lillie stood up and pushed the chair back, leaning over the desk and snatching up Quinn's cigar. She took a long puff, thinking on things, looking out the beaded glass of the window to the recreation area. It was Saturday afternoon, when families came to visit the folks in jail, setting up lawn chairs on the other side of the chain-link fence. They passed fried chicken and snack cakes through the fence, having family reunions, laughing, talking, arguing. One couple one time had tried to have sex through the chain links and it turned into a real mess.

"You found her," Quinn said. "Didn't you?"

"She's out in my vehicle now," Lillie said. "Why don't you try and give me a fucking challenge sometime. How'd you know?"

"How long we know each other, Lil?"

"Ansley won't come inside," Lillie said. "And she won't talk to me. I found her at her girlfriend's house over in Cordova. I never figured that girl to be a switch-hitter. But Ansley apparently is open to all kinds. Isn't that something? She wasn't happy to see me. Even said I could be a real raging bitch back in high school."

"Who would ever say such a thing?"

"I know," Lillie said. "Just fucking insane. Nearly made me want to slap the shit out of her."

"You think she'll talk to me?"

"She seemed to like you, Quinn," Lillie said. "There's something dark on that girl's mind. And you're gonna have to be the one to get it."

"You can't just show up like this," goddamn Bentley Vandeven said to Fannie. "Even if the senator wanted to see you, this isn't the place for a meet. Let's all just sit tight, let me make some phone calls, and agree on a better location."

Fannie Hathcock sat behind the wheel of her new Lexus LS 500 Sport, a little gift she'd given herself over the summer. Pearl white with black leather interior and chrome trim. She had the sunroof wide open on the drive down to Jackson, cracked now as she sat there with Bentley in the steakhouse parking lot, the kid trying to be cool and collected, a real fucking voice of reason.

"How's Pastor Colson doing?" Fannie said. "Any luck getting in her pants? I heard she's really locked that shit down. Doesn't drink or drug anymore. Not fun at all."

Bentley's face drained of color. His face and front of his blue-and-white gingham shirt nearly soaked through on an unusually warm October afternoon. He didn't wear any jewelry, only a gold watch that probably cost half as much as her goddamn Lexus. "What do you know about it?"

"I've known what you're about since you brought the tip jar up to Tibbehah County for your fat-cat friends," she said. "Remember, Bentley? I made it very clear I wasn't Johnny Fucking Stagg and didn't make political donations."

"My relationship with Caddy Colson isn't about business or politics," he said. "And I'd appreciate you staying out of my private life."

"Little too late for that, kid," Fannie said, cracking the electric windows. "Be a good boy and open that glovebox. Hand me the pack of Dunhills in there. Was your daddy hoping you getting tight with Miss Caddy would lead to some good dirt on the sheriff? Sure seems like a lot of goddamn work for a man your age. Grown-ass women are a little different from that Ole Miss cooze you're probably used to, all spray-tanned, manicured, and wide-eyed. You got to put in some real effort for a mature woman."

Bentley seemed taken aback for a moment, opening his mouth as if he didn't know what to say. But then he just shook his head, kneading his palm into his forehead and laughing a little. "I appreciate you driving down," Bentley said. "There's an Olive Garden right up the road. I'd be happy to buy you lunch and listen to any of your concerns."

"Bentley?"

"Yes, ma'am."

"Do I look like the kind of woman who eats at a fucking Olive Garden?" she asked. "I just drove two hours down from Tibbehah County to have a face-to-face meeting in y'all's little Honeycomb Hideout here. If the senator was ashamed to see me, he should've made it clear before I made the trip. I sure as shit am not about to drive back to Jericho without a meet."

"They won't see you."

"Bullshit," she said, blowing out a long stream of smoke, watching it float from her car out into the parking lot. "When did Vardaman start running y'all's show? I remember a time when the establishment wouldn't let a hick like him park cars at a place like this. You boys always liked making money, but when did you stop being any fucking fun? The hell of it is, I'm pretty sure Vardaman believes half the shit he's saying. Did y'all ever consider what's gonna happen to y'all when they open the barn doors and those crazy folks come to suck at the state tit?"

Bentley, God love him, seemed to be sweating even more. She loved making him nervous. He looked down at the face of his phone and across the parking lot to the steakhouse. He was so damn fidgety that he looked like a man who needed to take a leak bad. Being in a parked car with Fannie Hathcock might damage whatever political career the kid had imagined for himself.

"He's not here," Bentley said. "I don't know what you heard."

"Then get him here," Fannie said, looking down at the Cartier on her wrist. "I have all damn day to sit at the bar and make small talk with y'all's friends until he shows up."

"My father asked that you leave," he said. "He didn't like what you were saying up at the bar about a certain good friend of his and a Shetland pony."

"I was joking," Fannie said. "A Shetland pony's too good for that man. The fat son of a bitch couldn't get laid in a mannequin factory."

"I'll talk to my father," he said. "Can I relay your message to him? Personally."

Fannie shook her head, spewing more smoke. "No, sir," she said. "I'm sorry to have disturbed whatever circle jerk y'all had planned today. But I have something your dear ole daddy and Vardaman need to hear live and in person."

"Can you at least tell me what this is about?" he asked. "They'll want to know."

Fannie turned to him and patted his smooth face. "Back room, kid," she said. "Tell those boys to open their fucking ears and cover their nuts. Vardaman's world is about to get tossed inside out and Miss Fannie's the only one who can make things right."

"Did you ever tell Caddy we hooked up?" Ansley Cuthbert asked Quinn.

They'd stopped off on a county road between Providence and Carthage, a meandering logging road, skittering the edge of the National Forest. Ansley had told him where to go and where to stop, both of them not talking much since they left the sheriff's office.

"Somehow, it never came up," Quinn said, turning to Ansley as he sat behind the wheel, wondering what was so special about this stretch of road, five klicks from where they found Brandon's body, eight from where they found the girl, and about twenty from the Hawkins property. "Did she know?"

Ansley shook her head, looking a lot different from the last time he'd seen her, drinking Coors down along Sarter Creek one summer evening, four-wheelers and trucks parked along the sandy bottom. He and Anna Lee had broken up for a few weeks—again—and he'd found some companionship with Ansley, going for a long ride out into the hills and Big Woods, listening to George Strait, drinking beer and fooling around in the back of his truck. That had been more than twenty years ago but somehow seemed like last week. Back then, Ansley had been a blonde, but now she had raven black hair, pale skin, and a sleeve tattoo on her left arm. Looking nice in a black-and-white-checked shirt and skinny black pants, hair done up like women used to wear back in the forties. A pinup in motion.

"Always knew you'd go back to Anna Lee," she said. "I have to say, I'm kind of shocked y'all didn't get married."

"Yeah?" Quinn said, turning to her in the truck. "Me, too. Right up until the time she married Luke Stevens. And for a little while after."

"Never goes quite the way you think it will when you're a kid."

"Nope."

"We sure did have some fun that night," Ansley said, smiling. "You were a wild man. Driving like you did."

"We may have committed some violations."

"I only recall two," she said. "Damn. That was the summer before Brandon and all this mess."

"I'm sorry," Quinn said. "I always wondered why you dropped out and left Tibbehah."

"Your friend getting murdered will motivate you to keep moving," she said. "It was so damn horrible, Quinn. As bad as it gets."

Quinn didn't say anything. He figured her wanting to take a ride, telling him where to go, would be the start of something he couldn't force. Lillie used to tell him the best way to get a witness talking was to shut your damn mouth and listen. He didn't try to push her or fill the silences, only sat there behind the wheel, letting her mind take her back to November of 1997, months before Quinn's graduation, right before she'd leave Tibbehah altogether and make a life in Memphis.

"They killed him," she said. "I guess you know that already."

Quinn waited.

"Do you want me to take you to the spot I last saw him?" she said. "It's not two hundred feet from where we parked. Goddamn, my heart is beating so fast. I feel like I'm coming loose from my skin."

"You don't have to," Quinn said. "We can talk right here."

"I need to do it," she said. "Makes things right after I started all this back in motion. I got Shaina Taylor to reach out to those girls. I sent those letters to Maggie. It's disrespectful if I don't walk my ass back to where I saw him die. Christ Almighty."

They crawled out of the truck, Quinn, in his boots, hopping down to the gravel, Ansley leading the way over a little ditch and through some brush and vines into an endless pine forest, stretching up into the hills and for thousands of acres beyond Tibbehah County. The location wasn't completely lost to him now, knowing they were within two or three miles of Vardaman's lodge. He'd once crisscrossed this very road looking for escaped convicts named Esau Davis and Bones Magee.

"Brandon and me were just friends," she said, walking beneath the tall pines, feet soft on the copper-colored needles. "We might've fooled around a little. But mostly we were good pals, going to movies, hanging out at Mr. Phillips's house, playing gags on folks at church camp. That kid was a real joker, always looking to put his thumb in someone's eye."

She kept walking, moving faster than Quinn, stopping for a moment to find her place, sunlight coming down through the tall trees, spinning for a second and then finding her way again, heading up a hill and coming upon what looked to be an old cabin falling in on itself, the rock fireplace still standing tall. "I knew I could find it."

Quinn wanted to ask the who and the why but knew Ansley would get to it, her eyes shining with memories, false eyelashes fluttering, crying as she walked, wiping her tears with the back of her hand. "I'm the one who told him about the parties," she said. "Mr. Stagg would pay us just to be there. You didn't have to fool around or nothing. He said those men just liked pretty young faces bringing them barbecue and whiskey. Pleasant company. He said if you wanted to get frisky, it was all on you. You know how Mr. Stagg talks."

"Straight out his ass," Quinn said. Ansley had stopped down at the old house, nothing but rotten wood and a few panes of busted glass. Maybe a hunt cabin back in the day, or someone's little home, way out from Jericho and civilization. Quinn used to love discovering these old places as a kid, knowing from an early age how quickly nature could take back what man had tried to claim. No matter the abuse, the woods knew how to grow again and heal itself. That was one of the reasons he found so much solace and comfort walking among the trees, whether hunting or just hiking. A strange comfort coming over him now.

"I never told anybody what they did to Brandon, because I knew only two things could happen: they might put me in jail or they might kill me. And nothing would happen to them," she said. "At first, what we did was Brandon's idea. But I got in on it, too. Our families didn't have a lot of money and that fall we made more money than I could ever have imagined. We almost didn't know where to put it all."

"Brandon's father thought Mr. Phillips had given it to him."

"Mr. Phillips?" she said. "Brandon's father was a real asshole. He couldn't stand Brandon hanging out with adults outside his family. That man didn't even like his kids leaving the house. When he found Brandon's shoe box full of hundreds, he whipped the shit out of him. Gave him a black eye."

Quinn nodded, hands on hips, turning around, looking for a trail or path leading out. He dropped a pin on his GPS, knowing he'd be back here for a long while, taking pictures, documenting everything Ansley Cuthbert had to say.

"Brandon was a hell of a photographer," Quinn said. "Wasn't he?"

"I'd tell him where and when and he'd get that lens as long as your arm on his camera," she said. "He had fun doing it, laughing like hell about how fat and stupid those men were. It's how we got in with Skylar. She was our age but a dropout. I'm sure that wasn't her real name. I think she was from somewhere over in Alabama, another runaway who came down to Tibbehah to work at the Booby Trap. The girl was funny as hell. Knew damn-near everything. Kind of organized the young girls for their duties. She'd bring in boxes and boxes of

Victoria's Secret bikinis and all. Skylar would help us with our makeup and hair, making sure we looked just right at those parties."

"Did you know Vardaman?"

"I knew who he was and that the cabin was his place," she said. "But he really wasn't there too much. He'd more kind of host these things, make sure all his boys were having a good time, fine young tail serving them chilled shrimp and gallons of scotch. They'd shoot skeet and ride four-wheelers. The ones who weren't from Mississippi had the most fun of all. Tibbehah County for them was like going to the far side of the damn moon."

"How many times did you go to the lodge?" Quinn asked.

"I only did it once," she said. "Those men creeped me out. Skylar would call us when they'd be having another one of those rich daddy parties and I'd drive Brandon out to the woods and set on a time to meet back. I always got scared we were going to get caught. I think that was most of the fun for Brandon and me. He'd tell me what he'd saw and then we'd go back to the high school and develop those pictures. He'd set a meet and then we'd all split up the money. I guess that was my first dose of reality, the ways of the world. How men will do damn-near anything for sex."

"How long did y'all keep this up?"

"Maybe three months," she said. "Brandon was smart. He always had them leave the money in public places. Most of the time, the town square. And he never showed up himself. He had this old black man named Mooney do it for him. Mooney hung out at the pool hall and for five dollars would do anything you asked. Never once looked inside the bag. I remember me and Brandon one time skipped school and blew through five thousand dollars in a damn day up at the Galleria and the Peabody Hotel. He bought me a pair of diamond earrings."

"What happened to Skylar?"

Ansley looked to Quinn, nodding, black bangs chopped right above her eyebrows. "You know," she said. "Y'all were the ones who dug her out of that hole."

"Who did it?"

"It wasn't Vardaman," she said. "But it was his people. I was with Brandon when they caught him. We thought we were safe, hiding in that shack. It had a roof then, some kind of damn protection in the rain. We should have kept on running. Brandon walked out to protect me. After they took him away, I ran and ran. I was scared to death and never ever looked back."

"Did you see Brandon get shot?"

Ansley shook her head.

"But you saw them take him away?"

She nodded, crying hard now, her face a damn mess with the white makeup streaked with black eyeliner. Sobbing, almost retching, as she stood there with Quinn. He wrapped his arm around her and pulled her close.

"When we were hiding in the cabin, Brandon told me they made him watch as they buried Skylar," she said. "When he turned and ran, they hunted him like he was some kind of animal. He said they were having a hell of a time, yelling and hollering, chasing him on four-wheelers. We'd already agreed where to meet, here at the cabin, like always, Brandon hiking in the woods and leaving me with his truck. But they found the cabin. They didn't even know about me, had never seen me, so Brandon said he'd go out there and I should keep hiding. But they snatched him up, driving him off in his own truck. I guess that's how they got his hunting rifle. Most days, he kept it up under the front seat."

"You remember what Vardaman's people looked like?"

"Not really," she said. "Everything happened so damn fast and I was hiding when they found us. I tried to make myself as small as possible and didn't look out until I heard that old truck start up. I prayed that they'd let Brandon go."

"Why'd you reach out to the Taylors now?" Quinn said. "You've spent half your life hiding from the men who did this."

"When I saw that man's face on TV, running for governor of Mississippi, some old goddamn piece of me just broke. I had to stop hiding."

"Help yourself," Jimmy Vardaman said.

"I think I already have," Fannie said, reaching for the bottle of champagne she'd ordered from the back room hostess and pouring a second glass. Moët & Chandon imperial rosé. "Want to join me?"

"No, ma'am," he said. "Little early for me."

"Since when?" Fannie asked. "Probably don't screw with the lights on, either. Have the Baptists damn well neutered you, Vardaman? Goddamn. I know who you are. You can be yourself with Miss Fannie. Me and you together, straight fucking shooters."

"What's on your mind, Miss Hathcock?" Vardaman said, refusing to sit at the big oval conference table. Only he and Fannie in the back room of thc steakhouse, Bentley leaving them alone and heading back to the bar. "Now, how about we get to the fucking point. I had to skip a church fish fry over in Okolona."

"I heard you got yourself a little trouble and old Buster White won't man up to handle it."

"Who's Buster White?"

"Big, fat son of a bitch who talks like he's got jambalaya gagged down his craw hole and funds your whole campaign?" she said, tipping her glass. "You were just down at his casino a few days back. I got bitches everywhere. Why? Forget already?"

Vardaman, still standing, nodded and held the leather headrest of the catbird seat of the conference room. Someone had laid out a half-dozen bowls of nuts and potato chips to feed half the swinging dicks in the state senate. Guess no one informed them this was a private meet.

"You mind me asking how you did it?" Fannie said, setting down the flute of champagne, those fine-ass little bubbles rising to the top. "A few years ago, these old grits-in-the-mouth, secret-handshake douchebags wouldn't let you mow their goddamn lawns. Me and you ain't their kind of people, Vardaman."

Vardaman moved the headrest from side to side, the chair's wheels squeaking along the floor. "The party needed a little wake-up call," he said. "Mississippi has wandered way the hell out in the woods. Outsiders trying to make Mississippi something it's never been and never will be. This is a damn lovely state full of rich history, tradition, character. Look at what those folks did up at Ole Miss. Killing off Colonel Reb and not letting the band play "Dixie"? Like I tell my people, don't ever forget where you come from. We're a proud people who want to take all that back."

"I grew up on the Coast," Fannie said. "Wasn't too damn great for me. I've been working hot pillow joints since I started shaving my legs. It wasn't exactly Scarlett O'Hara and Tara down there. Fanciest thing I knew was my trailer park was called Camelot. But don't try and spoon-feed me a hot-shit sundae. I know your game here and it doesn't have damn thing to do with tradition. This ain't about a thing but old-fashioned money and power."

"Maybe," he said, grinning. "Mr. White bankrolled me when these people wouldn't take my phone calls. They laughed behind my back, called my supporters a bunch of dumb, uneducated rednecks. Hicks. Now they'll do anything to sign checks, kiss ass, and tee up every fucking ball on the fairway. And now I don't need them. Or Buster White. Or you."

Fannie took a sip of champagne, looking up at Vardaman. Staring up at his face, she decided he was one of the most unattractive men she'd ever met, and she had a long memory for ugly folks. Not just pure classic ugliness, but he had a weird symmetry of parts. His arms were too long, his hands too short. He had a big belly and a weirdly shaped head, like the face had been carved out of red country clay.

"You want to cornhole my fine ass on account of that third-string Baptist preacher Skinner," she said. "You think that old fossil can deliver Quinn Colson's nuts to you on a silver platter? Please. Jesus God. Skinner can't do anything of the kind. Not the way you want. All you did was fuck me and Buster White at the same time. All those lies and bonfires of bullshit he started didn't do a goddamn thing. Now what, Vardaman? You got two weeks until your election and, fuck a goddamn duck, you've hit a bunch of goddamn potholes. Two dead kids lost in the boogerwoods, a redneck Hansel and Gretel story. Damn, I'll give it to you. You sure know how to throw some parties."

Vardaman smiled, walking slow, lost in thought, around the table, coming up to Fannie at the end and offering her his small, bony hand. She also smiled and stood up, looking bad-ass in a sleeveless pink chiffon blouse, so thin you could see the lace of her black bra. Vardaman rested a hand on her bare, sunkissed shoulder. "And you can do better?"

"Nobody needs to know your troubles."

"This ain't your business, Fannie," he said.

Fannie nodded. She could smell his breath, his face in front of her, onions and charred meat. He reached out with his free hand and stuck it up under her dress, grabbing her quick and hard by the coot. "Now you listen to me," Vardaman said, squeezing tight. "Don't you ever come to my town and shit in my bed. You hear me? I tell Buster White what you're doing and your head will end up rolling up on Panama City Beach."

Fannie stared right into his face, reaching down into her Birkin bag and extracting her titanium framing hammer with its hickory handle. Before Vardaman could even see what was going on, she knocked the son of a bitch sideways, sending him tumbling down on the ground and howling. The door busted open and a small little honey in black running shorts and a white T-shirt three sizes too small came rushing in.

"Get some ice and towels," she said. "Man can't handle his liquor."

Vardaman was sprawled the fuck out on the ground, legs wide, holding a goose egg spreading through his fingers, blood spiderwebbing down his face.

"Now you listen up and you listen up good," she said. "I'm your best goddamn chance of packing up this Tibbehah County shitshow. I'll take care of your problems if you take care of me. Vienna's Place ain't going anywhere. You hear me? Buster White is so over the hill I hear he's already singing hymns about crossing the River Jordan. It's me, you, and the Chief now. *Understand?* I own your fucking bony ass now. Or do I need to give you another whack to get through that goddamn thick skull?"

Vardaman didn't answer.

**Tashi Coleman**
***Thin Air* podcast**
**Episode 8: THE WITNESS**

NARRATOR: Here at *Thin Air* we seldom use unnamed sources. We ask everyone we interview to use their real names in an effort to make them stand behind what is said. However, in cases of a source feeling that harm may come to them, we are able to make exceptions. The woman you are about to hear was a close high school friend of Brandon Taylor. She said she kept in constant contact with Brandon in the weeks and months that proceeded his death.

She also said something else: that she was an eyewitness to his murder.

She spoke to us on the condition of anonymity, fearing that those responsible would try to find her. Even twenty years later. At the timc of the killing, she was only fifteen. She said she's been running ever since. We were the first to speak to her about what happened. This was the second time we met, this time at an interstate rest stop before she made her way to a new city, adopting, she says, a new name.

> [CAR DOOR OPENS AND STARTS TO CHIME. DOOR SLAMS.]
>
> WITNESS: This is so hard to talk about.
>
> TASHI: Maybe we can begin with what happened later? Your life since Brandon died? And why you don't want us to use your name.

[HIGHWAY NOISES. TRUCKS WHOOSHING PAST. KIDS WALKING PAST CAR, LAUGHING.]

WITNESS: OK. [A SIGH.] Sure. I've tried to block it out for a long time. I saw a therapist when I lived in Memphis, trying to deal with all the garbage in my life. I had substance abuse issues, tons of toxic relationships, and was trying to get some clarity. It was maybe my third, fourth visit to see him when I started to talk about Brandon. About his death and having to leave Tibbehah.

TASHI: Did people know what you saw?

WITNESS: No. Not even my mother. I swore to myself I'd never tell a soul.

TASHI: So why did you? What made you come forward?

WITNESS: You want me to talk about that now? I thought that part came later, what we did and what we saw? Isn't that how these things work? You string your listeners along until the whole thing comes together.

TASHI: That comes in editing. But you were the one who wanted this case open? Right?

WITNESS: I reached out to Brandon's sister, Shaina, about a year ago and told her the family might ask some more questions. I didn't tell her the whole story, but I gave her enough. And didn't tell her my name. I didn't want to be involved. All I hoped for is that these people who killed Brandon would be exposed.

TASHI: Why didn't you just step forward to the police and tell them what you knew?

WITNESS: Are you kidding?

TASHI: Because you felt threatened?

WITNESS: Two friends of mine died because of what they knew. They were kids and were murdered. One of them dropped into a ten-foot hole and was lost for years. No one even looked for her. No one cared. I was given a gift: I got away alive. Even though it made me leave Tibbehah County and start my life over as a teenager, dancing in nude clubs, hustling. There wasn't any other way.

TASHI: And you fear these people would still want to do you harm?

WITNESS: Absolutely. You promised not to use my name. Right? You won't use my name. I can't have that.

TASHI: I promise.

WITNESS: Have you ever known a damn secret so bad and horrible that just thinking about it scared the hell out of you? Woke you up in the middle of the night, just trying to breathe. I would've done anything, and pretty much did, to escape living down in that shithole and getting found out. These people don't think like you and me. Tibbehah County is a dark, evil place, and I pray to God every damn day that I'll never have to go back.

TASHI: What if this all leads to a new investigation, a new trial?

WITNESS: I'll be long gone. After me and you talk right here, you'll never hear of or see me again. My car is packed with everything that I own. I've done it plenty of times before and I'm happy to do it again. That's how sure I am about what I'm about to tell you.

TASHI: Now? Are you sure?

WITNESS: Let's go. The light is red. Is that thing still on?

# TWENTY-SIX

"That's some real Caligula shit going on there, Quinn," Agent Holliday, aka Jon Ringold, said to Quinn. The men leaning against the tailgate of Quinn's F-150 outside Maxwell Federal Prison Camp in Montgomery, Alabama. Quinn had driven three and a half hours, leaving at daybreak, to meet the federal agent. "Only problem is that you and I both know that Johnny Stagg won't ever say shit about something with Vardaman. He and Vardaman threw in together a long time back. I talked to the prosecutor, and, sure, he's willing to make a deal with Stagg. But he's gonna have to come up with something real juicy and solid and worth our time."

"I know the when and where and why," Quinn said. "Just not the who."

"But you're sure it's not Vardaman?"

"Pulled the trigger?" Quinn said. "Yep, I'm sure. But who made the call? That's what I need Stagg to answer. Back then, he was king of north Mississippi."

"This kid had balls," Ringold said. "Trying to shake down a state senator and all his crooked shitbird pals. Damn. He must've had a pic of Vardaman screwing a billy goat."

"Maybe," Quinn said. "All I found were pictures of the hunt lodge and the woods around it."

"Anyone in them?"

"Nope," Quinn said. "And no damn goats, either."

"Stagg doesn't have to know what you've seen or haven't seen."

"No, sir," Quinn said, nodding. "He does not."

Holliday had grown his beard out long again, nearly down to his chest, his head clean-shaven, looking like some sort of hipster monk. He had on a black T-shirt and black leather biker jacket with jeans. Holliday had been undercover when he and Quinn first met, going as Jon Ringold, gun for hire, under Stagg's command out at the Rebel Truck Stop. There'd been a time when he nearly exposed himself to Stagg, saving Quinn's ass during a shoot-out with a motorcycle gang. Real fine folks called the Born Losers.

Quinn walked around to the passenger side of his truck and pulled out a box of Liga Privadas he'd been keeping for a special occasion. He handed them over to Holliday, offering his hand.

"Congrats on the marriage," Holliday said. "Should've known you'd make a good thing out of a bank robber case."

"Maggie and Brandon are the best thing that's ever happened to me."

"Sorry about your truck," Holliday said, shaking his head. "That was one good-looking pickup. Rest in peace, Big Green Machine."

Quinn leaned against the tailgate, looking over at the flat, one-story brick prison building and then back to Holliday. "I know you can't say much."

"We're working on it," he said. "You know Nat Wilkins? She and I have been talking regular about north Mississippi. After we shut down the Pritchards, things have just gotten worse. I can't talk about what we have, but I'm not exactly surprised about the relationship between Vardaman and the Syndicate boys. We've had eyes on Buster White's casino for a long while."

"Election's next week."

Holliday cut open the cigar box with a folding knife and pulled out a Liga Privada, pulling it loose from the cellophane and whittling a little hole at the tip. Quinn clicked open his old Zippo, offering him a flame.

"Let me know what you hear from Stagg," Holliday said. "We all got an end game in mind. You, me, Nat, and more folks in Oxford. You know how much damn time we've put in this whole thing? Sure was fun bringing down old Johnny Stagg's crooked ass. But it seems we missed this Mississippi shitshow by a goddamn mile."

"Wish that could happen before the election."

"Wish in one hand and shit in the other," Holliday said, puffing on the cigar, getting the tip glowing red.

"See which one gets full first," Quinn said.

"I appreciate you letting me tag along," Lillie Virgil said, riding shotgun with Reggie Caruthers in his cruiser. "I wouldn't miss seeing Fannie's face for anything in the world. Maybe we can get the DJ at Vienna's to play, 'The Night They Drove Old Dixie Down.'"

"Don't get me wrong," Reggie said, driving, turning down the long shot of Jericho Road, passing the Piggly Wiggly, old Hollywood Video, and headed toward signs pointing the way to Highway 45. "I don't care a bit for Fannie Hathcock. But don't you hate that this is Skinner's doing? Fannie is cutthroat, but Skinner is a moral train wreck."

"Might I remind you what that woman is all about?" Lillie said, drumming her fingers on the door handle, thrilled to be along for the ride. "Don't let the big tits and fancy perfume mess with your head. That woman deals in stolen goods and hijacked eighteen-wheelers. She runs most of the drugs in the state and trucks in underage girls, most of them from Central America or Vietnam. She doesn't give a good goddamn about anyone other than herself. She'd whore out her own grandmomma for a nickel."

Reggie nodded, listening to Lillie. "Miss Fannie might wonder why you're riding shotgun with me."

"I'll tell that bitch I heard some federal fugitives were getting peckers pulled in the VIP room," she said. "Who knows. Maybe I'll get lucky. That place is a baited trap for shitbirds."

"We're only serving the paper today," Reggie said. "Just the notice for a change in county law, saying that nude or topless dancing of any sort is illegal. Doesn't matter if they wear G-strings or pasties. But one way or another, Vienna's Place is done."

"Those poor truckers," Lillie said, making a yanking motion with her hand. "Now they're gonna have to shift their gears for themselves. So damn sad. Almost makes me want to cry."

"Yes, sir," Johnny Stagg said. "I said to myself just the other day, I bet I'll be seeing ole Quinn Colson soon. I figured you'd be driving over to Alabama to say hello with a whole mess of questions."

"Then you know why I'm here."

"Yes, sir," Stagg said. "I do."

"And you know that if you help out, I'll talk to the Feds for you."

"Sure was nice of you to bring me a sack of Krystal burgers and some peppermints," Stagg said, his face in a perpetual frozen grin, like a TV preacher filled with good news for man. "You must've stopped off at a truck stop on the way into Montgomery."

"Right off the Lonesome Highway," Quinn said. "Nothing's too good for you, Stagg."

Stagg looked amused by the situation, seated by the prison commissary at a little orange table like you'd see outside a fast-food franchise. He had on a denim prison jumpsuit, gray hair parted down the side like a respectable businessman. But he still had the craggy face of a filling station attendant, sunburned and wind-chapped, with teeth as big as tombstones. The man looking pretty much unchanged since being sentenced for drug running, racketeering, bribery, and making false statements to the IRS. That was by no means all of Stagg's business, but it had been enough to send him away for twenty years. He'd learned a quick hard lesson about doing business with local crooks like Larry Cobb who kept track of their bribes and hidden cash in a safe busted open by his own son-in-law and a two-bit moron and Alabama football superfan named Peewee Sparks.

"I'm sure you're aware, I still keep up with events in Tibbehah from time to time," Stagg said, reaching for the peppermints but leaving the sack of Krystals. Inmates sat at a dozen other tables scattered across the large room that resembled a high school cafeteria.

"Did you hear about the Tibbehah Cross?"

Johnny Stagg grinned even more. "That sure made me smile," he said. "That old bastard Skinner is a real piece of work. Won't be happy until he's buried in his Sears and Roebuck suit and lying in the box about to meet his maker."

"They're building it right out front of the old Booby Trap," Quinn said. "Skinner thinks it'll outshine all that red neon."

Stagg laughed, crunching the candy between his back molars. "Can't wait to see it, one of these days," Stagg said, looking around the open room. "I sure do miss Tibbehah County. My third wife divorced me. My son won't speak to me now that the money tit's gone dry. But I still got a few friends, some hardworking folks, still loyal. Send me Christmas cards and such."

At a nearby table, Quinn recognized the former CEO of what used to be one of the largest corporations in America. Down toward the security door sat a former wide receiver for the L.A. Rams with an attractive woman in a flowered silk dress and two young children. Quinn knew the player but couldn't recall what he'd done or why he was inside with a guy like Stagg.

"Yes, sir," Johnny Stagg said. "We got us a real all-star team in here. Half these sonsabitches flushed their life down the toilet for drugs. Funny, that's something that's never interested me. I have never had the inclination to so much as puff on one of them marijuana cigarettes."

"Never stopped you from moving that shit," Quinn said. "Weed, pills, dope. Was there anything you didn't move up Highway 45 through the Rebel?"

Stagg nodded. "Women," he said. "I didn't have no stomach for selling young ladies. If they come to me on their own volition, that was one thing. But that business running through my place now sure will turn your stomach. I never forced a girl to work the pole or hop up into a semi. That was their own doing."

Quinn told Stagg to hold that thought and walked over to the canteen for a Styrofoam cup of coffee. When he returned, Stagg had started in on the Krystal burgers, the old man's eyes shining with amusement as he chewed.

"I never liked working with them people on the Coast," Stagg said. "Whatever you thought of me, I knew my goddamn limits. Damn, this is some good stuff, Quinn. I always like the way the folks at Krystal steam the bun. Them little cooked onions. Almost makes you forget that you're getting yourself a sorry sliver of meat."

Quinn took a sip of the coffee, which tasted about what he'd expect from the Maxwell Prison commissary. Metallic and bitter. Still, it was coffee. It was a long drive back up to Birmingham, then over through Tupelo and on to Tibbehah County.

"How's your daddy doin'?" Stagg asked.

Quinn didn't answer.

"And your momma and them?" Stagg said, licking his fingers. "Damn, son. I heard you went and got yourself married. That sure is something. Good for you, Sheriff. About time for you to start a family. A wholesome and noble endeavor. Some real family values going on right there."

"Holliday thinks he can knock five years off your sentence," Quinn said. "If you want to assist."

"Assist?" Stagg asked. "Funny choice of words. Makes it all seem like some type of goddamn game. Only reason I'd assist is to get back at some folks I like even less than you. You and Holliday sure cornholed my ass to Hong Kong and back."

"You cornholed yourself, Johnny."

"Boy, if I can figure out a way a man could cornhole himself, I'd damn well make a million dollars," he said. "Especially in a place like this."

Stagg nodded toward the wide receiver, saying the man's name under his breath and listing all the teams he'd played with and some of his stats. Stagg said he could never imagine how a fella would go from ten million a year to selling damn dope from the back of his SUV. "I think he played ball in college with that other fella who murdered all them folks up in Boston. They say he'd gotten his damn brains bashed in and didn't know right from wrong."

"Lot of that going around these days."

"Bullshit," Stagg said. "Folks like Vardaman just realized they can feed the weak-minded bullshit for supper and call it a chocolate cake. Doesn't matter what they do. Deeds don't mean squat. Folks only care about what you say, preach up there in the political pulpit. You better heed that, son, as an elected official."

Quinn listened, not turning to see the football player at the other table but hearing his children laughing. He sipped on his coffee, waiting for Stagg to make up his mind. He looked forward to getting on the road back home, to the farm and Maggie. Wanting to be a decent father to Brandon, maybe teaching him some more survival skills. Every kid should know how to shoot a gun and follow a compass. Know right from wrong, truth from a sack of lies. "I need to know if you were there," he said. "At the hunt lodge. November 1997."

Stagg shook his head.

"How about Vardaman?"

Stagg shook his head again and sucked some meat from a tooth. "I heard he was there when they buried that girl. They used his personal backhoe and everything. Wish I could tell you more about who she was. But she was just a drifter, never using a real name, working on a cash-only basis. You were in the service. You know how those transactions go."

"What was her name?"

"You mean what did we call her?" Stagg asked, his mind drifting off somewhere else, looking sedate and somewhat listless. "Skylar. Skylar Cole. I liked her. She was a good worker. One of the best dancers the Booby Trap ever saw. Used to do this routine to Reba's 'Fancy' that melted your heart. I heard she might've been from over in Alabama somewhere. Or was it Georgia? I never met a stripper yet who could keep her backstory straight. Diddling stepdaddies, mean-ass fathers. Working to save up money for their three-legged momma's operations."

"Who killed her?"

"Damn, boy," Stagg said. "You're getting right to it. Barely have time to swallow my damn Krystal burgers."

Quinn just stared at him, elbows on the table, right hand around the disposable cup. The steam rising from the slick surface.

"You remember that old boy with the silver buzz cut that used to hang out at the Rebel?" Stagg said, saying the man's name. "He worked with the highway patrol just like Joe Roberts worked for the state in that Johnny Cash song? Sorry to let you know that. Since you done already killed that son of a bitch."

"You sent him to kill me," Quinn said. "He killed other people for you, too."

Stagg grinned. "Where'd you hear a damn lie like that?" he said. "I did no such thing. But I know for a damn fact Vardaman didn't like being blackmailed. He was truly fired up when he came to me with his problems. Madder than hell, spit flying from his mouth and wanting to hurt some folks. Believe it or not, I tried to talk reason with him. Even helped him facilitate those payments on the Jericho Square to keep down embarrassment of those fine visitors to Tibbehah County."

"How'd you help?"

"Oh," Stagg said, shrugging. "I paid that ole hush money for him, stuff in hundreds and twenties in a sack from the Piggly Wiggly. In return, this old black fella would hand over them negatives."

"Wait," Quinn said, holding up his hand. "Wait a second. You knew the man making the pickup but made the payment anyway?"

"Hell, Quinn," Stagg said. "You know Tibbehah County. Not a lot of stories that don't connect. Wasn't any of my damn business to shut down some young entrepreneur. I can't say I really minded having a little hold over Vardaman myself."

"Did he ever pay you back?"

"Vardaman?" Stagg asked, grinning. "Shit. That cheap son of a bitch? He figured it'd be my honor to take out the trash for him."

"Did you hand over those negatives direct to Vardaman?" Quinn asked. "Or was there another go-between?"

Stagg reached for another peppermint and unwrapped the candy, popping it on his tongue and grinning as he sucked on it. "You still don't like me much," Stagg said. "Do you? After all me and you been through together. All them trials and travails and you still hold a grudge. I'll tell you what the pastor in here tells us. *Repay no one evil for evil, but give thought to do what is honorable in the sight of all.*"

"Son of a bitch," Quinn said. "You kept those negatives. Didn't you?"

Stagg kept on sucking on the peppermint. "Why, of course not. Vardaman wanted them," he said. "He insisted on it. Burned them up as soon as he got 'em."

Quinn leaned forward, closer to the table. Stagg grinned, his eyes twinkling.

"But no one told me not to print some more pictures off of 'em."

"Where are the pictures?"

"Come on now, son," he said. "Like I said, you're moving too damn fast. If we was on a date, I wouldn't even get a peck on the cheek. You'd go right for the ole cooter. It's gonna take time for you and the federal folks to unwind all this shit. And before I lift another goddamn finger, I want my lawyer here and the federal prosecutor from Oxford who fucked me a hundred ways from Sunday. Yes, sir. I want his cocky, smiling ass on his knees and his mouth open wide before I share my hidey-hole with him. That's my goddamn trump card. My ace in the hole."

"I'll see what I can do," Quinn said.

Stagg didn't move, looking away from Quinn as if he was in deep thought over the matters they'd just discussed. "I heard Skylar's face done looked like ground chuck when the trooper was done teaching her a lesson. You know what? I don't think he meant to kill her. Man like that, born with that kind of defect brain, just like that pro ball player . . . Old boy just couldn't help himself."

Quinn stood but didn't offer his hand. "I'll be in touch."

"You do that, son." Stagg kept on grinning, lifting his pointed chin and sucking on a fresh mint. His old skin looked like a leather shaving strop. "Your uncle wasn't strong enough to handle the Mississippi way. You and I both know that's what killed him. I'll help you. But you better know it won't matter a pot of mule piss. The truth don't matter no more. Better square that in your mind, Sheriff. Vardaman's people say they want to turn back the clock? If they do that, you better start building gallows on the town square."

It had been a minute since Lillie Virgil had been in Vienna's Place, but stepping into the dim light and neon, tired girls half-ass dancing on stage and Midnight Man looming behind the bar, she realized not much had changed at all. She walked in with Reggie as Midnight Man polished a tray of shot glasses, his big eyes shifting up to the spiral staircase and the glass office at the end of the catwalk where Fannie did business. Lillie nodded back toward the big man, taking the lead, Reggie trailing her but getting stopped by two working girls who couldn't help but run their hands over his broad chest, one saying how much she liked his dimples. Overhead, the speakers played "Salt Shaker" by the Ying Yang Twins.

Upstairs, Fannie's door was open, Lillie spotting the woman herself sitting in a grouping of low-slung leather chairs, looking to be having a counseling session with a skinny Asian girl with hair the color of cotton candy. She had on white go-go boots and a pink lingerie getup.

"Well, damn," Fannie said. "You finally coming in for that free lap dance and tequila shot I offered you when you were sheriff?"

"I'll wait on you to improve your talent," Lillie said. "I think I saw a few pregnant gals working the pole. I was just waiting for a little hand to reach down out of her pussy and pick up a dollar bill."

Fannie didn't answer as Reggie followed Lillie into the glass office. The Asian woman with the pink hair excused herself, passing Reggie on the way out and giving him a bright smile and a wink. She recalled giving Quinn hell once about how working girls just loved a man in uniform.

He stepped up past Lillie and set a folded piece of paper on the black coffee table. A cigarillo smoldered in a nearby ashtray.

"What's this shit?" Fannie said.

"Board of supervisors met last night," Reggie said. "They're outlawing all nude dancing and liquor sales along the Highway 45 corridor and within the county."

"Bullshit."

"Nope," Lillie said. "It's time to pack up the G-string and your Traveling Cooter Salvation Show. You're gonna just have to make a hard living running all that cooze and dope throughout the Deep South. Tough break, Fannie. I know how much you love this place. Naming it after your dead grandmomma and all. Real class with a capital *K*. I'm sure she's sending you kisses from heaven."

Fannie tossed the county ordinance onto her glass-top desk and picked up her cigarillo, standing up and walking toe-to-toe with Lillie. She was several inches shorter than Lillie, all red hair and long red nails, so much perfume on her she smelled like the makeup counter at Macy's. Lillie didn't move, smelling the smoke and perfume, the woman's large breasts poking into her chest like she could make her back the hell up.

"Why do you keep on coming back to Tibbehah County?" Fannie asked. "Never figured you for a traditional woman, but it seems like you just can't stay away from the sheriff. Even after he turned his back on your big ass and found a sweet little freckly girl to shack up with. A real instant family going on with that kid named for that boy who shot himself. I know you never ask for my advice, Lillie Virgil, but I'd do the right thing and keep to your own business running down black kids in the housing projects and shooting down escaped convicts in the back. Colson's set up his own life."

Lillie took a step forward in her suede cowboy boots, hands on hips, pressing against Fannie hard as the woman smirked, cigarillo lifted up to her lips. She could see the crow's-feet just starting to form at the corners of Fannie's green eyes, smoker wrinkles around her lips. "They shut down this shitshow and it's gonna be hell with the IRS all over your ass. I have to admit, this was one hell of a money wash during its time. What do you think you'll use next? Maybe start up a megachurch to go with that big cross they're erecting outside?"

"Are you saying I run an illegal business?"

"Shit," Lillie said. "Everything you do is illegal, woman. You probably can't even pop a squat without breaking an international treaty. I think this is just a solid first step to shine the light on who you really are."

"And what's that, Lillie Virgil?"

"The most ruthless bitch in the South since Scarlett O'Hara hitched on a strap-on and took it to ole Rhett Butler's bony ass."

Lillie turned to Reggie, whose mouth hung open, looking uncomfortable standing there, a few of the working girls peeking into the narrow office from the metal platform. "OK," he said. "She's got the paper. We're done."

"Can't wait to see Skinner burn this place down," Lillie said. "Not that it'll matter much to you. It'll just make it much easier to see what you're really about. And when the Feds come knocking and you run, I'll track your ass down wherever you go. I can smell that cheap-ass perfume from a thousand miles away."

"You wouldn't know Chanel from a bottle of Jean Naté cooter splash, Lillie Virgil," Fannie said, blowing out smoke and pointing toward the door. "Y'all tell Skinner he'll be hearing from my attorney. Nude dancing is a First Amendment issue and we got every right to do our thing twenty-four/seven, three hundred sixty-four days a year. Even a stripper needs a break on Christmas."

"Like you cut Mingo a break?" Lillie asked. "Can't let anyone get close to you. Can you? That boy treated you better than he treated his own momma. And then one day he just up and disappears. Fell off the face of God's green earth. That's on you, woman. Your hands are filthy with that boy's blood."

"People come and go," Fannie said. "This is the service industry."

Lillie nodded to Fannie Hathcock, watching the woman give her a hard stare from behind the glass desk, cigarillo trembling in her fingers. "Stick to that tall tale, Fannie," Lillie said. "A simple businesswoman just trying to earn a dollar with jiggling boobies and watered-down cocktails. That's some real sob sister shit right there. Just don't forget a lot of folks know who you really are and that's gonna be your undoing. See you on the run. It's gonna be a hard-ass fall."

Quinn Colson had insisted Tashi and Jessica move out of the Traveler's Rest, knowing they didn't feel safe, weren't safe, and had few options in Tibbehah County. The only other motel was a place called the Golden Cherry across the street from the strip club, a flea trap renting rooms by the hour according to what people in Jericho had told her. The sheriff offered them a bed at his farm until they could get settled somewhere in town or else based out of Tupelo. Maggie Colson gave them her son's room, Tashi already thinking of the possibilities of telling part of the story from Brandon Taylor's namesake. The small room had a double bed, which Jessica and Tashi had shared for the last few nights, the walls decorated with pictures and posters of Westerns and Native American art. An old rifle that looked like a relic hung over the bed Maggie said had belonged to her great-grandparents. Old hardcover editions of *Huck Finn*, *Treasure Island*, *White Fang*, and *Kim* were stacked neatly on top of the headboard.

Tashi sat on the bed with her legs folded, MacBook in her lap, scrolling through scanned records of the Taylor file. Jessica was on the floor, headphones on, listening to the two-hour confidential interview they'd done with Ansley Cuthbert, speaking about her friendship with Brandon, taking money from Johnny Stagg for the "Daddy parties," and how she and Brandon threw in with a girl named Skylar Cole to blackmail the guests. All of it culminating with Skylar beaten to death and buried deep, Brandon being forced to watch and then running for his life to where he and Ansley hid in an abandoned house in the Big Woods. Ansley did not want to be named on the podcast. She'd remain anonymous, a friend of Brandon's only, someone the killers never knew existed.

Tashi closed the laptop and left Jessica listening to the interview, heading out into the first-floor hallway and through the screen door to the front porch. The door closed with a hard thwack, Maggie Colson looking up from where she sat in a metal glider with a huge black man who appeared to have a prosthetic arm.

Maggie introduced him as Boom Kimbrough, the sheriff's best friend.

"Quinn had to head over to Alabama," Maggie said. "He asked Boom to stick around while he's gone."

"Does he think those men will come back?"

Maggie shook her head and nodded toward Boom. "Boom was coming over to supper anyway," she said. "Quinn just asked him to come on over a little early."

Tashi couldn't help but notice a very large handgun in Boom Kimbrough's lap. It was big and silver and seemed as large as a cannon.

"Don't you worry," Boom said, smiling. "I'm a better shot now than when I had two arms. Ain't nobody getting on this porch without permission."

Tashi smiled but didn't say a word. She didn't like guns, never liked them, and hated the idea of being protected in such a way. She and Jessica shouldn't have to hide out like criminals in an effort to tell their story. Ansley Cuthbert shouldn't have to keep quiet and be afraid to speak out even twenty years after Brandon's death.

"Did Quinn go to see Johnny Stagg?" Tashi asked.

"I don't know," Maggie said, but Tashi could tell she was lying. Quinn had mentioned last night he'd put in a request to meet with Stagg, Stagg being the man in charge of north Mississippi back then. "Y'all are welcome to stay as long as you like."

"It shouldn't be long," Tashi said. "We're getting close."

"Is Ansley enough?"

"I wish she'd let us use her name," Tashi said. "It would give us a lot more credibility. But for now, it's all we have."

Boom stood up, sticking the large gun into a holster on his belt along his left hip, looking like one of the gunfighters from the movie posters in Brandon's room. *The Man from Laramie. Code of the West.* He walked to the edge of the porch, staring down the gravel road at the bridge spanning a meandering creek.

"Quinn said two of those boys followed you back from Tupelo."

"That's right," Tashi said. "They'd been in our motel room, too. They trashed some of our notes and wrote some nasty things on the mirror over the sink."

"What kind of things?" Boom said, looking to Maggie, moving back and forth on the glider. She was wearing jeans and a threadbare VOTE FOR COLSON T-shirt, no shoes.

"Mainly about us being outsiders," Tashi said. "And about me being Jewish."

"Wonder how they feel about a one-armed nigger carrying a big-ass gun?"

Tashi smiled, feeling an ease of the pressure she'd carried around for days. "Doubt they'd like it very much."

Boom grinned back at her. "Quinn ever tell you about the time me and him took on some peckerwood racists out at Hell Creek?"

"I heard a little bit about it," Tashi said.

"This was right when Quinn came home after his Uncle Hamp died," he said. "Town had pretty much turned to shit."

"Hold on," Tashi said. "We just got some new recording gear shipped to us. Let me get it."

Maggie stood up and said she'd put on some coffee. Boom kept still at the edge of the porch, nodding but continuing to watch the road. The man looked like a mountain, large and muscular, in ragged jeans and a faded flannel shirt, a CAT ball cap on his head. Back turned, he started to laugh.

"What's so funny?" she asked.

"Good times," Boom said.

"What?" Tashi said, opening the screen door.

"Putting those motherfuckers on the run," he said. "You got to do that from time to time. Let them know where they all stand."

# TWENTY-SEVEN

Quinn drove up through Birmingham and cut across the rest of Alabama and most of north Mississippi to talk to Vardaman. Vardaman wasn't hard to find. He posted all his rallies and appearances on his Facebook page, a small picture of himself grinning in front of Mississippi and American flags, promising a RETURN TO VALUES, a larger picture for the banner showing him speaking before a huge crowd of his supporters, many in Watchmen caps and holding up signs. THE SOUTH *WILL* RISE AGAIN. STOP REWARDING, START DEPORTING.

By the time Quinn arrived, the rally was over, but he spotted Vardaman's campaign bus parked outside the Landers Center. The flashing sign facing Interstate 55 advertising that CURIOUS GEORGE LIVE would be coming soon, as well as MONSTER TRUCK JAM and REPTICON: MEMPHIS REPTILE & AMPHIBIAN SHOW. Quinn stopped his truck sideways in a long stretch of open slots, Vardaman's bus being one of the last vehicles left, a few folks coming in and out of its door.

Quinn let down his window, watching the bus, and finished the cigar he'd been smoking since Tupelo, his tumbler of truck stop coffee gone cold.

He didn't have a warrant and hadn't given advance notice he'd be coming. Quinn wanted to catch Vardaman off guard. Within a few minutes, he spoke with three different handlers until a pudgy young guy in a rumpled blue suit with thick brown hair and a goatee led him up onto the bus and back toward a little booth situated by the rear windows. The guy said his name was Tudhope and that he broadcasted an AM talk radio show in Meridian.

"Wrote my first book when I was fifteen," Tudhope said, mopping the sweat off his brow with his tie. "It was called *Take Back My America*. Went to number eighteen on the *USA Today* bestsellers list. Maybe you remember it?"

Quinn didn't answer, following Tudhope's wide body between the seats to the back of the bus. Vardaman waved from the booth, dressed in a white dress shirt open at the throat, sleeves rolled up to the elbows. A woman sat with him in the little cove, lots of blonde hair, big teeth, and large, almost bovine blue eyes. Tudhope introduced her as the senator's press secretary. Quinn took off his ball cap, still standing, and nodded to them both.

"Little far from Tibbehah," Vardaman said. "Glad you stopped by, Sheriff. We never got to finish our talk at the Good Ole Boy."

"We finished it," Quinn said.

"All you said was 'Bullshit,'" Vardaman said. "Not exactly a productive conversation or spirited debate."

"Nope."

"Would y'all mind leaving me and Sheriff Colson alone for a few minutes?" Vardaman asked. "Looks like he's got something personal on his mind."

"Did you know a woman named Skylar Cole?" Quinn asked.

Vardaman gave an odd look, his face scrunched up, turning to each of his advisers. Tudhope nodded to the press secretary and squeezed his thick frame into the banquette behind the table. His pudgy face shone with sweat.

"We found her remains not far from your hunt lodge," Quinn said. "Someone had busted her skull."

"Sheriff," Vardaman said. "I don't know what the hell you're talking about."

"She would've died in 1997," Quinn said. He had no proof the body was Skylar Cole or even that it was from 1997. But he had enough to ask the question. "She was a regular at some of those house parties y'all liked to throw. Skeet shooting and whole hog barbecue. Whiskey and underage girls. Good ole times."

Vardaman's cocky smile dropped. He didn't look to either his adviser or press secretary. He reached up and loosened his knotted tie and stared hard at Quinn. His nostrils flared as he nodded, understanding now exactly why Quinn was here and what he wanted.

"Skylar Cole brought the girls," Quinn said. "They all came from Stagg's place. You know the Booby Trap?"

The blonde woman started to laugh and shake her head. "I think this is all over," she said. "Thank you for stopping by, Sheriff, but we have to be in Greenwood by tonight. He's got a donor dinner at Lusco's. They're serving steak and pompano from the Gulf. I'll walk you back to your truck."

Quinn didn't move, noting a nasty welt under Vardaman's silver hairline.

"Looks like someone already tried to set you straight, Senator," Quinn said. "Want to tell me where you got that bruise?"

Vardaman didn't answer as Quinn kept on staring at him, his

misshapen head and waxy-looking face folding into his true self, hard gaze and grinding jaw looking like he was chewing on something with his back teeth. He didn't stop staring until Quinn said the name of the old state trooper that used to work for him and took care of their special business in Tibbehah County. The trooper had been famously shot out in the Big Woods, disgraced and exposed as being a longtime bad seed in the highway patrol. A notorious bagman who was finally found out.

"I don't know that name," Vardaman said.

"You should," Quinn said. "He served as your bodyguard for years, as well as being the go-to guard for two Ole Miss football coaches. I've seen a lot of pictures of y'all together. Even a trip down to Louisiana to catch redfish."

Tudhope gripped Vardaman's arm and whispered into his ear. Quinn stood back, watching them and the blonde woman, who was playing with the tight pearl choker around her neck.

"I know Brandon Taylor blackmailed some of your guests," Quinn said. "I know that Skylar Cole helped set them up. Both were killed. Y'all wanted it to seem like that Taylor kid killed himself. I know who was at those parties. All about the history of Stagg and the Booby Trap. And I know you were the one who ultimately made the call to kill those kids."

"That's the craziest horseshit I ever heard," Vardaman said, still grinding his teeth, his face turning a deep purple. "I don't know a damn thing about any of that. I've tried time after time to be cordial to you, son. At every damn turn, you've worked to embarrass me and harass my supporters. You arrested one of my people just two days ago, violating his fucking Second Amendment rights. I don't know what kind of fantasy you've created in your mind about some cold case from twenty years back."

"Might take a little time to put the pieces together," Quinn said.

"But it's coming. Figured I'd just give you the option of dropping out of the race before you cause Mississippi further embarrassment."

"You ain't got shit, son," Vardaman said. "Because all this is just a fucking lie. Nothing but an old-fashioned witch hunt. You ain't got any facts. Just an outright fucking fabrication."

"Might have a few keepsakes, too," Quinn said. "Y'all sure none of those pictures are still around?"

Vardaman's face blossomed with even more color, spit on his lips, as he breathed out his flared nostrils. "Lies," he said. "Y'all just can't stand that I've already won. You'll do anything to slander my name."

"You gonna double down on that, Senator?" Quinn asked. "When this all shakes out?"

Tudhope mopped his brow again with his tie, turning to the press secretary, the woman just shaking her head back and forth, pushing Tudhope out of the booth. The fat man, nearly tumbling to the floor, reached for the headrest of the banquette to gather his feet, and told them to clear the bus.

"It's your call," Quinn said, his eyes not leaving Vardaman's. "But the election won't stop a damn thing. I just hate having to drive all that way to Jackson to arrest you."

"It'll never happen," Vardaman said.

Quinn nodded, picking up his cap from the table, little indentions in its flat top for poker chips and playing cards. A half-eaten bucket of KFC pushed toward the bus window.

"You'll be long gone by then, son."

"No, sir," Quinn said. "My time rousting your crooked ass has just started."

"That's a threat," Tudhope said, pointing, then reaching for his cell phone. "Y'all hear that? Say it again and you'll be all over the news. We got every news organization in the state on speed dial."

"Is that a fact?" Quinn nodded, turning. "So do I."

* * *

Caddy liked to clean. She liked the order of it, not caring if it was inside the string of little shacks she offered to homeless families and battered women or the dusty old barn that had been the heart of her ministry. Caddy wanted to concentrate on the barn today, focus on its rugged simplicity as the genesis of everything she hoped to accomplish. She remembered Jamey Dixon first finding the place, sitting there crooked, alone, and abandoned on some logged-out land along a dry creek bed. This was the place, he'd said. We'll start it all here. The fallow land, the crooked barn, all of it his rock to build upon. And now she had to drive down the road and see the bones of the big new outreach building that probably would never be finished. She wished like hell she'd never even started it. Being incomplete and useless up on the hill was a slight to everything Jamey had wanted.

She'd heard the car pull up as she started sweeping the wooden floor, rugged one-by-sixes they'd laid down a few years before, stripped from an old house, secondhand and repurposed like everything else. Caddy had been thinking about Jamey most of the day, wearing one of his flannel shirts that morning, feeling safe and comfortable back in the barn and prepping for tomorrow's Sunday service.

The big double doors of the barn were open, and she turned to see Bentley walk inside, hands in his pockets, hanging his head, not saying a word, just watching her work. She'd collected a pile of dirt in the center of the floor, the mismatched pews pushed off to either side while she swept.

"I tried to call."

Caddy didn't answer, only returned to her sweeping.

"I stopped by your mother's house," he said. "She told me you'd come out here. I know you're upset. I can't say I blame you."

Caddy didn't answer, sweeping, trying to forgive herself for being so almighty stupid as to trust someone like Bentley Vandeven. She'd let him into her private space out at The River, introduced him to her family, to her son, and brought him into her bed. So damn stupid. She wondered if anything he said had been true, running his hands over her body and telling her that her scars were so beautiful. Caddy came upon some broken glasses, pushing them into the pile of dirt, knowing the worst part of holding service in the barn was the cleanup. You never could quite clean up an old barn.

"I don't like what's happening," he said. "I don't like any of it. I've always done what my father has asked. I've always believed he had some kind of good business plan. He always dismissed Vardaman. He called him a joke, just some dumb hick with crazy ideas."

Caddy swept the pile onto a piece of cardboard and dumped the dirt and glass into the trash can. Bentley walked over and took the broom from her hands. Up close in the fading sunlight, she could tell he'd been crying. He didn't say a word, only turned from her and started on the floor, working as he had for the last several months, following along and trying to help with the chores.

"My father said they didn't have a choice," Bentley said. "He said it had gone too far and they had to work with a bad situation. They can't control Vardaman anymore. He's running everything now. But this thing I told you about? About your brother? I can't be a part of that. I told my father I'm done. I quit the foundation. I quit everything. I want to be here with you. I don't want their money. I don't want to be around my father ever again."

Caddy had been holding her breath, watching him sweep, sloppy and not even knowing how to gather the dirt, before she inhaled deeply. "Do I look like I give a damn about Vardaman?" she asked. Her mouth felt dry and dusty, and her own words sounded strange. "I want to know who the hell you think you are to con me and my family. To slip into my bed, whisper shit into my ear, spy on my damn brother. Who are these people you work for? What the hell do they want?"

"I can't stop what's happened," he said. "It was wrong."

"Damn straight it was wrong," she said. "This is a sacred place for me. I opened up to you and told you all about what I've been and what I hoped to do. That must've been damn funny to you. Some piece of country stripper trash who's found the Lord. Did you have to sleep with me or was it just something to do while you kept tabs on me down here? Maybe you were just bored?"

"I wanted to be with you, Caddy," he said. "I came here for the wrong damn reasons, but you set me straight. That's why I'm back here now. I wanted to tell you what I've done and warn you about Quinn. These folks are serious. Just let me stay here. I'll sweep the floors, I'll take out the garbage, I'll fix the roofs and do the laundry. Just forgive me."

Caddy snatched the broom out of his hands, tired of watching his bad technique. She held on to the handle and stared at him. "What do you know about Quinn? Or is that just another lie?"

"They want him gone."

"Who?"

"Vardaman," he said. "The Watchmen. Quinn's trying to make trouble for him for something that happened a long time back. With that kid Brandon Taylor. Quinn's trying to embarrass the senator about some parties he used to throw a long time ago. It could turn into a real mess, damage his time as governor."

"Sure hate to see that," Caddy said. "Such a fine man."

"I don't want to be a part of this anymore, Caddy," he said. "I'm finished. I swear to God. Just give me back the broom. I want to help you. I want to be part of your life. Me, you, and Jason."

Caddy looked at Bentley's smooth face—no wrinkles. His full head of hair without a single gray. He wore an earnest expression as he stood there in the sunlight cutting through the barn doors. She nearly felt sorry for him but was too disgusted. He'd been dumb enough to follow those people. They didn't give a damn about anyone or anything, only wanted to take and use whatever they could get. "Don't ever say my son's name again," she said. "Just go. Please just get the hell out of here and out of my life. You've humiliated me and my family enough."

"Please," he said. "Just listen to me."

"I hope you find your purpose, Bentley," Caddy said. "I really do. But it'll never be here. Or never be with me. For once in your life, you'll have to find your own way. Who the hell are you, anyway?"

Three days later, Quinn drove to Oxford to see Holliday. The federal agent arranged for them to meet at a law office on the Square. It was an old building with a plaque outside saying it was the first structure built after the town was burned during the Civil War. Quinn took the steps up to a wide porch looking out at the old courthouse, white Christmas lights strung from buildings around the structure up to the clock tower. Holliday was smoking one of the cigars Quinn had given him while looking out at the marquee to the Lyric Theatre.

"I felt guilty after I left you in Montgomery," Holliday said, looking down at the cigar. "Aren't I the one who should be giving you a wedding gift?"

"Sounds like you got one."

He followed Holliday around the corner to a small metal table where a manila folder sat waiting. Quinn pulled his own cigar from his pocket, fired it up with the Zippo, and flipped open the file.

"Stagg's one crooked, mean bastard," Holliday said. "But the son of a bitch delivered. He kept the copies in a safe-deposit box in a bank in Water Valley. It's there. Just like he said."

Quinn shuffled through several dozen black-and-white eight-by-ten photos of old flabby men in a variety of compromising positions with young women, most looking like very young teenagers. The photos were clear, taken by Brandon Taylor with a long lens, but Quinn didn't recognize a single face.

"Any IDs in Stagg's hidey-hole?"

"Nope," Holliday said. "We're working on it. Couple of those old fat fellas look like they're about to have a coronary. You see that one shot? That good ole boy resting his whiskey glass on top of the girl's head? Now, that is damn arrogance in motion."

"Just check the register of your local Jaycees."

"That's hard, Quinn."

"You don't believe it?"

"I believe this state deserves better."

"Ever read Faulkner?" Quinn said. "It's been like this for a long while. Mississippi was founded as a place to plunder. What kind of territory attracts folks like that?"

Holliday nodded, ashing his cigar off the white railing. Quinn closed the file and turned away.

"Take it," Holliday said. "That's your copy."

"Not much I can do with it."

"Yeah?" Holliday said, walking toward the other side of the building facing the Van Buren.

It was twilight, and the marquee to the Lyric Theatre cut on, flashing white lights, the sign reading HAPPY HALLOWEEN BASH. A couple of kids appeared in the bow window of an old storefront, now a taco shop, standing as still as mannequins to fool passersby.

"Remember what Faulkner said about Mississippi," he said. "'I don't hate it. I don't hate it.'"

"I don't hate it, either," Quinn said. "Or else I wouldn't have come back."

"Faulkner's brother Jack was an Army man and a longtime federal agent," Holliday said. "He was brought in from the El Paso office to Chicago by Melvin Purvis to help catch John Dillinger. He was there when they shot him down at the Biograph. Several agents shot Dillinger, but none of them wanted to know who killed him."

"I always heard nobody wanted to take the credit."

"I think they were just glad the son of a bitch was finally dead."

Maggie turned up the volume on the stereo while she cooked, flipping over the chicken in the black skillet, listening to Ray Stevens singing "Everything Is Beautiful" and thinking about her dad. She'd been dreaming a lot about him lately, about driving with him in The Blue Mule on his runs over to New Orleans or up to Memphis, that one time he brought her up to Jericho when Brandon died. Maggie Powers, not yet sixteen, standing there with folks she barely knew or hadn't met, staring at that slate-colored casket, closed and covered with flowers. *Jesus loves the little children of the world* . . . Ray Stevens somehow making it all better.

Jessica wandered into the kitchen in cutoff sweats and a T-shirt, grabbed herself a glass and filled it with water from the tap. She was barefoot and had a trucker cap down in her eyes, her hair pulled into a ponytail and threaded through the snap back.

"You're going native," Maggie said. "Real Mississippi style."

"I got the hat at the Salvation Army," she said. "Like it?"

"Perfect," Maggie said. "What's it say?"

"'Billy Beer,'" Jessica said. "Isn't that fantastic? I can't wait to show my dad. He used to have a can of it until it finally corroded and drained all over his bookshelf. It was a real mess. You ever smell beer that's forty years old?"

"Hope I never do," Maggie said. "You OK with chicken?"

"I thought you were vegetarian?"

"I am," she said. "But I've learned to cook for everyone. Not everyone is so much into a nice big salad for dinner . . . We have a full house tonight. You and Tashi. Boom. Brandon and hopefully Quinn."

"Do you know when he'll be back?"

"Soon." Maggie flipped over the chicken, which was turning a nice brown color, Maggie taking pride in her cooking even though she wouldn't touch it. She'd seen and read enough about the industrial farming complex to turn her stomach. But these birds had been local, raised and killed in Tibbehah County. Quinn always said it was more honest to look what you ate in the eye.

"Is he bringing liquor?" Jessica said, smiling. "He promised some good wine, too."

"He'll grab some in Oxford," Maggie said. "Always does. Good wine makes life tolerable."

"My head feels like it's going to explode," she said. "We've come so damn far with this. We've been down here for nearly three months and learned so much."

"It'll come together."

"It'll take us well into next year just to put together the podcast," Jessica said. "And then it may not run until this summer. Do you have any idea what it's like to sit on a story like this? We have to just sit back and watch Vardaman get elected and we can't do a damn thing about it."

"Quinn's not happy about it, either."

"Tashi and I talked about it," she said. "If we had more, we'd share the story. Take it to someone who could get the information out there. The papers in Jackson and Tupelo. Hell, I don't know. Maybe CNN. I mean, this is a big story. Do some damage to Vardaman's campaign. But Ansley won't go public. And all we really have is her word on what happened and some blurry pictures of the outside of that hunt lodge. We can tell this story in the podcast. But that'll take time. And then it'll be too late."

Maggie forked the chicken and set the pieces on some paper towels to soak up the grease. She reached down and wiped her hands on the apron she was wearing over her jeans. Looking pretty domestic except for the sleeveless Marc Bolan T-shirt. She'd been trying to keep it all slow and easy on the farm, keep the doors and windows open to the nice cool fall air, make sure everyone was fed and happy, and pretend like all of this wasn't so damn personal to her. She didn't want Brandon to feel a damn bit of how she felt at the moment.

"This will work out," Maggie said, walking over to the table, straightening the flowers she'd picked and put in an old whiskey bottle.

"How can you be so sure?"

"It takes time," Maggie said. "Quinn's reopened the case. He's talking to people. Making sure folks are accountable."

"But, Christ," Jessica said, waiting a moment to drink down some water. "Knowing something and being able to tell it are two different things. Brandon Taylor has been dead for twenty years."

Maggie held on to the edge of the sink and closed her eyes. "I know how long Brandon has been dead. He was my friend and I loved him. Still do. Y'all didn't even know him. It's just a story to you. Words and memories strung together."

Jessica was silent. Maggie reached up into the cabinets for some plates, the clatter reverberating in the still room, the Ray Stevens record hitting the center grooves, the needle going over and over the same spot with little clicks and whooshes.

"I'm sorry."

"It's fine."

"No," Jessica said. "It's not. It's the not knowing that's getting to us.

Maybe we shouldn't have come here. We've invaded your space and your life too long."

Maggie was about to answer when she heard Hondo barking from the front porch. That dog could hear Quinn's truck from a mile away. A minute later, she heard the truck door slam shut. She could hear Quinn talking with Boom outside, Hondo clambering down the steps and running out to greet him, barking and barking.

"I'm sorry."

"It's fine," she said. "We've all been through a lot. Help yourself to supper. I'll check on the wine."

Quinn moved into the room, tall and spit-shined, dressed in his sheriff's office shirt with the tin star and crisp dark blue jeans with cowboy boots. Maggie hugged him as he grabbed a piece of the chicken, nearly burning his fingers, and set it back down. He kissed her full on the lips, and she could smell his bay rum aftershave and feel his short-clipped hair in her hands.

"Did you bring wine?"

"Always."

Quinn looked over her shoulder and said hello to Jessica. "Time to change that record. What is it?"

"Ray Stevens," she said. "'Everything Is Beautiful.'"

Quinn smiled and nodded, knowing what that meant. She felt a pang of guilt for bringing all this into his life so soon after they got married. She watched as he walked over to the refrigerator and grabbed a can of Coors. "Join me outside for a moment?"

"I was just about to set the table."

"Let's let that chicken cool," he said, giving her a wink. He walked over to the kitchen table where Jessica was sitting with her half-full glass of water and dropped the manila folder right in front of her.

Jessica looked up at Quinn but didn't say anything. The folder within an inch of her right hand.

"Let us know when you're ready for supper," he said. "Might take a moment for me to finish this beer."

Maggie followed him out onto the porch. Quinn lifted the beer to his lips, looking out onto the rolling land. Boom was sitting on the tailgate of his truck, talking to Brandon, and Hondo had hopped up beside him.

"What's in that file?" Maggie asked.

"Damn-near everything," Quinn said. "Is Caddy still coming to supper?"

Maggie nodded, watching Quinn's face in the darkness of the porch. She walked over and cut on the multicolored lights that he had never managed to take down from last Christmas, saying he liked the way they looked no matter the time of year.

"You think she could recognize Bentley Vandeven's daddy, even twenty years back?" he asked. "I heard that man always keeps a whiskey glass nearby. No matter what he's doing."

Fannie was on the Natchez Trace south of Tibbehah County, out in the cold and the dark, smoking cigarillos and staring out at the big mounds where the Choctaws used to honor their dead. Only two cars had passed in the thirty minutes she'd been there, hands in the deep pockets of her red Burberry cashmere coat, thinking back on that cemetery where they buried Ray, the city of the dead down in Metairie. All those marble crypts and angel statues watching as they settled him into a mausoleum with the rest of his old Italian family. She couldn't wait to get the hell out of there, getting turned around on the way, the place like a beautiful fucking maze.

She wished she could've told Ray about Vardaman standing up to her and reaching out to grab her by the snatch. He would've found a lot of humor in the way she knocked his spray-tanned ass sideways with the framing hammer. Sitting there bleeding from his temple, all the son of a bitch could do was nod and nod, listening to what Fannie knew and what she could do about it. She held his fucking saggy nuts in the palm of her hand. And with him, Chief Robbie, and Marquis Sledge up in Memphis in line with her, Buster White didn't matter worth two shits. It had taken a while, but, goddamn, she had it all. Everything she wanted. And everything Ray had trained her for.

She heard a car coming in from the south and she watched it slow near the mounds, turning in and parking by her Lexus. Fannie couldn't see the make or model, some kind of black sedan, maybe a Cadillac or a Lincoln. A big man crawled out and closed the door. He had his head down, hands in his pockets, as he approached her. Fannie's hand reached for the little gun in her pocket, ready to pull and shoot if he made a false move. As he walked closer, she could tell it was the man the Chief had told her about, a big, strapping Indian with long black hair, a wide, flat face, black eyes, and a busted nose. He looked like old pictures of Jim Thorpe.

"Miss Fannie?"

She nodded.

"You wanted to talk in person?"

"That's right," she said. "You're a big one, aren't you? You look familiar as hell. Have me met?"

The man shook his head. His wore his hair pulled into a ponytail, a black leather jacket, jeans, and black cowboy boots. Chief Robbie had told her about the man and what he might do for her and for Vardaman. She didn't know his name but heard he was a military badass back in his day, some kind of Green Beret Special Forces dude that had come home to become the Chief's personal and loyal pit bull.

"How soon can you do it?" she asked.

"I will need help."

"OK."

"Someone good."

"I'll do my best."

The man stood there in the cold, a truck rambling past on the two-lane kicking up leaves and dirt, lights momentarily shining across his dark face. He kept staring at her, no expression at all.

"I do know you," she said. "Or you know me?"

"I know who you are, Miss Hathcock," the man said. "I've heard many stories about you."

Fannie shifted on her nice Italian booties, taking a drag of a cigarillo. "Whatever you heard about Miss Fannie has been greatly exaggerated."

"I heard many good things about you," he said. "Someone I know said you were a tough woman but loyal. And could be trusted. They thought very highly of you."

She nodded, thinking that this man had a nice, rugged face, like it had been carved from stone. He was older, maybe in his fifties, but looked like he kept in shape, strong and rough in the right way. Fannie had a hell of a hard time finding men who weren't soft. She walked up on him, close enough that he could smell her gardenia perfume, letting her red coat open up a little and letting him see what was working under her blue wrap dress. When this was all over, perhaps . . .

"The man I know was named Mingo," the dark man said. "Do you know him?"

Fannie felt a coldness spread across her back and down her legs. She felt her mouth twitch a little as she pulled on the cigarillo again, nodding.

"He disappeared two years ago," he said. "He worked for you?"

"Yes," she said. "He was a good worker. A good kid."

The man's eyes were dark and serious as he stared at her for a good long while. "Sometime after all this, I'd like to talk to you about him," he said.

"Of course," she said. "You knew Mingo on the Rez?"

The man didn't move at all, another car flying past, lighting up his face. Fannie's left hand in her coat, finger on the trigger of the gun, as she licked her lips and smiled.

"Yes," he said. "Mingo was my son."

# TWENTY-EIGHT

It was getting past six, Quinn supposed to be rolling off duty and meeting Maggie in town to go trick-or-treating with Brandon and Jason, laughing and talking, enjoying a night off with family. They planned to meet over at Caddy's house, Maggie's grandmother's old place, and then make a round down Stovall Street. They'd zigzag their way up to the Square, where some churches had organized a "trunk or treat" for the kids from out in the country and those who wished to keep the devil out of Halloween. Every year some pastor had convinced the kids not to go as ghosts and goblins but instead seek out their favorite biblical character. Jericho Square would be filled with Moseses and Jacobs, Ruths and Naomis, the prophet Elijah, and John the Baptist, before he lost his head.

"My momma wouldn't let us have Halloween at all," Reggie said, sitting in Quinn's office right before the day and night shifts traded off. "She said it was Satan's hour, time to tempt kids with all his wickedness."

"Y'all didn't do anything?"

"Nope," Reggie said. "No costumes. No pumpkins. No parties. I used to get real jealous of my friends loading up with all that candy. I'd ask my momma what was so wrong with just dressing up, knocking on a few doors? And she'd turn to me, mad as hell, with smoke coming out her ears, and say Halloween was a night when the devil rejoices."

"Hard to argue with that."

"Speak of that ole devil," Reggie said, leaning forward in his chair. "Don't know what to make of it, but I heard those two young ladies from New York been meeting with folks at the *Daily Journal* and some man at CNN. Is that true?"

"That's their business," Quinn said, shrugging. "Nothing changes for our work, making sense of what happened to that Taylor kid and the girl in that hole."

"For Maggie?" Reggie asked.

Quinn nodded, looking at his watch and standing up. Out the window, two of the county jail inmates were working in the parking lot, building a bookshelf for the common area. Miss Janice from over at the library had donated a pile of books for the inmates to read. Most of them self-help books, stuff like *7 Habits of Highly Effective People*, *The Secret*, and *Unlimited Power* by Tony Robbins. Quinn told Miss Janice he wasn't really sure he wanted dope dealers and serial thieves to be that much more effective in Tibbehah. He said his job was to feed and lodge until trial, not rehabilitate. But Miss Janice wouldn't take no for an answer and dropped off four full boxes of books. What could you do?

"I don't mean to get personal, Sheriff," Reggie said. "But I hope Maggie finds some comfort in the knowing. I heard she stayed away from Tibbehah for a long while after it happened. Couldn't have been easy."

"It was one of the first things we discussed when she moved back."

"I guess that helped draw y'all closer?"

"That and having a sociopath for an ex-husband," Quinn said, turning away from the window as Cleotha opened the office door. She put a hand on her big hip and made a sour face, holding up two call-back slips.

"That woman Dana Ray won't stop calling, Sheriff," Cleotha said. "I told her you off duty, but her crazy ass called three more times in the last hour."

"And what'd she say?"

"That peckerhead boyfriend of hers got out on bond and is messin' with her mind," Cleotha said. "I said, 'If he's threatening you or coming near your house, you give us a call, but until then I ain't setting up no chat line with Sheriff Colson.'"

"And this last time?" Quinn asked.

"She say ole Bradley Wayne called and said he's coming for his shit," Cleotha said. "He got himself a big-screen TV and one of them rowing machines. Some porno movies and beef jerky. Woman said it just like that. Like she's the star of her own goddamn Hallmark movie of the week. *The Stripper and the Shitbird*."

Quinn looked down at Reggie, who stood and opened his hand for the call-back slip. Quinn intercepted it, checking out the address. He hadn't realized Dana Ray had stuck so close, living up on Perfect Circle Road. "Y'all have enough on your plate," Quinn said. "And you're down a deputy tonight."

"Sheriff, I don't know why you mess with that trash," Cleotha said. "I seen that girl when she come in to press charges and, damn, if she didn't have a tattoo of a pistol aimed down at her privates. That's what I'd call asking for your own damn shit."

"Serve and protect, Cleotha," Quinn said. "If we cut out those who made some poor life choices, we all would be out of a job."

"I'll get Kenny to follow you out," Reggie said. "That fella sure has it in for you, Sheriff."

"Do I look concerned?"

"Petrified," Reggie said, smiling.

Quinn patted him on the arm and reached for his cap and jacket. A rough wind buffeted the windows, stirring up dirt in the jail yard. The sky filled with a weird orange glow.

"Sometimes I feel like we running a damn day care center in this county," Cleotha said, turning and heading back to her desk. "You doing the Lord's work. You hear me, Sheriff?"

Maggie and Boom sat in the gazebo on the Square, watching the kids running loose, filling pillowcases and little plastic pumpkins with candy from the back of cars and pickup trucks. Boom had insisted on coming along, Tashi and Jessica now headed back to Brooklyn to piece together their story, leaving some of the details with a few local reporters. The oak tree branches shook in the hard winds blowing across the Square. Maggie hoped they'd get enough trick-or-treating in before it started to rain.

"Wasn't like this when me and Quinn were kids," Boom said. "Miss Jean just kicked our asses outside and told us to get back before midnight. We'd knock on a few doors, but mainly we liked to fuck with people. Shooting out lights with BB guns. Rolling folks' houses. Putting shaving cream and eggs all over teachers' cars. We just ran wild."

"Y'all were lucky you didn't get arrested."

"Naw," Boom said. "We were just having a little fun. Real thin line between cutting up and being a juvenile delinquent. Me and Quinn walked that razor's edge."

"Y'all turned out just fine," Maggie said, watching Brandon, dressed as Spider-Man, fill up his pillowcase and then dart down the center path of the Square. Small orange lights blinking above, cutouts of ghosts and witches hanging in the trees and turning in the wind. "My grandmother didn't like me out late at night when I'd come visit. I had to promise to be home by dark or else she'd call the sheriff on me. I remember her waiting up, sitting on the couch, smoking Kool cigarettes, with a loaded .22 next to her."

"Ain't nothing wrong with that," Boom said, grinning, pulling back his plaid hunting coat to reveal the biggest damn gun she'd ever seen in her life. "I'll move along when Quinn gets here."

"We appreciate you, Boom," Maggie said, resting her hand on his metal hook. "I hope you know that. You gave Quinn a lot of comfort being at the house while he did his job."

"Ain't got much else to do."

"Sure you do," Maggie said. "You and Quinn—y'all always watched each other's back."

"Always."

Maggie turned to see Brandon running toward the gazebo while Caddy and Jason walked across the Square, Maggie not quite making out Jason's costume, maybe some type of pro wrestler. He had on a long black leather duster and wide-brimmed black hat. Brandon ran up to him, always admiring his older cousin, and laughing and saying something about The Undertaker. Jason had on eyeliner and a fake mustache and goatee. When he walked up the steps, he looked right at Boom and rolled his eyes back into his head. "You will rest in peace!"

Boom stood up and pounded fists with the kid. Caddy stepped up to join Maggie, her hair even shorter than usual, dressed in old jeans and boots, a threadbare barn coat over her narrow shoulders. She sat down and fired up a cigarette as Boom walked down with the boys, following them over to another row of trucks and cars to candy. They sat there in the dark for a moment, taking in the scene.

"Where's Quinn?"

"Out on a call," she said. "Said he'll head straight here when he's done."

"Weird night," Caddy said, looking up at the orange sky behind the old water tower, branches whipping back and forth, grit kicking up off the footpaths. "Better get these kids knocking on doors before the bottom falls out."

"Why'd you ask about Quinn?"

"Just thought he'd be here," she said. "Wasn't he working a day shift?"

"Sure."

Caddy blew out some smoke and smiled, patting Maggie on her leg. "How'd you like Jason's costume? I sewed it myself from a bunch of donations I had out at The River. Isn't he a damn trip?"

"I heard about Bentley," Maggie said. "You OK?"

Caddy shook her head and took a drag off the cigarette. "Let's talk about anything else," she said. "I should've seen that shitstorm coming from a mile away."

Quinn had agreed not to talk about Brandon Taylor until the news broke. And maybe not even then. The women had spoken to some local media, some Quinn knew and some he didn't, and headed north as quickly as they'd arrived. Tashi had apologized to him again, sorry for doubting what he said, for thinking that maybe he'd been involved in Brandon's death. It was just an ugly lie, Quinn had said, told by an ugly man. Quinn still not able to summon any grief for E. J. Royce's sorry ass, even if he wanted to find his killers.

The wind kicked up as he drove south on Sugar Ditch Road, the cotton fields dry and brittle in the bottomland, the sun going down in the distance, orange and black. Just as he turned onto Perfect Circle Road, the rain started, tapping light on his windshield, wind buffeting his truck as he slowed, hit the high beams, and searched for Dana Ray's trailer. He passed the old Blue Sky convenience store, now nothing but a burned-out shell, no one bothering to clean up or rebuild. He drove, winding his way deeper into the Ditch, past the little trailers up on the rolling hills or down in the bottomland, porch lights on, some decorated for Halloween with inflatable pumpkins or black cats. One woman, Miss Eubanks of Big Momma Bail Bonds, really did it up. Music, flashing strobes, and purple lights all down her chain-link fence.

Quinn looked down at the GPS on his phone and then back in his rearview mirror, Kenny following close behind in his patrol car. He was within a quarter mile of the address as he picked up the phone and called Maggie, letting her know it wouldn't be long. "How about dinner at El Dorado after?"

"Sounds good," she said. "I'll ask Boom."

"Margaritas?"

"Twist my damn arm."

Quinn rolled down a flat stretch of gravel, shooting down the other side of Perfect Circle Road, the loop making a sloping half oval. He spotted an older trailer with a handmade porch outside, a blue light on by the front door. He stopped his truck, Kenny pulling up beside him, his patrol car idling as he let down the window.

"Sit tight," Quinn said.

Kenny nodded as Quinn approached the front porch, walking up a homemade plywood ramp, buckled from sun and water damage, and pounded on the door. He could hear music playing inside, Miranda Lambert threatening to burn some shit down with kerosene.

Quinn knocked again, hearing some rustling inside, a shadow taking shape on the other side of the curtains. Quinn waited for the door to open as he heard the landing buckle and crack.

Three men in black approached from around the corner, sending Quinn into a crouch, reaching for his gun as he felt a weapon pressed into his spine, the man telling him to move slow and easy, raise those damn hands, or he'd be wandering about this world in a fucking wheelchair. Quinn recognized the voice as the short fella's from the Neshoba County Fair, turning his head to see Kenny out of the patrol car and on his knees in the flashing blue lights. Four men surrounded the deputy, lashing his wrists in zip ties and forcing him to the ground.

"Howdy, Sheriff," the man said into his ear, pulling the Beretta off Quinn's hip and pushing him down the ramp toward the gravel drive. Quinn counted out eight men in total, all outfitted in black combat gear and holding rifles, faces covered in balaclavas as if Quinn didn't know they were part of the Watchmen Society. He was twenty meters from the woods, maybe fifty to the road running along a creek bed. The wind shook the trees and loose roof of the trailer, Quinn turning back to see the shadow of the woman opening the front door, silhouetted in the frame as she spoke to one of the men. It was Dana Ray. She was holding a cigarette in her hands and looked scared.

"Where's Fannie?" Quinn said.

The man socked Quinn hard and fast in the back of his head, making him stumble forward, as another kicked out his legs, sending Quinn tumbling down on his back. He quickly found his feet and kicked one man straight in the groin. The fat, squat man had his face covered, but Quinn knew it was him, coming at him with the butt of his rifle, trying to take out Quinn's head like a piñata. Quinn ducked and rolled. Another man's boots finding his ribs and kicking hard, the others joining in with hard elbows and kicks, as Quinn got to his knees and covered his face. Some of the kicks connecting with bones and cartilage, Quinn tasting blood in his mouth, as fists and boots flew, taking out his legs every time he tried to get up.

Quinn tackled another man to the ground and punched him right in the throat. Three, four men on his back, trying to get him down. Guns were drawn, and they ordered him to quit fighting or they'd shoot.

In the silence, he heard Kenny yelling and then some scuffling sounds. Someone by Kenny's patrol car said, "Put that fat fucker in the trunk."

Quinn got to one knee and spit out some blood. He felt his eyes swell and sharp pain in his ribs with every panting breath. He looked up at the men, who had formed a ring around him, holding weapons. Quinn kept low, knowing what was about to come next. He'd have more luck taking a run right for the tree line. If they wanted to shoot him in the back, at least he'd have a damn chance.

Something caught the attention of the men and they all turned. A tall figure strode up, hands in the pockets of his coat, not bothering to hide his face. His face flat and wide, long black hair in a slick ponytail.

"Take him down to that creek," said the man, who looked like he'd just stepped off the Rez.

"We ain't through with him yet."

"You're through," the Indian said. "Walk him down there and leave us. This man killed my friend. Not yours."

"Leave?" the man said. "Shitfire. What the hell you talking about? You ain't gonna fuckin' kill him. Are you? We're just trying to teach this cocky bastard a lesson."

The Indian looked hard at the man as two others grabbed Quinn by the arms and force-walked him toward the winding creek, a gun in his back, the squat guy still trying to debate the Indian, saying he sure as shit wasn't gonna be any part of killing a cop. "Have y'all lost your fucking minds? That's not what we're about, Tonto. I ain't a part of this. *No siree.* No fucking goddamn way."

The men walking with him let go of Quinn's arms for a moment, the trees shaking in the violent wind shooting down through the cotton fields. A big harvest moon shone through the clouds for a moment. The blue light on the trailer porch went out, as did the light in the window.

"Get back in your goddamn car," the Indian said to the squat man. The others momentarily distracted.

Quinn dove into the brush and tangled weeds by the creek, sliding down into the rocky bed, running through the shallow water, keeping close to the bank and down in the shadows as shots fired behind him, earth and stones kicking up around him. He pushed himself against the sunken edge of the creek bed, catching a ragged breath with the cracked rib, his mouth tasting like pennies, staying silent as he watched four men up on the edge of the creek, pointing and making their way down.

He pushed himself deeper under a root ball exposed by the erosion, waiting for one of the men to get close enough. He steadied his breath, staying as quiet as possible, listening to a Watchman move through the bed, splashing up water as dead leaves shook from the tall cottonwoods and floated down toward the sandy bottom.

He was nearly close enough for Quinn to reach out and snatch his ass. And then Quinn's cell phone went off. "Everything Is Beautiful" rang out up and down the creek.

"Not answering," Maggie said.

"Where'd he go?"

"Remember that trouble out at Vienna's Place?" Maggie said. She and Boom waited at a booth at the El Dorado, Caddy taking the kids for one last stretch of door knocking a few blocks away. The restaurant smelled of tortillas and fried meat. At the next table, a woman from the bank was having a birthday party. The waiter put a sombrero on her head and served her a drink with the colors of an American flag.

"Sure," Boom said. "Boyfriend making trouble for one of the dancers. Pulled a gun on Quinn."

"That's the one," Maggie said. "So this guy bailed out and has been harassing this girl. She's had Quinn on her speed dial, calling Quinn every time he tries to make contact. But Quinn said she was shacking up with some new guy and that the old boyfriend didn't know where she lived. I don't know what happened, but he said he had to go out there. Tonight."

"She asked for him personal?"

"I guess."

Boom nodded, not saying anything, just kind of staring off into the street, all the pretty lights on the town square. Rain just starting to fall in Jericho, kids and parents making a run for it from the gazebo back to their cars. Some running into the El Dorado, looking for shelter. Several waiters and cooks walked up to the next table, singing "Feliz Cumpleaños." Shaking maracas, banging on the table, the whole damn deal.

"I'll call Cleotha."

Boom nodded.

"You don't like it."

"Call Quinn again," Boom said. "And then call dispatch."

"I'm sure he's fine."

"He's fine."

"I'm starting to get paranoid," Maggie said, dialing her phone as

Boom stood up and reached for his Carhartt jacket, sliding in his good arm, the right side pinned tight to the coat. The big gun stuck in his leather belt.

Quinn's phone went right to voicemail. Maggie called dispatch right away, getting Cleotha and asking where Quinn had called in from last. She looked up at Boom as she repeated the address out on Perfect Circle Road.

"Don't you worry," Cleotha said. "Kenny done gone with him. Make sure that crazy woman and her boyfriend don't give him no trouble. I'll get him on the radio and tell him to call, Miss Maggie."

Maggie put down the phone and looked up. Boom was already gone, darting across the slick streets to where he'd parked his GMC pickup. The trees blowing sideways as leaves shook loose and free like confetti.

The man was down, and Quinn had his gun. He left the man facedown and handcuffed to the root ball, moving out with what he'd confiscated: a folding knife and a fully loaded Glock 19. The other men had scattered, searching for Quinn in the woods and following the creek bed from high on the ridge, scanning the moonlit water. As they disappeared upstream, he dropped back down into the creek, the moon going back under the clouds now, raining like hell, soaking his shirt and jeans, feeling the creek's water seep into his cowboy boots, as he looked out for more Watchmen and for a place to pull himself up out of the bed and fight his way back to Kenny.

He'd made a call. Deputies were on their way.

At a bend in the creek, he saw a little outcropping where he could lift himself up, blue lights from Kenny's cruiser flickering over the lip of the bed. His ribs ached like hell as he pulled up, digging into the earth with his fingernails, trying to crest the hill. He spotted a gathering of Watchmen, their vehicles parked at the side of road. He spat some more blood from his mouth and gritted his teeth as he tried harder to pull himself up and out.

He heard the shots just as he felt the bullets tear into his back. His hands broke free, sending him tumbling down the muddy hill and rolling into the now rising creek, raindrops pinging the shallow water. Quinn dragged himself to the sandy bank as the big Indian tromped across the creek toward him, gun in hand, moving quick and with purpose, one of the Watchmen tagging alongside him, telling the Indian that they need to leave now, the cops had to be on their way and he was done with all this bullshit.

Quinn pushed himself up onto his elbows, trying to stand, to keep moving, but his body failed him. He gritted his teeth even more, telling himself this wasn't nearly as bad as that night fight in Kandahar, pitch-black and hand-to-hand, with some insurgent trying to cut his throat. Or as bad as getting shot in the back of his leg and shoulder during a raid of a Taliban compound, dirty, ragged faces multiplying and waiting, peeking out from the rocks, ambushing his team and the helicopter.

"Let's go," the short man said to the Indian. Quinn briefly remembered grabbing that man by his nose, bringing him to his knees. Now the man was trying to stop this Indian from firing the kill shot and taking him out. *Ain't life funny.*

"Sure," the Indian said. He turned and shot the man in the head, dropping him fast and hard, then came toward Quinn, gun raised and chin high, looking to finish it.

The Glock was lost, Quinn was bleeding out, and the bed was obscured with darkness and rain as he heard more shooting over the hill and a lot of yelling. So much goddamn pain that his mind couldn't process it. He was going into shock. Somewhere, a big motor revved, and there was crashing and the sound of glass breaking, and then the entire damn creek bed lit up with headlights as a truck went flying over Quinn into the little ravine, landing hard and mean in the water, doors flying open and Boom appearing with a big-ass gun in his hand. He raised it and began to fire. There was more yelling and then rain. And then, damn it. There was nothing but darkness as Boom called out to him.

*Quinn. Quinn. Goddamn you.*

# TWENTY-NINE

When Tashi Coleman heard that Quinn Colson had been shot, she flew straight to Memphis, rented a car, and drove the hundred miles down to Tibbehah County General. Quinn was alive and in the ICU, no visitors, no new information. Most of his family and friends were camped out in a sitting area outside the security doors. The light was dim, a television in the corner playing a new episode of *Dr. Phil*, the good doctor taking on a woman and her bratty daughter from Beverly Hills. The girl nearly in tears because her mother wouldn't buy her a Mercedes G wagon, costing the woman a quarter million, for her sweet sixteen. The girl said she wouldn't settle for anything less since the G's interior matched her Chanel purse.

Caddy was seated with her back to the television, her son Jason sleeping with his head in her lap and covered in a blue blanket. She looked up as Tashi walked in and took a seat across from her. Quinn's mother smiled from across the room, where she stood with Boom

Kimbrough, both of them speaking in quiet, personal tones. Boom looked up at Tashi and nodded to her, still continuing the conversation.

"I'm so sorry."

Caddy nodded, placing her hand on Tashi's knee, and smiled. "I had to turn off the news," Caddy said. "I can't stand to see that man's face on television. Smiling and grinning, talking about values and change. He's gonna win. Votes are pouring in for him."

"Nothing matters anymore," Tashi said. "Everything we did and exposed. The pictures of those parties Vardaman hosted out at his hunt lodge. No one cared. Everyone just said they were fakes trying to tarnish a great man's reputation."

"I saw the pictures," Caddy said, rubbing her sleeping son's head. "Those were as real as it gets. I bet a lot of divorce lawyers in Jackson had their phones lighting up."

"What about those men who shot Quinn?"

"Vardaman said they acted under their own volition," Caddy said. "He claims that the Watchmen Society is in no way affiliated or endorsed by his campaign."

"Bullshit," Tashi said, trying to keep her voice down. "They worked all his rallies. The one they found dead in that creek? He was the ringleader, hosted some kind of website that pushed all kinds of nutso conspiracy theories."

Caddy looked worn and tired, eyes red and heavy, as she touched a gold cross that hung around her neck. A heated debate going on in the television, more about the fifteen-year-old getting a job, maybe volunteering at a soup kitchen, and giving up her dream of owning that Mercedes. Dr. Phil telling the girl he once waited on cars at the A&W Root Beer while wearing roller skates. "Roller skates!" Dr. Phil repeated with pride.

"That man has no moral center," Tashi said. "He doesn't care what happened to Brandon. And apparently this state doesn't, either. They just want to hear him talk and promise they can return to a time that never existed. What's the point of reporting it? What's it all matter? Didn't make a damn bit of difference."

The bratty girl on television was arguing that a thousand-dollar allowance was nothing. She couldn't live like that. "When you indulge her," Dr. Phil said, "you're doing that to make yourself feel better. She doesn't need a job babysitting. This girl needs a job in the world." Thunderous applause, everyone in the studio audience pleased with Dr. Phil's direct and personal advice. Tashi was pretty sure the girl was screwed. She wasn't going to get that damn G wagon Mercedes.

"How's Quinn?"

Caddy didn't answer the question, just gave a soft smile, eyelids puffy and heavy. "I think you're wrong."

"About what?"

"That nothing matters," Caddy said. "It *all* matters. If nothing matters, we all better just give up and quit. I've done that before and I'm not doing it again."

"We're putting together the podcast now," Tashi said. "Some of the producers want to move it up a few months on account of everything that's happened. The coverage we've gotten about Vardaman's ties to Brandon. Maybe it will help."

"This isn't the end of that story."

"I know."

"What y'all did just kicked things off," Caddy said, staring straight ahead, beyond Tashi and over her shoulder. "Y'all did good. But there's a lot more to this than Brandon Taylor. These people in Jackson running things don't give a damn about anything except for filling their coffers while people go hungry."

"Quinn will be OK?" Tashi said. "I heard he's going to be OK."

"We all have a purpose," she said. "No matter how folks try and use us. We all are part of His will."

"And God will make things right?" Tashi said, not recording but recording everything in her mind. "That's what you believe?"

"Yes, ma'am," Caddy said, nodding, absolutely sure of it. "It has to. God would never leave us hanging like that. Never."

It was nearly midnight at Vienna's Place and most of the election results were in, Vardaman kicking the crap out of his competition, not even damn close, taking the state by more than eighty percent. Not that the news was unexpected, but Fannie poured herself another celebratory glass of pink Veuve Clicquot, the same stuff that Ray always had chilled for her. Tony Bennett on the stereo, the bed turned down with rose petals and chocolate on the pillows. Maybe a few new outfits from Agent Provocateur with all the bustiers, thigh highs, and little snaps and clasps that he liked. Fannie raised her champagne to Ray, that slam dunk election, and to her dearly departed grandmother who set her on the right career path. *Don't you ever take shit from anyone,* Vienna always said. *And don't you ever forget that a man keeps his brains in his shorts. Use that pecker like a steering wheel.*

Fannie had been working to be in control of her damn life since she was a knobby-kneed teenager, washing stains from the towels and sheets, bleaching all that shit clean, promising herself that she'd be the one calling the damn shots one day. And that she'd always, always be in control. Midnight Man reached across the bar and poured the last of the champagne, turning to the TV she was watching and then shaking his head as he walked off.

"Don't tell me you didn't see that coming?" Fannie said, smirking a bit. "Vardaman's political porn to these fuckwads."

"Yeah?" Midnight Man said in that low, hoarse whisper, almost to himself. "We always see that shit coming."

Fannie drank the champagne, tasting so sweet, bubbles tickling the back of her throat. Damn. She and the Chief were finally in charge. After the Chief's people paid Buster White a visit and laid down the fucking law, that fat bastard was of no more importance than a senile greeter at Walmart. She'd run north Mississippi and now part of the Coast over to New Orleans, and the Chief would take his cut and do his business through the Rez. The Chief had put the terms to Buster White, the son of a bitch not taking it so well, nearly having a heart attack himself, making threats, and promising retaliation that they all knew would come. When Vardaman was in charge, she'd have to keep that fucking leash tight, but she'd still be taking that man out for a walk every week.

Up on the television, the new governor of Mississippi stood on the dais with his wife, a fat, brassy blonde who looked zonked out of her mind, and two college-age kids, a boy and a girl. He was speaking to the crowd of his lunatics, using his hands to emphasize the words that Fannie couldn't hear. She could only see the scroll at the bottom of the screen. VARDAMAN WINS BY A LANDSLIDE.

Vienna's was in fine form tonight, a couple hundred guests ogling the girls, tossing dollar bills, feeling high-rumped waitresses and being led back to the VIP room to open up their wallets and throw down their credit cards for one more bottle, one more dance, so much fucking fun that those men never wanted it to end. And there was Fannie, the fucking queen of it all, sitting at the bar, anonymous and alone, winning at damn-near everything that she ever wanted. She had the state, the corridor, the drugs, the stolen shit, the fucking tractor trailer shipments, the Cartel contacts, the whores, domestic and international, and the promise of it all, that it would only get bigger and better. Ray was dead. Buster was nothing. She and the Chief and that grinning bastard on television.

Let that dumb son of a bitch Skinner try to close down her least profitable business and erect that cross. She'd hang that old fucker from it by his dick.

She sipped the last of her champagne, turning to see two teenage girls locked in an embrace on the center stage, that Katy Perry song "Roar" pounding on the speakers. *Eye of the tiger. Dance through the fucking fire.* Two men in their twenties, nicely dressed with good clothes and good teeth, stared down from the end of the bar at her. She looked down at the amazing display of cleavage she was sporting tonight in her little black dress and couldn't blame them. But, damn, if only those boys knew, she'd bring them both to their fucking knees and make 'em cry for Momma.

Fannie smiled, leaning back on her barstool, nodding to the music, as the DJ played another song. "Hey, Midnight Man," Fannie Hathcock said, turning back to the bar.

Midnight Man leaned over the bar to hear her better. "Yes, ma'am?"

"I like that," she said. "Tell him to play that shit again."

Maggie was the first one to see Quinn. The doctors and some of the other nurses had done their best to keep her up to date, talking to her straight and direct like a nurse and not like a stranger. She'd appreciated that and did her damn best to absorb the information and relay it to Quinn's mother and sister as she always did as part of her job. She lost any part of that, her clinical professionalism, and she felt like she just might curl into a ball and not get back up. She had to stay up for Brandon and Quinn and for herself. It was just like Quinn always said, always keep on the march, keep moving, don't let the enemy see you wounded. As a two-time military wife, even if the first one was to a professional asshole, she knew how to toughen up and keep on with the mission.

It was late, she and Caddy trying for the last hour to get Jean to please go home and get some rest and Jean not having any of it. She and Caddy were camped out in the waiting area with Boom and old Mr. Varner. Varner nearly getting ejected from the hospital for showing up at the front desk with an M4 carbine and telling security that he'd be standing guard for the night.

All of it. So much chaos and craziness. TV news crew outside. The two lengthy surgeries. The waiting, the praying, the details of Quinn's old injuries. His body had already been through so much. Shot up two days shy of his twenty-first birthday and then three times after that. The doctor had explained all the scar tissue they'd had to cut through to get to the four bullets. A collapsed lung, a shattered shoulder blade, so much lost blood.

She'd pulled a chair close to him. He was still asleep from the last surgery, tubes running into his nose and an IV drip in his arm. His vitals were good and strong. He could breathe on his own. He'd come awake for a while, right before the last surgery, and had joked about that Indian in the creek being a bad shot. That man getting away, state police and FBI out looking for him statewide.

"Come back, Quinn," she said. "Come back, please."

She felt something stir, Quinn's fingers moving in hers. Maggie started to cry but tried like hell to compose herself, biting her lip. Boom walked into the room, standing side by side with Maggie, placing his good arm around her back.

"How's your truck?" Quinn said, lips dry and voice weak.

"'Bout the same as yours," Boom said. "Looks like shit."

"These folks trying to get us to quit?"

"Yeah," Boom said. "Pretty fucking dumb."

"But we don't quit."

"Never," he said. "Our heads too goddamn thick."

Maggie leaned over and kissed Quinn on his cracked lips, his eyes opening briefly, and whispered into his ear that she loved him. Quinn's eyes closed again and he was fast asleep.

"What now?" Maggie said.

"Fun's just starting," Boom said. "We got those bastards on the run."

If you had to spend twenty years of your life in jail, FCI Beaumont in Texas wasn't a bad place to do it. It wasn't exactly Bible camp, but they did have competitive flag football and volleyball leagues, a good gym with stair-climbers and rowing machines, and a decent shop for leather crafts. That's pretty much a lot of what Donnie Varner had been doing since being sentenced seven years ago for stealing a few M4s from his National Guard unit and selling them to the Cartel. Or so the Feds had claimed. It was a little more complicated than that.

Ten days after the election in Mississippi, Donnie had been working on a hand-tooled belt for his father when one of the guards told him he had a visitor. It was strange, almost unheard of, to have a visitor after five, but he wasn't exactly looking forward to another night watching the goddamn *Golden Girls* with the boys in his unit. Two of them saying they were so damn horny they'd take on Blanche and that big gal Dorothy at the same time.

He left the belt, nearly done with etching in the SEMPER FI, LAND, SEA AND AIR and this tough-ass-looking bulldog holding a gun. His old dad, Luther, a Marine sniper during Vietnam, would sure as hell love it. He hoped to get it done and in the mail by Christmas. Maybe that'd make Luther feel a little bit better about having a two-bit convict for a son.

The guard led him down an endless corridor, his orange canvas shoes thwacking on the shiny buffed floors, fluorescent lights buzzing overhead. The guard unlocked a metal door and waited for Donnie to enter.

A man about his age in a black T-shirt was sitting at the table. He had a shaved head and a long brown beard, sleeve tattoos down both arms, and a real serious expression, looking like both a convict and the law at the same time.

"Whatever it is," Donnie said, "I didn't do it. I've been minding my own damn business, making fucking wallets and watch straps. Besides, it's time for my turkey dinner. Been waiting since June for that shit."

"Mr. Varner . . ."

"Oh, hell," Donnie said. "Here we fucking go. As soon as somebody calls me Mr. Varner, I know my ass is in trouble. I know I'm charismatic as hell, but y'all can't keep me in here forever."

The man didn't smile or identify himself. The steel door behind them closed. The tattooed man told him to take a seat. "Your buddy Quinn Colson has been shot."

"Yeah?" Donnie said, sitting up straight and leaning into the table. "Is he alive?"

The man nodded. "My name's Holliday," he said. "I am the federal agent in charge of north Mississippi. Quinn Colson is my friend."

"So what?"

"I know the folks who tried to kill him."

"And?"

"I've got an idea of how to get 'em."

"Wish I could help," Donnie said. "But I'm a little busy being rehabilitated. I'm not in that life no more. I deal in leather. I could make you one hell of a belt to go with those fancy boots."

"How'd you feel about getting right back in it?" the man said.

"Helping us. Helping Quinn. And, in the process, shaving some years off that sentence?"

Donnie leaned back in the hard prison chair, front legs lifting off the floor, as he scratched at his cheek. "Hmm," he said, shrugging a bit. "What exactly is it that you have in mind?"